# THE IONIAN MISSION

Patrick O'Brian, one of our greatest contemporary novelists, is the author of the acclaimed Aubrey–Maturin tales and the biographer of Joseph Banks and Picasso. His first novel, *Testimonies*, and his *Collected Short Stories* have recently been republished by HarperCollins. He has translated many works from French into English, among them the novels and memoirs of Simone de Beauvoir and the first volume of Jean Lacouture's biography of Charles de Gaulle. In 1995 he was the first recipient of the Heywood Hill Prize for a lifetime's contribution to literature. In the same year he was awarded the CBE. He lives in the South of France.

'For Patrick O'Brian's followers, the arrival of a new Jack Aubrey–Stephen Maturin novel ranks with the events of a year. I know of no novelist who excites such fierce loyalty from a following which is almost a brotherhood in the intensity of its feelings for the writer and his works . . . He is able to convey the detail of shipboard life without ever becoming tedious. Even when there is little action, when the plot is measured and easy, when he is merely describing a situation . . . he never fails to keep the reader. His mastery is not limited to being a good writer. He is much more than that.' KEVIN MYERS, *Irish Times*

# PATRICK O'BRIAN

# *The Ionian Mission*

HarperCollins*Publishers*

HarperCollins*Publishers*
77-85 Fulham Palace Road,
Hammersmith, London w6 8jb

This paperback edition 1996
1  3  5  7  9  8  6  4  2

Previously published in paperback by HarperCollins 1993
Reprinted twice

Also published in paperback by Fontana 1982
Reprinted five times

First published in Great Britain by
William Collins Sons & Co. Ltd 1981

ISBN 0 00 649922 8

Set in Imprint

Printed and bound in Great Britain by
Caledonian International
Book Manufacturing Ltd, Glasgow

# CONTENTS

# MARIAE SACRUM

*The sails of a square-rigged ship, hung out to dry in a calm.*

1  Flying jib
2  Jib
3  Fore topmast staysail
4  Fore staysail
5  Foresail, or course
6  Fore topsail
7  Fore topgallant
8  Mainstaysail
9  Main topmast staysail
10  Middle staysail
11  Main topgallant staysail

12  Mainsail, or course
13  Maintopsail
14  Main topgallant
15  Mizzen staysail
16  Mizzen topmast staysail
17  Mizzen topgallant staysail
18  Mizzen sail
19  Spanker
20  Mizzen topsail
21  Mizzen topgallant

# AUTHOR'S NOTE

The Royal Navy of Nelson's time was much given to
music and poetry: no wardroom was complete without
half a dozen German flutes and every month the *Naval
Chronicle* published several pages of verse by officers on
active service or half-pay. These poems presumably show
naval talent at its highest, and they provide excellent
material for a writer who wishes to show this perhaps
unexpected side of the sailor's life but who feels that his
own pastiches cannot possibly give the same impression of
authenticity. Yet the somewhat less accomplished pieces
that never reached print are even more valuable: I have
come across a certain number of them in the library at
Greenwich, but to my knowledge there is no mine so rich
as the *Memoirs of Lieutenant Samuel Walters, R.N.*,
which remained in manuscript until 1949, when the
Liverpool University Press published them, admirably
edited by Professor Northcote Parkinson, to whom I make
all proper ackowledgements for the lines I have borrowed.

# CHAPTER ONE

Marriage was once represented as a field of battle rather than a bed of roses, and perhaps there are some who may still support this view; but just as Dr Maturin had made a far more unsuitable match than most, so he set about dealing with the situation in a far more compendious, peaceable and efficacious way than the great majority of husbands.

He had pursued his strikingly beautiful, spirited, fashionable wife for years and years before marrying her in mid-Channel aboard a man-of-war: for so many years indeed that he had become a confirmed bachelor at last, too old a dog to give up his tricks of smoking tobacco in bed, playing his 'cello at odd untimely moments, dissecting anything that interested him, even in the drawing-room; too old to be taught to shave regularly, to change his linen, or to wash when he did not feel the need – an impossible husband. He was not house-trained; and although he made earnest attempts at the beginning of their marriage he soon perceived that in time the strain must damage their relationship, all the more so since Diana was as intransigent as himself and far more apt to fly into a passion about such things as a pancreas in the drawer of the bedside table or orange marmalade ground into the Aubusson. And then again his deeply-ingrained habits of secrecy (for he was an intelligence-agent as well as a physician) made him even more unsuited for domestic life, which withers in the presence of reserve. He therefore gradually retired to the rooms he had long retained in an old-fashioned comfortable shabby inn called the Grapes, in the liberties of the Savoy, leaving Diana in the handsome modern house in Half Moon Street, a house shining with fresh white paint and new-furnished with elegant but fragile satinwood.

9

It was in no way a parting; there was no sort of violence or ill-will or disagreement about Stephen Maturin's fading away from the intense social life of Half Moon Street to the dim, foggy lane by the Thames, where he could more easily attend the meetings of the Royal Society, the College of Surgeons, or the entomological or ornithological societies that interested him so very much more than Diana's card-parties and routs, and where he could more safely carry out some of the delicate business that fell to his lot as a member of the naval intelligence department, business that necessarily had to be kept from the knowledge of his wife. It was not a parting in any sense of unkindness, but a mere geographical separation, one so slight that Stephen usually covered it every morning, walking up through the Green Park to breakfast with his wife, most often in her bedroom, she being a late riser; while he nearly always appeared at her frequent dinner-parties, playing the part of host to admiration, for he could be as smooth and complaisant as the most civilized of her guests so long as he was not required to keep it up too long. In any case Diana's father and her first husband were serving officers and all her life she had been accustomed to separation. She was always delighted to see her husband and he to see her; they never quarrelled now that all reasons for disagreement were gone; and in fact this was probably the best possible arrangement for a pair with nothing in common but love and friendship, and a series of strange, surprising, shared adventures.

They never quarrelled, except when Stephen brought up the question of marriage according to the Roman rite, for their wedding had been performed in the brisk naval fashion by the captain of HMS *Oedipus*, an amiable young man and a fine navigator but no priest; and since Stephen, being of mixed Irish and Catalan parentage, was a Papist he was a bachelor still as far as the Church was concerned. Yet no persuasion, no kind words (and harsh ones he dared not use) could move Diana: she did not reason, but simply

10

and steadily refused. There were times when her obstinacy grieved him, for apart from his own strong feelings on the matter he seemed to make out some obscure superstitious dread of a strange sacrament mingled with the general English dislike of Rome; yet there were also times when it added a certain not wholly disagreeable air of intrigue to the connection. Not that this ever occurred to the eminently respectable Mrs Broad of the Grapes, who liked her house to be just so and who would countenance nothing whatsoever in the roving line, a landlady who would at once turn away any man she suspected of leading out a wench. Mrs Broad had known Dr Maturin for many years; she was thoroughly used to him; and when he told her that he meant to stay at the inn she only stared for a while, amazed that any man born could sleep away from such a ravishing lady; and then accepted it as 'one of the Doctor's little ways' with perfect calm. Some of his little ways had indeed been quite surprising in the past, seeing that they ranged from the quartering of badgers, rescued from a baiting, in her coal-shed to the introduction of separate limbs and even of whole orphans for dissection when they were in good supply towards the end of winter; but she had grown used to them little by little. The Doctor's 'cello booming through the night and skeletons in every cupboard were nothing now to Mrs Broad; and nothing now could astonish her for long. She also thoroughly approved of Diana, whom she had come to know well during her first startled stay at the inn, where Stephen had brought her when they landed in England. Mrs Broad liked her for her beauty, which she candidly admired, and for her friendliness ('no airs nor graces, and not above taking a little posset with a person behind the bar') and for her evident affection for the Doctor. Mrs Maturin was very often at the Grapes, bringing shirts, blue worsted stockings, shoe-buckles, leaving messages, darting in for small sums of money, for although Diana was far richer than Stephen she was even more improvident. It seemed a strange kind of marriage, but Mrs Broad had once seen

11

Mrs Maturin in one of the palace coaches with Lady Jersey – royal footmen up behind – and she had an indistinct notion that Diana was 'something at Court', which would naturally prevent her from living like mortals of ordinary flesh and blood.

Diana had been there still more often in recent days, because the Doctor was going to sea again with his particular friend Jack Aubrey, a post-captain in the Royal Navy, once known in the service as Lucky Jack Aubrey for his good fortune in taking prizes but now so miserably involved in his affairs that he was glad to accept an unenviable temporary command, the *Worcester* of seventy-four guns, one of the surviving Forty Thieves, that notorious set of line-of-battle ships built by contract with a degree of dishonesty in their scantlings, knees, fastenings – in their whole construction – that excited comment even in a time of widespread corruption: very strong comment indeed from those who had to take them to sea. She was to carry him to the Mediterranean, to Admiral Thornton's squadron and the interminable blockade of the French fleet in Toulon. And since Stephen was to go to sea, it was obviously necessary that his sea-chest should be prepared. He had packed it himself on a great many occasions before this and it had always satisfied his modest needs even when he was a great way from shore, let alone in the Mediterranean, with Malta or Barcelona only a few hundred miles to leeward, according to the wind; but neither Diana nor Mrs Broad could bear his method of tossing things in pell-mell, the more fragile objects wrapped in his stockings, and they both perpetually interfered: tissue-paper, orderly layers of this and that, neatness, even labels.

The brassbound chest was open now and Dr Maturin was fishing in it, hoping to find his best neckcloth, the frilled white neckcloth the size of a moderate studdingsail that he was to put on for Diana's farewell dinner. He fished with a surgical retractor, one of the most efficient instruments known to science, but nothing did he find;

and when at last the steel claws grated on the bottom he called out, 'Mrs Broad, Mrs Broad, who has hidden my neckcloth?'

Mrs Broad walked in without ceremony, the neckcloth over her arm, although Stephen was in his shirt. 'Why, oh why did you take it away?' he cried. 'Have you no bowels, Mrs Broad?'

'Mrs Maturin said it was to be new-starched,' said Mrs Broad. 'You would not like to have your frill all limp, I am sure.'

'There is nothing I should like better,' muttered Stephen, folding it about him.

'And Mrs Maturin says you are to put on your nice new pumps,' said Mrs Broad. 'Which I have scratched the soles.'

'I cannot walk to Half Moon Street in new pumps,' said Stephen.

'No, sir,' said Mrs Broad patiently. 'You are to go in a chair, like Mrs M said this morning. The men have been waiting in the tap this ten minutes past.' Her eye wandered to the open chest, as neat as an apple-pie not half an hour ago. 'Oh, Dr Maturin, fie,' she cried. 'Oh fie, Doctor, fie.'

'Oh fie, Stephen,' said Diana, tweaking his cravat straight, 'How can you be so intolerably late? Jagiello has been slavering in the drawing-room this last age, and the others will be here any minute.'

'There was a mad bull in Smithfield,' said Stephen.

'Does one really have to pass through Smithfield to reach Mayfair?' asked Diana.

'One does not, as you know very well. But I suddenly remembered that I was to call at Bart's. And listen my dear, you have never been in time in your life, to my certain knowledge; so I beg you will keep your irony for some more suitable occasion.'

'Why, Stephen, you are as furious as a mad bull yourself, I find,' said Diana, kissing him. 'And to think that I have bought you such a beautiful present. Come upstairs and look at it: Jagiello can receive any early worms.' As she passed the drawing-room she called in, 'Jagiello, pray do the civil for us if anyone should come: we shall not be a minute.' Jagiello was almost domesticated at Half Moon Street, an absurdly beautiful young man, an exceedingly wealthy Lithuanian now attached to the Swedish embassy: he and Stephen and Jack Aubrey had been imprisoned in France together and they had escaped together, which accounted for an otherwise unlikely close friendship.

'There,' she said proudly, pointing to her bed, where there stood a gold-mounted dressing-case that was also a canteen and a backgammon-board: little drawers pulled in and out, ingenious slides and folding legs transformed it into a wash-hand-stand, a writing desk, a lectern; and looking-glasses and candleholders appeared on either side.

'Acushla,' he said, drawing her close, 'this is regal splendour – this is imperial magnificence. The Physician of the Fleet has nothing finer. I am so grateful, my dear.' And grateful, infinitely touched he was: while Diana put the gleaming object through its paces, explaining how it worked and telling him how she had stood over the workmen, bullying them into finishing it in time – oaths, sweet persuasion, promises until she was hoarse, as hoarse as a God-damned crow, Stephen chéri – he reflected on her generosity, her improvidence (rich though she was, she never had any money to spend, and this was far more than even she could afford), and on her ignorance of naval life, of the damp, cramped cupboard that a surgeon lived in at sea, even the surgeon of a seventy-four, a ship of the line: this precious piece of misguided craftsmanship might do very well for a field-officer, a soldier with a baggage-wagon and a dozen orderlies, but for a sailor it would have to be wrapped in waxed canvas and struck down into the driest part of the hold. Or perhaps it might be allowed in the bread-room . . .

'But the shirts, dear Stephen,' she was saying. 'I am absolutely desolated about the shirts. I could not get the wretched woman to finish them. There are only a dozen here. But I will send the others down by coach. They may catch you in time.'

'God's love,' cried Stephen, 'there is no need, no need at all. A dozen shirts! I have never had so many at one time since I was breeched. And in any case I need no more than two for this voyage. Sure, it is almost over before it is begun.'

'I wish you were back already,' said Diana in a low voice. 'I shall miss you so.' And then, glancing out of the window, 'There is Anne Trevor's chariot. You will not mind her coming, Stephen? When she heard that Jagiello was dining here she begged and prayed to be invited, and I had not the heart to say no.'

'Never in life, my dear. I am all for the satisfaction of natural desires, even in Miss Trevor, even in a Judas-haired rack-renting County Kerry absentee landowner with a Scotch Anabaptist vulture by way of an agent, or bailiff. Indeed, we might go so far as to leave them alone for two minutes.'

'It seems a damned odd voyage to me,' said Diana, frowning at the pile of shirts. 'You never told me how it all came about. And it is all so sudden.'

'In the crisis of a war naval orders are apt to be sudden. But I am just as pleased: I have some business to deal with in Barcelona, as you know: I should have travelled to the Mediterranean in any case, Jack or no Jack.' This was true as far as it went; but Stephen had not seen fit to explain the full nature of his business in Barcelona, nor did he now say that he also had a rendezvous with French royalists no great way from Toulon, a rendezvous with some gentlemen who were heartily sick of Buonaparte, a rendezvous that might lead to great things.

'But it was understood that Jack was to have the *Blackwater* and take her to the North American station as soon as she was ready,' said Diana. 'He ought never to have been shoved into a temporary command in that rotten old *Worcester*. A man of his seniority, with his fighting record, ought to have been knighted long ago

15

and given a decent ship, perhaps a squadron of his own. Sophie is perfectly furious: so is Admiral Berkeley, and Heneage Dundas, and all his service friends.' Diana was well informed about Captain Aubrey's affairs, he being married to her cousin Sophie and an old friend into the bargain; but she was not quite as well informed as Stephen, who now said, 'You are aware of Jack's predicament, of course?'

'Of course I am, Stephen. Pray do not be an ass.' Of course she was: all Captain Aubrey's acquaintance knew that on coming ashore with his pockets full of French and Spanish gold he had fallen an even easier prey to the landsharks than most sailors, as being of a more trusting, sanguine disposition. He had made a disastrous plunge into the arms of a more than usually rapacious shark and he was now deep in law-suits, with the possibility of ruin at the end of them.

'I am speaking more of the most recent phase. It seems that he forgot the discretion his legal advisers urged him to observe, and it seems to them that an absence from the country is now essential for a while. I forget the details – mayhem, attorneys flying out of a two-pair-of-stairs window, glass damaged to the extent of several pounds, clerks put in fear of their lives, blasphemous words, a breach of the King's peace. That is why things are so sudden. And that is why he accepted this command. It is no more than a parenthesis in his career.'

'He will come back for the *Blackwater* then, when she is ready? Sophie will be so happy.'

'Why, as to that, my dear, as to that . . .' Stephen hesitated; and then, overcoming the passion for reserve that among other things made him so unsuitable a husband, he said, 'The fact of the matter is that he had very great difficulty in getting even this command: his friends were obliged to make the most pressing representations to those in power, reminding them of services rendered, of promises made by the late First Lord; and even with all that he might never have had it if Captain – if a

16

friend had not very handsomely stood aside. There is some hindrance, some personal grudge in the Admiralty itself; and in spite of his record he may be disappointed of the *Blackwater*, although he has been fitting her out so long. The parenthesis may close only to find him on shore, eating his heart out for so much as a rowing-boat that flies the King's flag.'

'I suppose it is his shocking old father,' said Diana.

General Aubrey was an opposition member of Parliament, a vehement enthusiastic loquacious Radical, a sad handicap to any son serving the Crown, whose ministers controlled appointment and promotion.

'Sure, that has something to do with the matter,' said Stephen. 'But there is more to it than that, I believe. Do you know a man called Andrew Wray?'

'Wray of the Treasury? Oh yes. One sees him everywhere: I was obliged to dance with him at Lucy Carrington's ball the day you went off to your old reptiles, and he was at the Thurlows' dinner. Listen: there is another carriage: it must be Admiral Faithorne. He is always as regular as a clock. Stephen, we are behaving abominably. We must go down. Why do you ask about that scrub Wray?'

'You think him a scrub?'

'Certainly I do. Too clever by half, like so many of those Treasury fellows, and an infernal blackguard as well – he treated Harriet Fanshaw so shabbily you would not believe it. A scrub for all his pretty ways, and a coxcomb: I would not touch him with a barge-pole.'

'He is now acting as second secretary to the Admiralty during Sir John Barrow's illness. But he was in the Treasury some time ago, when Jack told him he cheated at cards, told him quite openly, in his candid naval way, in Willis's rooms.'

'Good God, Stephen! You never told me. What a close old soul you are, upon my honour.'

'You never asked.'

'Did he call Jack out?'

'He did not. I believe he is taking a safer course.' A thundering treble knock on the front door cut off his words. 'I will tell you later,' he said. 'Thank you, my dear, for my beautiful present.'

As they went down towards the hall Diana said, 'You know all about ships and the sea, Stephen.' Stephen bowed: he certainly should have known a fair amount about both, having sailed with Captain Aubrey since the turn of the century, and in fact he could now almost always discriminate between larboard and starboard: he prided himself extremely on his acquaintance with fore and aft and some even more recondite nautical terms. 'Tell me,' she said, 'What is this barge-pole they are always talking about?'

'Ho, as for that, mate,' said Stephen, 'you must understand that a barge is the captain's particular boat, or pinnace as we say; and the pole is a kind of unarticulated mast.'

He opened the drawing-room door for her, disclosing not one young woman but two, alternately scorning one another and adoring Jagiello, who sat between them in his splendid Hussar's uniform, looking amiable but absent. On seeing Stephen he sprang up, his spurs clashing, and cried 'Dear Doctor, how happy I am to see you,' clasping him in both arms and smiling down on him very sweetly.

'Admiral Faithorne,' called the butler in a hieratic boom, and the clock struck the hour.

More guests arrived, and profiting by the frequently opened door the kitchen cat glided in, low to the ground, and swarmed up Stephen's back to his left shoulder, where it sat purring hoarsely, rubbing its ear against his wig. Still more guests, one of them being the banker Nathan, Diana's financial adviser, a man after Stephen's own heart, he too being wholly devoted to the overthrow of Buonaparte, using his highly-specialized weapons with singular efficiency. And although the ceremony was spoilt by an ugly scene when the butler removed the cat, they did at last move into the dining-room, where they sat down to

18

as good a meal as London could offer, for in spite of her sylph-like form Diana was rather greedy and in addition to an educated taste in wine she possessed an excellent cook. His talents had on this occasion been directed to the preparation of all Stephen's favourite dishes.

'May I help you to some of these truffles, ma'am?' said he to his right-hand neighbour, a dowager whose influential countenance had helped to re-establish Diana's reputation, damaged by ill-judged connections in India and the United States and only partially restored by her marriage.

'Alas, I dare not,' she said. 'But it would give me great pleasure to see you do so. If you will take an old woman's advice, you will eat up all the truffles that come your way, while your innards can still withstand 'em.'

'Then I believe I shall,' said Stephen, plunging a spoon into the pyramid. 'It will be long before I see another. Tomorrow, with the blessing, I shall be aboard ship, and then hard tack, salt-horse, dried peas and small beer must be my lot: at least until that Buonaparte is brought down.'

'Let us drink to his confusion,' said the dowager, raising her glass. The whole table drank to his confusion, and then at due intervals to Dr Maturin's return, to his very happy return, to the Royal Navy, to one another, and then standing – a point of some difficulty to Miss Trevor, who was obliged to cling to Jagiello's arm – to the King. In the midst of all this cheerfulness, of this excellent claret, burgundy and port, Stephen looked anxiously at the clock, a handsome French cartel on the wall behind Mr Nathan's head: he was to take the Portsmouth mail, and he had a mortal horror of missing coaches. To his distress he saw that the hands had not moved since the lobster bisque; like most of the clocks in Diana's house the cartel had stopped, and he knew that decency forbade even a sur-reptitious glance at his watch. Yet although he and Diana lived lives more independent than most married pairs they were very, very close in other respects: she caught his look and called down the table 'Eat your pudding in peace, my

19

dear; Jagiello has borrowed his ambassador's coach, and he is very kindly driving us down.'

Shortly after this she and the other women withdrew. Jagiello moved up the table to the dowager's place and Stephen said to him, 'You are a good-hearted soul, my dear, so you are. Now I shall see Diana for the best part of another twelve hours; and I shall not have to fret my mind over that infernal mail-coach.'

'Mrs Maturin tried to make me promise that she should drive,' said Jagiello, 'and I have given my word that she should, once the sun was up, subject to your approval.' He sounded uneasy.

'And did she submit to your condition?' said Stephen, smiling. 'That was kind. But you need not be concerned: she drives prodigiously well, and would send a team of camels through a needle's eye at a brisk round trot.'

'Oh,' cried Jagiello, 'how I admire a woman that can ride and drive, that understands horse!' And he went on at some length about Mrs Maturin's shining parts, which had needed only a thorough understanding of horses to be quite complete.

Stephen was aware of Nathan's amused, benign, cynical face on the far side of the table, smiling at Jagiello's enthusiasm: there was something about Jagiello that made people smile, he reflected – his youth, his cheerfulness, his abounding health, his beauty, perhaps his simplicity. 'None of these qualities are mine, or ever have been,' he said to himself. 'Are the Jagiellos conscious of their happiness? Probably not. Fortunatos nimium . . .' A yearning for coffee spurred his vitals, and seeing that the decanters had made their last round untouched by his pink and somewhat stertorous guests he said aloud, 'Perhaps, gentlemen, we might join the ladies.'

Jagiello's offer of the coach had come as a surprise, and the other carriages had been ordered early so that Dr Maturin should be able to make his farewells and reach the Portsmouth coach with half an hour to spare. The carriages therefore appeared at half past ten and rolled away,

20

leaving Stephen, Diana, and Jagiello with a delightful sense of holiday, of free, unexpected, unmortgaged time. Nathan was also left behind, partly because he had come on foot from his house just round the corner and partly because he wished to speak to Diana about money. She had brought some magnificent jewels back from India and the United States, many of which she never wore; and in the present state of war, with Napoleon's astonishing, horrifying victories over the Austrians and Prussians, their value had increased immensely. Nathan wanted her to take advantage of the fact and to put some of the rubies ('vulgar great things, much too big, like raspberry tarts' she said) into a select list of deeply depressed British stocks, a drug on the market – an investment that would yield splendid returns in the event of an Allied victory at last. However, he only smiled and bowed when she suggested that they should take the remains of the bombe glacée into the billiard-room and there eat it while they played. 'Because in any case Stephen must say goodbye to his olive-tree,' she observed. Hers was perhaps the only billiard-room in Half Moon Street to possess an olive: the room had been built out over the garden behind, and Stephen, prising up a flagstone by a convenient window, had set a rooted cutting from a tree growing in his own land of Catalonia, itself the descendant of one in the grove of Academe. He sat by it now, showing Nathan the five new leaves and the almost certain promise of a sixth. With another husband Nathan might have spoken about these stocks and shares; but Stephen would have nothing whatsoever to do with his wife's fortune – he left it entirely to her.

'Come, Stephen,' said she, putting down her cue. 'I have left you such a pretty position.'

Dr Maturin addressing himself to a shattered leg with a saw in his hand was a bold, deft, determined operator; his gestures were rapid, sure, precise. But billiards was not his game. Although his theory was sound enough his practice was contemptible. Now, having studied the possibilities at length, he gave his ball a hesitant poke, watched it roll deliberately into the top right-hand pocket without touching any of the others, and returned to his olive-tree. The other players belonged to a different world entirely: Nathan gathered the balls into a corner, nursing them in a long series of almost imperceptible cannons and breaking them only to leave his opponent in a most uncomfortable situation; Jagiello accomplished some surprising feats at the top of the table with a spot-stroke; but Diana favoured a more dashing game by far, delighting in the losing hazard. She walked round the table with a predatory gleam in her eye, sending the balls streaking up and down with a ringing crack. At one point, when she had already made a break of thirty-seven and needed only three to win, the balls were awkwardly placed in the middle. She hoisted her slim person on to the edge of the table and she was about to reach right out with her whole length poised over the baize when Stephen called 'Take the rest to it, my dear; take the long rest, for all love.' There was a strong possibility that she was with child, and he did not like the position at all.

'Bah,' said she, lowering her cue to her outstretched hand: she glared along it, her eyes narrowed, the tip of her tongue showing from the corner of her mouth; she paused, and then with a strong smooth stroke sent the red straight into the bottom right-hand pocket while her own ball shot into that on the left. She slipped off the table with such a lithe, easy grace and such an open delighted triumph that Stephen's heart stopped for a beat and the other men looked at her with the utmost fondness.

'Captain Jagiello's coach,' said the butler.

As far as real battlefields and beds of roses were concerned, Captain Aubrey was far better acquainted with the first, partly because of his profession, which, with enormous intervals of delay, often cold and always wet, brought him into violent conflict with the King's enemies, to say nothing of the Admiralty, the Navy Board, and bloody-minded superiors and subordinates, and partly

because he was a wretched gardener. For all his loving care
the roses at Ashgrove Cottage produced more greenfly,
caterpillars, mildew, rust, and grey mould than flowers –
never enough at any one time to make a bed for a dwarf,
let alone a six-foot sea-officer who tipped the beam at
sixteen stone. In the figurative sense, his marriage was a
good deal nearer the roses than most; he was a good deal
happier than he deserved (he was neither a sure provider
nor quite strictly monogamous) and although he was not
ideally happy, although he might secretly wish for a
companion with more sense of a man's carnal nature and
somewhat less possessive, he was profoundly attached to
Sophie: and in any case he was often away from home
for years on end.

He now stood on the poop of HMS *Worcester*, about
to set off again; and his wife sat a little way behind him,
on an incongruous elbow-chair brought on deck for the
occasion.

The ship had been at single anchor in Spithead these
long hours past, the Blue Peter as firmly established at
her foretopmast head as though it had been nailed there,
her foretopsail loosed, and her capstan-bars shipped and
swifted a whole watch ago, ready to send her on her way:
the entire ship's company was in a state of angry tension
– officers snappish, dinner delayed, all eyes indignantly
turned to the shore. She swung broad on the slackening
ebb, and Captain Aubrey moved over to the starboard
rail, his telescope still trained on Portsmouth. His face,
his naturally good-tempered, cheerful face, was set, dark,
and stern: the wind still served, but only just, and once
the tide began to make his ship might as well return to
her moorings – she would never get out against the tide.
He loathed unpunctuality; and unpunctuality it was, gross
unpunctuality, that was keeping him here; he had already
begged a long, long breathing-space from the port-admiral,
who was devoted to Mrs Aubrey, but this could not last
and any moment now a hoist would break out on that
flagstaff over there, the *Worcester*'s signal to proceed to

23

sea, and then sail she must, surgeon or no surgeon, leaving her gig's crew to find their way as best they might.

Dr Maturin's sea-chest had come aboard, and his well-remembered 'cello-case, brought in good time from the Portsmouth mail; but no Doctor had come with them. It was in vain that Bonden, the Captain's coxswain, badgered the coachman and the guard: no, they had not seen a little ill-looking sallow cove in a full-bottomed wig; no, they had not left him by accident at Guildford, Godalming or Petersfield, because why? Because he was never on the bleeding coach to begin with, cully. Bonden might put that in his pipe and smoke it, or stuff it up his arse, whichever he preferred; and there was eighteenpence to pay on the bass fiddle, as being unnatural baggage, unaccompanied.

'How I do loathe unpunctuality,' said Captain Aubrey. 'Even by land. Forward there: belay that smiting-line.' This last was delivered in a voice so strong that it echoed from the walls of Noman's Land Fort, and the words 'that smiting-line' mingled faintly with his next remark, which was addressed to his wife. 'Really, Sophie, you would think that a fellow of Stephen's parts, a prodigious natural philosopher, could be brought to understand the nature of the tide. Here is the moon at her perigee, in syzygy, and near the equator, as I showed you last night, and you smoked it directly, did you not?'

'Oh, perfectly, my dear,' said Sophie, looking wild: at least she had a clear recollection of the pale crescent over Porchester Castle.

'Or at least he might grasp its importance to seamen,' said Jack. 'And a full-blown spring tide at that. Sometimes I despair . . . My dear,' looking at his watch again – 'I am afraid we must say goodbye. If ever he should appear at Ashgrove Cottage, you will tell him to post down to Plymouth. Mr Pullings, a bosun's chair, if you please, a whip for the dunnage, and pass the word for the children.'

The cry ran through the ship 'Children aft – children report to the Captain – all children aft' and Jack's two little girls came running from the galley, grasping massy half-eaten slabs of cold plum-duff, followed by George, their younger brother, in his first pair of pantaloons, carried by a hairy quartermaster. But George's full-moon face was anxious and preoccupied; he whispered into the seaman's hairy ear. 'Can't you wait?' asked the seaman. George shook his head: the seaman whipped off the pantaloons, held the little boy well out over the leeward rail and called for a handful of tow.

On the poop itself Jack was still gazing through the innumerable masts – half the Channel fleet and countless transports, with smallcraft of every shape and size plying between them and the shore. He had the Sally Port clear in his glass, with the men-of-war's boats going to and fro, and his own gig waiting there, his coxswain sitting in the stern-sheets, eating bread and cheese with one hand and haranguing his shipmates with the other: behind the Sally Port the rough unpaved triangular square and the Keppel's Head inn at the far side, with its broad white balcony. And as he watched a coach and four took the corner at breakneck speed, scattering officers, seamen, Marines and their attendant trollops, and drew up, still rocking perilously, in the middle of the open space.

'Our number, sir,' said the signal-midshipman, his glass trained on the flagstaff. 'And now *Worcester proceed to sea.*' Another hoist, and the midshipman searched madly in his book. *'Without further . . . further . . .'*

*'Delay,'* said Jack without taking his eye from his telescope. 'Acknowledge. Mr Pullings: strike the Blue Peter. All hands to weigh.' He saw a woman pass the reins to a man, leap from the box and run down to the boats, followed by a small black figure from the body of the coach, carrying an enormous parcel. 'Sophie,' he said, loud over the bosun's pipes and the pounding of feet, 'ain't that Diana?'

'I am sure it is,' said she, looking through the glass. 'I can recognize her sprigged muslin from here. And that is poor Stephen, with the parcel.'

'At last,' said Jack. 'At last. The usual hell-fire drama.

Thank God he has someone to look after him, even if it is only Diana. Mr Pullings, our skeleton crew may take some time to win the anchor, though I am sure it will be done with every appearance of alacrity. Sweetheart, it is over the side with you, alas.' He handed her down to the quarterdeck, where the bosun's chair was swung inboard, waiting to lower her into the *Arethusa*'s barge, lent by their friend Billy Harvey.

'Goodbye, my dearest,' she said, smiling as well as she could, the great tears welling. 'God bless and keep you.'

'God bless you too,' said Jack, and in a hard, unnatural voice he called 'A whip for the children.' One by one they were lowered down like little bundles to their mother, their eyes closed and their hands tightly clasped. 'Mr Watson,' he said to the midshipman in charge of the boat, 'be so good as to speak my gig as you pull in, and tell 'em to spread more canvas, to spread every stitch they possess. My compliments and best thanks to Captain Harvey.'

He turned to give the orders that would carry the *Worcester* into the offing on the very tail of the ebb: he had ten minutes in hand, which might just suffice with this breeze, Bonden being a capital smallcraft sailor; and these ten minutes must be spent in persuading the sharpest eyes in the Navy that the *Worcester* was in fact obeying orders with all imaginable zeal rather than sitting there with her hands in her pockets. Ordinarily he would have left all this to Tom Pullings, his first lieutenant, an old and trusted shipmate; but he knew that there was not a man aboard who was not perfectly well aware of his motions, the ship having a small temporary crew of old experienced hands, all men-of-war's men, and since the seamen delighted in deception, above all any deception intended to blear the port-admiral's eye, he was afraid they might overact their parts. It was a ticklish business, managing this tacit connivance at disobeying a direct order while at the same time maintaining his reputation as an efficient officer, and perhaps there was a little too much brisk running about to be quite convincing. At one point a gun from the shore brought his heart into his mouth, much as it had leapt when he was a youngster and the same Admiral, then a commander, had caught him playing the fool rather than attending to the exact trim of the outer jib; but it was only the great man emphasizing his desire that *Andromache* should send a lieutenant to his office: *Andromache* had spent more than forty seconds hoisting out a boat. Even so, Jack dared not risk the same reproof in the face of the fleet, and the *Worcester* was well under way, her best bower catted, her topsails sheeted home (though faintly), and her topgallants loose in the brails by the time the gig crossed her wake under a press of canvas and shot up her starboard side. Out here the flood was cutting up an awkward, high-chopping sea against the breeze and hooking on would require the most accurate judgement. However, Bonden *was* a most accurate judge of these things: he might decide to wait until the ship was clear of the Wight, but in any case there was no danger of the boat being stove alongside.

Jack was still angry: he was also cold and unhappy. He glanced down at the heaving boat, the bowman poised with his hook, Bonden at the tiller gauging the scend of the sea, alternately filling a trifle and then luffing up, and at Stephen, looking meek in the stern-sheets, nursing his box: he sniffed, and went below without a word. The Marine sentry at the cabin door changed his smile to a look of remote wooden respect as he passed.

On the quarterdeck Mr Pullings said to a midshipman, 'Mr Appleby, jump down to the purser and ask him for half a pint of sweet oil.'

'Sweet oil, sir?' cried the midshipman. 'Yes, sir, directly,' he said, seeing a hint of brimstone in the first lieutenant's eye.

'Pin her, Joe,' said Bonden. The bowman hooked on at the mainchains, the big lugsail came down with a run, and speaking in a curt, official voice Bonden said, 'Now, sir, if you please. We can't hang about all day under the barky's lee. I'll look after your old parcel.'

The *Worcester* was a wall-sided ship and the way into her was a series of very shallow smooth wet slippery steps that rose vertically from the waterline, with no comfortable tumblehome, no inward slope, to help the pilgrim on his way; still, they had manropes on either side and this made it just possible for very agile, seamanlike mariners to go aboard: but Dr Maturin was neither agile nor yet seamanlike.

'Come on, sir,' said the coxswain impatiently as Stephen crouched there, hesitating with one foot on the gunwale. The gap between the ship and the gig began widening again and before it should reach proportions of a chasm Stephen made a galvanic spring, landing on the lowest step and grasping the manropes with all his might. Here he stood, gasping and contemplating the sheer height above: he knew he had behaved very ill, and that he was in disgrace. Bonden, though an old friend, had greeted him without a smile, saying 'You have cut it precious fine, sir. Do you know you have very nearly *made us miss the tide*? And may yet.' And in the passage from the shore he had heard a good deal more about 'missing the tide, and a roaring great old spring-tide too,' and about the Captain's horrid rage 'at being made to look a ninny in the face of the whole fleet – like a flaming lion all through the ebb; which if he misses of it at last, there will be all Hell to pay, and with boiling pitch at that.' Harsh words from Bonden, and no kindly stern-ladder or even bosun's chair to bring him aboard . . . here the *Worcester* gave a lee-lurch, heaving her ugly larboard flank so high that the copper showed, while the starboard, with Stephen on it, sank to a corresponding depth. The cold sea surged deliberately up, soaking his legs and the greater part of his trunk. He gasped again, and clung tighter.

As she rolled back again vigorous, impatient hands seized his ankles, and he found himself propelled up the side. 'I must remember to pay the proper compliment to the quarterdeck,' he reflected, when he was very nearly there. 'This may attenuate my fault.' But in his agitation he forgot that he had earlier pinned his hat to his wig, to preserve it from the wind, and when on reaching the holy space he pulled it off – when both rose together – his gesture had more the appearance of ill-timed jocularity than of respect, so much so that some of the young gentlemen, two ship's boys, and a Marine, who did not know him, dissolved in honest mirth, while those who did know him did not seem mollified at all.

'Upon my word, Doctor,' said Mowett, the officer of the watch, 'you have cut it pretty fine, I must say. You very nearly made us miss our tide. What was you thinking of? And you are all wet – sopping wet. How did you get so wet?'

Mr Pullings, standing by the weather rail, looking stiff and remote, said, 'The rendezvous was for the height of flood two tides ago, sir,' with no kind word of greeting.

Stephen had known Mowett and Pullings since they were mere snotty reefers of no consequence whatsoever, and at any other time he would have snapped them as tight shut as a snuff-box; but now their vast moral superiority, the general strong mute disapprobation of the *Worcester*'s company, and his own wet misery left him without a word, and although in the depths of his mind he was half aware that this harshness was at least in part assumed, that it belonged to the naval idea of fun he had so often suffered from, he could not bring himself to respond.

Pulling's grim expression softened a little. He said, 'You got a ducking, I see. You must not stand there in wet clothes: you will catch your death of cold. Has it reached your watch?'

Very, very often in Dr Maturin's career, it – that is to say the sea, that element so alien to him – had reached his watch when he came aboard, and indeed sometimes it had closed over his head; but every time the fact astonished and distressed him. 'Oh,' he cried, groping in his fob, 'I believe it has.' He took out the watch and shook it, shedding still more water on the deck.'

'Give it here, sir,' said Pullings. 'Mr Appleby, take this watch and put it in the sweet oil.'

The cabin door opened. 'Well, Doctor,' said Jack, looking even taller than usual and far more intimidating. 'Good morning to you, or rather good afternoon. This is a strange hour to report aboard – this is cutting it pretty fine – this is coming it tolerably high, I believe. Do you know you very nearly made us miss our tide? Miss our tide right under the Admiral's front window? Did not you see the Blue Peter flying all through the forenoon watch – nay, watch after God-damned watch? I must tell you, sir, that I have known men headed up in a barrel and thrown overboard for less: far less. Mr Mowett, you may round in and set the jib and forestaysail at last. At last,' he said with heavy emphasis, looking at Stephen. 'Why, you are all wet. Surely you did not fall in, like a mere lubber?'

'I did not,' said Stephen, goaded out of his humility. 'The sea it was that rose.'

'Well, you must not stand there, dripping all over the deck; it ain't a pretty sight, and you may take cold. Come and shift yourself. Your sea-chest is in my cabin: at least *it* had some notion of punctuality.'

'Jack,' said Stephen, shedding his breeches in the cabin, 'I beg your pardon. I am very sorry for my lateness. I regret it extremely.'

'Punctuality,' said Captain Aubrey: but then, feeling that this, the beginning of a homily on the great naval virtue, was hardly generous, he shook Stephen's free hand and went on, 'Damn my eyes, I was like a cat on hot tiles all through this vile morning and afternoon; so I spoke a little hasty. Join me on deck when you are shifted, Stephen. Bring the other glass, and we will take a last look at the shore before we round the Wight.'

The day was sparkling clear, the powerful telescopes showed the Sally Port sharp and bright, the inn and its white balcony, and on the balcony Sophie and Diana side by side, Jagiello tall on Diana's arm, his arm in a sling, and next to Sophie a diminishing row of heads that must be the children: a flutter of handkerchiefs from time to time. 'There is Jagiello,' said Stephen. 'I came down in his coach. That was the source of the trouble.'

'But surely Jagiello is a most prodigious whip?'

'Sure he is Jehu come again: we fairly swept out of London, and he driving in the Lithuanian manner, standing up and leaning out over his team, encouraging them with howls. This was very well for a while, and Diana and I were able to have a word in peace, because he and his cattle spoke the same language; but when we came to change horses the case was altered. Furthermore, Jagiello is not used to driving in England: Lithuania is an aristocratic country where the common people get out of the way, and when the slow wagon from Petersfield declined to pull over he was so displeased that he determined to shave it very close, by way of reproof. But the wagoner fetched the off-hand leader such a puck with his whip that we swerved, took a post and lost a wheel. No great harm, since we did not overturn, and once we had roused out a smith and he had lit his forge all was well in a couple of hours, apart from Jagiello's arm, which had a sad wrench. I have rarely seen anyone so vexed. He told me privately that he would never had exceeded a hand-canter if he had known he was to drive in a mere howling democracy. That was scarcely just; but then he was horribly cast down, with Diana watching.'

'Excitable foreigners,' said Jack. 'Jagiello is such a fine fellow that sometimes you almost forget it, but at-bottom he is only a foreigner, poor soul. I suppose you took the coach on?'

'I did not. Diana took it, so she did, the sun being up by then. She is a far better fist with a four-in-hand than I am, the creature.'

He had the creature clear in his glass, and the sun full on her. All the years he had known her she had struggled against unkind circumstances: an expensive, fashionable way of life in her girlhood with no money to support it; then worse poverty still, and dependence; then difficult, troublesome, passionate and even violent lovers; and all this had worn her spirited temper, rendering it mordant and fierce, so that for a great while he had never associated Diana with laughter: beauty, dash, style, even wit, but not laughter. Now it had changed. He had never known her so happy as she had been these last few months, nor so handsome. He was not coxcomb enough to suppose that their marriage had a great deal to do with the matter; it was rather her setting up house at last, with a wide and varied acquaintance around her and the rich easy life she led there – she adored being rich; yet even so a visible, tangible husband was not without an effect, even if he were not of the right race, birth, shape, religion, or tastes – even if he were not what her friends might have wished her at an earlier time. Jack was perfectly silent, wholly concentrated on Sophie far over the water: she was now stooping to the little boy at her side; she held him up high, clear of the rail, and he and his sisters all waved again. He caught the twinkle of their handkerchiefs through the yards of *Ajax* and *Bellerophon*, and behind the eyepiece of his telescope he smiled tenderly, an expression rarely seen by his shipmates. 'Do not suppose,' said Stephen, continuing his inward discourse, 'that I am in any way favourable to children' – as though he had been accused of a crime – 'There are far too many of them as it is, a monstrous superfluity: and I have no wish, no wish at all, to see myself perpetuated. But in Diana's case, might it not settle her happiness?' As though she were conscious of his gaze she too waved to the ship, and turning to Jagiello she pointed over the sea.

The *Agamemnon*, homeward-bound from the Straits, crossed their field of view, a great cloud of white canvas; and when she had passed Portsmouth was gone, cut off by a headland.

Jack straightened, snapped his telescope to, and looked up at the sails: they were trimmed much as he could wish, which was scarcely surprising since he himself had formed young Mowett's idea of how a ship should be conducted, and they were urging the *Worcester*'s one thousand eight hundred and forty-two tons through the water at a sedate five knots, about all that could be expected with such a breeze and tide.

'That is the last we shall see of the comforts of shore for some considerable time,' observed Stephen.

'Not at all. We are only running down to Plymouth to complete,' said Jack absently, his eyes fixed aloft: the *Worcester*'s pole-topgallantmasts were too taunt, too lofty by far for her slab-sided hull. If he had time in Plymouth he would try to replace them with stumps and separate royal-masts.

He deliberately set his mind to the problem of shipping these hypothetical royals abaft the cap and quite low, to relieve the strain on the notoriously ill-fastened ship in the event of a Mediterranean blow: he knew the wicked force of the mistral in the Gulf of Lions, and the killing short seas it could raise in under an hour, seas quite unlike the long Atlantic waves for which these ships were presumably designed. He did so to deaden the pain of parting, so much stronger than he had expected; but finding the sadness persist he swung himself up on to the hammock-netting and, calling to the bosun, made his way aloft, high aloft, to see what changes would have to be made when his stump topgallantmasts came aboard.

He was still aloft, swinging between sea and sky with the practised, unconscious ease of an orang-utang, close in technical argument with his dogged, obstinate, conservative, greybearded bosun, when a hundred feet and more below him the drum began to beat Roast Beef of Old England for the officers' dinner.

Stephen walked into the wardroom, a fine long room with a fine long table down the middle, lit by a great stern-window right across its breadth, a room which, despite the lieutenants' cabins on either side, offered plenty of space for a dozen officers, each with a servant behind his chair, and as many guests as they chose to invite. Yet at the moment it was sparsely inhabited: three Marines in their red coats by the window, the master standing in the middle, his hands on the back of his chair, quite lost in thought, the purser looking at his watch, Pullings and Mowett by the door, drinking grog and evidently waiting for Stephen.

'Here you are, Doctor,' cried Pullings, shaking his hand. 'On time to the second.' He was smiling all over his tanned friendly face, but there was more than a hint of anxiety in his eye, and in a low voice he went on, 'Poor Mowett is afraid he upset you, sir, playing off his humours when you came aboard: it was only our fun, you know, sir, but we were afraid you might not have twigged it, being, as I might say, so uncommonly damp.'

'Never in life, my dear,' said Stephen. 'What are you drinking?'

'Two-water grog.'

'Then pray give me a glass. William Mowett, your very good health. Tell me, when will the other gentlemen appear? I was deprived of my breakfast, and I raven: have they no sense of time, at all?'

'There ain't no other gentlemen,' said Pullings. 'We only have a skeleton crew, and so,' – laughing heartily, since the conceit had only just come to him – 'we have only a skeleton wardroom, ha, ha. Come, let me introduce the others right away: I have a surprise for you, and I long to show it. I fairly gripe to show you my surprise.' Mr Adams the purser had seen the Doctor in Halifax, Nova Scotia, at the Commissioner's ball, and was very happy to see him again; Mr Gill the master, a sad contrast to the purser's fat round-faced jollity, claimed an acquaintance from the days when he was a master's mate in the *Hannibal*, and Stephen had repaired him after the battle of Algeciras – 'though there were too many of us for you to remember me,' he said. Captain Harris of the Marines was amazingly glad to be sailing with Dr Maturin: his cousin James Macdonald had often spoken of the Doctor's skill in taking

34

off his forearm, and there was nothing so comfortable as the thought that if one were blasted to pieces there was a really eminent hand aboard to put one together again. His lieutenants, very young pink men, only bowed, somewhat awed, for Stephen had a great reputation as a raiser of the dead and as the invariable companion of one of the most successful frigate-captains in the service.

Pullings hurried them away to table, took his place at the head, dashed through his soup – the usual wardroom soup, Stephen noticed, quite useful for poultices; though at the same time he did notice a familiar, exquisite, yet unnameable scent on the air – and then called out to the steward, 'Jakes, is it done?'

'Done, sir, done to a turn,' came the distant answer, and a moment later the steward raced in from the galley with a golden pie.

Pullings thrust in his knife, thrust in his spoon, and his anxiety gave way to triumph. 'There, Doctor,' he said, passing Stephen his plate. 'There's my surprise – there's your real welcome aboard!'

'Bless me,' cried Stephen, staring at his goose and truffle pie – more truffle than goose – 'Mr Pullings, joy, I am amazed, amazed and delighted.'

'I hoped you might be,' said Pullings, and he explained to the others that long ago, when first made lieutenant, he had seen that the Doctor loved trubs, so he had gone out into the forest, the New Forest, where he lived by land, and had dug him a basket, by way of welcome aboard: and Mowett had composed a song.

'Welcome aboard, welcome aboard,' sang Mr Mowett
'Sober as Adam or drunk as a lord
Eat like Lucullus and drink like a king,
Doze in your hammock while sirens do sing,
Welcome, dear Doctor, oh welcome aboard,
Welcome aboard,
Welcome aboard.'

The others ground their glasses on the table, chanting

35.

'Welcome aboard, welcome aboard,' and then drank to him in the thin harsh purple liquid that passed for claret in the *Worcester*'s wardroom.

Thin though it was, the claret was nothing like so disagreeable as the substance called port that ended the meal. This probably had the same basis of vinegar and cochineal, but Ananias, the Gosport wine-merchant, had added molasses, raw spirit, and perhaps a little sugar of lead, a false date and a flaming lie by way of a label.

Stephen and Pullings lingered over the decanter when the others had gone, and Stephen said, 'I do not like to sound discontented, Tom, but surely this ship is more than usually damp, confined, awkward, comfortless? The mould on the beam that traverses my cabin is two inches thick, and although I am no Goliath my head beats against it. Sure, I have known better accommodations in a frigate; whereas this, if I do not mistake, is a ship of the line, no less.'

'I do not like to sound discontented neither,' said Pullings, 'nor to crab any ship I belong to; but between you and me, Doctor, between you and me, she is more what we call a floating coffin than a ship. And as for the damp, what do you expect? She was built in Sankey's yard, one of the Forty Thieves: twenty-year-old wood and green stuff with the sap in it all clapped together promiscuous and fastened with copper – precious little copper – and then overmasted to please the landsmen's fancy, so that when it comes on to blow her timbers all sprawl abroad. She is British-built, sir, and most of what we have sailed in, you and I, have been Spanish or French. They may not be very clever at fighting or sailing 'em, but God love us, they do know how to build.' He put down his glass and said, 'I do wish we had a can of Margate beer. But beer ain't genteel.'

'It might be more healthy,' said Stephen. 'So we are to put in at Plymouth, I hear?'

'That's right, sir: to complete. You will have your two mates – and don't I wish they may like it, when they see the dog-holes where we must stow them – and we must find the best part of our crew, three hundred hands or so. Lord, Doctor, how I hope we can get hold of some right seamen! The Captain can always fill half a frigate with good men come volunteerly, but they won't amount to much in a ship of the line – no prize-money in a ship of the line on blockade. And of course we are to have three more lieutenants and maybe a chaplain: the Captain is against it, but Admiral Thornton likes to have chaplains aboard and we may have to carry half a dozen out for the fleet. He is rather a blue-light admiral, though a good fighting-man, and he thinks it encourages the hands to have a proper funeral, with the words said by a real parson. Then we must have midshipmen, and this time the Captain swears he will enter none but what are regularly bred to the sea, none but what can hand, reef and steer, work their tides and take double altitudes, and understand the mathematics; he is not going to take a floating nursery, says he. For although you may scarcely believe it, Doctor, a dozen good seamanlike reefers are very useful aboard, learning the raw hands their duty; we are sure to have a good many – raw hands I mean – and they must learn their duty pretty quick, with the French grown so bold and the Americans coming right up into the Channel.'

'Are not the Frenchmen all shut up in Rochefort and Brest?'

'Their ships of the line: but when it comes on to blow hard from the east and our squadrons have to run for Torbay, their frigates slip out and chew up our merchantmen something cruel. I dare say we shall have a convoy to see down to the Straits. And then there are the privateers too, very presumptuous reptiles in the Bay. Still, the receiving ships may give us some decent drafts: the Captain has good friends in Plymouth. I hope so indeed, because there is no man in the service to work them up into a smart crew like the Captain, and a smart crew will offset an unweatherly slab-sided old ship. She has the guns, after all, and I can just see him sending her smack into the French line, if only they come out of Toulon, smack into the middle, both broadsides roaring.' The port, in addition to cochineal, contained a good deal of impure alcohol, and Pullings, a little elevated, cried 'Both broadsides into the thick of 'em – breaks the line – takes a first-rate – takes another – he is made a lord, and Tom Pullings a commander at last!' He turned his glowing, radiant face to the opening door.

'Well, sir, I am sure you shall be before long,' said Preserved Killick. He was the Captain's steward, a coarse, plain, ugly seaman, still quite unpolished in spite of his years of office, but a very old shipmate and therefore entitled to be familiar in an empty wardroom.

'Preserved Killick,' said Stephen, shaking his hand, 'I am happy to see you. Drink this,' – handing him his glass – 'it will do you good.'

'Thankee, sir,' said Killick, tossing it off without a wink; and in an official voice, though without changing his uncouth, easy posture, he went on, 'Captain's compliments and whenever Dr M has the leisure and inclination for a little music, would welcome his company in the cabin. Which he is a-tuning of his old fiddle this minute, sir.'

# CHAPTER TWO

At a broad table on the *Worcester*'s quarterdeck sat her
first lieutenant, with the Captain's clerk, the surgeon, the
purser, the bosun, and her other standing officers on either
side of him. Over to starboard stood a vague heap of men,
most of them poorly clothed, most of them looking lost and
miserable, all of them smelling of soap, the receiving-ship
having scrubbed them until they shone; but a few seemed
quite at home, and when Mr Pullings called out 'Next'
one of these stepped up to the table and touched his
knuckles to his forehead and stood there swaying gently,
a middle-aged man in loose trousers and a torn blue jacket
with metal buttons, a bright red handkerchief round his
neck. He looked horribly dissipated and he had certainly
been fighting the night before; Pullings gazed at him with
great satisfaction and said, 'Well, Phelps, are you come to
add to our burden?'

'That's right, sir,' said Phelps, and then very rapidly to
the clerk, 'Ebenezer Phelps, born at Dock in sixty-nine,
dwelling at Gorham's Rents, Dock, thirty-four years at
sea, last ship *Wheel 'em Along*, sheet-anchor man.'

'And before that *Circe* and *Venerable*,' said Pullings.
'And a damned bad character from both. Rate him able.
Phelps, you had better take a caulk below, before the
Captain sees you. Next.'

A powerful bosun's mate led up a pale knock-kneed
man in breeches and part of what was once a coachman's
greatcoat: his name was William Old.

'What was your trade, Old?' asked Pullings kindly.

'I don't like to boast,' said Old, gathering confidence,
'but I was a trifler.' There was a momentary hush; the
clerk looked up from his book with a frown; the bosun's
mate whispered 'Mind your luff, mate,' in a hoarse growl,

39

and Old added, 'Not a sadware man, sir, nor a hollow-ware man, but a trifler, a journeyman trifler. But the whole pewter trade, sadware and all, is gone to the dogs, and –'

'Have you ever been to sea?' asked Pullings.

'I once went to Margate, sir.'

'Rate him landman, if he passes the Doctor,' said Pullings. 'He may be some use as armourer's crew. Next.'

'Oh sir,' cried the journeyman trifler, about to be led off by the bosun's mate, 'Oh sir, if you please: may I have my bounty now, your honour? My wife is waiting there on the quay, with the children.'

'Explain to him about the ticket, Jobling,' said Pullings to the bosun's mate. 'Next.'

Now it was the turn of the pressed men, several right seamen among them, some taken far out in the offing from homeward-bound merchant ships by Mowett in the barge, others captured ashore by the gang. The first of them, a man called Yeats, looked more like a prosperous gardener, which indeed he was, as he explained to the lieutenant: a nurseryman. He had half an acre under glass – his business going well – would be ruined if he were pressed – his wife did not understand the trade, and she was expecting. His extreme distress was evident; so was his sincerity.

'What is that anchor doing on your hand?' asked Pullings, pointing to the mark, tattooed blue and red. 'You have been to sea: do not deny it.'

Yes, he had been to sea when he was a boy, five months in *Hermione*, sick almost all the time, and when she was paid off here in Hamoaze he had walked inland as far as ever he could and had never come near the shore again until Thursday, when the press-gang took him as he was crossing the bridge to visit an important customer at Saltash. His business would be ruined if he did not go home.

'Well, I am sorry for it, Yeats,' said Pullings. 'But the law is the law: any man that has used the sea may be pressed.' In cases like this some officers would make observations about the necessity for manning the fleet, about serving – preserving – the country, even about patriotism, for the general edification of the ship's company: others would turn harsh or gruff. Pullings only said 'Go along with the Doctor,' shaking his head. Yeats cast a desperate look at the seated men, clasped his hands, and went along without another word, too disheartened to speak.

Behind the canvas screen Stephen told him to take off his clothes, poked him in the belly and groin, and said, 'You lift heavy weights in your trade.'

'Oh no, sir,' said Yeats in a low spiritless voice, 'we only carry –'

'Do not presume to contradict me,' said Stephen sharply. 'You answer questions when they are asked and not before, do you hear?'

'Beg pardon, sir,' said Yeats, closing his eyes.

'You lift heavy weights. Here are the signs of an incipient hernia. I am afraid we shall have to refuse you. It is not serious yet, but you are to drink very little ale or wine, and no strong waters at all; you are to forswear tobacco, that nasty vice, and are to be let blood three times a year.'

In the great after-cabin, the Captain's drawing-room, music-room, refuge and delight, Jack paced to and fro, dictating to a knowing old confidential clerk, lent by his friend the Commissioner: 'Captain Aubrey presents his best compliments to Lord Alton and very much regrets that the *Worcester* is not a suitable ship for a young gentleman the age of his lordship's son; she carries no schoolmaster, and the nature of her present duties precludes – precludes my acting as a goddam dry-nurse: use that excellent expression you thought of for the others, Mr Simpson, if you please. But if the boy were put to a good mathematical school when he is twelve and taught the rudiments of trigonometry, navigation, English and French grammar for a year or so, Captain Aubrey would be happy to attend to his lordship's wishes in the event of his being appointed to some more eligible command.'

'Lord Alton has a good deal of interest with Government you know sir,' observed the clerk, an acquaintance of many years standing.

'I am sure he has,' said Jack, 'and I am sure he will soon find a more biddable captain. Now much the same to Mr Jameson: but in this case his boy is too old. He may be very good at Latin and Greek, but he does not know the difference between a logarithm and a log; besides, very few young fellows take well to the sea at fifteen. What next? Tell me, do you know anything about this nephew of Admiral Brown's?'

'Well, sir, he seemed a heavy young gentleman to me: his last captain turned him on shore, and I am told he failed to pass for lieutenant at Somerset House.'

'Ay, I dare say. I saw him make a sad cock of putting the yawl about when he was in *Colossus*: he was drunk at the time. But I believe I must take him. His uncle was very good to me when I was a boy. We will try to sharpen his wits: then he may pass at Gibraltar, and perhaps the Admiral will make him for his uncle's sake – they were shipmates in the time of the Spanish Armament, I recall,' said Jack, gazing out of the stern-window and seeing the Hamoaze of more than twenty years ago, just as crowded with men-of-war even then, and himself a bran-new lieutenant, shedding happiness all round him like the rising sun, taking the two officers in question ashore in the gig. 'I will write that letter myself,' he said. 'As for young Savage and Maitland, they may certainly come. But now there is this very delicate confidential semi-official letter to Admiral Bowyer about the remaining lieutenants: Mr Collins and Mr Whiting I know nothing of, except that they are very young, near the bottom of the list; but Mr Somers I will not have if I can possibly avoid it.'

'The Honourable Mr Somers,' said Simpson in a significant tone.

'No doubt, but he is an idle fellow and no seaman at all – too rich for his own good or the comfort of the mess he is in – cannot hold his wine and has not the mother-wit

42

to leave it alone. Imagine him taking the middle watch in dirty weather on a lee-shore – imagine sending him away with the boats on a cutting-out expedition – that would be sporting with men's lives indeed. I have no notion of people making the service a mere convenience for themselves, as if it were a public establishment for loungers. No. We must phrase it with great care, pointing out most respectfully that we will be damned if we receive him on board rather than one of the two other gentlemen we have put in for, Thorneycroft and Patterson: they are both on shore, as I know very well.'

'Mr Widgery of the Yard to see you, sir,' said Killick.

'Oh yes,' said Jack, 'that will be about my topmasts. Mr Simpson, you may think it as well to advise with the Commissioner about this letter; and perhaps you would let me see your draft this evening. There is not a moment to lose: the hound may report aboard any day, and then it will be much harder to get rid of him. And please tell Mrs Fanshaw, with all proper expressions, that I should be very happy to dine with her and the Commissioner on Sunday. You will take a glass with Mr Widgery before you go?'

'You are very kind, sir. But before I forget it, Captain Fanshaw begs you will enter his sister's grandchild on the books, before the muster is made up. Name of Henry Meadows, rising eight, a likely lad.'

'Of course,' said Jack. 'What rating? Captain's servant looks as well as any. Killick, show Mr Widgery in, and bring the madeira.'

The evening gun boomed out over Hamoaze, Catwater and the Sound; lights began to twinkle from Plymouth, from Dock, and from the floating town of men-of-war, each one a village in itself. Those from the *Worcester*'s great cabin showed brighter than most, because her captain still had a great deal of paper-work to do, and he had lit his patent Argand lamp: statements from the receiving-ships lay on his table, together with indents for carpenter's, gunner's and bosun's stores, huge rolls from the Victualling Yard, and the first outline of a watch-list, the result of some hours of close consultation between him and his first lieutenant; but superimposed upon these neat heaps lay some sheets of music in manuscript, his violin beside them; and it was these that he was studying when Stephen walked in.

'There you are, Stephen,' said Jack. 'Killick, Killick there. The toasted cheese, d'ye hear me? Stephen, I am happy to see you.'

'Sure, you look quite happy, too. Have you had a good day?'

'Tolerable, I thank you, tolerable. I must say the Commissioner has done us proud for once: we have something not far from our complement of hands, and he has promised to turn over half the Skates when she pays off tomorrow.'

'The little small ship that came in after us, with a shark's tail nailed to its prow? With all your eager hopeful greed for men you can hardly expect many out of a mere floating band-box.'

'To be exact, brother, she is a brig; and although her ship's company may not amount to a very great many, they have served a four-year commission together in the West Indies under young Hall, a very fine seaman; they have seen a mort of action, and I dare say every man-jack can be rated able. We are most uncommon lucky to be able to snap 'em up, I do give you my word.'

'Perhaps the Skates may esteem themselves less fortunate, turned over without seeing their friends after four years away.'

'It is hard,' said Jack. 'Very hard. But then war is a very cruel hard business.' He shook his head, but brightening again he said, 'And the Yard has done the handsome thing about my stump topgallants and separate royals – quite agreed with me about their lessening the strain, and will let me have them in the morning, out of the old *Invincible*.'

'Wittles,' said Killick. 'Which I have put 'em in the dining-cabin. Not an inch of room on this here table,' – looking angrily at the papers.

'Indeed,' said Jack as they ate their supper, 'I do not remember an easier, more satisfactory manning. We have a good third of our people seamen, able and ordinary confounded, not counting the Skates; and many of the others look stout, promising material.'

'There were many sad brutish grobians among those I examined,' said Stephen, who was feeling disagreeable and contradictory: he loathed the whole business of impressment.

'Oh, of course there are always some odd fish among the quota-men sent by the magistrates; but this time we have very few downright thieves: only one parricide, that was found incapable of pleading and sent to the Navy; and after all he will scarcely carry on his capers here – he will scarcely find another father aboard. And much the same applied to the poachers. Upon the whole, I am very pleased: what with the old leaven and the new, as it says in the Bible, I do not doubt but we shall have a tolerable brisk crew by the time we reach the flag. And to encourage 'em I have laid in a fine stock of private powder, the stock of a fireworks-maker lately deceased, a most prodigious bargain. It was the clerk of cheque that gave me wind of it – he means to marry the widow – and although it is a little mixed with red orpiment and so on the ordnance-master swears it is sound. The only thing between me and perfect felicity,' said Jack, thrusting the cloud of legal troubles still farther back into the recesses of his mind, 'is the threat of these parsons and the absence of the other lieutenants: manning always means a prodigious amount of work, and far too much of it falls on poor Pullings. We must have more lieutenants at once. Pullings is quite worn out, and the next few days will be rough going indeed.'

'So he is too: and grown strangely snappish from want of repose. He rounded on me with inconceivable

45

ferocity for turning a small paltry handful of men away:
his appetite for hands is unmeasured, insatiable, inhuman.
I must give him a comfortable dose tonight. Seventy-five
drops of the tincture of laudanum, and tomorrow he will
be the complaisant amiable obliging Thomas Pullings we
have always known: otherwise it must be the blue pill for
him. Blue pill and black draught.'

'With any luck the others should appear tomorrow,
and that will take some of the load off his shoulders: and
the Commissioner has a plan for sending the parsons in a
merchantman. Your mates came aboard this afternoon, I
collect: I hope you are pleased with them?'

'I have no doubt that they are as competent as their
certificates state them to be, as competent as we have
any right to expect in surgeons.' Stephen was a physician, and surgeons (though worthy souls often enough,
taken individually) had not yet lived down their long,
long association with barbers. 'But even if the one had
been Podalirius and the other Machaon I should still have
preferred to be alone.'

'Are they not quite the thing?' asked Jack. 'I will
try to arrange a transfer if you do not like them.'

'You are very good; but it is not that I have taken
any disgust either to the young man or to the old. It
is only that I dislike the whole notion of subordination.
The corporal lurks in almost every bosom, and each man
tends to use authority when he has it, thus destroying his
natural relationship with his fellows, a disastrous state of
affairs for both sides. Do away with subordination and you
do away with tyranny: without subordination we should
have no Neros, no Tamerlanes, no Buonapartes.'

'Stuff,' said Jack. 'Subordination is the natural order:
there is subordination in Heaven – Thrones and Dominions take precedence over Powers and Principalities,
Archangels and ordinary foremast angels; and so it is in
the Navy. You have come to the wrong shop for anarchy,
brother.'

'Be that as it may,' said Stephen, 'I had far rather

sail alone; yet with some six hundred souls crammed into this insecure and mouldy wooden vessel, many verminous, many poxed, and some perhaps harbouring the seeds of the gaol-fever, I need some assistance even in the ordinary daily course, to say nothing of action, God forbid. And in point of fact, since I am likely to be absent some of the time, I have taken peculiar pains to come by an exceptionally well-qualified, well-recommended senior assistant. But listen, why are you so opposed to these clergymen? Surely you are no longer so weak as to set store by superstition?'

'Of course not,' said Jack quickly. 'It is only for the sake of the hands,' – his invariable reply. 'Besides,' he said after a pause, 'you cannot talk bawdy with parsons. It ain't fitting.'

'But you never do talk bawdy,' said Stephen. It was true, or at least almost true: although no kind of a prude, Jack Aubrey was a man who preferred action to talk, fact to phantasm, and although he did possess a small stock of lewd stories for the end of dinners when imaginations grew warm and often lubricious he usually forgot them, or left out the point.

'Oh well,' said Jack: and then, 'Did you ever meet Bach?'

'Which Bach?'

'London Bach.'

'Not I.'

'I did. He wrote some pieces for my uncle Fisher, and his young man copied them out fair. But they were lost years and years ago, so last time I was in town I went to see whether I could find the originals: the young man has set up on his own, having inherited his master's music-library. We searched through the papers – such a disorder you would hardly credit, and I had always supposed publishers were as neat as bees – we searched for hours, and no uncle's pieces did we find. But the whole point is this: Bach had a father.'

'Heavens, Jack, what things you tell me. Yet upon

recollection I seem to have known other men in much the same case.'

'And this father, this old Bach, you understand me, had written piles and piles of musical scores in the pantry.'

'A whimsical place to compose in, perhaps; but then birds sing in trees, do they not? Why not antediluvian Germans in a pantry?'

'I mean the piles were kept in the pantry. Mice and blackbeetles and cook-maids had played Old Harry with some cantatas and a vast great Passion according to St Mark, in High Dutch; but lower down all was well, and I brought away several pieces, 'cello for you, fiddle for me, and some for both together. It is strange stuff, fugues and suites of the last age, crabbed and knotted sometimes and not at all in the modern taste, but I do assure you, Stephen, there is meat in it. I have tried this partita in C a good many times, and the argument goes so deep, so close and deep, that I scarcely follow it yet, let alone make it sing. How I should love to hear it played really well – to hear Viotti dashing away.'

Stephen studied the 'cello suite in his hand, booming and humming *sotto voce*. 'Tweedly-tweedly, tweedly tweedly, deedly deedly pom pom *pom*. Oh, this would call for the delicate hand of the world,' he said. 'Otherwise it would sound like boors dancing. Oh, the double-stopping . . . and how to bow it?'

'Shall we make an attempt upon the D minor double sonata?' said Jack, 'and knit up the ravelled sleeve of care with sore labour's bath?'

'By all means,' said Stephen. 'A better way of dealing with a sleeve cannot be imagined.'

Neither had at any time been more than a fairly accomplished amateur: of recent years neither had had much leisure for practice, and various wounds (an American musket-ball in Jack's case, a French interrogation in Stephen's) had so slowed down their fingers that in places they were obliged to indicate the notes by hooting; and as they felt their way through the difficult sonata time after time they made the night so hideous that Killick's indignation broke out at last and he said to the Captain's cook, 'There they go again, tweedly-deedly, tweedly-deedly, belly-aching the whole bleeding night, and the toasted cheese seizing on to their plates like goddam glue, which I dursen't go in to fetch them; and never an honest tune from beginning to end.'

Perhaps there was not: but after a particularly difficult, severe and abstract passage the last movement ended with a triumphant summing-up and resolution that they could both play at first sight and that they repeated again and again; and the grave happiness of the music was still with Captain Aubrey when he walked on to his quarterdeck in the bright morning to see his stump topgallantmasts and their attendant royals come aboard, followed almost immediately by the *Tamar*'s barge bringing a score of glum but resigned and obviously competent Skates to the larboard side and by a Plymouth wherry with two pink-faced young men, very carefully shaved, wearing identical uniforms, their best, and solemn expressions. The wherry hooked on to the starboard mainchains: the young men ran up the side in order of seniority – two whole weeks lay between them – saluted the quarterdeck and looked quickly fore and aft for the officer of the watch. They saw no calm dignified figure pacing up and down with a telescope under his arm and an epaulette on his shoulder, but after a moment a very dirty tall thin man in tarry trousers and a round jacket stepped towards them from the busy crowd at the foot of the foremast; his eyes were rimmed with red, his expression stern, as well it might be, Pullings having been obliged to keep watch as well as carry out all his other duties since the *Worcester* left Portsmouth. The first young man took off his hat and said in a humble voice, 'Collins, sir, come on board, if you please.'

'Whiting, sir, if you please: come on board,' said the other.

'You are very welcome, gentlemen,' said Pullings. 'I

will not give you my hand, it being covered with slush; but you are very welcome. There is a mortal deal of work to be done, if ever we are to put to sea. There is not a moment to lose.'

Jack was speaking to the gunner at the time, explaining that the private powder in the kegs marked X was mixed with red orpiment, and XX with antimony or copper, while still others had lycoperdium or camphor or strontium, but he noticed with satisfaction that neither of the two young men did in fact lose a moment. Their sea-chests were scarcely aboard before they were out of their fine clothes, actively forwarding the work on the foretopgallantmast, as deep in slush as any of those concerned with easing its head through the awkward trestle-trees and cap. 'It may not be fighting-powder, Mr Borrell,' said Jack, 'but it will answer very well for practice. Let a dozen rounds be filled for each gun. I should like to see how the people shape as soon as we put to sea: perhaps tomorrow, on the evening tide.'

'A dozen rounds it is, sir,' said the gunner with deep approval. Captain Aubrey belonged to the school of Douglas and Collingwood, men who believed that a ship's prime purpose was to bring cannon within range of the enemy and then to fire with extreme speed and accuracy, and Borrell supported this view with all his heart. He walked off to fill cartridge with his mates in the magazine and Jack looked up at the rising foretopgallantmast with a smile: there was order in that apparent chaos of men, spars and ropes, and Tom Pullings had the whole operation well in hand. He looked down, and his smile faded: a small boat crammed with parsons was approaching the ship, followed by another with a lady in mourning, a small boy by her side.

'I had hoped to persuade her to put the boy to school,' said Jack to Stephen after supper, as they sat down to a comparatively simple Scarlatti piece that they both knew well. 'I had hoped to convince her that a voyage of this kind, a few months on the Toulon blockade, a relieving turn with no future in it – a mere parenthesis, as you said the other day – would be no use to her boy, and that there were many other captains, with schoolmasters and a long commission ahead of them: I named half a dozen. And I had hoped to ship no first-voyagers this time, no squeakers, no use to me and I no use to them. But she would not be denied – wept, upon my word; shed tears. I have never been so wretched in my life.'

'Mrs Calamy is an officer's widow, I collect?'

'Yes. Edward Calamy and I were shipmates in *Theseus*, before he was made post into the *Atalante*. Then they gave him the *Rochester*, seventy-four, just such a ship as this: she was lost with all hands in the great autumn blow of the year eight. If I had told her that we came from the same yard, she might have taken the little brute away.'

'Poor little brute. Pullings found him bathed in tears, and comforted him: the child led him downstairs, *below*, and gave him a large piece of plum-cake. This argues a grateful heart in Mr Calamy. I hope he may thrive, though he is so puny, so very puny.'

'Oh, I dare say he will, if he is not drowned or knocked on the head. Mrs Borrell will look after him – the Navy is equipped to breed up squeakers, after all. But I tell you what, Stephen, I tell you what: the Navy is not equipped to deal with a whole God-damned – a whole blessed convocation of clergy. It is not six parsons that are come aboard but seven: seven, upon my sacred honour. How I hope this breeze holds true for three more tides, so that we may put to sea before they send us half the bench of bishops.'

The wind did not hold true. The *Worcester* had barely shipped her new stumps, rattled down the shrouds, completed her water and received the port-admiral's visit before an ominous swell set in, causing her to pitch and roll even in the sheltered Hamoaze and foretelling the great grey swathes of rain driving in on a strong south-wester whose force steadily increased day after day, emptying the Sound, pinning the men-of-war to their moorings in

Hamoaze and the merchant ships in Catwater, driving the Brest team off their blockade into Torbay, and scattering the shores with driftwood, much of it ancient wreckage, English, French, Spanish, Dutch, and neutral. But some was recent, and this was mostly English, for not only were there now far more English merchantmen than foreigners to be wrecked, but the Royal Navy, keeping the sea in all weathers, the whole year round, was fast wearing out, and although new ships were continually being built as fast as limited treasure and supplies would allow, many others had to be kept in active service when they were no longer seaworthy – thirteen had been lost this year, quite apart from those taken by the Americans or the French.

Yet at least this delay gave the *Worcester* time for all kinds of last-minute arrangements, such as a provision of soap or blotting-paper, so often forgotten in even the best-ordered ships until they have sunk the land and with it all sources of supply: it also allowed still more people to put off with requests to Captain Aubrey, still more letters to come aboard for Admiral Thornton's squadron and for the *Worcester* herself. Some of these were addressed to her Captain; long, intricate and not particularly encouraging letters from his lawyer, letters that made Jack look careworn and old. 'How I do loathe this hanging about,' he said. 'It is a kind of enforced unpunctuality. And the damned thing about it is that Sophie could perfectly well have come down for a week or so: and Diana too I dare say. Yet at least it has brought you acquainted with your new messmates. You must be pretty crowded down there, but I hope you find them good company, learned and so on?'

Jack had not yet dined with the wardroom and its new inhabitants: not only had he been extremely busy with a restowing of the hold, to improve the *Worcester*'s trim, but partly out of custom and partly out of a desire to forget his legal worries he had also dined with other captains almost every day: fine hard-drinking parties, most of them, and a moderately good way of overlaying care for the while.

He had also travelled quite far inland to pay his respects to Lady Thornton and to ask whether he might carry anything from home to the Admiral. 'Yet now I come to think of it,' he went on, 'one of them, the Scotchman, is not a parson at all, but a professor of moral philosophy, to be delivered to Port Mahon, where presumably they are in need of his services. *Moral* philosophy. How does that differ from your kind, Stephen?'

'Why, natural philosophy is not concerned with ethics, virtues and vices, or metaphysics. The fact that the dodo has a keel to her breastbone whereas the ostrich and her kind have none presents no moral issue; nor does the dissolution of gold by aqua regia. We erect hypotheses, to be sure, some of us to a most stupendous height, but we always hope to sustain them by demonstrable facts in time: these are not the province of the moralist. Perhaps it might be said that your moral philosopher is in pursuit of wisdom rather than of knowledge; and indeed what he is concerned with is not so much the object of knowledge as of intuitive perception – is scarcely susceptible of being known. Yet whether wisdom can be any more profitably pursued than happiness is a question. Certainly the few moral philosophers I have known do not seem to have been outstandingly successful in either, whereas some natural philosophers, such as Sir Humphrey Davy . . .' Stephen carried on to the end of his long, his very long sentence, but a great while before he stopped it was apparent to him that Captain Aubrey was meditating a joke.

'So I suppose,' he said, smiling so broadly that his blue eyes were not more than twinkling slits in his red face, 'that you and Sir Humphrey could be described as immoral philosophers?'

'Sure there may be some poor thin barren minds that would catch at such a paltry clench,' said Stephen. 'Pothouse wits that might, if their beery genius soared so high, also call Professor Graham an unnatural philosopher.'

Captain Aubrey heaved silently for a while – few

53

men relished their own wit more than Jack – and then, smiling still, he said, 'Well, at all events, I hope he is good company. I can imagine an unnatural and an immoral philosopher arguing the toss for hours, to the admiration of all hands, ha, ha, ha.'

'We have barely exchanged a dozen words; he seems a reserved gentleman, and perhaps a little deaf. I have hardly formed any opinion of him; though he must be widely read, sure, to occupy a chair in a respectable university. I believe I have seen his name to a recent addition of the Nicomachean Ethics.'

'And what of the others, the parsons proper?'

Ordinarily they did not exchange their views about Stephen's fellow-members of the wardroom mess; Jack, for example, had not said a word about his extreme displeasure at the arrival of Mr Somers rather than either of the lieutenants he had applied for, nor of his intimate conviction that the young man had been in Plymouth for several days, reporting aboard only when the hard labour of fitting the *Worcester* for sea was done. But the parsons were no part of the ship's company; they were passengers; they might be discussed, and Stephen described them briefly. One was a West Country rector, an invalid who hoped to find health in the Mediterranean, where his cousin commanded the *Andromache*. 'I wish he may get there, at all: such a cachexy I have rarely seen ambulant' – all the others were unbeneficed clergymen: two had been ushers in schools for young gentlemen, and thought any other life preferable to that, even on shipboard; two had tried long and hard and unsuccessfully to live by their pens – they were pitifully thin and shabby – and one, from the West Indies, had ruined himself by the invention of a double-bottomed defecator.'It appears that the machine, which is designed to purify sugar, requires only the investment of a little more capital to sweep the board; and that any gentleman with a few hundreds to spare might set up his coach on the profits within a very short space of time. But come, joy, are we ever to attack

Scarlatti, the poor soul, or are we to sit here until the crack of doom, as windbound as our unhappy argosy?'

'There is not a moment to be lost,' said Jack, reaching for his bow. 'Let the battle begin.'

The grey days crept by with continual heavy rain and the gale working up a sea that made the *Worcester* pitch and roll at her moorings to such a degree that most of the black coats deserted the wardroom table and even ship-visiting came to a stop. But on the afternoon of Tuesday the wind backed into the east, just far enough to allow the *Worcester* to warp out into the Sound and shape a course, every staysail set, topsailyards braced up cracking taut, all seamen on deck, all landsmen ordered below, for Penlee Point. Then, shaving the headland so close that the quarterdeck held its collective breath, while Stephen privately crossed himself, she edged away, brought the breeze on to her larboard quarter, dropped her courses, and ran clear out into the Channel under all plain sail, the first to leave Plymouth apart from a revenue cutter since the blow began.

'The skipper is in a hell-fire hurry,' observed Somers to Mowett, as Jack cast a look at Rame Head, looming through the rain on the starboard beam, and stepped purposefully below.

'Wait until you see him at quarters,' said Mowett. 'There will be an exercise tonight, and you will have to rattle your guns out pretty brisk to please him.'

'Oh, as for that,' said Somers, 'I am not at all afraid. I know how to make my men skip, I believe.'

Jack was indeed in a hell-fire hurry. Not only did he always long to be at sea, and even more so this time than usual, out of lawyers' reach and before he could be saddled with a convoy, but he knew very well that the Brest squadron had been blown off their station and that he had a fair chance of snapping up any French privateer that might take advantage of their absence and of the easterly wind to run into the ocean, there to cruise for British merchantmen: privateers, or even with great luck a frigate. For although any French frigate he had ever seen would surely have the legs of the *Worcester*, which added sloth to unresponsiveness and lack of beauty, his ship could throw a broadside of 721 pounds from her long guns alone, enough to disable any frigate at long range, if only they were pointed straight and fired briskly.

He was in a hurry, but a cheerful hurry: he had brought his ship to sea after a delay far shorter than many he had known, in spite of the time spent in reducing her masts to something more near his liking; thanks to Fanshaw's kindness and Mowett's zeal his people amounted to 613 souls, only twenty-seven short of the *Worcester*'s official complement, with a far higher proportion of seamen than he had any right to expect; and although thanks to her Captain's weakness she carried the usual nursery of very young gentlemen, some useless mids, and a lieutenant he did not care for, Jack had upon the whole been let off very lightly.

With his first lieutenant and the gunner he plunged down into the familiar reek of the lower deck: bilge-water, cable-slime, mould, hard-worked unwashed men. Well over five hundred hands slept here, close-packed; and since it had been impossible to open the gunports or pipe up hammocks this last week and more the reek was even stronger than usual although the long low space was empty now, apart from a couple of heaps of hopelessly sea-sick landsmen, apparently dead, and a few swabbers. But Jack was not concerned with them, nor with the stench, a part of life from his earliest days: his business was with the ship's main armament, the two tiers of massive guns, thirty-two pounders, stretching fore and aft in the gloom, bowsed tight up against the side, uttering squeaks and groans as the roll shifted their concentrated three tons an inch or so in spite of the well-heaved frapping. With the light crew that brought the *Worcester* down he had not been able to fire the lower-deck guns, but he was confident that with the weather clearing he should do so later in the day and he was eager to begin – gunnery

was his passion and he could not rest easy until he had
at least started the long and arduous process of working
up the gun-crews to his own exacting standards of rapid
and above all accurate fire. Holding a lantern he walked
bent low along the tiers, each gun neat and square with
its sponge, worm, rammer, powder-horn, bit, quoin and
handspikes laid just so; he listened attentively to Borrell's
account of each and to Pullings' provisional arrangements
for the crews, and once again he blessed the luck that
had given him reliable officers, as well as enough right
men-of-war's men to provide at least an experienced first
and second captain for every piece.

'Well,' he said at the end of their tour, 'I believe
we may have some live practice this evening. I hope
so, indeed. We can afford quite a number of rounds:
my Dock powder was a most amazing bargain, and we
fairly cleared the widow's shop. You have plenty filled,
Mr Borrell?'

'Oh yes, sir. But I was obliged to fill promiscuous,
which some of the kegs had no marks and others two
or three; and very old-fashioned some of it smelled and
tasted, too. Not that it was not very fine-corned and bold
and dry, sir: I mean no reflection.'

'I am sure you do not, master gunner. But I hope you
did not taste much of the powder with antimony in it.
Antimony is ticklish stuff, they say. It is most uncommon
damp down here,' he added, pushing his finger deep into
the mould on the beam over his bowed head. 'We certainly
need a thorough house-warming, as you might put it.'

'Much of the wet comes through the hawse-holes and
the manger, sir,' said Pullings, who was very willing to
find some virtue in his ship. 'The bosun has a party
there with extra hawse-bags. But upon the whole, sir,
she is pretty tight – tighter than I had expected, with
this swell. She certainly labours much less with these new
topgallantmasts, and she scarcely heaves under the chains
at all.'

'Oh, a swell like this don't put her out,' said Jack.

'As far as she was designed at all, she was designed for the Atlantic. But what she will do in those short steep Mediterranean seas that cut up so quick – well, it will be interesting to find out. And it will be interesting to see the effect of antimony. The effect on the guns, I mean, Mr Borrell; I am sure you would have to eat a peck of it to do a man of your constitution any harm.'

'Pray, Dr Maturin,' he said on the quarterdeck, 'what is the effect of antimony?'

'It is a diaphoretic, an expectorant and a moderate cholegogue; but we use it chiefly as an emetic. You have heard of the everlasting antimony pill, sure?'

'Not I.'

'It is one of the most economical forms of physic known to man, since a single pill of the metal will serve a numerous household, being ingested, rejected, and so recovered. I have known one handed down for generations, perhaps from the time of Paracelsus himself. Yet it must be exhibited with discretion: Zwingerius likens it to the sword of Scanderberg, which is either good or bad, strong or weak, as is the party that prescribes or uses it, a worthy medicine if it be rightly applied to a strong man, otherwise it may prove but a froward vomit. Indeed, the name is said to signify monk's bane.'

'So I have always understood,' said Jack. 'But what I really meant was its effect on guns, was a little mixed with the powder.'

'Alas, I am wholly ignorant of these things. But if we may go by analogy, it should cause the piece to vomit forth the ball with more than common force.'

'We shall soon know,' said Jack. 'Mr Pullings, I believe we may beat to quarters.'

It was common knowledge throughout the *Worcester* that something was up, and none of the seamen was particularly surprised when after a preliminary running in and out of the guns the Captain walked forward along the gangway through the hush of a ship stripped for battle, all hands silent at their action-stations, the

58

officers and midshipmen by their divisions, deck after deck, the powder-boys sitting on their cartridges behind each gun, the slow-match smouldering in the tubs and sending its heady scent eddying along the deck as the tensely expectant *Worcester* lay to in the grey and empty Channel, heaving high but easy on the swell. They were not particularly surprised when on reaching the starboard bow-chaser, whose first captain was his own coxswain, Barret Bonden, he took out his watch and said, 'Three rounds: fire on the roll.'

The usual crashing roar, the stab of flame, and the usual furious ordered activity of the crew in the billowing smoke, sponging, reloading with the practice powder, ball and wad rammed home, the gun heaved up and primed, everything directed at cutting a few seconds off the time between the discharges. For this was the gun-crew that was to set the standard by which the rest would be compared. No surprise here, though a keen appreciation of their speed: but amazement, sheer amazement fore and aft, when in fifty-one seconds flat Bonden clapped his match to the priming of the second charge and the gun uttered an enormously loud high-pitched unnatural screeching bellow, jetting out a vast tongue of brilliant white light, in which the fragments of wad showed momentarily black.

It was a miracle alone that prevented the astonished crew from being crushed by the recoiling gun, and Jack had to tally on to the train-tackle to stop it running out again unchecked on the downward roll. He too wore the same blank look of wonder as those about him, but quicker than the rest he changed it to the Olympian calm appropriate to a captain, and when Bonden took the rope, muttering 'Beg pardon, sir: I wasn't expecting . . .' he returned to the counting of the seconds and observed, 'Come, Bonden, you are wasting time.'

They did their best, they heaved valiantly, but their rhythm, their coordination was upset and a full two minutes passed before the gun was run up, primed and pointed, and Bonden bent over it with an expression of ludicrous apprehension on his tough, battle-hardened face, his mates all edging as far from the piece as was decent or even farther, in an atmosphere of the most lively tension. His hand came down: this time the gun belched crimson, a noble, long-lasting crimson flame and crimson smoke, a deep, solemn, musical boom; and all along the deck the exact discipline of the gun-crews dissolved in delighted laughter.

'Silence fore and aft,' cried Jack, cuffing a contorted powder-boy, but his voice trembled as he said, 'Stop your vent. House your gun. On the roll, fire three.'

After the first dull blast of the regulation powder with which it had been loaded, number three produced a splendid blue, a splendid green; and so it went throughout the ship, deck after deck: exquisite colours, strange unheard-of bangs, infinite mirth (though sternly repressed) and a truly wretched performance in point of time.

'That was the most cheerful exercise I have ever known in my life,' said Jack to Stephen in the after-cabin. 'How I wish you had seen Bonden's face, just like a maiden aunt made to hold a lighted squib. And it was almost as good as a real action for pulling the people together – Lord, how they were laughing on the lower deck when hammocks were being slung. We shall make a happy ship of her, for all her faults. If the wind holds, I shall take her in close tomorrow evening, and let them break some glass.'

In his long career Captain Aubrey had observed that of all the forms of great-gun exercise there was none that came anywhere near firing at a fixed mark on land, above all if it had windows. Until the gun-crews were quite steady they tended to throw away many of their shots in full-blown action, and although firing at barrels laid out by the boats was very well in its way – infinitely better than the dumb-show of merely heaving cannon in and out that was usual in many ships – it lacked the high relish, the point of real danger, of smashing valuable defended

60

property, and whenever circumstances allowed he would take his ship close to the enemy shore to bombard some one of the many small posts and batteries strung all along the coast to guard harbours, estuaries, and places where the Allies might land. Now, the breeze having come well north of east with every sign of backing farther still, he fixed his position by two exact lunar observations and altered course to raise the Ile de Groix a little before the break of day. Although the night turned thick and troubled in the middle watch – no moon to be seen, still less a star – he was confident of his calculations, precisely confirmed by the mean of his three chronometers, and although his chief hope was of some privateer slipping out of Brest or even a commerce-raiding frigate, if he missed of them, he would at least be able to provide his people with a fine selection of posts to batter.

A little before two bells in the morning watch he came on deck. The idlers had not yet been called and the quiet night-time routine still had some while to run before the washing of the decks began, and the tumult of holystones great and small. The swell had diminished and here under the remote but effective lee of Ushant far astern the breeze made no more than a steady, regular song in the rigging as it came in three points abaft the larboard beam. She was under courses and topsails, no more. Since the arrival of the other lieutenants Pullings no longer kept a watch, but he was already up, talking to Mowett by the larboard rail: both had their night-glasses trained south-east.

'Good morning, gentlemen,' said Jack.

'Good morning, sir,' said Pullings. 'We were just talking about you. Plaice, on the forecastle lookout, thought he saw a light. Mowett sent a sharp man aloft: he can make nothing of it, but sometimes we seem to catch something on the lift, and we were wondering whether to call you yet. It is all wrong for the Groix lighthouse.'

Jack took the telescope and stared hard and long. 'So God-damned thick . . .' he muttered, wiping his eye and staring again.

The half-hour glass turned, two bells struck, the sentries called 'All's well', the midshipman of the watch heaved the log, reported 'Five knots one fathom, sir, if you please,' and chalked it on the board, a carpenter's mate stated that there was two foot four inches in the well – the *Worcester* made a good deal of water – and Mowett said 'Relieve the wheel: forecastle hands spell the afterguard at the pumps; call the idlers.'

'There, sir,' cried Pullings. 'No, much nearer.' And at the same moment the forecastle lookout and the masthead roared 'Sail on the larboard beam.'

The mists of the dying night had parted, showing not only a stern-lantern and a toplight but the whole of a ghostly ship, sailing large, standing south, and not two miles away. Jack had just time to see that she was taking in her foretopgallant-sail before she vanished, vanished entirely.

'All hands,' he said. 'Dowse the lights. In driver: main and fore topgallants, forestaysail, outer jib. Pass the word for the master.' He caught up the log-board and strode into the master's day-cabin with its charts spread out, the *Worcester*'s course pricked to the last observation. Gill came running, frowsty and dishevelled, a glum companion but a Channel pilot and a fine navigator; and between them they worked out the ship's position. Lorient lay due east, and the day would show them the Ile de Groix fine on the starboard bow. If the weather cleared at all they would see its light well before true dawn.

'A considerable ship, sir?' asked the master.

'I hope so indeed, Mr Gill,' said Jack, walking out of the cabin. He was in fact certain of it, but he did not like to anger luck by saying that what he had seen was either a heavy frigate or even something far better, a ship of the line stealing down the coast to Rochefort: in either case a man-of-war, and necessarily a French man-of-war, since the *Worcester* had such a head-start over the blockading squadron.

The decks were filling rapidly with the watch below,

blundering about half-clothed and stupid, snatched from their short hour's sleep, but brightening wonderfully when they heard there was a ship in sight.

'A two-decker, sir,' said Pullings with a delighted grin. 'She took in her maintopgallant before she disappeared again.'

'Very good, Mr Pullings,' said Jack. 'Clear for action. Let the people go quietly to quarters: no drum, no calling out.'

It was clear that the stranger, now looming faintly through the haze from time to time, had reduced sail to watch for the blink of the Groix light: a further proof that she was bound for Rochefort or the Bordeaux stream, since if her destination had been Lorient she would have borne in with the land an hour ago.

The sky was lightening in the east, and he stood there with his glass considering his course of action amidst the strange silence of the deck – men absurdly whispering as they stood by their guns, the guns themselves eased gently out, orders passing in an undertone. Below he could hear the cabins going down as the carpenter's crew made a clear sweep from stem to stern. The cry of a parson untimely roused came up through the hatchway, where they were laying the fearnought screens and wetting them.

There was still the possibility of the stranger's being a storeship or a transport, in which case she would bear up for Lorient the moment she saw the *Worcester*. He also observed with grave concern that with no more than courses and topsails she was gliding along at a remarkable pace: a clean-bottomed ship no doubt, and one that could probably give the *Worcester* mainsail and topgallants once all canvas was aboard. But if she was what he hoped, and if she showed fight, he must draw her down well south of Lorient, right to leeward, so that with this wind she could never make that port and the protection of its tremendous batteries. To be sure, that would mean playing long bowls with the Frenchmen for a while, and although they might not be the best seamen in the world they were often capital gunners; and his ship's company lacked experience. With a sudden stab at his heart he remembered that he had forgotten to order fighting cartridge instead of practice-powder at the last recharging of the guns: this was dead against his principles, but in fact it did not signify – he had carefully observed the fall of the shot, and the coloured powder threw its ball as well as the King's best Red L.G. In any case, as soon as the stranger was another mile to leeward, too far to fetch Lorient, he must close. He had the immense advantage of being ready, cleared for action, all hands on deck, guns run out, and already Pullings had the studding-sail booms and royals laid along. It would be strange if after the surprise and hurry and confusion aboard the Frenchman during the seven or eight minutes needed to gain that mile – it would be strange if he did not manage to lay her alongside, above all with the island and its shoals lying so awkwardly in her path.

'Mr Whiting,' he said, 'prepare the French colours, the number seventy-seven, and some kind of an answer to their private signal. Let it jam in the halyards.'

The near haze lifted and there she lay, a seventy-four, high, taut and handsome. Probably the *Jemmapes*: at all events no ship to decline battle. Yet they were strangely inactive aboard her: the *Worcester* was coming up on them fast, steering for their starboard quarter, running off that precious distance south of Lorient; but they never stirred. Suddenly he realized that every man-jack aboard her was staring for the Groix light. It came sharp and clear, a double flash. She dropped her topgallantsails, and while they were sheeting home someone caught sight of the *Worcester* – he distinctly heard trumpets aboard the Frenchman, trumpets and the urgent thunder of a drum. His eyes were so used to the half-light that even without a glass he could see people hurrying about on her decks. After a few moments her colours ran up and she changed helm to cut the *Worcester*'s course. 'Edge off two points,' said Jack to the master at the con. This would bring them still farther south. 'Mr Whiting, French colours if you please. Mr Pullings, battle-lanterns.'

Battle-lanterns aboard the Frenchman too, lights showing in every port, guns running out. The French number and private signal: the *Worcester*'s slow and evasive reply, which did not deceive the enemy for more than a few moments. Yet even those few moments carried the two ships a furlong farther south, and in a very short while now the *Jemmapes* – for the *Jemmapes* she was – would no longer be able to haul up for Lorient. Not that she showed the least sign of wishing to do so: far from it. Her commander was bringing her out in the most handsome manner, evidently determined to join issue as soon as possible, as though he had heard Lord Nelson's maxim 'Never mind manoeuvres: always go straight at 'em.'

In earlier years Jack would have lain to for the *Jemmapes* in much the same generous spirit, but now he wanted to make doubly sure of her; he wanted her to try for the weather-gage, and he kept the *Worcester* away another point and a half, watching the enemy intently as the two ships ran, each abreasting the sea with a fine bow-wave. Hammocks were racing up on deck aboard the *Jemmapes*: her waist and forecastle was a pretty scene of confusion, and in that man's place, with such a clean-bottomed swift-sailing ship, Jack would have held off until his people were more nearly settled: but not at all, out she came as fast as she could pelt, and Jack saw that his estimate of her speed had been short of the mark. She was indeed a flyer, and once the vital mile was run off he would have to close as fast as ever he could, while he still had the advantage of wind and readiness – close and board. He had never known it fail. All along the *Worcester*'s decks the arms-chests lay open: pistols, cutlasses, wicked boarding-axes.

He saw the flash of the Frenchman's chaser, the cloud of smoke torn away ahead, and a white plume rose from the grey sea well beyond the *Worcester*'s starboard bow.

'Our colours, Mr Whiting,' he said, fixing the enemy quarterdeck in his telescope. And much louder, 'Maintop there: hoist the short pennant.'

He saw the shift of helm that would bring the *Jemmapes* broadside on: she turned, turned and vanished in a cloud of smoke billowing to her topsails, the single timber-shattering discharge that only a stout new ship could afford. The line was good, but they had fired a trifle past the height of the roll and their well-grouped shot tore up a broad patch of sea a hundred yards short. A dozen ricochets came aboard, one smashing the blue cutter; a hole appeared in the mainsail and some blocks fell to the deck behind him – there had been no time to rig netting. A subdued cheer from the forecastle and waist and many an eye looked aft for the order to fire. On the edge of his field of vision he saw Stephen standing by the break of the poop in his nightshirt and breeches: Dr Maturin rarely went to his action-station in the cockpit until there were casualties for him to deal with. But Jack Aubrey's mind was too taken up with the delicate calculations of the coming battle for conversation: he stood there, wholly engrossed, working out the converging courses, the possible variants, the innumerable fine points that must precede the plain hard hammering, when everyone would be much happier. On these occasions, and Stephen had known many of them, Jack was as it were removed, a stranger, quite unlike the cheerful, not over-wise companion he knew so well: a hard, strong face, calm but intensely alive, efficient, decided, a stern face, but one that in some way expressed a fierce and vivid happiness.

A full minute passed. The second French broadside must be rammed home by now. He would have to suffer two or three of them, and at shortening range, before he could carry out his plan: but a fresh crew hated being fired at without making a reply. 'One more,' he said in his strong voice. 'One more, and then you shall serve them out. Then wait for the word and fire at her tops. Fire steady. Do not waste a shot.' A fierce growl all along, then the Frenchman's roaring fire and almost at the same moment the great hammer-crash of round-shot hitting the *Worcester*'s hull, splinters flying across the deck, wreckage falling from aloft. 'Do not do that, youngster,' said Jack to little Calamy, who had bent double when a shot crossed the quarterdeck. 'You might put your head in the way of a ball.' He glanced fore and aft. No great harm, and he was about to give the order to bear up fire when the wounded maintack tore free. 'Clew up, clew up,' he said, and the wild flapping stopped. 'Starboard three points.'

'Three points a-starboard it is, sir,' said the quarter-master at the wheel, and in a long smooth glide the *Worcester* brought her guns to bear. She was head-on to the swell, a fair pitch but no roll. 'Wait for it,' he called. 'At her tops. Waste not a shot. At the word from forward aft.' The wind sang through the rigging. The Frenchmen would be almost running out their guns again: that was the moment to catch them. He must get his broadside in first, fluster them, and hide his ship in smoke. 'Bow guns stand by. Fire.'

From forward aft the long rolling fire, an enormous all-pervading roar; and a freak of the wind brought the dense smoke eddying back – red smoke, green, blue, crimson and orange, with unearthly tongues of intensely brilliant coloured flame in the greyness. He leapt on to the hammock-cloths to pierce the cloud, the unnatural cloud, yet still it lingered: and no reply from the *Jemmapes*: 'God love me, what's amiss?' he said aloud, while below him the gun-crews sponged, loaded, rammed and heaved like fury, fresh powder running up from the magazines.

The smoke cleared at last, and there was the *Jemmapes* stern-on, running fast, apparently unhurt apart from a small green fire blazing on her poop, running close-hauled for Lorient, shocked and appalled by these new secret weapons – she was already packing on more sail.

The guns were run out again. At three degrees of

elevation he gave her another broadside, a raking broadside at her defenceless stern, a broadside delivered with a fierce, savage cheer. But though several shots struck her hull they did not check her speed; nor did the now-normal flash of the *Worcester*'s fire induce her to lie to; and by the time Jack called 'Hard a-starboard' to go in chase she had gained a quarter of a mile, while fools were capering on the forecastle, cheering, bawling out 'She runs, she runs! We've beat her!'

The *Worcester* hauled her wind, the sail-trimmers leapt to the braces and flew aloft to set the upper staysails, but she could not lie as close to her quarry by nearly a whole point, nor, without her mainsail, could she run on a bowline so fast by two knots and more. When the *Jemmapes* was so far ahead that the bow-chaser could hardly reach her, Jack yawned, gave her one last deliberate, sullen broadside at extreme range, and said 'House your guns. Mr Gill, course south-south-west: all plain sail.' He realized that it was day, that the sun was rising over Lorient, and added 'Dowse the battle-lanterns.' As he spoke he saw Pullings' face and the cruel disappointment on it: had they held their opening fire another five minutes the *Jemmapes* could never have reached Lorient. With the wind, the Ile de Groix, its reefs, and the shore all lying just so, a close action could have been forced whether the *Jemmapes* held her course or no: five minutes longer and Pullings would either have been a commander or a corpse. For a successful, evenly-matched action was certain promotion for a surviving first lieutenant: Pullings' only possible chance of promotion from the long and over-crowded lieutenants' list, since he had no pull, no interest or influence of any kind, no hope apart from his patron's luck or superior ability; and Jack Aubrey had misjudged the situation, one that might never arise again in Tom Pullings' whole career. Jack felt a sadness rise, far greater than his usual depression after a real battle, and looking at the dangling maintack he said in a hard voice, 'What are our casualties, Mr Pullings?'

'No dead, sir. Three splinter wounds and a crushed foot, no more. And number seven, lower deck, dismounted. But I am sorry to tell you, sir, I am very sorry to tell you, the Doctor has copped it.'

# CHAPTER THREE

Dr Maturin had taken part in many actions at sea, and although he had twice been captured and once wrecked he had never copped it yet, because as a surgeon he spent most of the time below the water-line, sheltered from splinters, round-shot and grape, in comparative safety if not in comfort. But now he had been wounded in three several places: first a falling shoulder-block knocked him down, then a jagged lump of elm from the hounds of the mizen topmast ripped off half his scalp, and lastly one of a shower of eighteen-inch splinters driven from the *Worcester*'s quarterdeck berthing by a thirty-two-pound ball struck both his feet as he lay there, struck them flatwise, piercing the list slippers and his soles. The wounds were spectacular and he left an uninterrupted trail of blood as he was carried below, but they were not serious; his assistants sewed him up again – Lewis, the elder man, was a rare hand with a needle – and although the pain was singularly shrill and insistent, Stephen's favourite tincture of laudanum dealt with that. He could take it now with a clear conscience, and with the tolerance resulting from long abuse he drank it by the pint. It was not the wounds, therefore, nor the loss of blood, nor the pain that brought him so low, but rather the incessant flow of visitors.

His assistants left him pretty well alone, apart from attending to his dressings, for not only was he a dangerous patient, stubborn, dogged and even violent if attempted to be dosed according to any system but his own, but he was also their superior in naval and in medical rank, being a physician and the author of highly-esteemed works on seamen's diseases, an officer much caressed by the Sick and Hurt Board: furthermore he was no more consistent

70

than other men and in spite of his liberal principles and his dislike of constituted authority he was capable of petulant tyranny when confronted with a slime-draught early in the morning. But he had no authority over the *Worcester*'s passengers, and with regard to them the social contract was fully binding. It was their duty to visit the sick unless they were being sick themselves (and poor Dr Davis was prostrated by the slightest roll or pitch); they had nothing else at all to do; and throughout their leisurely, almost windless and unnaturally calm passage across the Bay of Biscay and down the coast of Portugal they succeeded one another in the Captain's dining-cabin, where Stephen's cot had been set up. Nor were they alone. His old shipmates Pullings and Mowett sat with him every day, and very welcome they were; but all the other members of the wardroom came in from time to time, walking on tiptoe and suggesting remedies in low, considerate tones. Men who had listened to him with respectful attention when he was well now gave him advice quite fearlessly; and Killick hovered near at hand with fortifying broth, possets made by the gunner's wife, and galley receipts for strengthening the blood. Had it not been for the blessed opium that allowed him to plane above his irascibility some of the time his wellwishers would have worried him into his coffin, a hammock with two round-shot at his feet, before they raised the Rock of Lisbon; for although he could put up with pain tolerably well he had always found boredom mortal, and the purser, the Marine Captain (strangers to him) and two of the parsons droned on and on. Apart from the inventor of the double-bottomed defecator, whose history he had heard seven times, they had nothing to say, and they said it for what seemed hours, while his smile grew more fixed and rigid until at last it came to resemble the risus sardonicus.

But in latitude thirty-eight degrees north he began to recover; the feverish petulance left him, he became equable and mild, and his complaisance was no longer a matter of strong self-restraint. He discovered agreeable qualities in two of the clergymen and Professor Graham. When Cape St Vincent showed misty on the larboard bow he was well enough to be carried on deck in an elbow-chair with two capstan-bars lashed to its sides, sedan-fashion, to be shown the desert of grey ocean in which Lieutenant Aubrey, Sir John Jervis, and Commodore Nelson had defeated the greatly superior Spanish fleet on St Valentine's Day in 1797. And when the *Worcester* lay alongside the New Mole in Gibraltar, taking in fresh supplies and waiting for the levanter to blow out, the strong east wind that prevented her from passing the Strait into the Mediterranean, he sat luxuriating in the sun in the stern-galley, his bandaged feet on a stool, a glass of fresh orange-juice in his hand, and Professor Graham by his side: for although the Scotchman was a grey, somewhat positive, humourless soul he had read a great deal, and now that he had overcome at least some of his initial reserve he was a grateful companion, a man of obvious parts, and in no way a bore. Stephen had received the visit of several acquaintances from the shore, the last of these bringing him specimens of four uncommon cryptogams that he had always longed to see; he gazed at them now with such pleasure, such intensity, that it was some moments before he answered the Professor's question 'What was the language you were speaking with that gentleman?'

'The language, sir?' he said with a smile – he was feeling unusually cheerful, even merry, 'It was Catalan.' He had been tempted to say Aramaic, out of a spirit of fun; but Graham was too learned, too much of a linguist to swallow that.

'So you speak the Catalan, Doctor, as well as the French and Spanish?'

'I have spent much of my life on the shores of the Mediterranean,' said Stephen, 'and in my malleable youth I came by a certain knowledge of the languages spoken at its western end. I do not possess your command of Arabic, however; still less of your Turkish, God forbid.'

'To revert to our battle,' said Graham, having digested this. 'What I do not understand is why Captain Aubrey should have shot off those extraordinary coloured balls in the first place.'

'As for that,' said Stephen, smiling at Graham's notion of a battle – from their noble balcony they had the whole bay spread out before them, with Algeciras on the farther shore, where he had taken part in a real action: a hundred and forty-two casualties in HMS *Hannibal* alone: blood and thunder all day long – 'You must know that in their wisdom the Lords of the Admiralty have laid down that for the first six months of his commission no captain may presume to fire more shot a month than one third the number of his guns under various heavy mulcts and penalties; and after that only half as many. Whitehall supposes that the mariners know how to direct their pieces accurately and shoot them off at great speed while the ship is tossing on the billows by instinct: the captains who do not share this amiable illusion buy their own powder, if they can afford it. But powder is costly. A broadside from a ship of this size uses up some two hundredweight, I believe.'

'Hoot, toot,' said Graham, deeply shocked.

'Hoot, toot, indeed sir,' said Stephen. 'And at one and tenpence farthing the pound, that comes to a considerable sum.'

'Twenty, nineteen, five,' said Graham. 'Twenty pounds English, nineteen shillings and five pence.'

'So you will understand that captains seek the best market for their private powder: this came from a fireworks manufactory – hence the unusual colours.'

'There was no intention to deceive, then?'

'*Est summum nefas fallere*: deceit is gross impiety, my dear sir.'

Graham stared: then his grave grey face adopted a somewhat artificial smile and he said, 'You speak facetiously, no doubt. But the false colours, the French flag, was certainly intended to draw the enemy closer, so that he might be more readily destroyed; and it almost succeeded. I wonder we did not raise the signal of distress, or even pretend to surrender: that would have brought them closer still.'

'To the nautical mind some false signals are falser than other false signals. At sea there are clearly-understood degrees of iniquity. An otherwise perfectly honourable sea-officer may state by symbol that he is a Frenchman, but he must not state that his ship has struck upon a rock, nor must he lower his colours and then start to fight again, upon pain of universal reprehension. He would have the hiss of the world against him – of the maritime world.'

'The end proposed is the same in either case, the deception equal. I should certainly hoist all the colours in the spectrum, were it to advance the fall of that wicked man by five minutes. I refer to the self-styled Emperor of the French. War is a time for efficient action, not for the display of fine feelings, nor the discussion of the relative merits of forgery and false pretences.'

'It is illogical, I admit,' said Stephen, 'but this is the moral law, as perceived by the nautical mind.'

'The nautical mind,' said Graham. 'Hoot, toot.'

'The nautical mind has its own logic,' said Stephen, 'and although it may disobey many of the Articles of War with a clear conscience – swearing is forbidden, for example, and yet we daily hear warm, intemperate language, even blasphemous and obscene; so is the sudden spontaneous beating of men who are thought to move too slowly, or *starting*, as we call it. But you may see a certain amount of it even in this ship, which is more humane than most. Yet all these transgressions and many more, such as that stealing of stores which we term capperbar, or the neglect of religious feasts, are carried only to certain clearly-understood traditional limits, beyond which it is mortal to go. The seamen's moral law may seem strange to landsmen, even whimsical at times; but as we all know, pure reason is not enough, and illogical as their system may be, it does enable them to conduct these enormously complex machines from point to point, in spite of the elements, often boisterous, often adverse, always damp and always capricious.'

'It is a perpetual source of wonder to me that they arrive so often,' said Graham. 'And I remember what a friend of mine wrote on the subject. Having taken proper notice of the complexity of the machine, as you so rightly observe, the infinity of ropes and cords, the sails, the varying forces that act upon them, and the skill required to manage the whole, directing the vessel in the desired direction, he went on to this effect: what a pity it is that an art so important, so difficult, and so intimately concerned with the invariable laws of mechanical nature, should be so held by its possessors that it cannot improve but must die with each individual. Having no advantages of previous education, they cannot arrange their thoughts; they can scarcely be said to think. They can far less express or communicate to others the intuitive knowledge which they possess; and their art, acquired by habit alone, is little different from an instinct. We are as little entitled to expect improvement here as in the architecture of the bee or the beaver. The species cannot improve.'

'Perhaps your friend was unfortunate in his sea-going acquaintance,' said Stephen, smiling. 'As unfortunate as he was in his reference to the bee and her building, which is surely confessed by all mathematicians to be geometrically perfect, and therefore not susceptible of improvement. But leaving the bee aside, for my part I have sailed with mariners who were not only active in improving the architecture of their machines and the art of conducting them, but who were only too willing to communicate the knowledge they possessed. Such tales have I heard of Captain Bentinck's palls, or rather shrouds, and his triangular courses, of Captain Pakenham's newly-discovered rudder, of Captain Bolton's jury-mast, of improved iron-horses, dogs, dolphins, mouses – or mice as some say – puddings . . .'

'Puddings, my dear sir?' cried Graham.

'Puddings. We trice 'em athwart the starboard gumbrils, when sailing by and large.'

'The starboard gumbrils . . . by and large,' said Graham, and with a passing qualm Stephen recalled that the Professor had an unusually good memory, could quote long passages, naming the volume, chapter and even page from which they came. 'My ignorance is painful to me. As an old experienced seafarer you understand these things, of course.'

Stephen bowed and went on, keeping to slightly safer ground, 'Not to mention the countless devices to measure the speed of the vessel through the water by means of rotating vanes or the pressure of the circumambient ocean – machines as ingenious as the double-bottomed defecator. That reminds me: pray, what qualifications are called for in an Anglican clergyman, what attendance at a seminary, what theological studies?'

'I believe he must have taken his degree at one of the universities, and certainly he must have found a bishop willing to ordain him. My impression is that nothing more is required – no seminary, no theological studies – but I am sure you know more of the Anglican polity than I, since like so many of my countrymen I am a Presbyterian.'

'Not I, since like so many of mine I am a Catholic.'

'Indeed? I had supposed that all officers in the Navy were obliged to forswear the Pope.'

'So they are too, the commissioned officers: but surgeons are appointed by a warrant from the Navy Board. I forswore nothing, which was a comfort to be sure; yet on the other hand without renouncing the Bishop of Rome I can scarcely look forward to being an admiral and hoisting my flag. The height of naval ambition is denied me.'

'I do not understand. Surely a gentleman in the physical line can never hope to be an admiral? But you are pleased to be jocose, I have no doubt.' Jocularity did not please Professor Graham; he looked somewhat offended, as though he had been trifled with, and shortly afterwards he took his leave.

But he was back again the next afternoon, and he and Stephen now gazed upon the Rock at short range, the *Worcester* having been removed to make room for the *Brunswick* and *Goliath*, and Pullings having swung her stern-on so that her starboard side could be scraped and painted. It was one of those days when some particular quality in the light and not merely the brilliance of the sun makes colours glow and sing: a military band was playing on the Alameda, its brasses blazing like gold beneath the shade, while through the gardens and up and down the Grand Parade flowed an easy crowd of red coats, blue jackets, and a wonderful variety of civilian clothes from Europe, Morocco, the Turkish provinces of Africa, Greece and the Levant, and even from much farther east. White turbans and the pale, dust-blue robes of Tangier Copts, the dark red and broad straw hats of Berbers and the black of Barbary Jews moved in and out among the pepper-trees, mingling with tall Moors and Negroes, kilted Greek seamen from the islands, red-capped Catalans, and small Malays in green. On Jumper's Bastion stood a group of the *Worcester*'s young gentlemen, some long and thin, others very small indeed, and Stephen noticed that they seemed to be gathered about a monstrous dog; but as they moved off it became apparent that the creature was a calf, a black bull-calf. Other Worcesters wandered among the geraniums and castor-oil plants: these were the select bands of liberty-men, those who had had the time and the foresight to provide themselves with white or black-varnished low-crowned hats with the ship's name embroidered on the ribbon, watchet-blue jackets with brass buttons, spotless white duck trousers, and little shoes; each had had to pass the master-at-arms' inspection, for although the *Worcester* was not yet a crack ship or anything remotely like one, Pullings was very jealous of her reputation and he acted on the principle that the appearance of virtue might induce its real presence. Few

77

of them were drunk yet, and most of their mirth – clearly audible at half a mile – was the effect of pure unaided gaiety. Beyond them and the variegated crowd rose the grey and tawny Rock, green only at its lower rim, and above its long crest the strange fog or breeding cloud brought into being by the levanter, a breeding cloud that dissipated there in the blazing light of the western side. Stephen had Mount Misery clear in his telescope, and sharp against the whitish sky an ape: high, high above the ape a vulture hanging on the wind. Both Stephen and the ape gazed at the bird.

Professor Graham cleared his throat. 'Dr Maturin,' he said, 'I have a cousin who occupies a confidential post under Government: he is concerned with the gathering of information more reliable than newspaper or mercantile or even consular reports and he has asked me to look out for gentlemen who might assist him. I know little of these things – they are far outside my province – but it occurs to me that a medical man, fluent in the Mediterranean languages, with a wide acquaintance scattered about these shores, would be unusually well suited for such purposes, above all if he were of the Romish persuasion; for it appears that most of my cousin's colleagues are Protestants, and clearly a Protestant cannot enter into the intimacy of Catholics as well as their co-religionists. Allow me to add, that my cousin disposes of considerable funds.'

The distant ape shook its fist at the vulture: the enormous bird tilted and gliding sideways crossed the strait to Africa without a movement of its wings – a fulvous vulture, Stephen observed with satisfaction as the colour showed upon the turn. 'Why, as for that,' he said, putting down his telescope, 'I am afraid I should make but an indifferent source of information. Even in a small town – and you must have noticed how closely a ship resembles a small crowded town, with its hierarchy, its people all knowing one another, its particular walks and places of refreshment for the different classes, its perpetual gossip – even in a town a medical man rarely gets away. But a ship is a town that carries its walls with it wherever it goes. A naval surgeon is tied to his post, and even when the ship is in port he is still much taken up with his patients and with paper-work, so that he sees little of the country or its inhabitants. Oh, it is the pity of the world to travel so far and to see so little.'

'Yet surely, sir, you do go on to dry land from time to time?'

'Not nearly as often as I could wish, sir. No. I am afraid I should be of little use to your cousin; and then again the necessary dissimulation, the disguise, the lack of candour, I may even say the deceit called for in such an undertaking would be mighty distasteful. But now that I come to think of it, would not a naval chaplain answer your purpose very well? He has far more time to spare on shore. There are our clerical shipmates, as you see, walking about as free as air with others of their kind. There, just by the dragon-tree. No, my dear sir, that is a common plane: to the right of the date-palms – the dragon-tree, for all love.'

Beneath the dragon-tree's green shade paced twelve clergymen, six from the *Worcester*, six from the garrison, all clean-shaved, discreetly admiring the majestic beards, Arabian, Hebrew and Berber, that passed them on the parade.

'We say farewell to all of them but one,' observed Professor Graham. 'The wardroom will seem strangely bare.'

'Indeed?' said Stephen. 'Five at one blow? I had heard that Mr Simpson and Mr Wells were to leave us, *Goliath* and *Brunswick* having arrived, but what is to become of the others, and who is to remain?'

'Mr Martin is to stay.'

'Mr Martin?'

'The one-eyed gentleman. And Mr Powell and Mr Comfrey are to go straight to Malta in that storeship over there.'

'The xebec, or the polacre?'

'The vessel to the right,' said Graham somewhat testily.

79

'The vessel that is so busy, with sailors creeping up the masts. And Dr Davis has decided to go home, by land as far as ever he can. He finds the sea does not suit his constitution, and is casting about for a suitable conveyance.'

'He is quite right, sure: for a man of his age, and in his state of health, it would be death to be boxed up in a confined moist uneasy tossing habitation, either airless or with so much of it that one's whole person is battered and assailed; to say nothing of the falling damps, so fatal to those that have passed the climacteric. No: to go to sea a man needs youth, an adamantine health, and the digestion of a hyena. But I hope the poor gentleman will be able to attend the farewell dinner? Great preparations are making, I am told. The Captain is coming, and I look forward eagerly to the feast myself; I am sick of eggs and bonny-clabber, and that villain' – nodding in the direction of Killick, who was banging chairs about in the great cabin behind them, before bringing in a host of swabbers to make the place a wet, spotless misery – 'will bring me nothing else.'

Dr Davis was not able to attend: he was in a Spanish diligence with eight mules drawing him as fast as they could away from everything connected with the sea. But he sent his excuses, his best compliments, his best thanks, and his best wishes, and they filled his chair with a lean, deserving young master's mate called Honey, Joseph Honey. As the church clocks of Gibraltar struck the hour Captain Aubrey walked into the crowded wardroom full of blue coats, red coats and clerical black. His first lieutenant welcomed him, and proposed a glass of bitters. 'I am afraid our company is not quite complete, sir,' he said; and turning he silently gibbered at the wardroom steward.

'Can it possibly be that the Doctor is late?' asked Jack. But even as he spoke there was a muffled thumping, two or three vile oaths, and Stephen came in on his bandaged feet, his elbows supported by his servant, a quarter-witted but docile and sweet-natured Marine, and Killick. They greeted him, not indeed with a cheer, for the Captain's presence was a restraint upon them, but very cheerfully; and as they sat down Mowett said, smiling across the table at him, 'You are looking wonderfully well, dear Doctor, I am happy to see. But it is not surprising, for

> Even calamity, by thought refined,
> Inspirits and adorns the thinking mind.'

'Why you should suppose that mine requires any adornment I cannot tell, Mr Mowett,' said Stephen. 'You have been cultivating your genius again, I find.'

'You remember my weakness then, sir?'

'Certainly I do. And to prove it I will repeat certain lines you composed in our first voyage together, our first *commission*:

> Oh were it mine with sacred Maro's art
> To wake to sympathy the feeling heart,
> Then might I, with unrivalled strains, deplore
> Th'impervious horrors of a leeward shore.'

'Very good – capital – hear him, hear him,' cried several officers, all of whom had experienced the impervious horrors not once but many times.

'That's what I call poetry,' said Captain Aubrey. 'None of your goddam – your blessed maundering about swains and virgins and flowery meads. And since we are on calamities and leeward shores, Mowett, tip us the piece about woe.'

'I don't know that I quite remember it, sir,' said Mowett, blushing now that the whole table was attending to him.

'Oh surely you do. The piece about not whining – plaintless patience, you know: I make my little girls recite it.'

'Well, sir, if you insist,' said Mowett, laying down his soup-spoon. His normally cheerful, good-natured expression changed to a boding, portentous look; he fixed his eyes on the decanter and in a surprisingly loud moo began:

'By woe, the soul to daring action swells;
By woe, in plaintless patience it excels:
From patience, prudent clear experience springs
And traces knowledge through the course of things;
Thence hope is formed, thence fortitude, success,
Renown – whate'er men covet and caress.'

Amid the general applause, and while the soup gave
way to an enormous dish of lobsters, Mr Simpson, who sat
at Stephen's side, said, 'I had no idea that the gentlemen
of the Navy ever wooed the Muse.'

'Had you not? Yet Mr Mowett is exceptional only in
the power and range of his talent; and when you join the
*Goliath* you will find the purser, Mr Cole, and one of the
lieutenants, Mr Miller, who often contribute verses to the
*Naval Chronicle*, and even to the *Gentleman's Magazine*.
In the Navy, sir, we drink as much of the Castalian spring
as comes within our reach.'

They also drank even headier liquors, and although the
*Worcester*'s wardroom, being poor, could afford only the
fierce local wine known as the blackstrap, there was plenty
of it within reach; and this was just as well, because after
its spirited beginning the dinner-party came dangerously
near the doldrums: those who had not sailed with Captain
Aubrey before were somewhat awed by his reputation, to
say nothing of his rank, while the presence of so many
parsons called for a pretty high degree of decorum from
all hands: and even remarks about the *Brunswick*'s old-
fashioned way of carrying her mizentopmast staysail *under*
the maintop were out of place when so many of the company could not tell a staysail from a spanker. The junior
officers sat mute, eating steadily; Somers applied himself
to the blackstrap, and although he sniffed it scornfully, as
one used to decent claret, he drank a great deal; the Marine
captain launched into an account of a curious adventure
that had befallen him in Port of Spain, but realizing that
its scabrous end was utterly unsuitable for this occasion,
was obliged to bring it to a pitifully lame and pointless

though decent conclusion; Gill, the master, tried hard to overcome his settled melancholy, but he could manage little more than a bright, attentive look, a fixed smile: both Stephen and Professor Graham had retired into private contemplation; and while the company ate their mutton little was to be heard but the sound of their powerful jaws, some well-intentioned, ill-informed remarks on tithes by Captain Aubrey, and a detailed explanation of the working of the double-bottomed defecator at the far end of the table.

But Pullings sent the bottles round with more urgency than before, crying 'Professor Graham, a glass of wine with you, sir – Mr Addison, I drink to your new floating parish. – Mr Wells, I give you joy of the *Brunswick* in a bumper, sir: bottoms up.' Jack and Mowett seconded him, and by the time the pudding came in the temperature of the gathering had risen to something more nearly what Pullings could have wished.

The pudding was Jack's favourite, a spotted dog, and a spotted dog fit for a line-of-battle ship, carried in by two strong men.

'Bless me,' cried Jack, with a loving look at its glistening, faintly translucent sides, 'a spotted dog!'

'We thought as how you might like one, sir,' said Pullings. 'Allow me to carve you a slice.'

'Do you know, sir,' said Jack to Professor Graham, 'this is the first decent pudding I have had since I left home. By some mischance the suet was neglected to be shipped; and you will agree that a spotted dog or a drowned baby is a hollow mockery, a whited sepulchre, without it is made with suet. There is an art in puddings, to be sure; but what is art without suet?'

'What indeed?' said Graham. 'But there are also puddings in art, I understand – in the art of managing a ship. Only yesterday I learnt, to my surprise, that you trice puddings athwart the starboard gumbrils, when sailing by and large.'

Graham's surprise was nothing to that of the wardroom:

'By *and* large?' they said. 'Gumbrils? starboard gumbrils?' Jack's spotted dog hung in his gullet for a moment before he understood that someone had been practising upon the Professor's credulity, an ancient naval form of wit, played off many and many a time on newly-joined young gentlemen, on himself long, long ago, and by Pullings and Mowett on Dr Maturin in former years; but never to his knowledge on any man of Graham's eminence. 'Puddings we have, sir,' he said, swallowing his own, 'and plenty of 'em. There is the wreath of yarns tapering towards the ends and grafted all over that we clap about the fore and main masts just below the trusses before we go into action, to prevent the yards from falling; then there is the pudding on a boat's stem, to act as a fender; and the puddings we lay round the anchor-rings to stop them chafing. But as for the gumbrils, why, I am afraid someone must have been practising on you. They do not exist.' The words were scarcely out of his mouth before he wished them back: he knew Stephen extremely well, and that detached, dreamy expression could only mean a consciousness of guilt. 'Unless,' he added quickly, 'it is some archaic term. Yes, I rather think . . .'

But it was too late. Captain Harris, the Marine, was already explaining by and large. With a piece of fresh Gibraltar bread and arrows drawn with wine he showed the ship lying as close as possible to the breeze: '. . . and this is sailing by the wind, or as sailors say in their jargon, on a bowline; whereas large is when it blows not indeed quite from behind ut say over the quarter, like this.'

'Far enough abaft the beam that the studdingsails will set,' said Whiting.

'So as you see,' continued Harris, 'it is quite impossible to sail both by and large at the same time. It is a contradiction in terms.' The expression pleased him, and he repeated, 'A contradiction in terms.'

'We do say by and large,' said Jack. 'We say a ship sails well by and large when she will both lie close when the wind is scant and run fast when it is free. No doubt that is what your informant meant.'

'I think not, sir,' said Graham. 'I think your first supposition was correct. I have been practised upon. I am content. I shall say no more.'

He did not look content; indeed he looked thoroughly displeased, in spite of a formal appearance of complaisance; but he did say no more, no more at least to Dr Maturin, except on one occasion. The dinner ran its course, the wine did its cheerful work, and by the time the port was on the table the wardroom was filled with the comfortable noise of a party going well, laughter and a great deal of talk; the young officers had found their tongues – a decent loquacity – and riddles were propounded; Mowett obliged the company with a piece about dealing with light airs abaft the beam, beginning:

With whining postures, now the wanton sails
Spread all their charms to snare th'inconstant gales.
The swelling stud-sails now their wings extend,
The staysails sidelong to the breeze ascend.

And Stephen, aware that he had not only behaved badly but that his bad behaviour had been discovered, took advantage of a pause between two songs to say that unless the wind came fair tomorrow he intended to go ashore to buy a raven at the shop of the Jew-man from Mogador, famous for birds of all kinds, including ravens, 'to see whether it was true that they lived a hundred and twenty years' – a pale, flabby little joke, but one that had made people laugh for two thousand five hundred years. It made them laugh now, after a moment's consideration; but Dr Graham said, 'It is very unlikely that you will live so long yourself, Dr Maturin. A man already so advanced in years, and with such habits, cannot pretend to live to such an age. A hundred and twenty years, forsooth.'

These were the last words he said to Stephen until the *Worcester* was lying off Port Mahon in Minorca, having sailed from Gibraltar the moment the wind came far enough north of east. She now had a leading breeze for Mahon itself, but nothing, not even his respect for learning and his consideration for Professor Graham, would induce Jack to take her into that long harbour, easy to enter but the very devil to leave except with a northerly air. Many a time he had seen line-of-battle ships windbound there in former days, when he in his little weatherly brig could just beat out, but only just; and with Admiral Thornton's squadron not two days' sail away if the breeze held true he did not intend to lose a minute, even if begged to do so by a choir of virgins on their knees. The *Worcester* lay to, therefore, off Cape Mola, and Mr Graham was lowered into a boat; though at least he was indulged in the relative comfort of the pinnace. He gave Stephen a cold 'Good day to you,' and was gone.

Stephen watched the pinnace hoist its sails and speed away over the short choppy sea, sprinkling its occupants at every plunge and soaking them quite often: he was sorry that he had offended Graham, who was a strong, intelligent man, no cloistered scholar, and no sort of a bore at any time. But such a degree of resentment was unamiable and he saw him go without much regret. 'And in any event,' he reflected, 'he will never again think of me as a potential intelligence-agent; still less as one in fact, dear Mother of God.'

'Shearwaters!' cried a voice beside him. 'Surely they cannot be shearwaters here?' Stephen turned and saw Mr Martin, the only remaining parson, the thinner and shabbier of the two literary gentlemen. 'Certainly they are shearwaters,' he said. 'Do they not nest in holes on Cape Mola over there? To be sure, they are less sharply black and white than those of the Atlantic, but they are shearwaters for all that – the same voice by night in their burrows, the same solitary white egg, the same grossly obese chick. See how they turn with the wave! Certainly they are shearwaters. You have studied birds, sir?'

'As much as ever I could, sir; they have always been my great delight, but since I left the university I have had little leisure, little opportunity for reading, and I have never been abroad.'

What with his wound and the superabundance of clergymen, Stephen had had almost no contact with Mr Martin, but now his heart warmed to this young man who shared his passion, who had learnt a great deal, and who had paid for his learning with long journeys on foot, nights spent in byres, haystacks, sheepcotes, even prisons when he was taken up for a poacher, and with the loss of an eye, destroyed by an owl. 'The poor bird only meant to protect her brood: she could not tell I meant them no harm – I was culpably abrupt in my movements. Besides, it is convenient, when looking through a spy-glass, not to have to close the other eye.' They exchanged accounts of the bustard, the osprey, the stilt, the cream-coloured courser; and Stephen was describing the great albatross with an eagerness approaching enthusiasm when he heard Captain Aubrey say, in a tone of strong displeasure, 'Loose the foretopsail. Give him a gun.'

It was the conduct of the returning pinnace that caused these remarks. To Stephen it seemed to be coming along well enough, beating into the wind, tacking briskly from time to time, but it was clear from the look of the other officers on the quarterdeck that Mr Somers was not handling the boat to their satisfaction. At one point they all shook their heads in unison, frowning with disapproval, and in fact a moment later a spar carried away – a spar that might be replaced in Malta, but not much nearer at hand. When the pinnace came alongside with a rending crack, Captain Aubrey said, 'Mr Pullings, I should like to see Mr Somers in the cabin,' and walked off.

Somers came out of the cabin ten minutes later, red-faced and sullen. The quarterdeck was full of officers and young gentlemen, watching Minorca dwindle on the larboard quarter as the ship stood north-east for her rendezvous with the Admiral: a glance showed Somers' state of mind, and they all studiously avoided his eye as he paced up and down for a while before going below.

He was still in a surly, resentful mood when the wardroom met for supper, and they tried to cheer him up. It had long been obvious to all the sailors present that he was no seaman, but they all knew the importance of good relations in a small community, tight-packed, always on top of one another, with no possibility of getting away throughout the whole length of the commission: but Somers did not choose to be brought into a happier state of mind. Where he had served his time they could not tell, but it must have been in some ship that did not observe the conventions they had always known, one of which was that any unpleasantness on deck was forgotten – at least pretended to be forgotten – at table. Towards the end of the meal he grew more conversable, talking to Mr Martin and the younger Marine lieutenant, Jackson, who admired him for his good looks, his comparative wealth, and his connections: without mentioning any names he explained to them the difference, as he saw it, between bosun-captains and gentleman-captains, the first being those who paid great attention to mechanical duties, the province of mere mariners, the second being the true soul of the Navy, high-spirited men who left such things to their inferiors, reserving all their energies for a superior general direction and for battle, in which they led their men (who respected, almost worshipped them) incomparably well. He grew almost as enthusiastic about gentlemen as Stephen had been about the wandering albatross – the common people instinctively recognized blood and accepted its superiority – they knew that a man of ancient lineage was as it were of another essence, and they could distinguish him at once, almost as though he wore a halo. Young Jackson abounded in his sense, applauding his higher flights, until he happened to look along the table and saw the grave faces of his companions, when a certain doubt came over him, and he fell silent. By this time Somers was too drunk to notice that, or to attend to the strong, determined conversation that drowned his voice. He was in fact so drunk, drunk even by naval standards, that he was obliged to be bundled into his cot: this was usual enough, and since he had no watch to keep that night there was no adverse comment (the purser was regularly speechless by lights out, though the *Worcester* was not reckoned a hard-drinking ship by any means). But his state the next morning was far from usual: he was so unwell that Stephen, having prescribed three drachms of Lucatellus' balsam, told him that he might perfectly well decline the Captain's invitation to dinner, on grounds of health. Somers was touchingly grateful for Dr Maturin's attentions, and as he walked off Stephen reflected that he had often known men who were showy and arrogant in public – men with little instinctive social tact – to be pleasant enough with only one companion. He offered this reflection, in general terms, to Mr Martin as they sat on the poop under a cloudless sky after their dinner with the Captain, gazing at the white-flecked pure blue sea and the various gulls that wantoned in the wake; but Martin was too full of the bustard, the great Andalusian bustard bought in Gibraltar, that had formed the main dish, to give more than a civil assent before returning to that noble fowl. 'To think that I should have lain three nights in a shepherd's hut on Salisbury Plain – a hut on wheels – in the hope of seeing one at dawn, to say nothing of my vigils in Lincolnshire, and that I should have found a cock-bird on my plate in the bosom of the ocean! It is very like a dream.'

He was also full of enthusiasm for the Navy: Such kindness in the Captain, such cordial hospitality – none of the cold formal distance or hauteur he had been led to expect – and the gentlemen of the wardroom were so friendly and considerate – he could not speak too highly of Mr Pullings' and Mr Mowett's amiability. The other officers had been very good to him too, while the comfort of his little cabin in spite of the enormous gun, and the – he might almost say the *luxury* of their fare, with wine every day, quite astonished him.

Stephen glanced to see whether he were speaking

ironically, but all he could detect was honest pleasure and satisfaction, together with a rosy gleam from Captain Aubrey's port. 'Sure, we are fortunate in our shipmates,' he observed, 'and I have noticed that many sea-officers, nay the majority, are of the same cheerful, good-natured, liberal stamp. Coxcombs are rare; reading men not unknown. Yet from the physical point of view the nautical life is usually represented as one of hardship, discomfort, and privation.'

'All things are relative,' said Martin, 'and perhaps some years of living in a garret or a cellar and working for the booksellers is no bad preparation for the Navy. At all events it is the life for me. Both as a naturalist and as a social being, I am –'

'By your leave, sir,' said the captain of the afterguard, coming up the poop-ladder with a horde of swabbers.

'What's afoot, Miller?' asked Stephen.

'Which we hope to raise the flag before long,' said Miller, 'and you would not wish the Admiral to see the deck all covered knee-deep with filth, sir, would you now? With remarks passed through all the fleet?'

The filth was not discernible to a landsman's eye, unless it were for a very slight dusting of little pieces of worn tow fallen from the rigging and gathered under the lee of the rail, but Stephen and the parson were chivvied off the poop to the quarterdeck. Five minutes later the tide of powerful cleaners dislodged them once again and they moved on to the gangway. 'Should you not like to go below, sir?' asked Whiting, the officer of the watch. 'The wardroom is almost dry by now.'

'Thank you,' said Stephen, 'but I wish to show Mr Martin a Mediterranean gull. I believe we shall go to the forecastle.'

'I will have your chair sent forward,' said Pullings. 'But you will not touch anything, will you, Doctor? Everything is quite clean, fit for the Admiral's inspection.'

'You are very good, Mr Pullings,' said Stephen, 'but I can walk and stand quite well now. I do not need the chair, although I am sensible of your attention.'

'You will not touch anything, Doctor?' called Pullings after them: and on the forecastle a midshipman and two elderly sheet-anchor men desired them to take great care, and to touch nothing. They were unwelcome and in the way, but after a while Joseph Plaice, an old shipmate of Stephen's and a forecastle-hand, brought them each a cheese-shaped bag of bow-chaser wads and there they sat in some comfort, touching neither the beautifully flemished falls nor the gleaming gun-sights.

'The Navy is the life for me,' said Martin again. 'Quite apart from the excellent company – and I may say that as far as I have seen, the ordinary sailormen are quite as obliging as the officers.'

'I have certainly found it so, in many cases. Aft the more honour, forward the better man, as Lord Nelson put it,' said Stephen. 'Aft being the officers and young gentlemen, forward the hands – the container for the contents, you understand. Yet I think that by forward we are to take him to mean real sailors; for you are to observe that in a crew such as this a great many scrovies are necessarily swept in, froward dirty disreputable rough good-for-nothing disorderly ragabashes and raparees to begin with, and sometimes for ever.'

Martin bowed, and went on, 'Apart from that, and only to be mentioned long after, there is the material aspect. I must beg pardon, sir, for alluding to such a subject, but unless a man has earned his bread by a calling in which he must rely on himself alone, in which any failure of invention, any bout of sickness, is fatal, he can scarcely appreciate the extraordinary comfort of a certain hundred and fifty pounds a year. A hundred and fifty pounds a year! Good heavens! And I am told that if I consent to act as schoolmaster to the young gentlemen, an annual fee of five pounds a head is due for each.'

'I conjure you to do no such thing. There is a Mediterranean gull, just perched on the long pole running out in front: you see her heavy dark-red bill, the true blackness of her head? Quite different from ridibundus.'

'Quite different. At close range there is no possible confusion. But pray, sir, why must I not teach the young gentlemen?'

'Because, sir, teaching young gentlemen has a dismal effect upon the soul. It exemplifies the badness of established, artificial authority. The pedagogue has almost absolute authority over his pupils: he often beats them and insensibly he loses the sense of respect due to them as fellow human beings. He does them harm, but the harm they do him is far greater. He may easily become the all-knowing tyrant, always right, always virtuous; in any event he perpetually associates with his inferiors, the king of his company; and in a surprisingly short time alas this brands him with the mark of Cain. Have you ever known a schoolmaster fit to associate with grown men? The Dear knows I never have. They are most horribly warped indeed. Yet curiously enough this does not seem to apply to tutors: perhaps it is scarcely possible to play the prima donna to an audience of one. Fathers, on the other hand –'

'Mr Pullings' compliments, sir,' said a young gentleman, 'and begs Dr Maturin will take his feet off the fresh paint.'

Stephen gazed at him and then at his feet. It was quite true: the glistening surface of the carronade that served him for a footstool gleamed not as he had supposed with polish nor yet with spray but with jet-black paint, newly laid on. 'My compliments to Mr Pullings,' he said at last, 'and pray desire him to let me know, at his leisure, how I am to take my feet off the fresh paint without instantly and indelibly marking both the deck here and at every step I take to the main staircase. These bandages are not lightly to be taken off. And in any case, sir,' – to Mr Martin – 'the question hardly arises, for as you remarked yourself, you found the Pythagorean proposition impossible to be understood; and the education of the young gentlemen aboard is almost all a matter of trigonometry: even of algebra, Heaven preserve us.'

'Then I must abandon my midshipmen, I see,' said Martin smiling. 'But still I feel that the Navy is the life for me – an ideal life for a naturalist.'

'To be sure, it is a very fine life for a young man with no ties on land and with a robust constitution, a young man who is not over-nice about his victuals, and who does not make a god of his belly. And I am of your opinion entirely, in believing the better kind of sea-officer to be excellent company: though there are others; and the poison of authority can sap a captain, with the unhappiest effects upon the whole ship's company. Then again, if it is your misfortune to have a bore or a petulant coxcomb aboard, you are penned up with him for months and even years on end, so that his shortcomings grow exquisitely tedious and the first words of his often-repeated anecdotes a hellish torment. And as to its being a life for a naturalist, why, it has advantages to be sure; but you are to consider that the Navy's prime function is to take, burn, or destroy the enemy, not to contemplate the wonders of the deep. The utmost power of language is not enough to describe the frustration a naturalist must endure in this jading pursuit of merely political, material ends: had we been allowed some days ashore at Minorca, for example, I could have shown you not only the black wheatear, not only the curious Minorcan chat, but Eleanora's falcon! The bearded vulture!'

'I am sure what you say is profoundly true,' said Martin, 'and I bow to your experience – I shall nourish no illusions. And yet, sir, you have seen the great albatross, the southern petrels, the penguins in their interesting diversity, sea-elephants, the cassowary of the far Spice Islands, the emu scouring the sultry plain, the blue-eyed shag. You have beheld Leviathan!'

'I have also seen the three-toed sloth,' said Dr Maturin.

'Sail ho,' called the lookout at the foremasthead. 'On

deck, there, four sails of ships, six sail, a squadron, fine on the larboard bow.'

'That will be Sir John Thornton's fleet,' said Stephen. 'Presently we must make ourselves trim: perhaps we might call the ship's barber.'

Captain Aubrey, as trim as his newly-brushed best uniform could make him, the Nile medal in his buttonhole, the regulation sword at his side (Admiral Thornton was a stickler for etiquette) went down the *Worcester*'s side with the full naval ceremony, preceded by a midshipman with several packets under his arm. He was grave and silent as the barge pulled along the broad expanse of sea between the two ranges of towering line-of-battle ships stretching ahead and astern of the *Ocean*, each exactly in station, two cable lengths apart. Although this was only a parenthesis in his career, a routine turn on the everlasting Toulon blockade, with little likelihood of action, there was always the sea to cope with, the sudden savage winds of the Gulf of Lions; and the unexpected was always at hand. Admiral Thornton was himself an outstanding seaman; he required a very high degree of competence in his captains; he never hesitated to sacrifice individuals when he thought the good of the service was at issue – many an officer had he set on the beach for ever – and although Jack could hardly hope to distinguish himself during this parenthesis it was quite possible that he might take a fall, particularly as Admiral Harte, the second in command, did not love him. His thoughts were more sombre, his face far less cheerful than usual. After the first few very active weeks of getting the *Worcester* into shape, weeks in which he had brought her gunnery to a moderately high standard of efficiency, the ship had settled into the steady naval way of life, a happy ship upon the whole; and since he had an excellent first lieutenant in Tom Pullings he had had plenty of time to worry about his affairs at home, his horribly involved and dangerous legal affairs. He had retained little Latin from his brief, remote, and largely ineffectual days at school, but one tag still ran through his head and the substance of it was that no ship could outrun care. The *Worcester* had run some two thousand miles as fast as he could drive her, yet care still sat there, dispelled only by the great-gun exercise and his evenings with Stephen, Scarlatti, old Bach and Mozart.

Bonden brought the barge kissing alongside the flagship. Jack was piped aboard with even greater ceremony, bosun's calls howling, Marines presenting arms with a fine simultaneous clash; he saluted the quarterdeck, observed that the Admiral was not there, saluted the Captain of the Fleet, shook hands with the captain of the *Ocean*, took the packets from his midshipman, and turned to a man in black, the Admiral's secretary, who led him below.

The Admiral looked up from the innumerable papers on his broad desk, said 'Sit down, Aubrey. Forgive me for a moment,' and went on writing. His pen squeaked. Jack sat there gravely, as well he might, for the man in front of him, brilliantly lit by the Mediterranean sun coming in through the stern-window, was a pale bald bloated ghost of the Admiral Thornton he had known, a man without any glorious fleet-action to his name but with a great reputation as a fighting captain and a greater one as an organizer and a disciplinarian, a man with a personality as strong as St Vincent's and not unlike him, except that he loathed flogging and paid much attention to religious observance – and that he was happily married. Jack had served under him, and although he had known many admirals since those days he still found him as formidable as ever, shockingly aged and sick though he was. Jack sat there, considering the passage of time and its mutilations; he stared, hardly aware of what he was seeing, at the Admiral's pale bald head with a few long streaks of grey hair on either side until an old, old pugdog, suddenly waking, set up a furious little din, waddled straight at his chair and bit him in the leg, if so nearly toothless a nip could be called a bite.

'Quiet, Tabby, quiet,' said the Admiral, scratching on.

The pug retreated, snorting and growling, rolling her eyes and defying Jack from her cushion under the desk. The Admiral signed his letter, put down his pen and took off his spectacles: he made as if to rise, but sank back. Jack sprang to his feet and the Admiral stretched out his hand over the papers, looking up at him without much interest. 'Well, Aubrey,' he said, 'welcome to the Mediterranean. You have made a fairly good passage, considering the levanter. I am glad they sent me a real seaman this time: some of the people they wish on us are sad loobies. And I am glad to see you managed to persuade them to let you have sensible masts. Taunt, heavy-sparred ships, above all if they are wall-sided, will never do for winter service here. Tell me, how do you find the *Worcester*?'

'I have her statement of condition here, sir,' said Jack, taking one of his packets. 'But perhaps first you will allow me to deliver this: when I did myself the honour of waiting upon her before we sailed I promised Lady Thornton that it should be the first I gave you.'

'Bless me, letters from home,' cried the Admiral, and his dull, glaucous eyes took on their old life and gleam. 'And a couple from my girls, too. This is an epocha – I have not heard from them since *Excellent* came in. Bless me. I take this very kindly in you, Aubrey, upon my word I do.' This time he rose from his chair, heaving his thick body up on his stick-like legs to shake Jack's hand again; and as he did so he noticed the torn silk stocking, the little spot of blood. 'Has she bit you?' he cried. 'Oh, I am so sorry. Tabby, you vile cur, for shame,' he said, bending to cuff the pug: she snapped at him without the least hesitation, never stirring from her cushion. 'She grows fractious in her old age,' said the Admiral. 'Like her master, I am afraid. And she pines for a run on shore. Do you know, Aubrey, it is thirteen months since I let go an anchor?'

When the Admiral had leafed through the several covers and had glanced at his official correspondence to see whether there were any particularly urgent matters, they returned to the *Worcester* and Jack's wound. The ship did not detain them long; they both knew her and most of the other Forty Thieves, and Jack was aware that the Admiral longed to be left alone with his letters. But Thornton repeatedly expressed his concern about the wound and the torn stocking: 'At least I can assure you that Tabitha ain't mad,' he said; 'Only wanting in wits and discrimination. If she had been mad there would scarcely be a flag-officer left in the squadron, since she has nipped Admiral Harte, Admiral Mitchell, and the Captain of the Fleet again and again. Particularly Harte. And not one of them has fallen into convulsions that I know of. But she *is* fractious, as I say, like her master. A good set-to with the French would set us both up – make us young again, and let us go home at last.'

'Is there any likelihood of their coming out, sir?'

'Maybe there is. Maybe. Not immediately, of course, with this southern air and a steady glass; but the inshore squadron has reported a good deal of activity these last weeks. Lord, how I hope they make a dash for it,' cried the Admiral, clasping his hands.

'God send they do, sir,' said Jack, standing up. 'God send they do.'

'Amen to that,' said the Admiral, and rising with the roll of the ship he walked to the door with Jack, observing as they parted, 'We are to have a court-martial tomorrow, I am afraid. You will attend, of course. There is one particularly ugly case that I do not choose to leave over for Malta, and we will deal with the others at the same time. I wish it were done with. Oh, and I believe you have a Dr Maturin aboard. I should like to see him at noon, and so would the Physician of the Fleet.'

# CHAPTER FOUR

Jack Aubrey dined with his particular friend Heneage Dundas, captain of the *Excellent*. They had been midshipmen and lieutenants together; they could speak quite openly, and when the scrappy meal was over – the *Excellent*'s least meagre hen, boiled not to tenderness but string – and they were alone, Jack said, 'I was shocked to see the Admiral.'

'I am sure you were,' said Dundas. 'So was I when I first came out and went aboard the flag. I have hardly set eyes on him since then, but they say he has grown much worse – scarcely comes on deck except for half an hour or so in the cool of the evening and hardly ever entertains. How did you find him?'

'Worn out, completely worn out. He could barely get up from his chair – legs as thin as broomsticks. What is the matter with him?'

'Keeping the sea is the matter with him. Keeping up this infernal blockade as strictly as ever he can, with old battered ships, most of them undermanned and all of them short of stores, a worn-out squadron with some damned awkward troublesome captains and an incompetent second-in-command. I tell you, Jack, it will be the death of him. I have only been here these three months, and I am not half his age, but you know what a strict blockade is – another world, quite cut off; short commons, brown shirts, foul weather, the people bored and harassed with keeping exact station under the admirals' eyes – and already the ship is like a prison. He has had years of it, far more than any other Commander-in-Chief.'

'Why don't he go home, then? Why don't they relieve him?'

'Who could take over? Harte?'

They both gave a scornful laugh. 'Franklin?' suggested Jack. 'Lombard? Even Mitchell. They are all seamen; they could manage a blockade. Franklin and Lombard did very well off Brest and Rochefort.'

'But it is not only the blockade, you blockhead,' cried Dundas. 'The Admiral could manage the blockade with one hand tied behind his back. If it were only the blockade, he would be as plump and rosy as you or me. Though I may say in passing, Jack, you seem to have lost a good deal of your blubber since last I saw you: I doubt you weigh thirteen or fourteen stone. No, if it were only the blockade, a score of men could relieve him. But quite apart from the French he has the whole Mediterranean on his hands and everything that touches it: Catalonia, Italy, Sicily, the Adriatic, the Ionian, and the Turks, Egypt, the Barbary States – and I may tell you, Jack, the Barbary States are the very devil to deal with. I was sent to reason with the Dey, and I did so pretty well, although our consul tried to put a spoke in my wheel. I was very pleased with myself until I put in again a few weeks later about some Christian slaves and found that my Dey had been murdered by the soldiers and that there was a new one in the palace, wanting a new agreement and a fresh set of presents. Whether the consul or the men with him had engineered the affair I do not know, but the Foreign Office have some people there: Ned Burney recognized a cousin of his dressed up in a sheet.'

'Surely civilians cannot poach on our ground – on the Commander-in-Chief's preserves?'

'They are not supposed to, but they do. So does the army, at least in Sicily. And that makes things even more complicated, though they were complicated enough in the first place, in all conscience, with dozens of rulers, great and small. You never know where you are with the Barbary States, but they are essential for our supplies; while the Beys and Pashas in Greece and up the Adriatic almost never obey the Turkish Sultan –

they are practically independent princes – and some of them are quite prepared to play booty with the French to gain their ends. The Sicilians cannot be relied upon; and apart from the fact that we must not provoke him at any price for fear of the French, I do not know just how we stand with the Turks. But the Admiral does. He has the whole cat's-cradle of strings in his hands – you should see the feluccas and houarios and half-galleys that come aboard him – and it would not be easy for any new man to pick them up, particularly as instructions take so long coming out. We are often months and months without orders from the Admiralty, and without post either, and the Admiral has to play the ambassador and diplomat right left and centre, keeping all these rulers steady, as well as look after the squadron.'

'It would be difficult to replace him, of course. But they cannot really mean to leave him here till he works himself to death? If he dies, a new man must be sent out, and with no one to ease him into the command he would be very much at a loss. In any case, people say he has asked to be relieved several times. Lady Thornton told me so herself.'

'Yes, he has,' said Dundas; and he hesitated. His elder brother was First Lord, and he was wondering how much confidential information he could decently pass on. 'Yes, he has. But between you and me, Jack, between you and me, he has always left a loophole – he has always asked to be relieved in such a manner that they could press him to stay and he could yield. He has never sent in an ultimatum, and I do not believe the Admiralty knows how sick he is. They have sent him reinforcements, they have promoted his officers, and they have made him Major-General of the Marines; and they think the situation is dealt with.'

'Yet he longs to go home,' said Jack. 'A rum business.'

'I think the explanation is this,' said Dundas. 'He longs to go home, and he ought to go home; but he longs even more for a fleet-action with the French. While there is a possibility of that, and there is a very real possibility

100

since they outnumber us, it is my belief that he will stay. He will either have his battle or die aboard his ship.'

'Well,' said Jack, 'I honour him for it.' And once again he said, 'God send the French come out.' After a pause he stood up: 'Thank you for my dinner, Hen,' said he. 'I have rarely drunk such capital port.'

'It was very good of you to come,' said Dundas. 'I have been fairly pining for someone to talk to – glum as a gib cat and sick of my own company. There is precious little ship-visiting on blockade. Sometimes I play chess, right hand against left hand; but there ain't much fun in that.'

'What is your wardroom like?'

'Oh, they are a very decent set, upon the whole. They are mostly young men, of course, except for the premier, who is old enough to be my father: I invite them in turn, and dine with them on Sundays, but they are not men I can unbend with, not as who should say really talk to; and the evenings drag on and on, unfriended, melancholy, slow,' said Dundas with a laugh. 'They are people with whom you have to pose as a demi-god from one noon-observation to the next. I get very tired of it, and I doubt I play the part convincingly. You are most uncommon lucky to have Maturin. Give him my regards, will you? I hope he will find time to come across.'

Maturin had every intention of coming across, being fond of Captain Dundas, but first he had to wait on the Admiral and the Physician of the Fleet. He was ready early in the morning: his uniform, having been thoroughly revised and brushed by Killick, had been passed by Jack at breakfast, and now he stood on the quarterdeck, talking to Mr Martin. 'The ensign at the top of the middle mast indicates that Sir John Thornton is an admiral of the white,' he said. 'And as you perceive, the ensign itself is also white; whereas that on the rear mast, or *mizen* as we say, of the large vessel to the left is red, from which we are to understand that Mr Harte is a rear-admiral of the red squadron. Then again, could we see the flagship of Mr Mitchell, who commands the inshore squadron, we should find that it flies a blue flag, also on the rear mast, from which we should conclude that he is a rear-admiral of the blue and therefore subordinate to both Sir John Thornton and Mr Harte, the order of the squadrons being the red, the white, and the blue.'

'Three cheers for the red, white and blue,' said Mr Martin, his spirits raised high by the spectacle of so many glorious men-of-war assembled under the brilliant morning sky: no less than eight towering three-deckers and four more ships of the line besides the smaller vessels. Exactly-squared yards, fresh paint and shining brass concealed the fact that many of them were fast wearing out under the perpetual stress of weather, that some indeed were already beyond their useful lives; and though a sailor would have noticed fished masts and twice-laid stuff in the rigging, a landsman's eye saw no more than a hint of their true state in the patched sails and wind-frayed pennants. 'And the Union Jack on the Admiral's ship signifies the supreme command, no doubt?'

'I believe not, sir,' said Stephen. 'I am told that it is rather an indication of a court-martial having to be held in the forenoon. Perhaps you would like to attend? Anyone may listen to the proceedings, and it might give you a more comprehensive view of the Royal Navy.'

'It would be deeply interesting, I am sure,' said Martin, more soberly.

'Captain Aubrey is good enough to take me in his boat: it is preparing now, as you see, a capacious vehicle. I am sure that he would make room for you; and you would not find the flagship very difficult to get into. It is what we call a three-decker, and has a convenient door in the middle, termed an entry-port. I will ask him, if you wish, when he appears.'

'That would be very kind, if you are sure I should not be importunate.' Martin broke off, and nodding towards the place not far from the hen-coops where some sheep and a lugubrious bloodhound were being aired, he said,

'That child with the bull-calf, I see him every morning when I am up early enough – pray, is it another naval custom?'

'I am afraid it is, in a way. The puny young gentleman is Mr Calamy. He longs to grow huge and powerful, gigantically strong, and some wicked older members of the midshipmen's birth have told him that if he carries the calf on his shoulders a certain distance every day, his frame will insensibly become accustomed to the brute's gradually increasing weight, so that by the time it is a full-grown bull he himself will be a second Milo of Crotona. It was a bishop's son that first set him on, I regret to say. See, he falls again – how eagerly he takes up his burden – they cheer him, the Judas-band – it is a shame to abuse the poor lad so – the calf has kicked him – he masters the calf – he staggers on. And I am sorry to say the officers encourage it: even the Captain encourages it. And here is the Captain, ready to the moment.'

Captain Aubrey was not in fact quite ready. Rats had got at his best cocked hat in the night – they were very troublesome and enterprising in the *Worcester*, but a few months of blockade would deal with that, since the foremast hands and the midshipmen would eat them – and Killick was busy on the gold lace. Automatically he glanced aloft, taking in the state of the sky, the trim of the sails and the rigging, then fore and aft: his eye caught the little group on the larboard gangway, he smiled and called out in his strong cheerful voice, 'Clap on, Mr Calamy. Never say die. Perseverance does it.' The hat appeared; Jack clapped it on and in reply to Stephen's request said, 'Certainly, certainly. Smith, give Mr Martin a hand down the side. Come, Doctor.'

The barge shoved off, one of many converging upon the flagship for the court-martial; the captains gathered and Jack greeted several old acquaintances, some of them men he cordially liked. But he hated these occasions, and when the court assembled, when the Captain of the Fleet

103

had taken his seat as president, with the deputy judge-advocate and the members around him, and when the clerk had delivered to each a list of the cases to be tried, his face grew dark. There was the usual string of crimes too serious for a captain to deal with on his own, since most of them carried the death-penalty – desertion, real or attempted, striking superiors, murder, sodomy, theft on an ambitious scale – perhaps inevitable when some ten thousand men were brought together in these circumstances, many of them against their will. But there was also a series of accusations made by officers against officers: one member of a wardroom against another, captains against lieutenants or masters for neglect of duty, disobedience or disrespect, lieutenants against captains for oppression and tyranny or language scandalous and unbecoming to the character of an officer or drunkenness or all three. He hated these cases, the evidence of bad blood and rancour in a service where decent relations were essential to efficiency, to say nothing of happiness among the people. He knew very well that men on a long blockade, almost entirely cut off from contact with home and the outside world, apparently forgotten, badly supplied, badly fed, keeping the sea in all weathers, were likely to grow sour, and that small offences rankling could grow to monstrous proportions; but even so he was distressed to see the length of this second section of the list. All the trouble came from three ships, the *Thunderer*, Harte's flagship, the *Superb*, and the *Defender*; their officers must have been at loggerheads with one another and with their captains for months and months. 'At least,' he reflected, 'we shall not have time to get through more than a few of them, and then, what with exchanging and cooling down, most of the smaller charges will be withdrawn.'

Upon the whole he was right, a court-martial at sea being an exceptional affair, quite unsuited to the usual leisurely procedure in port; but even so they dealt with many more cases than he had expected, the judge-advocate – here the Admiral's secretary, Mr Allen – being a keen-witted, energetic, methodical, quick-thinking man of business.

They ran through the earlier, more routine cases with remarkable speed: and the sentences to death or to being flogged round the fleet with two, three and even four hundred lashes (which amounted to much the same thing, on occasion) plunged Jack's heart in gloom. Then, it appearing that the clerk accused of comforting the King's enemies, a most unusual case and no doubt the reason for this most unusual sitting, had killed himself, the court proceeded to some of these nasty wardroom quarrels. In a way Jack was relieved: he knew nothing of the clerk's case, but it might well have proved as monstrous as the one he had heard in Bombay, when a surgeon, an able, respected, but free-thinking man, was hanged for saying that he approved certain aspects of the revolution in France; and he wished to hear no more of the ghastly solemnity with which the judge-advocate told a wretched culprit that he was to be put to death – the more so since he knew that the Commander-in-Chief, a man as hard to others as he was to himself, would probably confirm every sentence.

The disgruntled officers followed one another in a most disagreeable public washing of very dirty linen. Fellowes, the captain of the *Thunderer*, appeared no less than three times, either as accused or accuser, a big, angry-looking man with a red face and black hair; Charlton of the *Superb* and Marriot of the *Defender* twice each. The court dealt with these cases tenderly: often, when the proceedings were resumed after the members' deliberation, the judge-advocate would say 'The court having maturely and deliberately considered the evidence finds these charges partly proved: the sentence of this court is that you be reproved for petulance and admonished to be more circumspect and not to offend in a like manner for the future; and you are accordingly hereby reproved and so admonished.' But one young man was dismissed his ship and one, who had been provoked into giving Fellowes a very rash answer, was broke – dismissed the service.

They were both from the *Thunderer*, and the conclusive evidence, the interpretation of the lieutenant's attitude and unwise gesture, came from Harte, who spoke with evident ill-will. They turned to yet another case, a plain drunken murder on the lower deck this time, and as Jack listened sadly to the familiar evidence he saw Martin watching with a tense, shocked expression on his white face. 'If he wanted to see the dirty side of the Navy, he could not have come to a better place,' he reflected, as a seaman bearing witness rambled on: 'Which I heard the deceased abusing of the prisoner in a most dreadful manner; he first called him a Dutch galliot-built bugger, damned him, and asked how he came to be in the ship, or who brought him into her; then he damned the person whoever did bring him. I could not afterwards make out what the deceased said, as he was in a horrid passion, but Joseph Bates, yeoman of the sheets, bade him kiss his arse – he was no seaman . . .'

While the earlier cases were being heard Stephen was with Dr Harrington, the Physician of the Fleet, an old and esteemed acquaintance, a learned man with very sound ideas on hygiene and preventive medicine but unhappily somewhat too gentle and timid for full effectiveness at sea. They talked of the squadron's remarkably good state of health: no scurvy, Sicily and its orange-groves being near at hand; little venereal disease, the ships being so rarely in port and the Admiral forbidding all but the most unexceptionable women aboard and very few even of them; no casualties from action, of course, and surprisingly few of the maladies usual to seamen, except in *Thunderer*, *Superb*, and *Defender*. 'I put it down largely to the use of wind-sails to bring at least some fresh air below,' said Harrington, 'to the continual serving-out of antiscorbutics, and to the provision of wholesome wine instead of their pernicious rum; although it must be admitted that happiness, comparative happiness, is a most important factor. In this ship, where there is often dancing on the forecastle, and stage-plays, and an excellent band, we have almost no sickness: in the three ships I have mentioned, where the diet, the wind-sails and the antiscorbutics are exactly the same, the surgeons have their hands full.'

'Indeed, the effect of the mind on the body is extraordinarily great,' observed Stephen. 'I have noticed it again and again; and we have innumerable authorities, from Hippocrates to Dr Cheyne. I wish we could prescribe happiness.'

'I wish that we could prescribe common sense,' said Harrington. 'That might be at least a first step towards it. But there is so strong a resistance to change in the official mind, with so stubborn and dogged a clinging to tradition, however evil, in the seamen, that sometimes I grow discouraged. Yet I must admit that the Admiral, though a difficult patient himself, supports me in all the reforms I try to introduce.'

'A difficult patient?'

'I should scarcely go too far if I were to say an impossible patient. Disobedient, masterful, doses himself. I have ordered him home I do not know how many times: I might as well have spoken to the ship's figurehead. I regret it extremely. But he tells me that he has consulted you before – you must know what kind of a patient he is.'

'What is his present state?'

Harrington made a hopeless gesture. 'When I have said that there is a tabes of the inferior members and a generalized severe and progressive lowering of the whole constitution I have said all I can usefully say.' He nevertheless went on to give a more detailed picture of decline: great loss of physical strength in spite of adequate digestive and eliminatory functions, a wasting of the legs, little or no exercise, occasional seasickness – disturbing after so many years at sea and dangerous in such a reduced condition – lack of sleep, extreme irascibility.'

'Is there any imbecility of will?'

'Heavens, no! His mind is as sharp and clear as ever it was. But his task is beyond the powers of a man his age

107

– it is beyond the powers of a man of any age, that is not in perfect health. Can you imagine dealing not only with the management of a large and often troublesome fleet, but with all the affairs of the Mediterranean as well? Particularly of the eastern Mediterranean, with its devious, shifting politics? He is at it fourteen and fifteen hours a day, hardly finding time to eat, still less to digest. And all this is required of a man whose education has been that of a sailor, no more: it is required of him for years on end. I wonder the strain has not killed him before this. My prescriptions, my bark and steel, may do some good; but short of going home there is only one thing that will set him squarely on his feet again.'

'What is that?'

'Why, an action with the French, a victorious fleet-action with the French. You spoke of the effect of mind upon matter just now: I am convinced that if the French were to come out of Toulon, and if they could be brought to action, Sir John would throw off his weakness; he would eat again, he would take exercise, he would be happy, vigorous, and young. I remember the change in Lord Howe after the First of June. He was about seventy and old for his age, sitting in an elbow-chair on the old *Charlotte*'s quarterdeck at the beginning of the battle, mortally tired from want of sleep: by the end he was in the prime of life, following every move, giving the clear exact orders that won the victory. And so he continued, for years and years. Black Dick, we used to call him . . .' Dr Harrington looked at his watch. 'However,' he said, 'you will be seeing our patient in a little while, and perhaps you will put your finger on some peccant organ that I have missed. But before that I should like to show you a very odd case; a case, or rather a cadaver, that puzzles me.'

He led the way below, and there in a small triangular room lit by a scuttle, lay the case in question, a young man arched backwards so that only his head and heels touched the deck, his face set in so agonized a grin that his mouth reached almost to his ears. He was still in irons, and the ship being on an even keel the broad leg-shackles kept him in position.

'He was the Maltese clerk,' said Harrington, 'a linguist employed by the Admiral's secretary for Arabic documents and so on. There was some question of his having made a wrong use of them. I do not know the details, but they would have come out at the court-martial had he lived to stand his trial. What do you make of it?'

'I should have said tetanus without hesitation,' said Stephen, feeling the corpse. 'Here is the most characteristic opisthotonos you could possibly wish, the trismus, the risus sardonicus, the early rigor. Unless indeed he could have taken a wild overdose of St Ignatius' beans, or a decoction of their principle.'

'Just so,' said Harrington. 'But how could he have come at the draught with his hands in irons? It puzzles me.'

'Pass the word for Dr Maturin – pass the word for Dr Maturin.' The cry ran along the decks from the Admiral's cabin and reached them as they stood gazing at the corpse.

Stephen had seen a good deal of the Admiral in earlier years, when Sir John was a member of the Board of Admiralty, a junior lord who had to do with Intelligence. He knew the reason for Stephen's presence in the Mediterranean and he said, 'I understand your possible rendezvous on the French coast is not for the immediate future, and that you wish to go to Barcelona before that. Now as far as Barcelona is concerned, there is no difficulty: any one of the victuallers can set you down and bring you back to Mahon when you wish. But the French coast is clearly a matter for a man-of-war, and as I am very short of sloops and avisoes, I have it in contemplation to make the return of one of the ships of the line to Mahon coincide with your visit. Perhaps the *Thunderer* is most in need.'

'If her need is not particularly urgent, sir,' said

Stephen, 'I should infinitely prefer it if the *Worcester* might be sent. Indeed, from my point of view that would be the ideal solution. Taking me and those I may bring with me off that coast is likely to be a delicate business, and Captain Aubrey is used to expeditions of this kind: we have nearly always sailed together. He is also a very discreet man, which is a point of great importance for any future undertaking of a similar character.' The pug had been staring at Stephen from the time he came in, sniffing in his direction: now she walked across the deck, bowing and wagging what tail she possessed. She made a heavy spring into his lap, and sat there wheezing, gazing into his face and smelling strong.

'I know he is a fine seaman, and no one can possibly question his courage,' said the Admiral, with something like a smile lighting his grey face, 'but I do not believe that I have heard him called discreet before.'

'Perhaps I should have added the qualification *at sea*. Captain Aubrey is very discreet at sea.'

'Very well,' said the Admiral, 'I shall see what can be done.' He put on his spectacles, made a note, held it at arm's length, and placed it on one of the many heaps of exactly-squared documents. Then, wiping his spectacles, he said, 'Tabby likes you, I see: she is a rare judge of character. I am very glad that you are come out, Maturin; I am sadly at a loss for intelligence, although Mr Allen, my secretary, has gathered a certain amount of local talent, and we had Sir Joseph's colleague, Mr Waterhouse, until the French caught him on shore and shot him. That was a shocking loss.'

'Did he know that I was coming out?'

'He knew that a gentleman was coming, no more. But if he had known that the gentleman was Dr Maturin, I do not think you need fear any disclosure: Waterhouse was the most secret man I have ever known, though he seemed so open – *volte sciolto, pensieri stretti* indeed. Allen and I learnt a great deal from him. But even so, we are often far to seek, and the French have some very

110

clever fellows in Constantinople and Egypt; and even in Malta, I am afraid. Allen had a Maltese clerk who must have been selling them copies of our papers for months before we caught him. They will be trying him today,' he said, glancing upwards to the captain's great cabin, where the court-martial sat, 'and I must admit I am most uneasy about the outcome. We cannot ask a gathering of English sea-officers to accept the *raison d'Etat*; yet we cannot hang him without their sentence: on the other hand we cannot produce the documents – there is far too much loose talking already – nor can we gag the fellow to prevent him from giving evidence that will reveal too much. How I hope Allen will handle the matter cleverly; he came along surprisingly under Mr Waterhouse's tuition.'

'I am sure he did,' said Stephen. 'I understand Mr Allen is an able, determined man.'

'He is both, thank God: and he does his very best against the interlopers who make a difficult situation even worse.'

'You allude to the gentlemen of the Foreign Office, I collect?'

'Yes. And to those from Lord Weymouth's service. The army gives me a certain amount of trouble too, with strange unauthorized alliances and promises, but that is only in Sicily and Italy, whereas the consuls and the people in the consulates are to be found everywhere, each with his own little plot and his local allies, trying to put in a ruler of his own, particularly in the smaller Barbary States . . . bless me, you would think that we were pursuing half a dozen different policies at once, with no central direction or authority. They order these things better in France.'

Stephen mastered a strong desire to contradict and said, 'Now, sir, by no means the least important reason for my being aboard this ship is to consult with Dr Harrington about your health. I have heard his views: now I must examine you.'

'Another time,' said the Admiral. 'I go along well enough for the moment: anno Domini and too much paper-work is the only trouble – I have not half an hour to call my own. But Mungo's Cordial keeps me in reasonable trim. I understand my own constitution.'

'Please to take off your coat and breeches,' said Stephen impatiently. 'Personal inclination is neither here nor there: the health of the Commander-in-Chief is of great concern to the entire fleet, to the entire nation. Nor is it to be left in unqualified hands. Let us hear no more of Mungo's Cordial.'

No single peccant organ did he find in his long and careful examination, but rather a general malfunction of the entire being, harassed beyond its power of endurance. 'When I have consulted with Dr Harrington,' he said at last, 'I shall bring some physic over, and I will see it drunk. But I must tell you, sir, the French are the cure for disease.'

'You are in the right of it, Doctor,' cried the Admiral. 'I am sure you are in the right of it.'

'Is there any probability of their coming out in the next two or three months? I say two or three months advisedly, sir.'

'I believe there is. But what haunts me is the thought that they may slip out without our knowing. What the gentlemen in London cannot be made to understand is that the blockade of a port like Toulon is a very chancy thing. The French have but to carry their telescopes up to the heights behind the town when the wind blows hard in the north – when we are blown off our station – to see how we bear and so avoid us. With a northerly breeze the air is almost always clear, and they can see for fifty miles up there. I know that two of their ships slipped out last month, and there may be more. If their fleet escaped me it would break my heart; much more than that, it might turn the scale of the war. And time is against me: the squadron is fast wearing out. Every time the mistral blows we lose some spars, our precious masts are sprung and our ships strain even more, while the French sit tight in port, building as fast as ever they can. If the French don't beat

112

us, the weather will.' As he put on his clothes he nodded to the deck above and said, 'They are taking a devilish long time about it.'

He sat at his desk again, collecting his thoughts. 'I will deal with these while we wait for Mr Allen,' he said, breaking the seal of a letter. He stared at it, said 'I must get stronger spectacles. Read me this, will you, Maturin? If it is what I hope for, I must begin preparing my answer at once.'

'It is from Mohammed Ali, Pasha of Egypt,' said Stephen, taking the letter and helping the pug on to his knee again. 'It was dated from Cairo on the second of this month, and it runs, "To the excellent among the chiefs of the Christian Powers, the Moderator of the Princes of the religion of Jesus, the Possessor of sage counsel and luminous and abundant talent, the Expounder of the truth, the Model of courtesy and politeness, our true and real friend, Thornton, Admiral of the English fleet. May his end be happy, and his course marked with brilliant and great events. After many compliments to your Excellency, we inform you, most illustrious friend, that we have received your kind letters translated into Arabic, and have read them, and understand your advice (as beautifully expressed as it is wise) respecting the management and defence of our ports. Your assurance that you preserve a regard for an old and sincere friend, and your sage counsels, have given us infinite content and joy. You shall ever have proofs of our abundant friendship and of our respectful attention; and we implore God to give effect thereto, and to preserve you ever in respect and esteem." '

'Civil,' said the Admiral. 'But he evades the issue, of course: not a word about the real point of my communication.'

'I see that he speaks of letters in Arabic.'

'Yes. In principle the Navy writes to foreigners in English; but where I want things done quick I send them unofficial copies in a language they can understand whenever I can. Even without that wretched Maltese we have clerks for Arabic and Greek: French we can manage for ourselves, and that answers for most other purposes; but we are very much at a loss for Turkish. I should give a great deal for a really reliable Turkish translator. Now this one, if you will be so good.'

'From the Pasha of Barka. He gives no date, but begins, "Thanks to God alone! To the Admiral of the English fleet, peace be to you, etc. We are told of the amicable way in which you treat our people, and we are informed of the truth of it, and that you deal friendly with the Moors. We shall serve you in any thing that may be possible with the greatest pleasure. Before this time another Pasha had the command; but now he is dead, and I have the command; and everything that you may be in want of will be attended to, please God. The Consul of your nation residing here treats us in a very bad way, and we wish that he may behave and speak with us in a better manner, and we will act accordingly, as we always did. It is customary, when a new Pasha is appointed, to send some person to congratulate him. Mohammed, Pasha of Barka." '

'Yes,' said the Admiral, 'I have been expecting this. Mohammed sounded us some time ago, to find whether we should help him to depose his brother Jaffar. But it did not suit, Jaffar being a good friend of ours, while as we knew very well, both from his reputation and from intercepted letters, that Mohammed was hand in glove with the French, who promised to set him up in his brother's place. It is probable that the ships that got out of Toulon went there for the purpose.' He considered for a while. 'I must find out whether the French are still there, which is very likely,' he went on. 'Then I rather think I can confound his knavish tricks by provoking them into a breach of his neutrality. Once they fire a shot he is committed, and I can send a powerful detachment, restore Jaffar, who is in Algiers, and perhaps catch the Frenchmen at the same time. Yes, yes. The next, if you please.'

'The next, sir, is from the Emperor of Morocco, and it is addressed to the King of England, by the hand of the Admiral of his glorious fleet. It begins, "In the name of God, amen. He is our first, our father, and all our faith is reposed in Him. From the servant of God, whose sole confidence is in Him, the head of his nation, Suliman, offspring of the late Emperors Mahomet, Abdallah, and Ismael, Sheriffs from the generation of the faithful, the Emperor of Great Africa, in the name of God and by His order, the Lord of his Kingdom, Emperor of Morocco, Fez, Taphelat, Draah, Suez, etc. To His Majesty of the United Kingdom of Great Britain and Ireland, King George the Third, Defender of the Faith, etc., etc., and worthiest and best of kings, commanding Great Britain, Ireland, etc., etc., etc., the Glory of his Country, Duke of Brunswick, etc., etc. May the Lord grant him long life, and happiness throughout his days. We had the honour to receive your Majesty's letter, which was read before us, and were happy to be assured of your friendship, which we had before learned from your favours and attention to our wishes concerning our agents and subjects; for which please to accept our warmest and most sincere thanks. Your Majesty may rely on it, that we shall do everything in our power to assist your subjects in our dominions, and also your troops and vessels which may touch at our ports. We pray to the Almighty never to dissolve the friendship which has subsisted between our ancestors for so many years, but that it may be increased to the end of our generations: and we are always ready, at your Majesty's command, to do any thing that may contribute to your happiness or that of your subjects. Before we had written this, our express orders were, that all British ships that might touch at any of our ports should be supplied with a double allowance of provisions, and all that they might stand in need of; and we are ever ready, as we before said, to attend to your commands. We conclude with our most fervent prayers for your Majesty's health, peace, and happiness." '

'I am heartily glad of that,' said the Admiral. 'These sources of supply are of the first importance to us, and the Emperor is a man one may rely upon. How I wish I could say the same of the Beys and Pashas of the Adriatic, to say nothing of certain European rulers – ah, Allen, here you are at last. Dr Maturin, allow me to name Mr Allen, my secretary – Dr Maturin.' They bowed, looking attentively at one another. 'How did the court go?' asked the Admiral.

'Very well, sir,' said Allen. 'We got through a surprising amount of business, and I have some death-sentences for your confirmation. It was not necessary to try the Maltese: he died before his case came up. It is supposed he poisoned himself.'

'Poisoned himself?' cried the Admiral, fixing Allen with a stern, penetrating look. Then the life faded: he muttered, 'What does one man matter, after all?' and bent his grey face over the sentences, confirming them one by one with his careful signature.

The calm lasted through the night, and in the morning, despite a threatening sky, a falling barometer, and a prophetic swell from the south-east, the sentences were carried out. Mr Martin's ship still being absent, he had spent the night with two condemned men aboard the *Defender*, which had no chaplain: he walked beside each through the entire ship's company assembled, boats from the whole squadron attending, in a heavy silence, to the point under the foreyardarm where each had his last tot of rum before his hands were tied, his eyes blindfolded, and the noose was fitted round his neck. Martin was much shaken by the time he returned to the *Worcester*, but when all hands were called on deck to witness punishment he took what he conceived to be his place among them, next to Stephen, to watch the horrible procession of armed boats escorting those men who were to be flogged round the fleet.

'I do not think I can bear this,' he said in a low voice as the third boat stopped alongside their ship and the provost-marshal read out the sentence for the seventh

116

time, the legal preliminary to another twenty lashes, this time to be inflicted by the *Worcester*'s bosun's mates.

'It will not last much longer,' said Stephen. 'There is a surgeon in the boat, and he can stop the beating when he sees fit. If he has any bowels he will stop it at the end of this bout.'

'There are no bowels in this pitiless service,' said Martin. 'How can those men ever hope for forgiveness? Barbarous, barbarous, barbarous: the boat is awash with blood,' he added, as though to himself.

'In any case, this will be the last, I believe. The wind is rising: see how the Captain and Mr Pullings look at the sails.'

'God send it may blow a hurricane,' said Mr Martin.

It blew, it blew: not indeed a hurricane, but a wet wind out of Africa that came at first in heavy gusts, tearing the spray from the top of the rollers, clearing some of the degrading filth from the boats used for punishment. The flagship threw out the signal for hoisting all boats in, for making sail, for taking station in line abreast, for steering west-north-west; and the squadron headed for the coast of France, raising the topsails of the inshore squadron within two hours, the hills behind Toulon looming through the rain on the horizon, a little firmer than the clouds; and there a caique from the Adriatic found the flagship with still more letters for the Admiral's overloaded desk.

Encouraging news from the inshore squadron, however: the frigates that plied continually between Cape Sicié and Porquerolles, standing right in to the extreme range of the guns on the hillside whenever the wind served, reported that the French had moved three more ships of the line into the outer road and that they now lay there with the rest, yards crossed and ready for sea. On the other hand it was confirmed that one seventy-four, the *Archimède*, and one heavy frigate, probably the *Junon*, had slipped out in the last blow but one, their destination unknown. This still left Emeriau, the French admiral, a theoretical twenty-six sail of the line, six of them three-deckers, and six forty-gun frigates, as against Thornton's thirteen of the line and a number of frigates that varied so much according to the Admiral's needs in remote parts of the Mediterranean that he could rarely count on more than seven at any one time. It was true that several of the French ships were newly launched and that their crews had little experience apart from cautious manoeuvring between Cape Brun and the headland of Carquaranne, and that others were undermanned; but even so the enemy could certainly bring out a superior force, something in the nature of seventeen efficient line-of-battle ships. And since Emeriau had recently been sent a capable, enterprising second-in-command, Cosmao-Kerjulien, it was by no means unlikely that they should do so.

But they did not do so with the offshore squadron in sight, nor did they do so when the Commander-in-Chief withdrew over the rim of the horizon, taking Admiral Mitchell's flagship with him, to cruise in those middle waters that he called the sea of hope deferred.

The squadron cruised in strict formation under the eye of a most punctilious Captain of the Fleet and under the far more dreaded supervision of the unseen Admiral. It was not unlike a perpetual full-dress parade, and the least mistake led to a public reproof, a signal from the flag requiring the erring ship to keep her station, a message that could of course be read by all the rest. And since each ship had her own trim, her own rate of sailing and her own amount of leeway this called for incessant attention to the helm, jibs and braces, as wearing as the incessant vigilance by day and night, the searching of the sea for Emeriau in line of battle. For the Worcesters it was not so bad as for those who had been at it for months and even years; it had something of novelty, and there were quite enough man-of-war's men aboard for her not to disgrace herself. There was a great deal of necessary work to keep them busy: for most these were not yet routine tasks, already done so often that they were second nature; and unlike the other ships' companies the Worcesters had not been at sea so long that the absence of female company was a matter of almost obsessive concern. And although the gunner's wife, a plain, sober, middle-aged lady, had received a number of propositions – propositions that she rejected firmly but without surprise or rancour, being used to men-of-war – the idea of substitution had hardly spread at all. The ship was blessed with a long spell of fine weather to ease her in, and in a surprisingly short time this exactly-ordered, somewhat harassing but never idle existence seemed the natural way of life, pre-ordained and perhaps everlasting. Jack knew most of his six hundred men and boys by now, their faces and capabilities if not always their names, and upon the whole he and Pullings found them a very decent crew; some King's hard bargains among them and more who could not stand their grog, but a far greater number of good than bad: and even the landsmen were beginning to take some tincture of the sea. His midshipmen's berth he was less pleased with: it was the weakest part of the ship. The *Worcester* was entitled to twelve oldsters or midshipmen proper; Jack had left three places vacant, and of the nine youths aboard only four or perhaps five had the evident makings of an officer. The others were amiable enough; they walked about doing nobody any harm, gentlemanly young fellows; but they were not seamen and they took no real pains to learn their profession. Elphinstone, Admiral Brown's protégé, and his particular friend Grimmond, were both heavy, dull-witted, hairy souls of twenty and more; both had failed to pass for lieutenant and both were fervent admirers of Somers, the third lieutenant. Elphinstone he would keep for his uncle's sake; the other he would get rid of when he could. As for the youngsters, the boys between eleven and fourteen, it was harder to form an opinion, they being so mercurial: harder to form an opinion of their capabilities, that is to say, for their attainments could be summed up in a moment, and a more ignorant set of squeakers he had never seen. Some might be able to parse until all was blue or decline a Latin noun, but parsing never clawed a ship off a lee shore. Few understood the Rule of Three; few could multiply with any certainty, nor yet divide; none knew the nature of a logarithm, a secant, a sine. In spite of his determination not to run a nursery he undertook to show them the rudiments of navigation, while Mr Hollar the bosun, a far more successful teacher, made them understand the rigging, and Bonden the right management of a boat.

His classes were tedious in the extreme, since none of these pleasant little creatures seemed to have the least natural bent for the mathematics, and they were awed into even deeper stupidity by his presence; but the lessons did at least keep him from worrying about what the lawyers might be doing at home. Of recent weeks his mind had tended to run out of control, turning over the intricate problems again and again: a sterile, wearing, useless activity at the best of times and far worse between sleeping and waking, when it took on a repetitive nightmarish quality, running on for hours and hours.

It was after one of these sessions with the youngsters and their multiplication table that he stepped on to the quarterdeck and took a few turns with Dr Maturin while his gig was hoisting out. 'Have you weighed yourself lately?' asked Stephen.

'No,' said Jack, 'I have not.' He spoke rather curtly, being sensitive about his bulk: his more intimate friends would exercise their wit upon it at times, and Stephen looked as if he might be on the edge of a *bon mot*. But on this occasion the question was not the prelude to any satirical fling. 'I must look into you,' said Stephen. 'We may all of us entertain an unknown guest, and I should not be surprised if you had lost two stone.'

'So much the better,' said Jack. 'I dine with Admiral Mitchell today: I have two pair of old stockings on, as you see. Larboard mainchains,' he called to his coxswain, and almost immediately afterwards he ran down into the waiting gig, leaving Stephen strangely at a loss. 'What is the connection between the loss of two stone and the wearing of two pair of old stockings?' he asked the hammock-netting.

The connection would have been clear enough if he had gone aboard the *San Josef* with Jack. Her quarterdeck had a large number of officers upon it, which was natural enough in a flagship: officers tall, medium and short, but all of them remarkably lean and athletic – no sagging paunches, no dewlaps in the *San Josef*. From among them stepped the Admiral, a small compact man with a cheerful face and the pendulous arms of a foremast-hand. He wore his own grey hair, cut short in the new fashion and brushed forward, which gave him a slightly comic air until one met his eye, an eye capable of a very chilling glance indeed, though now it expressed a cordial welcome. He spoke with a pleasant West Country burr, and he rarely pronounced the letter H.

They talked about some improvements in the tops, the provision of a new kind of swivel-gun with little or no recoil; and as Jack had expected the Admiral said, 'I tell you what, Aubrey, we will have a look at them; and then while we are about it let us race to the jack-crosstrees – there is nothing like it for a whet to your appetite – the last man down to forfeit a dozen of champagne.'

'Done, sir,' said Jack, unbuckling his sword. 'I'm your man.'

'You take the starboard ratlines, since you are the guest,' said the Admiral. 'Away aloft.'

The captain of the maintop and his mates received them calmly and showed them the working of the swivel-guns. They were perfectly used to the sudden appearance of the Admiral, who was famous throughout the fleet as an upperyardsman and as one who believed in the virtue of exercise for all hands; they looked covertly at Captain Aubrey's face for signs of the apoplexy that had struck down the last visiting commander and they were gratified to see that from a pleasing red Jack's face had already turned purple from keeping pace with the Admiral. But

Jack was a tolerably deep file: he loosened his collar and asked questions about the guns – the guns interested him extremely – until he felt his heart beat easy with the coming of his second wind, and when the Admiral cried 'Go' he sprang into the topmast shrouds as nimbly as one of the larger apes. With his far greater reach and length of leg he was well ahead until half-way to the topmast bibs, where the Admiral drew level, swung out on the mizen flagstaff stay and began swarming up the frail spider's web that supported the *San Josef*'s lofty topgallantmast with the jack-crosstrees at its head, up and up hand over hand, no ratlines here for their feet. He was at least twenty years older than Jack, but he led by a yard when he reached the crosstrees, writhed round them and took up a strategic position that effectually stopped Jack's progress. 'You must stand on them with both feet, Aubrey,' he said without a gasp. 'Fair's fair,' and so saying he leapt outwards on the easy roll. For a split second he was in the air, free as a bird, two hundred feet above the sea: then his powerful hands grasped the standing backstay, and the immensely long rope that plunged straight from the mast-head to the ship's side by the quarterdeck at an angle of some eighty degrees; and as the Admiral swung to clasp it with his legs so Jack set both feet on the crosstrees. Being so much taller he could reach the corresponding stay on the other side without that appalling leap, without that swing; and now weight told. Fifteen stone could slide down a rope faster than nine, and as they both shot past the maintop it was clear to Jack that unless he breaked he must win. He tightened his grip above and below, felt the fierce burning in his hands, heard his stockings go to ruin, gauged his fall exactly, and as the deck swept close he dropped from the stay, landing at the same instant as his opponent.

'Pipped on the post,' cried the Admiral. 'Poor Aubrey, beat by half a nose. But never mind; you did very well for a cove of your uncommon size. And it has clawed some of the jam off your back, hey? Given you an appetite, hey,

hey? Come and drink some of your champagne. I will lend you a case until you can pay me back.'

They drank Jack's champagne, the dozen between eight of them; they drank port and something that the Admiral described as rare old Egyptian brandy; they told stories, and in a pause Jack produced the only decent one he could remember. 'I do not set up for a wit,' he began.

'I should think not,' said the Captain of the *San Josef*, laughing heartily.

'I cannot hear you, sir,' said Jack, with a vague recollection of legal proceedings; 'But I have the most amazingly witty surgeon: learned, too. And he once said the best thing I ever heard in my life. Lord, how we laughed! It was when I had *Lively*, keeping her warm for William Hamond. There was a parson dining with us, that knew nothing of the sea, but someone had just told him that the dog-watches were shorter than the rest.' He paused amid the general smiling expectancy. 'By God, I must get it right this time,' he said inwardly, and he concentrated his gaze on the broad-bottomed decanter. 'Not so long, if you understand me, sir,' he went on, turning to the Admiral.

'I believe I follow you, Aubrey,' said the Admiral.

' "So the dog-watches are shorter than the rest," says the parson, "very well. But why *dog*, if you please?" As you may imagine, we looked pretty blank: and then in the silence the Doctor pipes up. "Why, sir," says he, "do you not perceive that it is because they are *cur-tailed*?" '

Infinite mirth, far greater than on the first occasion long ago, when it had had to be explained. Now the company had known that something droll was coming; they were prepared, primed, and they exploded into a roar of honest delight. Tears ran down the Admiral's scarlet face: he drank to Jack when he could draw breath at last, he repeated the whole thing twice, he drank to Dr Maturin's health with three times three and a heave-ho rumbelow; and Bonden, who had regained the gig with his crew half an hour before, having been kindly

123

entertained by the Admiral's coxswain, said to his mates, 'It will be the gallery-ladder this tide. Mark my words.'

The gallery-ladder it was, a humane device discreetly let down so that captains who did not choose to face the ceremony of piping the side might come aboard unseen, giving no evil example to those they might have to flog for drunkenness tomorrow; and it was by the gallery-ladder that Captain Aubrey regained his cabin, sometimes smiling, sometimes looking stern, rigid and official. But he had always had a good head for wine, and although he had lost some weight there was still a fine bulk in which wine might disperse: after a nap he woke in time for quarters, perfectly sober. Sober, but grave, rather melancholy; his head ached; his hearing seemed unnaturally acute.

The great-gun exercise was not what it had been: a ship on blockade, sailing in formation, could hardly blaze away as the *Worcester* had done in the lonely ocean. But Jack and the gunner had devised a framework of laths with a mark hung in the middle by a network of lines whose meshes were just smaller than a twelve-pound ball, so that the exact flight of the shot could be traced and the angle corrected; this was boomed out from the fore yardarm and different crews fired at it from the quarterdeck twelve-pounders every evening. They still used Jack's curious private powder, which excited a good deal of ribald comment in the squadron – laborious signals about Guy Fawkes, and was the *Worcester* in serious distress? – but he persisted, and by now it was rare that any crew failed to cut the lines near the mark, while often they struck the bull's eye itself, to the sound of general cheering.

'I suppose, sir, that we may dispense with the firing today,' said Pullings in a quiet, considerate voice.

'I cannot imagine why you should suppose any such thing, Mr Pullings,' said Jack. 'This evening we shall fire six supplementary rounds.'

By an unhappy chance it so happened that the powder filled for this evening's practice was the kind that

124

gave a blinding white flash and an extraordinarily loud high-pitched bang. At the first discharge Jack clapped his hands tight behind his back to prevent himself from putting them to his head; and long before the last of the additional rounds he regretted his petulance with all his heart. He also regretted clasping his hands so tight, since his childish sliding on the flagship's backstay had scorched them cruelly, and in his sleep the right-hand palm had swelled in a red and angry weal. However, the marksmanship had been unusually good; everybody looked pleased; and with a haggard, artificial grin he said 'A creditable exercise, Mr Pullings. You may beat the retreat.'

After a barely decent interval while his cabin was being put to rights – for the *Worcester* was one of the few ships that stripped every evening, a clear sweep fore and aft – he retreated himself.

The first thing that met his cross-grained nose was the smell of coffee, his favourite drink. 'What is that pot doing here?' he asked in a harsh, suspicious voice. 'You do not imagine that I am in need of coffee at this time of day, do you?'

'Which the Doctor is coming to look to your hand,' said Killick with the surly, aggressive, brazen look that always accompanied his lies. 'We got to give him something to whet his whistle, ain't we? Sir,' he added, as an afterthought.

'How did you make it? The galley fire has been out this half hour and more.'

'Spirit-stove, in course. Here he is, sir.'

Stephen's ointment soothed Jack's hand, the coffee soothed his jangling soul, and presently the normal sweetness of his nature made a veiled appearance, though he still remained unusually grave. 'Your Mr Martin carries on about the harshness of the service,' he observed after the fourth cup, 'and although I must confess that a flogging round the fleet is not a pretty sight, I feel that perhaps he may carry it a trifle high. He may exaggerate.

It is unpleasant, to be sure, but it is not necessarily death and damnation.'

'For my part I should prefer hanging,' said Stephen.

'You and Martin may say what you like,' said Jack, but there are two ends to every pudding.'

'I should be the last to deny it,' said Stephen. 'If a pudding starts, clearly it must end; the human mind is incapable of grasping infinity, and an endless pudding passes our conception.'

'For example, I dined today with a man who was flogged round the fleet; and yet he flies his flag.'

'Admiral Mitchell? You astonish me: I am amazed. It is rare, perhaps all too rare, that an admiral is flogged round the fleet. I cannot recall an instance in all my time at sea, though the Dear knows I have seen a terrible lot of punishment.'

'He was not an admiral at the time. Of course he was not, Stephen: what a fellow you are. No. It was a great while ago, in Rodney's day I believe, when he was a young foremast-jack. He was pressed. I do not know the details, but I have heard he had a sweetheart on shore and so he deserted again and again. The last time he refused his captain's punishment and applied for a court-martial, just at the wrong moment. There had been a great deal of trouble with men running and the court decided to make an example of poor Mitchell – five hundred lashes. But, however, he survived it; and he survived the yellow jack when his ship was ordered to the Spanish Main, when her captain and half the people died of it in less than a month. The new captain took a liking to him, and being precious short of petty-officers rated him midshipman. Well, not to be tedious, he minded his book, passed for lieutenant, was appointed to the *Blanche* right away, and was acting second when she took the *Pique*, her captain being killed. That gave him his step, and he had not commanded his sloop half a year before he ran into a French corvette at dawn, boarded her and carried her into Plymouth: he was made post for that, about twelve years before I was; and having the luck not to be yellowed he hoisted his flag not long ago. Luck was with him all the time. He is an excellent seaman, of course, and those were the days when you did not need to pass for a gentleman, as they say now; but he needed luck too. I have noticed,' said Jack, draining the pot into Stephen's cup, 'that luck seems to play fair, on the whole. It gave Mitchell a damned ugly swipe early on, and then made it up to him: but, do you see, I had amazing good luck when I was young, taking the *Cacafuego* and the *Fanciulla* and marrying Sophie, to say nothing of prizes; and sometimes I wonder . . . Mitchell began by being flogged round the fleet: perhaps that is how I shall end.'

# CHAPTER FIVE

The *San Josef* sailed away, taking the hospitable Mitchell back to the inshore squadron, and the *Worcester*'s long spell of kind weather came to an end with a shrieking nine-day mistral that blew the fleet half way to Minorca over a torn white heaving sea that did almost as much damage as a minor action. Yet even if this and their laborious beating up to latitude 43°N had not put an end to social intercourse, Jack would still have led a tolerably isolated existence. It was not a sociable squadron. Admiral Thornton did not entertain; the Captain of the Fleet preferred all commanders to remain in their ships so long as there was any way upon them and he disliked ship-visiting in other officers as a relaxation of discipline, while in ratings he looked upon it as a probable prelude if not a direct incitement to mutiny; and although Rear-Admiral Harte did give an occasional dinner-party when weather permitted he did not invite Captain Aubrey.

Jack had paid his duty-call on the Rear-Admiral on joining and he had been civilly received, even to the extent of expressions of pleasure at his being in the squadron; but although Harte was a practised dissembler these expressions deceived neither Jack nor anyone else. Most of the captains were aware of the bad blood that had existed between the two ever since Jack's liaison with Mrs Harte, long before his marriage, and those who did not know were soon told.

Jack's social life would therefore have been even more meagre than that of the rest of the captains, if he had not had some particular friends in the squadron, such as Heneage Dundas of the *Excellent* or Lord Garron of the *Boyne*, who could afford to disregard Harte's ill-will: and, of course, if he had not had Stephen already on board. But in any case his days were quite well filled: the ordinary running of the ship he could leave to Pullings with total confidence, but he did hope to improve the *Worcester*'s seamanship as well as her gunnery. He observed with pain that the *Pompée* could shift her topgallantmasts in one minute fifty-five seconds and hoist out all her boats in ten minutes forty seconds, although she was by no means a crack ship, while the *Boyne*, which habitually took a reef in her topsails after quarters in fine weather, did so in one minute and five seconds. He pointed out these facts to his officers and to those very able seamen the captains of the forecastle, the tops, and the after guard, and from that time on the lives of the less nimble members of the crew became miseries to them.

Miseries, that is to say, in the horribly active daytime: many of them, with rope-scarred hands and weary, aching backs, took to hating Captain Aubrey and the vile watch in his hand. 'Infernal bugger – fat sod – don't I wish he may fall down dead,' said some, though very discreetly, as the jibboom flew in and out or topgallantmasts were struck for the sixth time. But after quarters the longed-for drum would beat the retreat, tension would slacken, and hatred die away, so that by the time the evening gun roared out aboard the Admiral something like benevolence returned, and when he came forward to watch the dancing on the forecastle on warm, still, moonlit nights, or to see how the band was coming along, they would greet him very kindly.

There was a surprising amount of musical talent aboard. Quite apart from the fiddler and the Marine fifer who ordinarily played to encourage the hands at the capstan by day and for the hornpipes in the evening, at least forty men could play some instrument or other, and many more could sing, often really well. A decayed bagpipe-maker from Cumberland, now a swabber belonging to the starboard watch, helped remedy the lack of instruments, but although he and his fellow north-countrymen set up a spirited shrieking, the band would not be much of a credit

129

to the ship until one of the victuallers brought Jack's order from the music-shop in Valetta; and the *Worcester*'s chief present joy lay in her choir.

Mr Martin's ship, the *Berwick*, had still not rejoined from Palermo, where her captain was known to be much attached – moored head and stern – to a young Sicilian lady with bright chestnut hair: he therefore remained in the *Worcester*, taking service every Sunday that church could be rigged, and he had noticed the full-throated rendering of the hymns. To the more full-throated he suggested that they should make an attempt upon an oratorio: the *Worcester* carried no scores of any oratorio whatsoever, but he thought that with industry and recollection and perhaps some verses from Mr Mowett something might be achieved. However, the word had hardly spread in the lower deck before it was reported to the first lieutenant that the ship possessed five men from Lancashire word-perfect in Handel's *Messiah*, they having taken part in it again and again in their native wastes. They were poor thin little undernourished creatures with only a few blue teeth among them, though young: they had been taken up for combining with others to ask for higher wages and sentenced to transportation; but as they were somewhat less criminal than those who had actually made the demand they were allowed to join the Navy instead. They had in fact gained by the change, particularly as the *Worcester* was a comparatively humane ship; yet at first they were hardly aware of their happiness. The diet was more copious than any they had ever known. Six pounds of meat a week (though long preserved, bony and full of gristle), seven pounds of biscuits (though infested) would have filled them out in their youth, to say nothing of the seven gallons of beer in the Channel or seven pints of wine in the Mediterranean; but they had lived so long on bread, potatoes and tea that they could scarcely appreciate it, particularly as their nearly toothless gums could hardly mumble salt horse and biscuit with any profit. What is more, they were the very lowest

130

form of life aboard, landlubbers to the ultimate degree – had never seen even a duckpond in their lives – ignorant of everything and barely acknowledged as human by the older men-of-war's men – objects to be attached to the end of a swab or a broom, occasionally allowed, under strict supervision, to lend their meagre weight in hauling on a rope. Yet after the first period of dazed and often seasick wretchedness they learnt to cut their beef right small with a purser's jack-knife and pound it with a marlin-spike; they learnt some of the ways of the ship; and their spirits rose wonderfully when they came to sing.

Musical gifts cropped up in the most unexpected places: a bosun's mate, two quarter-gunners, a yeoman of the sheets, a loblolly boy, the aged cooper himself, Mr Parfit, and several more were found to be able to sing a score at sight. Most of the others could not read music, but they had true ears, a retentive memory, a natural ability to sing in part, and they were rarely out when once they had heard a piece: the only trouble (and it proved insuperable) was that they confused loudness with excellence, and passages that were not so pianissimo as to be almost inaudible were taken with the utmost power of the human voice. In singing the immense difference between Mr Parfit, with two pounds five and sixpence a month plus perquisites, and a landsman with one pound two and six minus deductions for his slops was abolished, and as far as the vocal part of it was concerned the *Messiah* came along nobly. They most delighted in the Halleluiah Chorus, and often, when Jack walked forward to lend his powerful bass, they would go through it twice, so that the deck vibrated again and he sang away in the midst of that great volume of true ordered sound, his heart lifted high.

But most of his musical pleasure was on a less heroic scale, and he took it much farther aft, in his great cabin with Stephen, the 'cello singing deep in its conversation with the violin, sometimes plain and direct, sometimes immensely intricate, but always profoundly satisfying in the Scarlatti, Hummel and Cherubini that they knew very

131

well, more tentative and still exploratory as they felt their way far into the manuscript pieces that Jack had bought from London Bach's young man.

'I beg pardon,' said Stephen, as a lee-lurch made him slur his C sharp into a quarter-tone lower than a lugubrious B. They played on to the end of the coda, and after the moment's triumphant silence, the tension dying, he laid his bow on the table, his 'cello on a locker, and observed, 'I am afraid I played worse than usual, with the floor bounding about in this irregular, uneasy fashion. It is my belief we have turned round, and are now facing the billows.'

'Perhaps we have,' said Jack. 'The squadron wears in succession at the end of every watch, you know, and it is now just a little after midnight. Shall we finish the port?'

'Gule, or gluttony, is a beastish sin,' said Stephen. 'But without sin there can be no forgiveness. Would there be any of the Gibraltar walnuts left, at all?'

'If Killick has not blown out his kite with them, there should be plenty in this locker. Yes. Half a sack. Forgiveness,' he said thoughtfully, cracking six together in his massive hand. 'How I hope Bennet may find it, when he rejoins. If he has any luck he will come into the fleet tomorrow. The Admiral is less likely to blast him on a Sunday, and this is still a fine leading wind from Palermo.'

'He is the gentleman who commands Mr Martin's ship?'

'Yes. Harry Bennet, who had *Theseus* before Dalton. You know him perfectly well, Stephen: he came to Ashgrove Cottage when you were there. The literary cove, that read Sophie a piece about the school at Eton and teaching the boys how to shoot, while she was knitting your stockings.'

'I remember him. He made a particularly happy quotation from Lucretius – *suave mare magno*, and so on. Why should he be blasted, so?'

'It is common knowledge that he stays in Palermo

132

far, far longer than he should because of a wench, a red-haired wench. The *Spry* and two victuallers saw the *Berwick* at single anchor, yards crossed, ready for sea on Monday, and yet there was Bennet driving up and down the Marina in an open carriage with this nymph of his and an ancient gentlewoman for decency's sake, looking as pleased as Pontius Pilate. No one could mistake that flaming hair. In all sober earnest, Stephen, I do hate to see a good officer-like man such as Bennet jeopardize his career, hanging about in port for a woman. When he rejoins I shall ask him to dinner: perhaps I could drop a few tactful hints. Perhaps you could say something in the classical line, about that fellow who contrived to hear the Sirens, listening to them while seized to the mainmast, the rest of the ship's company having their ears blocked with wax: it happened in these waters, I believe. Could you not bring it in by some reference to Messina, the Straits of Messina?'

'I could not,' said Stephen.

'No. I suppose not,' said Jack. 'It is a most infernally delicate thing to take notice of, even to a man you know very well.' He thought of the time when he and Stephen had competed for Diana's quite unpredictable favours; he had behaved much as Harry Bennet was behaving now, and he had savagely resented anything in the way of tactful hints on the part of his friends. His eye rested on the dressing-case she had given Stephen: it had long since been confided to Killick, to be kept dry and shipshape, and it now lived in the cabin, where it acted as a music-stand, an unbelievably polished music-stand. Its candles shone on the gold mountings, the gleaming wood, with an unearthly radiance. 'Still,' he said, 'I do hope he comes in tomorrow. Psalms may dull the Admiral's edge.' Stephen walked into the quarter-gallery, the cabin's place of ease; and coming back he said, 'Great bands of migrant quails are passing northwards: I saw them against the moon. God send them a kind wind.'

Sunday morning broke fine and clear, and the *Berwick*

133

was seen a great way off, crowding sail for the squadron on the larboard tack. But long before church was rigged, long before Mr Martin had even looked out his surplice, the breeze began to veer northwards, so that it was a question whether she might not be headed and set well to leeward. As for the quails there was no question at all. Presently the unvarying path of their migration led them straight into the wind's eye, and the poor birds, worn out with their night's flying, began to come aboard, dropping on deck in their hundreds, so tired they could be picked up. But this was shortly after the bosun's mates had piped down the hatchways, roaring, 'Clean up for muster at five bells – clean shirt and shave for muster at five bells – white frocks and trousers – muster-clothes at divisions,' and only those few men who had had the foresight to pin the ship's barber as soon as the idlers were called in the first grey light and to make sure that their clothes-bags, their quarters and their persons would pass the coming inspection could trouble with quails. Few were so provident as to have shaved with Etna pumice and to have combed out their pigtails in sheltered corners during the dark hours of the middle or morning watch; but few as they were, there were too many for Mr Martin. He skipped about the upper deck, his one eye alive with concern, moving quails to safe places, forbidding the men to touch them: 'Yes, sir: no, sir,' they said respectfully, and as soon as he hurried on they stuffed more birds into their bosoms. He ran down to Stephen in the sick-bay and begged him to speak to the Captain, the master, the first lieutenant – 'They have come to us for shelter – it is impious, inhuman to destroy them,' he cried, pushing Dr Maturin up the ladder at a run. But as they reached the quarterdeck, thrusting their way through a dense red mass of Marines hurrying to form on the poop, the officer of the watch, Mr Collins, said to the mate of the watch, 'Beat to divisions,' and the mate of the watch turned to the drummer, standing three feet away, his drumsticks poised, and said, 'Beat to divisions.'

The familiar thunder of the general drowned their words and brought all quail-gathering to a stop. Encouraged by cries of 'Toe the line, there,' and sometimes by shoves and even kicks for the very stupid, all the *Worcester*'s people gathered in ordered ranks with their clothes-bags, all as clean as they could manage with sea-water, all shaved, all in white frocks and trousers. The midshipmen of their divisions inspected the hands, the officers of the divisions inspected hands and midshipmen and then, pacing carefully through the ever-increasing flocks of quails, reported to Mr Pullings that 'all were present, properly dressed, and clean,' and Mr Pullings, turning to the Captain, took off his hat and said 'All the officers have reported, sir, if you please.'

Jack took a quail from his epaulette, set it on the starboard binnacle with an abstracted air, and replied, 'Then we will go round the ship.'

They both of them cast a disapproving glance at Stephen and Mr Martin, neither of whom was properly dressed nor yet in his right place, and set off on the long tour that would take the Captain past every man, boy and even woman in the ship through the steady gentle fall of exhausted birds.

'Come,' whispered Stephen, plucking Martin by the sleeve as Jack, having done with the Marines, approached the first division, the afterguard, and all hats flew off. 'Come, we must go to the sick-bay. The birds will come to no harm for the present.'

Jack carried on past the waisters, the gunners, the foretopmen, the boys, the forecastlemen: a slower progress than usual, since he had to edge little round birds out of the way at every step. There was still a great deal of room for improvement: there were still far too many sloppy Joes; the monoglot Welsh youth among the waisters he privately called Grey Melancholy, being unable to retain his name, was obviously finding life unbearable; the three idiots seemed no wiser, although at least they had been scrubbed this time; and young Mr Calamy appeared to have shrunk rather than grown, in spite of his noble perseverance with the bull-calf; but perhaps that was only because his best gold-looped round hat came down over his ears. Yet even so, almost all hands looked cheerful, pretty well fed, and at the order 'On end clothes' they showed an adequate array of slops.

'Sure a quail is a very acceptable dish,' said Stephen to his first assistant, 'but, Mr Lewis, I cannot recommend the eating of her in her *northward* migration. Apart from the moral issue at this particular juncture, apart from the impiety that Mr Martin so rightly abhors, you are to observe that the quail, eating noxious seeds on the African main, may well be noxious herself. Remember Dioscorides' words; remember the miserable fate of the Hebrews . . .'

'Quails are coming down the ventilator,' said the second assistant.

'Then cover them gently with a cloth,' said Mr Martin.

Jack reached the galley, inspected the coppers, the harness-casks, the slush-tubs, the three hundredweight of plum-duff preparing for Sunday dinner; and with some satisfaction he noticed his own private drowned baby simmering in its long kettle. But this satisfaction was as private as his pudding: the long habit of command and the necessary reserve combined with his tall erect person in full-dress uniform made him a somewhat awful figure and this impression was strongly reinforced by a scar down the side of his face that in certain lights turned his naturally good-humoured expression to one of brooding ferocity. This light shone upon it now, and although the cook knew that even Beelzebub could not justly find a fault with the galley today he was too flustered to answer the Captain's remarks: his replies had to be interpreted by the first lieutenant, and when the officers passed on he turned to his mates, wiping imaginary sweat from his brow and wringing out his handkerchief.

On through the whole length of the lower deck, with candles burning between the great thirty-two-pounders to show the exact arrangement of swabs, worms, rammers, fire-buckets, shot-garlands and their scrupulous cleanliness. On, and at last to the sick-bay, where Dr Maturin, having greeted him formally and reported the few cases under his care (two ruptures, two gleets, a fractured clavicle) said, 'Sir, I am concerned about the quails.'

'What quails?' asked Jack.

'Why, sir, the quails, the round brown birds,' cried Mr Martin. 'They are landing by hundreds, by thousands . . .'

'The Captain sees fit to be jocose,' said Stephen. 'I am concerned, sir, because they may represent a threat to the people's health; they may be poisonous, and I desire you will be so good as to order proper measures to be taken.'

'Very well, Doctor,' said Jack. 'Mr Pullings, make it so, if you please. And I believe we may now hoist the church pennant, if it is already flying aboard the flag.'

The pennant was indeed flying aboard the flag, and the moment the *Worcester*'s Captain returned to his quarter-deck it was transformed into a place of worship: that is to say three arms-chests covered with a Union flag were arranged to form a reading-desk and pulpit for the chaplain, chairs were set for the officers, mess-stools and benches made of capstan-bars laid athwart match-tubs for the men, and Mr Martin put on his surplice.

Jack was by no means a blue-light captain – he had never brought a tract aboard in his life – nor was he what would ordinarily have been called a religious man: his only touch of mysticism, his only approach to the absolute, was by means of music; but he had a strong sense of piety and he attended gravely to the familiar Anglican service, conducted with a fine decorum in spite of the multitudes of quails. Yet at the same time the sailor remained keenly alert, and he noticed that the breeze had not only diminished but that it was fast backing to its original quarter. The birds had stopped landing, though they were still thick on the deck. The *Berwick* now had the wind two points free and she was tearing along under skysails and kites, a remarkable display of canvas and of zeal. 'He don't

137

spare the dimity,' Jack reflected: he frowned and shook his head at Mr Appleby, who had induced a quail to sit on his shining, tasselled Hessian boot, and glancing beyond him he saw the *Berwick*'s signal break out aboard the flagship.

They sang a hymn – it blended strangely with those coming from the ships within earshot – and then sat down to hear the sermon. Mr Martin had a low opinion of his powers as a preacher and usually he read a sermon by South or Tillotson, but this time he was to expound a text of his own. While he was searching for it – the marker had blown away during the last hymn but one – Jack noticed Stephen on the forecastle: he was directing the *Worcester*'s other Papists, her two Jews and the Lascars she had inherited from the *Skate* to gather quails in baskets and launch them over the leeward side. Some flew off quite strongly: others returned.

'My text,' said Mr Martin at last, 'is from the eleventh chapter of the Book of Numbers, verses thirty-one to thirty-four: "And there went forth a wind from the Lord, and brought quails from the sea, and let them fall by the camp, as it were a day's journey on this side, and as it were a day's journey on the other side, round about the camp, and as it were two cubits high upon the face of the earth. And the people stood up all that day, and all that night, and all the next day, and they gathered the quails: and he that gathered least gathered ten homers: and they spread them all abroad for themselves round the camp. And while the flesh was yet between their teeth, ere it was chewed, the wrath of the Lord was kindled against the people, and the Lord smote the people with a very great plague. And he called the name of that place Kibroth-hattaavah, because there they buried the people that lusted." Now Kibroth-hattaavah, in Hebrew, signifies the graves of those that lusted, and from this we are to understand that lust is the gateway to the grave . . .'

Church was over. The remaining quails, now regarded

with deep suspicion as Jonahs, were encouraged to leave
the ship, and the *Worcester*'s people began to look forward with keen anticipation to their Sunday pork and
plum-duff. The *Berwick*'s barge left the flagship, her
captain looking extremely grave; as it came within hail
Jack asked Bennet to dinner, observing, as his guest came
up the larboard side without ceremony, 'I shall be able to
introduce your new chaplain: he is aboard of us. Pass the
word for Mr Martin. Mr Martin: Captain Bennet. Captain
Bennet: Mr Martin. Mr Martin has just given us a most
impressive sermon.'

'Not at all,' said Martin, looking pleased.

'Oh yes, yes: I was immensely struck by the consequences of lust, by the graves of those that lusted,' said
Jack, and it occurred to him that there could be no better
prelude to the more or less veiled warning that it was his
duty as a friend to give Harry Bennet.

The prelude was perfect, yet the warning never followed. Bennet had had an extremely disagreeable quarter
of an hour, but it was only with the Captain of the
Fleet, the Admiral being engaged with some Oriental
gentlemen, and his spirits revived as soon as he had a
glass of Hollands in him. They rose still higher at table,
and from the beginning of the meal to his red-faced, jolly departure he entertained Jack with a detailed account
of Miss Serracapriola's charms, physical, intellectual and
spiritual; he showed him a lock of her very surprising
hair, and spoke of his progress in Italian, the extraordinary
beauty of her voice, her skill in playing the mandolin, the
pianoforte, the harp. 'Nelson kissed her when she was a
child,' he said on taking his leave, 'and you may do so,
once we are married.'

Jack usually slept very well, unless legal worries filled
his mind, but swinging in his cot to the south-eastern
swell and staring at the tell-tale compass over his head
by the light of a small constantly-burning lantern, he
said, 'It is a great while since I kissed anyone.' Bennet's
glowing account of his Sicilian had moved Jack strangely;

he could see her supple form, the particular warmth of southern beauty; he remembered the scent of a woman's hair, and his thoughts wandered to Spanish girls he had known. 'It is a very great while since I kissed anyone,' he said as he heard three bells strike in the middle watch and the discreet cry of the nearer lookouts, 'Life-buoy – starboard quarterdeck – starboard gangway', 'and it will be even longer before I do so again. There is no duller life on earth than a blockade.'

Sometimes the squadron wore every watch, sometimes every two, according to the wind, as the ships beat to and fro across the likely paths of the Toulon fleet, and far out on either wing lay what frigates or brigs the Admiral could spare. Sometimes they stretched across to raise Sardinia when the breeze might let Emeriau come out eastwards; sometimes almost down to Mahon in line abreast when the mistral blew; and sometimes they stood in to speak to the inshore squadron. Day after day of much the same manoeuvres, continually looking out; but nobody did they see, never a sail but for the odd rigs from up the Mediterranean for the Admiral, otherwise only sea and sky, perpetually changing but still essentially sea and sky. Never a victualler, never a word from the outside world.

Unseasonable drizzling weather from the south brought them fresh water to wash their clothes, but it stopped the dancing on the forecastle, and although the oratorio boomed on between decks, the deeper passages echoing like an organ, Jack felt the general tone of the ship sink half a tone.

Some stood the monotony better than others. The midshipmen's berth did not seem aware of it: with some of the younger officers they were preparing a stage-play; and Jack, recalling his own youth, recommended *Hamlet*. There was no dramatic poet he preferred to Shakespeare, he said. But Mr Gill, the master, grew sadder still, a dead weight at the wardroom table, and Captain Harris of the Marines, who had far less to do than Gill, increased his already heavy drinking; he was never drunk, never anything but amiably hazy, but he was never wholly sober. Somers, on the other hand, was often unsteady, incoherent, and disagreeable: Pullings did his best to check him, but no one could take the private bottles from his cabin.

He had the afternoon watch at a time when Jack, Pullings and the purser were busy with the ship's books and accounts in the fore-cabin. The squadron was sailing in line abreast under all plain sail, the moderate northwest breeze one point free, when the signal came to tack together, an unusual order, since the Admiral almost always required them to wear, as being kinder to the older, more battered ships – as being more economical in every way, seeing that tacking involved risks to material that wearing did not. Jack heard the cry of 'All hands about ship', but his mind was taken up with the question of changing the people's rations from wine to grog and he thought no more of it until a passionate bawling on deck and a pounding of feet jerked him from his chair. Three strides brought him on to the quarterdeck and one glance showed him that the *Worcester* had missed stays. She still had a good deal of way on her, though the foretopsail was braced to, and she was about to run her bowsprit over the *Pompée*'s waist. In the thunderous shaking of canvas hands gazed aft for orders: Somers stared, bemused. 'Back the foretopsail,' called Jack. 'Port your helm. Flat in forward, there.' The ship's way was checked but even so the gap narrowed: narrowed horribly, yet not quite to disaster. The *Worcester*'s bowsprit passed six inches astern of the *Pompée*'s taffrail. 'Bartholomew Fair,' shouted her captain as she drew clear and the *Worcester* gathered sternway. Jack wore his ship round on to the larboard tack, let fall his topgallantsails and ran her up to her rightful station. He turned to Somers, who was looking red and sullen, visibly unsteady: 'How did this lubberly state of affairs come about?' he asked.

'Anyone can miss stays,' said Somers in a thick, heavy voice.

141

'What kind of an answer is this?' said Jack. 'You are playing with your duty, sir.' He was very angry indeed: the *Worcester* had been made to look a fool in front of ten thousand seamen. 'You put your helm hard a-lee. You braced the foretopsail hard to. Of course you did: do not deny it. This is not a cutter, sir, but a ship of the line, and a dull-sailing ship of the line at that, one that must be luffed up handsomely to lose no way, as I have said a hundred times. A disgraceful exhibition.'

'Always finding fault – always finding fault with me – whatever I do is wrong,' cried Somers, suddenly very pale; and then breaking out still louder, 'Tyranny and oppression, that's what it is. Damn your blood, I'll show you who I am.' His hand moved towards a belaying-pin in the fife-rail but at the same moment Mowett gripped his arm. In the stunned silence Jack said, 'Mr Pullings, order Mr Somers to leave the deck.'

Some time later Pullings came into the cabin and asked, awkwardly enough, whether Somers was under arrest. 'No,' said Jack. 'I do not mean to bring him to a court-martial. If he chooses to ask for one, that is his affair; but when he is sober even he will see that any court would certainly break him, whoever his father may be. Break him or worse. But I am determined he shall never do duty in my ship again. He may invalid or exchange, anything he likes; but he shall never serve under me.'

Mr Somers' conduct was a nineteen days' wonder in the *Worcester*. Even when it was found that he was neither to be hanged nor flogged to death, as had been confidently foretold, the appalling scene was told over again and again, commented upon, and universally censured: it remained a wonder even after a felucca from Malta had brought trumpets, trombones, flutes, oboes and a bassoon and the oratorio began to take on its full dimensions; even after the *Worcester*'s wine ran out and she changed over to the far stronger, far more popular grog, with its usual consequence of far more fighting, disobedience, ineptitude, accidents, naval crime and naval punishment.

For part of this time the atmosphere in the ward-room was extraordinarily disagreeable. On coming to his senses the day after his outburst the wretched Somers had been exceedingly alarmed: he wrote Jack an abject letter of apology, and begged Stephen to intercede for him, promising to leave the service 'if this unfortunate incident' were overlooked. Then, finding that he was not to be brought before a court-martial, he began to feel aggrieved: he told his unwilling listeners that he would not bear this treatment – that his father would not bear it either – that his family controlled seven votes in the House of Commons as well as two in the Lords – and that no one could slight him with impunity. Some of his vague, minatory words seemed to hint at an intention of asking Captain Aubrey for satisfaction, of calling him out; but his listeners were few; they paid little attention, and even his former admirers were heartily relieved when he disappeared, having negotiated an exchange with Mr Rowan of the *Colossus*, a lieutenant of the same seniority.

His departure was a sad disappointment to those hands who had been preparing their testimony for the trial. Some of them were old shipmates of Jack's, and they were perfectly ready to swear through a nine-inch plank so long as their evidence led in the right direction: the court would have heard a lively description of the Honourable Sod's furious assault upon the Captain with a brace of pistols, a boarding-axe, a naked sword and a topmast fid, together with all the warm or pathetic expressions used on either side, such as Somers' 'Rot your vitals, you infernal bugger,' and Jack's 'Pray, Mr Somers, consider what you are about.' Now, until the oratorio should be ready, all they had to look forward to, to break the unvarying monotony of their days, was the coming performance of *Hamlet*; though indeed the play was said to be as good as bear-baiting at Hockley-in-the-Hole, with a very satisfactory ending, lit with Bengal lights regardless of the cost. Parties of volunteers under the captain of the hold were getting up gravel from the *Worcester*'s ballast, far,

far below – an arduous and a very smelly task – for the grave-diggers' scene, and the ship's butcher was already setting his tubs aside, it being understood that whenever a tragedy was performed in one of His Majesty's ships an appropriate amount of blood should be supplied.

The role of Hamlet came to the senior master's mate by right, and Ophelia had obviously to be Mr Williamson, the only young gentleman with a tolerable face who could sing and whose voice had not broken; but the other parts were distributed by lot, and that of Polonius fell to Mr Calamy.

He often came to Stephen to be heard his words and he was adjuring him neither to borrow nor to lend, to dress soberly but very rich, and to have little or nothing to do with unfledg'd companions in a high breathless chant with no punctuation when the signal midshipman came below with the Captain's compliments to Dr Maturin, 'and if he were at leisure, would like to show him a surprise on deck.'

It was a gloomy day with a low grey sky, spitting rain from the south-south-east, the squadron close-hauled under treble-reefed topsails, beating up to keep their offing; yet there was an extraordinary cheerfulness on the quarterdeck. Pullings, Mowett and Bonden on the leeward side were beaming all over their faces and talking away as though they were in a tavern: to windward Jack stood with his hands behind his back, swaying to the *Worcester*'s cumbrous lift and roll, his eyes fixed upon a ship some five miles away.

'Here is my surprise,' he said. 'Come and see what you make of her.'

For many years Jack, Pullings and Mowett had made game of Dr Maturin in the nautical line; so, more discreetly, had Bonden, Killick, Joseph Plaice and a variety of other mariners, foremast hands, midshipmen and officers. He had grown wary, and now, staring long, he said, 'I should not like to commit myself, but at a casual glance I should take it to be a ship. Conceivably a man-of-war.'

'I am altogether of your opinion, Doctor,' said Jack.

'But will you not look through this glass, to see whether you can make out even more?'

'A man-of-war, with little doubt. But you need not be afraid, with all this powerful fleet around you; and in any case, I perceive it has only one row of guns – a frigate.' Yet even as he spoke there seemed something familiar about that distant ship, racing towards them with a broad white bow-wave on either side, and she growing larger every minute.

'Stephen,' said Jack in a low, happy tone, 'she is our dear *Surprise*.'

'So she is too,' cried Stephen. 'I recognize that complexity of rails in front – I recognize the very place I slept on summer nights. God love her, the worthy boat.'

'It does my heart good to see her,' said Jack. She was the ship he loved best, after the *Sophie*, his first command: he had served in her as a midshipman in the West Indies, a time he remembered with the liveliest pleasure, and years later he had commanded her in the Indian Ocean; he knew her through and through, as beautiful a piece of ship-building as any that had been launched from the French yards, a true thoroughbred, very fast in the right hands, weatherly, dry, a splendid sailor on a bowline, and a ship that almost steered herself once you understood her ways. She was old, to be sure; she had been much knocked about in her time; and she was small, a twenty-eight-gun frigate of under six hundred tons, little more than half the weight of the thirty-six and thirty-eight-gun ships that were usual now, to say nothing of the recent heavy frigates built to match the Americans: indeed, she was scarcely a frigate at all to modern eyes. But she had teeth for all that, and with her speed and quickness of turn she could take on ships of far greater bulk: she had even had one perilous brush with a French ship of the line, giving almost as good as she got. If Jack were ever enormously rich, and if she were sold out of the service, there was no other ship in the Royal

Navy he would sooner buy, as the most perfect yacht in existence.

Her present captain, Francis Latham, had made no important changes: she still had that towering thirty-six-gun frigate's mainmast and the doubled travelling-backstays that Jack had endowed her with. And although he might have a most unfortunate reputation as a man who could not maintain discipline, Latham handled her well. She was under topgallants and full topsails with windward studdingsails on the main and fore: it looked dangerous, but it was a trim that suited the *Surprise* and she was running her ten or even eleven knots without the least risk to her spars.

The combined speed of the squadron and of the frigate brought them together at a splendid pace, yet to those who so longed for post and for news of home and the war by land the formalities of her making her number, making the private signal, and heaving to the wind to salute the flag with seventeen guns seemed exceedingly tedious. The flagship returned the civility with a quick, barking thirteen and immediately afterwards threw out a signal requiring the *Surprise* to strike her topgallantmasts: it was said that the Admiral had rather lose a pint of blood than a spar, and certainly he hated to see any ship endanger masts, yards, cordage or canvas when these might be needed for the supreme effort at some unknown moment – tomorrow, perhaps.

The *Surprise*, looking stumpy with topmasts alone, ran under the Admiral's stern. Her captain was seen to go aboard him in a barge containing five sacks, presumably of mails: the dispatches would be the sailcloth packet he held in his hand. Now the time dragged more painfully still, even though there was the diversion of another sail seen on the blurred southern horizon, a puzzling sail, until the clearing weather showed it to be two, a sloop and a Spanish victualler. Those who possessed watches looked at them; others came aft on various pretexts to peer at the sand in the half-hour glass; the Marine in charge gave it a privy jerk to hasten the sand in its fall. Endless surmises, vain conjectures as to the cause of the delay: the general opinion was that Captain Latham was being told that he was the kind of officer who should never sail without a store-ship in company; that he knew as much of seamanship as the King's attorney-general; and that the Admiral would not trust him with a boat in a trout-stream. But just at the one moment when the signal-midshipman had taken his eye from the flagship's mizen-peak twenty voices all around him uttered a meaning cough, and turning he saw the hoist break out: '*Boyne*, a boat and a lieutenant to repair aboard the flag. *Defender*, a boat and a lieutenant to repair aboard the flag,' and so it ran, hoist after hoist, until at last the *Worcester*'s turn came round. Throughout the squadron the boats splashed down and pulled double-banked at racing speed for the Admiral, returning with infinitely welcome post and the scarcely less welcome newspapers from home.

Apart from the watch on deck, the Worcesters retired to what privacy they could find in a man-of-war, where those who could read learnt something of that other world they had left, and those who could not had it spelled out to them. Jack was far more favoured than the majority in this respect as in most others, and inviting Stephen to come and share a pot, he walked into his great after-cabin, where each could have a corner and an easy chair to himself. He had a fine comfortable packet of letters from Sophie: all was well at home, apart from the chicken-pox and Caroline's teeth, which had been obliged to be filed by a dentist in Winchester; a strange blight had struck the roses, but on the other hand his new plantation of oaks was shooting up amazingly. They had seen a good deal of Diana, who was often driven down by Captain Jagiello, to whom Mrs Williams, Sophie's mother, was absolutely devoted, declaring that he was the handsomest man she had ever beheld, and so beautifully rich; and their new neighbour, Admiral Saunders, was most kind and attentive – all their neighbours were kind and attentive. And

147

there were laboriously-written notes from the children themselves hoping that he was quite well; they were quite well: and each told him it was raining and that Caroline had had her teeth filed by a dentist in Winchester. But the whole packet was domestic, from the first letter to the last: not a single word, good or bad, from his lawyers. Having read his home-letters over again, smiling as he did so, he pondered over this silence: a favourable omen or not? He took a guinea from his pocket, tossed it, missed his catch and sent the coin flying across to the table where Stephen was dealing with his correspondence, some cheerful, ill-spelt scrawls from Diana, describing a very active social life in London and observing, in a casual aside, that she had been mistaken about her pregnancy; some miscellaneous communications, mostly of a scientific nature; a note from the Admiral enclosing a friendly, even an affectionate letter to 'my dear Maturin' from Sir Joseph Blaine, his chief in Intelligence, together with two reports and a coded despatch. He had digested the reports and he was reading one of the unscientific communications when the guinea landed on the coded dispatch. On the face of it the letter in his hand called for no deciphering: in plain terms and an obviously disguised hand an anonymous correspondent told him that he was a cuckold and that his wife was deceiving him with a Swedish attaché, Captain Jagiello. He nevertheless hoped to make out the writer's identity, to break the code, as it were; there were few English men or women who would have spelt his name with an h, although it was usual in France; and he had already picked out some other significant details. The letter, and the puzzle, amused him: the malignancy and its transparent covering of righteous indignation were perfect of their kind and but for his ingrained sense of secrecy he would have shown it to Jack. In the event he did no more than return the guinea with a private smile.

They exchanged the essence of their family news and then Stephen observed that he intended leaving for Spain in the morning: 'The Admiral tells me that as soon as the

148

victualler shall have discharged its cabbages, onions and tobacco, it will carry me to Barcelona.'

'Lord, Stephen,' cried Jack, his face falling, 'So soon? Damn me, I shall miss you.'

'We shall soon meet again, with the blessing,' said Stephen. 'I expect to be in Mahon before very long.'

In the momentary silence they both heard the sentry hail an approaching boat and the boat's reply *'Dryad'*, signifying that the *Dryad*'s captain was coming aboard.

'Damn him,' said Jack, and in answer to Stephen's questioning look, 'She is that slab-sided sloop that came in with the victualler while we were reading our letters, a horrible old little lumpish round-sterned Dutch tub, captured about the time of the Spanish Armada and madly over-gunned with her fourteen twelve-pounders. I do not know who has her now. However,' he said, standing up, 'I suppose I must do the civil: do not stir, Stephen, I beg.'

Within seconds he was back again, strong pleasure shining in his face, and before him he urged a small, compact, round-headed officer, as pleased as himself, a gentleman who had served under him as a first-class volunteer, midshipman and lieutenant and who was now, largely because of Jack, a commander, the captain of that lumpish ill-looking tub the *Dryad*.

'William Babbington, my dear,' cried Stephen, 'I am delighted to see you, joy. How do you do?'

The *Dryad*'s captain told them how he did with all the ease and freedom and detail of a long and intimate acquaintance, a friendship as close as the difference in their ages would allow – a difference that had grown less important with the passing of the years. Having drunk half a pint of madeira, having made all proper enquiries after Mrs Aubrey, the children, and Mrs Maturin, and having promised to dine aboard the *Worcester* tomorrow (weather permitting) in the company of his old shipmates Pullings and Mowett, he sprang to his feet at the sound of three bells. 'Since *Dryad* is to be attached to the squadron,' he said, 'I must wait on Admiral Harte. It would never do to put a foot wrong with him. I am deep enough in his bad books already.'

'Why, William, what have you been at?' asked Jack. 'You can hardly have vexed him in the Channel?'

'No, sir,' said Babbington. 'It was not really a service matter. Do you remember his daughter Fanny?'

Both Jack and Stephen had a vague recollection of a thickset, swarthy, hirsute, spotted girl: their hearts sank. From his earliest youth, from a shockingly precocious age, Babbington had pursued the fair; and that was well enough, perfectly in the naval tradition; but although an excellent seaman, he lacked discrimination by land and he reckoned almost anything clothed in a skirt as one of the fair. Sometimes he attacked ravishing creatures with success, though surrounded with rivals, for in spite of his stunted form women found his cheerfulness, his singular charm and his unfailing ardour agreeable; but sometimes he set about angular maidens of forty. During his brief stay in New Holland he had enjoyed the favours of a she-aboriginal and in Java those of a Chinese lady of fifteen stone. Miss Harte's swarthiness, acne and hair would be nothing to him. '. . . so finding us in this posture, do you see, he cut up most uncommon rough and forbade me the house. And rougher still when he found she took it somewhat to heart, and that we corresponded. Said, if I was looking for a fortune I might go and try my luck with French prizes, and that I might kiss his breech too – she was meat for my master. Surely, sir, that was a pretty illiberal expression?'

'Kissing his breech, do you mean, or meat for your master?'

'Oh, kiss my breech is in his mouth every day, perfectly usual: no, I meant meat for my master. In my opinion that was low.'

'Only a scrub would say it,' said Stephen. 'Meat – pah! Suff on him.'

'Precious low,' said Jack. 'Like an ostler.' And then,

considering, 'But how could you be taxed with fortune-hunting, William? You do not have to live on your pay and you have expectations; and surely the lady had never been looked on as an heiress?'

'Oh Lord yes she is, sir: a twenty-thousand-pounder at least. She told me so herself. Her father inherited from old Dilke, the money-man in Lombard Street, and now he aims very high: they are arranging a match with Mr Secretary Wray.'

'Mr Wray of the Admiralty?'

'That is the man, sir. If Sir John Barrow don't recover – and they all say he is at the last gasp, poor old gentleman – Wray will succeed as full-blown Secretary. Think of that by way of influence for a man in the Rear-Admiral's position! I believe he got them to order *Dryad* to the Mediterranean to get me out of the way. He can keep an eye on me here while they are haggling about the dowry: the marriage will come off the minute the writings are signed.'

# CHAPTER SIX

As far as creature comforts were concerned, Jack Aubrey
was far, far better off than anyone else in the *Worcester*.
He had privacy, he had space: as well as the great cabin in
which he took his ease or entertained or played his fiddle
and the stern-gallery in which he took the air when he
chose to take it alone rather than on the thickly-populated
quarterdeck, he had a dining-cabin and a sleeping-cabin,
the fore-cabin where he taught his youngsters and attended to his paper-work, and quarter-galleries as lavatory and
place of ease. He had his own steward and his own cook, a
great deal of room for his private livestock, provisions and
wine, and enough in the way of pay and allowances for a
provident single man to lay in an adequate supply.

It was ungrateful in him to be discontented, as he
admitted in the long rambling letter that he wrote day
by day to Sophie – a letter, or rather an instalment of
the letter, in which he described Stephen's departure.
Ungrateful and illogical: he had always known that the
Navy was given to extremes and most of the extremes
he had experienced himself, beginning with that truly
startling lack of space that had faced him early in his
career when an angry captain disrated him, so that from
one day to the next he was no longer a midshipman but
a foremast hand, a common sailor required to sling his
hammock on the *Resolution*'s lower deck at the regulation
fourteen inches from his neighbours'. Since the *Resolution* was a two-watch ship, with half her people on deck
when the other half were below, in practice these fourteen inches increased to twenty-eight; but even so Jack's
bulky neighbours touched him on either side as they all
rolled together on the swell, part of a carpet of humanity,
some hundreds strong, unventilated, unwashed apart from

hands and faces, given to snoring, grinding their teeth, calling out in their short troubled sleep, never more than four hours at a time and rarely so much. Disrating was a rough experience and it had seemed to last for ever, but it was of great value, teaching him more about the men and about their attitude towards officers, work, and one another than he could ever have learnt on the quarterdeck: teaching him a very great many things, among them the value of space.

Yet here he was with space to be measured by the rod, pole or perch rather than by the square inches of the midshipmen's berth or the square foot of his days as a lieutenant – space and even headroom too, a point of real importance to a man of his height and a rare privilege in ships designed for people of five foot six. He had space and to spare; and he did not appreciate it as he should have done. One of the troubles was that it was uninhabited space, since by another of the Navy's rules of extremes he now ate and lived quite alone, whereas on the lower deck he had dined in the company of five hundred hearty eaters and even in his various gunroom and wardroom messes with a dozen or so – never a meal alone until he reached command; but from that time on never a meal accompanied, except by express invitation.

He did of course invite his officers quite often, and although in the present anxious unsettled state of his affairs he dared not keep the lavish table of earlier, richer days, it was rare that Pullings and a midshipman did not breakfast with him, while the officer of the forenoon watch and a youngster or a Marine would often share his dinner: and the wardroom entertained him once a week. Breakfast and dinner, then, were reasonably companionable; but Jack dined at three, and since he was not a man who turned in early that left a great deal of time, far more than the concerns of a ship on blockade could fill, a ship with a thoroughly efficient first lieutenant, plying to and fro off Toulon, all decisions taken by the flag.

The familiar tedium of blockade made these spacious,

lonely evenings lonelier and more spacious by far, but in one form or another they were the lot common to all captains who respected tradition and who wished to maintain their authority. Some dealt with the situation by having their wives aboard, in spite of the regulations, particularly on the longer, quieter passages, and some took mistresses; but neither would do in a squadron commanded by Admiral Thornton. Others sailed with friends, and although Jack had known this answer fairly well, generally speaking it seemed that few friendships could stand such close, enforced proximity for many weeks, let alone months or even years. There were also men who took to drinking too much, while some grew strange, crotchety and absolute; and although the great majority became neither confirmed drunkards nor eccentrics, nearly all captains with more than a few years' service were deeply marked by it.

So far Jack had been unusually lucky in this respect. From his first command he had nearly always sailed with Stephen Maturin, and it had proved the happiest arrangement. As her surgeon, Dr Maturin was very much part of the ship, having his own independent function and being, one no more than nominally subject to the captain; but since he was not an executive officer their intimacy caused no jealousy or ill-feeling in the wardroom: and although he and Jack Aubrey were almost as unlike as men could be, unlike in nationality, religion, education, size, shape, profession, habit of mind, they were united in a deep love of music, and many and many an evening had they played together, violin answering 'cello or both singing together far into the night.

Now when the fiddle sang at all it sang alone: but since Stephen's departure he had rarely been in a mood for music and in any case the partita that he was now engaged upon, one of the manuscript works that he had bought in London, grew more and more strange the deeper he went into it. The opening movements were full of technical difficulties and he doubted he would ever be able to do them anything like justice, but it was the great chaconne which followed that really disturbed him. On the face of it the statements made in the beginning were clear enough: their closely-argued variations, though complex, could certainly be followed with full acceptation, and they were not particularly hard to play; yet at one point, after a curiously insistent repetition of the second theme, the rhythm changed and with it the whole logic of the discourse. There was something dangerous about what followed, something not unlike the edge of madness or at least of a nightmare; and although Jack recognized that the whole sonata and particularly the chaconne was a most impressive composition he felt that if he were to go on playing it with all his heart it might lead him to very strange regions indeed.

During a pause in his evening letter Jack thought of telling Sophie of a notion that had come to him, a figure that might make the nature of the chaconne more understandable: it was as though he were fox-hunting, mounted on a powerful, spirited horse, and as though on leaping a bank, perfectly in hand, the animal changed foot. And with the change of foot came a change in its being so that it was no longer a horse he was sitting on but a great rough beast, far more powerful, that was swarming along at great speed over an unknown countryside in pursuit of a quarry – what quarry he could not tell, but it was no longer the simple fox. But it would be a difficult notion to express, he decided; and in any case Sophie did not really care much for music, while she positively disliked horses. On the other hand she dearly loved a play, so he told her about the *Worcester*'s performance. 'Neither the oratorio nor *Hamlet* has come off yet, and I think that for beginners we aimed a little high, since both call for a world of preparation. I have no doubt we shall hear them in the end, but in the mean time we content ourselves with much less ambitious entertainments: we have them once a week, weather permitting, on the evenings of make-and-mend day – a surprisingly good band of ten performers, some

155

dancers good enough for Sadler's Wells, short dramatic pieces, and a kind of farce that carries on from one week to the next – very popular – in which two old forecastle hands show a fat, stupid landsman the duties of a sailor and the customs of the Navy, banging him with bladders every time he does wrong.' He smiled again, remembering the massive laughter of five hundred close-packed men as the fool, beaten on both sides, fell into the bucket for the seventh time: then, as he brought his paragraph to a close, his mind drifted back to his sonata. It was not music that he would have chosen to play when he was alone and low in his spirits: but he was not allowed to change or give up once he had fairly started on a piece, so when he played at all it was this partita that he worked upon, playing in a non-committal way and attending chiefly to the technical aspect of the thing. 'At least I shall be word-perfect when Stephen comes back,' he said. 'And I shall ask his opinion of it.'

Upon the whole Jack Aubrey was not much given to lowness of spirits, and circumstances far more adverse than these had not disturbed his cheerful mind; but now a slowly-maturing cold, the monotony of the blockade, the unvarying sight of the *Pompée* ahead and the *Boyne* astern on the starboard tack and the other way about on the larboard, a long and most unseasonable, un-Mediterranean spell of dismal weather, combined with his loneliness and isolation to bring him down. He let his mind run over his complicated affairs at home – a very useless exercise, since the legal issues were obscure to experts, let alone to sailors, whose law was contained in the thirty-six Articles of War – and over his position here. On taking command of the *Worcester* he had known that she was bound for the Mediterranean and that Harte was second in command to Admiral Thornton on that station: but the Admiral Thornton he and all his friends had always known had so very strong and dominant a personality that his second would count for very little, particularly when he was so small a man as Harte. Had Jack known how likely it was that Harte might inherit the supreme command he would have pressed hard for another ship.

These reflections were running through his mind as he leant on the stern-gallery rail a few days later, holding a handkerchief to his streaming nose, looking sometimes at the *Worcester*'s grey and turbid wake, sometimes at the *Pompée*'s bows, a cable's length astern, and sometimes at the *Dryad*, Babbington's slab-sided tub, stationed well out to the leeward to repeat signals up and down the line. A diminished line, since the Admiral had run down to Palermo for a few days and the inshore squadron had been reinforced, but even so it covered a mile of sea as the squadron stood eastwards through the gloom and the task of repeating was no sinecure, particularly as they were hauled close to the wind – a wretched angle for a signal-lieutenant – and as Harte was perpetually fiddling with his flags.

By this time Jack was perfectly well acquainted with the numbers of all the ships in the squadron, and although from his place in taut-drawn line he could see little beyond the *Pompée* and odd glimpses of the *Achilles* directly in her wake, he caught all Harte's loquacity echoed from the *Dryad* and he saw the *Culloden* required to make more sail, the *Boreas* told to keep her station, and a distant frigate, the *Clio*, repeatedly ordered to alter course. And as he watched, nursing his red nose in a red-spotted handkerchief, he saw a number that he did not recognize together with a hoist requiring the ship in question to take a position astern of the *Thetis*. Some newcomer had joined the fleet. For a moment he had a wild hope that she might have come out from home, bringing letters and news, but then he realized that in such a case Pullings would certainly have sent to tell him. Still, he felt a curiosity about the stranger and he turned to go on deck: at the same moment Killick came out of the cabin with a bucket full of handkerchiefs to dry on his private line. 'Now sir, what's all this?' he cried angrily. 'No greatcoat, no cloak, no bleeding comforter even?'

157

Ordinarily Captain Aubrey could quell his steward with a firm glance, but now Killick's moral superiority was so great that Jack only muttered something about 'putting his nose out for a moment, no more,' and walked into the cabin with its unnecessary hanging stove, heated cherry-red. 'Who is come into the fleet?' he asked.

'What the Doctor would say, was he here, I do not know,' said Killick. 'He would carry on something cruel about folk risking the pulmony: he would say you ought to be in your cot.'

'Give me a glass of hot lemon shrub, will you, Killick?' said Jack. 'Who is come into the fleet? Bear a hand.'

'I got to hang the wipes out first, ain't I?' said Killick. 'Only *Niobe* from off of Alex – spoke to the Admiral off of Sicily – sent on here.'

Jack was sipping his hot lemon shrub and reflecting upon moral superiority, its enormous strength in all human relationships but even more so between husband and wife – the contest for it in even quite loving couples – the acknowledgement of defeat in even the least candid – when he heard a boat hailed from the quarterdeck. The answer 'Aye aye' made it clear that an officer was coming aboard and it occurred to Jack that it might be Mr Pitt, the *Niobe*'s surgeon, a great friend of Stephen's perhaps coming over to see him, not knowing he was gone – a man he would be happy to see: but as he passed through the door to the quarterdeck he gathered from Pullings' expression that it was not Mr Pitt, nor anything agreeable at all.

'It is Davis again, sir,' said Pullings.

'That's right, sir,' cried a huge dark seaman in a hairy coat. 'Old Davis again. Faithful and true. Merry and bright. Always up to the mark.' He stepped forward in a blundering, lurching movement, thrusting the cheerful young lieutenant from the *Niobe* aside, clapping his clenched left hand to his forehead and holding out the other. It was not usual in the Navy for anyone much under flag-rank to initiate conversation with a captain on

158

his quarterdeck, still less to grasp his hand; but Captain Aubrey, a powerful swimmer, had had the misfortune to rescue Davis from the sea, perhaps from sharks, certainly from drowning, many years before. Davis had at no time expressed any particular gratitude, but the fact of the rescue had given him a kind of lien upon his rescuer. Having rescued him, Jack was obliged to provide for him: this seemed to be tacitly admitted by all hands and even Jack felt that there was some obscure justice in the claim. He regretted it, however: Davis was no seaman although he had spent his whole life afloat, a dull-witted, clumsy fellow, very strong and very dangerous when vexed or drunk, easily vexed and easily intoxicated; and he either volunteered for Jack's various ships or managed to get transferred to them, his other captains being happy to see the last of a troublesome, ignorant, untameable man. 'Well, Davis,' said Jack, taking the hand and bracing his own to resist the bone-crushing grasp, 'I am happy to see you.' Less he could not say, the relationship being what it was, but in the faint hope of evading the gift he was telling the *Niobe*'s lieutenant that the *Worcester* was so short of men that he could not possibly spare a single one in exchange, no, not even a one-legged boy, when the *Dryad* repeated the signal *Worcester : captain repair aboard flag*.

'My barge, if you please, Mr Pullings,' said Jack, and as he stayed to have a civil word with the *Niobe*'s officer and to ask after Mr Pitt, he saw Davis plunge in among the hands who were preparing to hoist the boat out and then thrust one of its crew aside by brute force, passionately asserting his right to be one of the captain's bargemen again. Jack left Bonden and Pullings to deal with this by themselves and stepped aft for a last draught of hot lemon. How they did so without a scene he did not know, but as he sat in the barge, wrapped in his boat-cloak, with a supply of warm dry handkerchiefs in his lap and a ludicrous woollen comforter round his neck, he noticed that Davis was rowing number three, pulling with his usual very powerful, jerky, inaccurate stroke and wearing a look of surly triumph on his ill-natured and even sinister face. Whether he was staring straight at his captain Jack could not decide, seeing that one of Davis's eyes had a wicked cast in it.

Captain Aubrey repaired aboard the flag with all possible dispatch, pulling for three-quarters of a mile through a cold and choppy sea against the wind; but the flag was not ready to receive him. The Flag-Captain was a hospitable soul, however, and at once took him, together with the Captain of the Fleet, into his cabin, where he called for drinks. 'Though now I come to think of it, Aubrey,' he said, examining Jack's face, his red, bottle-shaped nose, with narrowed eyes, 'you seem to have a cold coming on. You want to take care of these things, you know. Baker,' he called to his steward, 'mix a couple of glasses of my fearnought draught, and bring 'em hot and hot.'

'I saw you swimming the other day,' said the Captain of the Fleet. 'Swimming in the sea. And I said to myself, This is madness, stark, staring madness; the fellow will catch cold directly and then go wandering about the squadron like a mad lunatic, spreading infection far and wide, like a plague-cart. Swimming, for God's sake! In a sheltered cove, under proper supervision, on a warm calm day with the sun veiled and on an empty stomach but not too empty neither, I have nothing against it; but in the open sea, why, it is just asking for a cold. The only cure is a raw onion.'

The first glass of the fearnought draught came in. 'Drink it while it is hot,' said the Flag-Captain.

'Oh, oh,' cried Jack the moment it had gone down. 'God help us.'

'I learnt it in Finland,' said the Flag-Captain. 'Quick, the second glass, or the first is mortal.'

'It is all great nonsense,' said the Captain of the Fleet. 'Nothing could be worse for you than boiling alcohol, pepper, and Spanish fly. An invalid should never touch alcohol: nor Spanish fly, neither. What you want is a raw onion.'

'Captain Aubrey, sir, if you please,' said a deferential young man.

Admiral Harte was sitting with his secretary and a clerk. In an impressive tone he said, 'Captain Aubrey, there is a service of great importance to be performed, and it is therefore to be confided to a reliable, discreet officer.' Jack sneezed. 'If you have a cold, Aubrey,' said Harte in a more natural voice, 'I will thank you to sit farther off. Mr Paul, open the scuttle. A service of great importance . . . you will take the *Dryad* under your orders and proceed to Palermo, where you will find the armed transport *Polyphemus* with presents for the Pasha of Barka and a new envoy aboard, Mr Consul Hamilton. You will carry this gentleman and the presents to Barka with the utmost dispatch. As you are no doubt aware, the benevolent neutrality of the rulers of the Barbary States is of the first importance to us, and nothing whatsoever must be done to offend the Pasha: on the other hand, you are not to yield to any improper demands nor sink the dignity of this country in the least degree, and you are to insist upon satisfaction in the matter of the Christian slaves. You will also carry these dispatches for our consul at Medina. They will be put aboard the *Dryad* when you are a day's sail from Medina: Captain Babbington will stand in, deliver them to the consul, and rejoin you and the transport on your passage east. It is clear, is it not, that *Dryad* is to part company a full day's sail from Medina?'

'I believe so, sir, but in any case I shall read my orders over and over again, until I have them by rote.' Like many other captains, Jack knew that in dealing with Admiral Harte it was as well to have everything in writing, and since this was one of the few points on which a captain was entitled to run counter to a flag-officer's wishes he carried the day, though not without wrangling. Harte was badly placed, since he had an audience perfectly well acquainted with the rules of the service, and after some remarks about unnecessary delay and waste of a fair breeze, urgent service and foolish punctilio, the clerk was told to draw up

161

a summary of Captain Aubrey's orders as quickly as he could. While it was being written out Harte said, 'Was you to be bled, it would help your cold. Even twelve or fourteen ounces would do a great deal, and more would really set you up: cure you for good and all.' The notion pleased him. 'Cure you for good and all,' he repeated in a low, inward voice.

The *Worcester* and the *Dryad* had hardly sunk the squadron's topsails below the western horizon before the sun came out and the breeze increased so that the sparkling blue was flecked with white horses.

'Buttons, the French call them,' observed Captain Aubrey in his thick, cold-ridden voice.

'Do they indeed, sir?' said Captain Babbington. 'I never knew that. What a very curious notion.'

'Well, you could say that they are as much like sheep as they are horses,' said Jack, blowing his nose. 'But sheep ain't poetical, whereas horses are.'

'Are they really, sir? I was not aware.'

'Of course they are, William. Nothing more poetical, except maybe doves. Pegasus, and so on. Think of the fellow in that play that calls out "My kingdom for a horse" – it would not have been poetry at all, had he said sheep. Now here are the orders: read them while I finish my letter, and commit the piece that concerns you to heart. Or copy it out, if you prefer.'

'Well, sir,' said Babbington as Jack laid down his pen, 'my part seems plain sailing: I part company a day's sail from Medina, run in, deliver the dispatches to the consul there, and rejoin. Indeed, the whole trip seems pretty straightforward: Palermo, Medina, Barka and back.'

'Yes,' said Jack. 'So it seems to me; and at the time I wondered at the Rear-Admiral saying it was an important service, calling for a discreet officer that could be relied upon – at his saying it with such a knowing look.'

There was a short silence. Jack and Babbington

had much the same opinion of Admiral Harte, and each knew the other's mind; but neither acknowledged this by so much as a glance. 'As pretty a run as you could wish,' said Babbington. 'We are sure to be able to pick up some pickled tunny at Barka, let alone other stores, and then there is always the possibility of a prize – a fat merchantman from the Levant, creeping between Pantellaria and the main at dawn, and we bringing up the breeze!'

'I have almost forgotten what a prize is like,' said Jack; but then the fine piratical gleam died out of his eyes and he said, 'But those days are pretty well over, I am afraid, except maybe in the Adriatic or farther east. At this end what few ships there are that are fair prize crowd sail for the African coast the moment they see one of our cruisers, and once in with the land they are safe. These Beys and Pashas are so' hellfire touchy about their neutrality and their goodwill is so important to us at this stage that the Admiral would break any man that cut out a prize on their shores, even if it were bursting with silk and pearls, gold, myrrh, and frankincense. I know that Harvey, in the *Antiope*, chased a very rich ship into a cove to the westward of Algiers, a cove with a paltry little tower in it, and left her there, for fear of upsetting the Dey. The Rear-Admiral spoke about that this morning, and I see the clerk put something in the orders: poor fellow, he was so badgered on all sides he wrote down the essence of everything that was said. At the bottom of page two.'

' "Scrupulous respect will be paid to the laws of neutrality." '

'Wittles in ten minutes,' said Killick, coming crablike in against the ship's strong leeward heel, carrying a tray of drinks. 'Which the gents are coming aft this moment. Give the door a shove with your knee,' he called out in his polished way. A muffled thump, the door flew open, Pullings and Mowett walked in, very fine in their roastbeef coats, and pleasant it was to see their frank, open delight

163

at finding their old shipmate Babbington. They had all three been midshipmen in Jack's first command; they had sailed together in some of his later ships; and although Babbington, the youngest, was already a commander and likely to be made a post-captain in a year or two, while the others were only lieutenants and likely to remain in that rank for the rest of their lives unless they had the luck to take part in a successful action, there was not the least sign of jealousy, nor of any repining at a system that, with merit roughly equal, would probably make Babbington a comfortably-housed admiral by the end of his career while they lived on a half-pay of a hundred and nine pounds ten shillings a year. The only word that showed any awareness at all came late in the cheerful meal, when Jack, having observed that if this breeze held and that if the transport did not keep them hanging about at Palermo they should make an amazingly brisk passage, asked, 'Who has the *Polyphemus* now?'

No one knew. A Transport Agent or even a Transport Commander was a desperately obscure person, outside all hope of promotion, almost outside the service. 'Some broken-winded old lieutenant, I dare say,' said Pullings, and then with a wry grin he added, 'Not but what I may be precious glad to hoist a plain blue pennant and command a transport myself, one of these days.'

The transport did not keep them hanging about. They found her standing off and on well north of Cape Gallo, obviously waiting for them and keeping as sharp a lookout as any man-of-war. They exchanged numbers, and Jack, standing on under easy sail, signalled the *Polyphemus* to join him. The transport dropped her topgallants and flashed out jib and staysails in a most seamanlike manner; but since she had to beat up, tack upon tack, to fetch the *Worcester*'s wake, he had plenty of time to observe her.

This he did, quite casually at first, as he sat drinking hot lime-juice in the great cabin. His telescope lay on the locker beside him, and quite early he had recognized the transport's commander, an elderly lieutenant by the name of Patterson who had lost an arm in an unsuccessful cutting-out expedition at the beginning of the war. He was now sailing the *Polyphemus*, a weatherly flush-decked ship, with great skill, keeping her as close to the wind as ever she would lie in the last long leg that would cut the *Worcester*'s course; but it was not Patterson's steel winking in the sun nor his exact judgement of the increasing breeze that made Jack stare more and more but rather something exceedingly odd that was going on amidships. It was as though the transport's people were trundling a gun up and down: but a grey gun, and a gun far larger than any first-rate would carry even on her lower tier. He could not make it out from the cabin, nor from the stern-gallery, nor from the poop. On the quarterdeck he said to the signal midshipman, 'Desire the transport to pass within hail, Mr Seymour,' and to the officer of the watch, 'We will lie to for a moment, Mr Collins, if you please.'

The *Polyphemus* crossed the *Worcester*'s wake, shot up under her lee, backed her foretopsail and lay there, rising and falling on the lively sea, her commander standing with his hook fast round the aftermost mainshroud, looking attentively up at the ship of the line. He was a lean, elderly man in a worn, old-fashioned uniform and his bright yellow scratch-wig contrasted oddly with his severe, humourless, sun-tanned face; but once again it was not Mr Patterson who fixed Jack's gaze, and the gaze of every Worcester who could decently look over the side. It was the rhinoceros that stood abaft the foremast, motionless amidst its motionless attendants, the two ships being frozen into respectful silence while their captains conversed over the water like a couple of well-conducted bulls.

For propriety's sake Jack first asked for news of the Admiral – sailed on Thursday evening, *Melampus* in company – for Mr Consul Hamilton – was aboard and would wait on Captain Aubrey as soon as he could stand: was somewhat incommoded by the motion at present – and

165

then he said, 'Mr Patterson, what is that creature abaft the foremast?'

'It is a rhinoceros, sir: a rhinoceros of the grey species, a present for the Pasha of Barka.'

'What is it doing?'

'It is exercising, sir. It must be exercised two hours a day, to prevent its growing vicious.'

'Then let it carry on, Mr Patterson: do not stand on ceremony, I beg.'

'No, sir,' said Patterson, and to the seaman in charge of the party, 'Carry on, Clements.'

As though some spring had been released the rhinoceros and its crew started into movement. The animal took three or four twinkling little steps and lunged at Clements' vitals: Clements seized the horn and rose with it, calling out, 'Easy, easy there, old cock,' and at the same moment the rest of the party clapped on to the fall of a travelling burton, hoisting the rhinoceros clear of the deck. It hung by a broad belt round its middle, and for a while its legs ran nimbly on: Clements reasoned into its ear in a voice suitable to its enormous bulk and thumped its hide in a kindly manner, and when it was lowered again he led it forward to the foot of the foremast, holding it by the same ear and advising it 'to step lively, watch for the roll, and mind where it was coming to, not to crush people with its great fat arse.' Here it was hoisted up, swung round, lowered, and led aft, walking quite meekly now with only an occasional skip and thrust of its horn or wanton flirt of its rump: hoisted again, turned and led forward: to and fro under the fascinated eyes of the Worcesters until at last it was brought to the main hatchway. Here it looked expectant, with its ears brought to bear, its dim eyes searching, its prehensile upper lip pointing from side to side. Clements gave it a ship's biscuit, which it took delicately and ate with every appearance of appetite. But then the hatches were removed and the creature's aspect changed: Clements blindfolded it with his black neckerchief, and by way of explanation Mr Patterson called out

166

'It is timid. It fears the darkness, or perhaps the depth.'

'Handsomely, now,' said Clements. He and the rhinoceros rose a foot, travelled over the hatchway and vanished downwards, the seaman with one hand on the rope, the other over the animal's withers, the rhinoceros with its four legs held out, stiff, its ears drooping, the image of grey anxiety.

'Lord, how I wish the Doctor were here,' said Jack to Pullings, and in a louder voice, 'Mr Patterson, I congratulate you on your management of the rhinoceros. Will you dine with me tomorrow, weather permitting?'

Mr Patterson said that *if* the weather permitted, he should be happy to wait on Captain Aubrey; but he said so in a doubtful bellow, with a shake of his head to windward, where there was every appearance of wind brewing up. And in the event Jack dined alone, the three ships running east-south-east under courses and reefed topsails over a sea too rough for boats to be launched with any comfort: he was just as glad, for although the breeze was fair, and although there was a general feeling of holiday, they being away from the squadron, his cold had so increased upon him that he was scarcely fit for company. Again he said to Pullings at breakfast 'I wish the Doctor were here.' He felt that it would be disloyal to Stephen to summon Mr Lewis, and before dinner he tried some of the remedies that had been suggested: they, or the wine he drank, may have done some good, for as they approached the Pantellaria channel and he spread his forces in the faint hope of a prize, he found his spirits rise to a fine point of cheerfulness. The hope was faint indeed, yet it had a reasonable existence: there were still some ships that would risk the eastern run for the sake of the enormous profits, and although these were fast, knowing craft upon the whole, often in the privateering or the smuggling line, this was one of the few sea-lanes in which they were less rare than elsewhere; and in this stretch of sea with this south-west wind a blockade-runner, beating up for home, would be at a great disadvantage.

He was so hoarse that Pullings was obliged to relay his orders, but it was with real satisfaction that he saw the *Dryad* steer south and the *Polyphemus* north until they were spread out so that in line abreast the three of them could survey the great part of the channel – a sparkling day, warm in spite of the wind, a truly Mediterranean day at last with splendid visibility, white clouds racing across a perfect sky, their shadows showing purple on a sea royal-blue where it was not white: an absurd day to have a cold on.

'Should you not go below for a while, sir?' said Pullings to him privately. 'It is perhaps a little damp.'

'Nonsense,' said Jack. 'If everybody started taking notice of a cold, good Heavens, where would one be? The war might come to an end. In any case we can only sweep for a little while: we lose *Dryad* once we are a day's sail from Medina, say at the height of Cape Carmo.'

All day long they sailed, searching the sea from their mastheads, and nothing did they find, apart from a group of tunny-boats out of Lampedusa, who sold them some fish and told them that a French Smyrna-man, the *Aurore*, had passed the day before, deeply-laden and somewhat crippled, having been mauled by a Greek pirate from Tenedos. They took it philosophically, as sailors must if they are not to run mad, being so subject to wind and tide and current; and with the sun going down astern while the full moon rose ahead, the *Worcester* sent the *Dryad* away for Medina, called the *Polyphemus* in and stood eastward with her, the breeze abating with the close of day. An easy sail and a flowing sheet: and while Jack consoled himself with Gluck and toasted cheese the hands gathered on the forecastle and danced in the warm moonlight until the setting of the watch, and, by Pullings' leave, beyond it. They were heartier still, since Jack had his skylight open and the wind had hauled forward; but it was a cheerful sound, one that he loved to hear, as signifying a happy ship. The confused distant noise, the familiar tunes, the laughter, the clap of hands and the rhythmic thump of feet was full of memories for him too, and as he wandered up and down his spacious, lonely domain, cocking his ear to the sound of *Ho the dandy kiddy-o*, he cut a few heavy, lumbering steps, in spite of his cold.

When he lay in his cot, swinging to the *Worcester*'s lift and roll, his mind drifted back to the days when he too had belonged on the forecastle, when he too had danced to the fiddle and fife, his upper half grave and still, his lower flying – heel and toe, the double harman, the cut-and-come-again, the Kentish knock, the Bob's a-dying and its variations in quick succession and (if the weather was reasonably calm) in perfect time. To be sure there was a golden haze over those times and some of the gold was no doubt false, mere pinchbeck at the best; but even so they had an irreplaceable quality of their own – perfect, unthinking health, good company upon the whole, no responsibility apart from the immediate task in hand – and he was thinking of the rare, noisy, strenuous, good-natured fun they had had when hands were piped to mischief as he fell asleep, smiling still. His sleeping mind often strayed far away, sometimes home to his wife and garden, sometimes to beds less sanctified, but now it scarcely stirred from the ship and he woke with the word Thursday in his ears, as clearly as if it had been shouted.

Of course it was Thursday: hammocks had been piped up early, well before sunrise, at the end of the middle watch, and his unconscious being had no doubt recorded the fact. Long, long ago he too would have been required to rise and shine, to show a leg and rouse out there in the dark, cold or no cold: now he could take his ease.

On Thursdays the *Worcester* presented her less glorious, less martial, more domestic face. Unless the weather was extraordinarily foul or unless the ship was in action, she washed her clothes that morning in enormous tubs and rigged clothes-lines fore and aft, while in the afternoon all hands were piped to make and mend. It was also the day when Jack was invited to dine in the wardroom,

169

and as he went there at the appointed hour by way of the quarterdeck and the companion-ladder he surveyed as fine a show of washing as the heart could desire: a thousand shirts and more, five hundred pair of duck trousers, countless handkerchiefs and smalls all waving and fluttering in the breeze. It was true that they were all washed in sea-water, the *Worcester* being short of fresh, that since the soap would not lather they were not very clean, and that they were harsh and salty to the touch, but they made a brave, many-coloured show, a cheering sight.

In the wardroom itself his presence had less of a damping effect than usual: there were few officers who had not either a cure for a cold or an account of a very shocking long-lasting bout, caught on some particular and clearly-defined occasion such as the leaving off of a waistcoat, the wearing of a Magellan jacket on watch one night and not on the next, standing talking to a woman with one's hat off, rain falling on one's hair, sitting in a draught, an untimely sweat; and these topics carried the meal on to the more informal stage of general conversation. Jack said little: he could not, being almost voiceless, but he looked and indeed felt amiable, and being adjured on all hands 'to feed a cold, sir, and starve a fever,' he ate a great deal of the fresh tunny that graced half the table's length, so welcome a change from salt pork. At the same time he listened to the talk at his end of the table: rhinoceroses, how best stowed, their probable weight, their diet – the one-horned kind and the two, where found – anecdote of a Sumatra rhinoceros belonging to HMS *Ariel*, its appetite for grog and unhappy end – the properties of powdered rhinoceros-horn, taken inwardly – regret at Dr Maturin's absence – a health to the absent Doctor – Barka, and the possibility of renewing their livestock, at least in sheep and poultry – the likelihood of the Pasha's coming it the handsome in the article of bullocks, in view of the rhinoceros and a cargo of no doubt equally valuable presents. At the far end however Mowett and Rowan, the man who had replaced the lubberly Somers, seemed to be in disagreement, strong and even acrimonious disagreement. Rowan was a round-faced, bright-eyed young fellow with a rather decided air: Jack had seen enough of him to know that although he was a man of little formal education – a West-Country shipwright's son – he was a competent officer and a great improvement on Somers; but apart from that he had gathered little and now, during a momentary pause in the talk on either side of him, he was surprised to hear Rowan say 'I may not know what a dactyl is, but I do know that *Will you take A piece of cake* is poetry, whatever you may say. It rhymes, don't it? And if what rhymes ain't poetry, what is?'

Jack quite agreed; and he was morally certain that Mowett did not know what a dactyl was either, though he loved him dearly.

'I'll tell you what poetry is,' cried Mowett. 'Poetry is . . .'

The midshipman of the watch came darting in. 'Beg·pardon, sir,' he said at Jack's elbow. 'Mr Whiting's duty and *Dryad* is in sight from the masthead, sir, two points on the starboard bow. At least, we think it is *Dryad*,' he added, quite ruining the effect.

It would be strange if there could have been a mistake about the *Dryad*, with her man-of-war's pennant and her distinctive rig; but it would also be strange, the breeze being what it was, if the *Dryad* could possibly have reached such a position without carrying an extraordinary press of sail.

'What is she wearing?'

'Skyscrapers, sir.'

That was decisive. No man-of-war would be flying out from the land, cracking on to that perilous degree, unless she were the *Dryad*. 'Very well, Mr Seymour,' he said. 'My compliments to Mr Whiting, and he may make sail to close the *Dryad*, if *Dryad* she be. I shall come on deck after dinner.' And in an aside to Pullings he added 'It would be a pity to waste a crumb of this glorious treacle-crowdy.'

*Dryad* she was, coming along as fast as ever her ungainly form would allow her: with a fine breeze on the beam and every sail that she could possibly bear she made very nearly nine knots, trembling as she did so and from the utmost limit of signalling distance flying a request to speak to the *Worcester*. For her part the *Worcester*, on the opposite tack, ran ten knots clean off the reel once she had stowed her remaining laundry away, and the two therefore approached one another over that empty brilliant sea so fast that they were within hailing distance before the inhabitants of the wardroom had been on deck, digesting their dinner, for more than half an hour. This was the first time, apart from practice, that the *Worcester* had spread her royals and loftier staysails since she came into the Mediterranean – the first time that her present complement had ever done so in more than a capful of wind – and although the fine urgent leeward lean of the ship, the strong rush of water along her side, and the white bow-wave spreading wide lifted Jack's heart, he looked very thoughtful indeed as he watched some of the orders being carried out. Many of the midshipmen and some of the upper-yardsmen did not understand their duty, and the setting of the mizen topgallant staysail would have cost one youngster a terrible fall if not his life but for the captain of the top, who caught him by the hair. And then when the ship was to fold her wings, as it were, her multiplicity of wings, to lie to for Babbington to come aboard he saw some very odd sights, such as two leading members of the Halleluia chorus heaving upon a rope with immense zeal and good will in the wrong direction until a distracted bosun's mate beat them off – better judges of Handel than the finer points of seamanship. There were not enough real seamen aboard, that was the trouble: these inland fellows, if properly shoved into place, could go through the ordinary motions well enough by now, or at least without disgrace, but in anything like an emergency many of them would be all to seek, quite lost without direction. The ship brought by the lee at night, for example, or laid on her beam-ends in a squall, or closely engaged with a determined enemy, spars, blocks and even masts falling about their ears. A crew of able seamen or even of ordinary seamen was not formed in a few months; and the only way of growing used to storm and battle was to work through both. He wondered how some of his people would behave on their first introduction to either, for he did not count what few blows they had had so far or the trifle of gunfire as emergencies, still less as storm or battle. These thoughts were prompted in part by the excellent seamanship displayed by the *Dryad*, and they were now dispelled by the sight of her captain coming aboard the *Worcester* as though there were not a moment to be lost. And to judge by his shining face as he came up the side it was good news that he was bringing.

'The French are in Medina, sir,' he said, the moment they were in the cabin.

'Are they, by God?' cried Jack, stopping short.

'Yes, sir. A seventy-four and a thirty-six-gun frigate.' He had come upon them suddenly as he turned the dog-leg into the Goletta, the long channel leading up to the port of Medina. There they lay, moored under the larger of the two batteries guarding the entrance to the Goletta, and if he had not instantly hauled his wind the *Dryad* must have been carried past them, into the channel, her escape cut off.

'Did they fire?' asked Jack.

'No, sir. I fancy they were as taken aback as I was, and I did not leave them much time to recover their surprise. I clawed off as quick as ever I could: *Dryad* came about beautifully, though we had only one reef out of our topsails; we weathered the cape with ten yards to spare and then cracked on regardless to join you, so that we could go back and destroy them together.' Babbington seemed to entertain no sort of doubt about the destruction of the French ships: none about the propriety of his conduct. Presumably his dispatches would be delivered to the consul in Medina once the destruction had taken place.

'Lord, sir,' he said, 'how I hope they are still there!'

'Well, William,' said Jack, 'we shall soon find out.'

For his own part he hoped they had put to sea. Quite apart from the whole thorny question of neutrality, an action against moored ships was not unlike a soldiers' battle: the unpredictable sea-changes were not there. Superior seamanship could not seize upon a shifting slant of wind, the tail of a current or a shoal and turn it into a decisive advantage, but would have to fight a motionless opponent, one unaffected by the breeze or lack of it, with all his hands free to fire the great guns or repel boarders. At sea there was room for manoeuvre, room for luck: and he was a great believer in luck. If the Frenchmen had put to sea, as he hoped, their course would almost certainly be for the Straits; yet with this breeze they could not yet have worked to the windward of Cape Hamada, and there was every likelihood that by steering west-south-west he would find them under his lee in the morning. He would have the weather-gage and with it the initiative, the power of choosing the moment and the closeness of action; all sorts of possibilities would be open to him; and to make the odds more nearly even he would need every happy turn that offered. For although the *Worcester* could probably deal with an average French seventy-four by a short battering and then by boarding her, the *Dryad* and the *Polyphemus* could not possibly undertake a well-handled frigate except by clever manoeuvring, so that at least one raked her while the *Worcester* brought her other broadside to bear. It could be done: the engagement, though unequal, could be brought to a successful end, given luck and less skilful opponents. Luck had nearly always been with him in battle, or at least rarely against him; but there was no guarantee that these Frenchmen would be less skilful or that they would let themselves be outmanoeuvred and destroyed piecemeal. There were inept French sailors, to be sure, but not nearly so many as people in London seemed to believe and as far as he was concerned the French sea-officers he had come into

174

contact with had usually been thoroughly able, wily, and courageous. As the three ships ran west-south-west under all the sail the slowest could bear, he sat snorting and gasping over his charts, drinking lemon-shrub hot and reflecting upon some of the French commanders he had known: the formidable Linois, who had taken him in the Mediterranean and who had very nearly sunk him in the Indian Ocean; Lucas, who had fought the *Redoubtable* so brilliantly at Trafalgar; Christy-Pallière . . . many others. On the other hand these ships had almost certainly escaped from Toulon in one of the recent blows, and although their officers might be capable enough it was unlikely that their crews would have much experience: yet were his own people much better? If he did meet the French at sea, and if things went as he hoped they would, with the *Worcester* between the seventy-four and the frigate, he would obviously have to fire both broadsides at the same time – that would be the whole point of the manoeuvre. But so far the Worcesters had had almost no training at all in that unusual operation.

'That can be remedied however, at least to some small extent,' he said aloud in a hoarse croak; and for the rest of the day laundry, ironing, making and mending were all laid aside, while the people went through the motions of fighting both sides of the ship at once, the gun-crews running from starboard to larboard as fast as ever they could, sweating in the afternoon sun, heaving guns in and out, in tearing high spirits from beginning to end.

Labour lost, however, for the *Polyphemus* spoke to an Algerine galley, an old and trustworthy acquaintance, and learnt that the Frenchmen had not sailed from Medina, had no intention of sailing, but had warped closer to the Goletta mole.

Mr Patterson brought this information himself, and Jack observed that his eyes were as bright as his steel hook, his whole ungainly person filled with fresh youth: there was the same elation on the *Worcester*'s quarterdeck, through-out the ship indeed, and Jack wondered at his own lack of joy. This was the first time that the prospect of action had not moved him like the sound of a trumpet: it was not that he dreaded the outcome, although this engagement was of that uncomfortable sort called a point-of-honour fight – an action where one's force was just too great to allow a decent, unblameable retreat yet not great enough to give much reasonable hope of success – but rather that he did not look forward to it with his usual eagerness. His heart did beat higher, but not very much higher, his mind being too much oppressed by material worries to do with the ship, with the conduct of a battle of this kind, and with the probable attitude of the Bey of Medina to be able to take much active pleasure in the prospect. 'It will be all right once the dust starts to fly,' he said to himself, and he gave the order that would carry the three ships to Medina as fast as the stiff breeze would carry them.

Dawn showed Cape Malbek fine on the starboard bow, and by the time the decks were washed and flogged dry the ships had opened the deep bay with Medina far away at the bottom of it. The wind slackened with the rising sun, but it was still as fair as could be wished and they stood in towards the distant town, keeping close to the western shore, gliding by the long line of salt lagoons so close that they could see the files of camels with their shining loads. At one point an undulating cloud of flamingoes wafted over the sea, showing scarlet as they all wheeled together, ten or twenty thousand strong. 'How I wish the Doctor were here,' said Jack once more, but Pullings only returned a formal 'Yes, sir,' and Jack was strongly aware of the many eyes turned upon him from the crowded quarterdeck and, somewhat more furtively, from the poop, the gangways, the maintop, and points forward. The last patches of deck were clean and dry, the last falls had been coiled down; there was no immediate task in hand and the ship was extraordinarily silent – hardly a sound but the even song of the breeze in the rigging and the hiss of the smooth water running down the *Worcester*'s side. He knew that the hands were longing to clear her for action;

the moral pressure was as perceptible as the warmth of the sun, and after a moment's listening to a sudden outburst of goose-like gabbling from the flamingoes he said 'Mr Pullings, let the hands be piped to breakfast: when they have finished, we may go to quarters. And we should be well advised to take advantage of the galley fires ourselves, before they are . . .' He would have added 'put out' if a fit of sneezing had not prevented him, but the missing words were clearly understood and in any case the bosun's mates had already started their calls.

Usually Jack asked Pullings and a midshipman or two to breakfast with him, but today, after a sleepless night, most of it on deck, he really felt too jaded for even Pullings' conversation and he retired alone, blowing his reddened nose as he went and murmuring 'Oh dear, oh dear. God damn and blast it,' into his handkerchief.

It was his rule always to eat hearty before an action or the probability of an action and Killick set a dish of bacon on the table, with four fried eggs, saying apologetically that 'that was all there was so far this morning, but the speckled hen might lay any minute now.' He ate them mechanically, but neither they nor even his coffee had their natural savour and when Killick came triumphantly in with the fifth egg he could not look at it with any pleasure. He tossed it privately out of the quarter-gallery scuttle, and as he followed its flight he saw the sea turn brown, then clear again. In their eagerness to be clearing the ship and casting loose their guns, the hands had started their tubs of cocoa over the side.

'Chips,' said Killick, jerking his thumb over his shoulder, and a moment later the carpenter came in, followed by some of his crew and the captain's joiner. Rather more civilly than the steward, he asked if he might begin. 'Just let me down this cup, Mr Watson,' said Jack, drinking the last of his ill-tasting coffee, 'and the place is yours. You will take particular care of the Doctor's – the Doctor's object, will you not?' he added, pointing at Stephen's dressing-case, now doing duty as a music-stand.

'Never you fret, sir,' said the carpenter, pointing at the joiner in much the same manner. 'Pond here has made a special case for it, lined with junk.'

'It is not an article that should ever have gone to sea,' said the aged joiner in a discontented voice. 'Still less into action.'

As Jack left the cabin he heard them attack the bulkheads, knocking out the wedges with a splendid zeal and rolling up the chequered canvas deck-cloth: before he had taken half a dozen turns on the quarterdeck Stephen's object and all the cabin furniture, crockery and glass had been struck down into the hold, the bulkheads had vanished and with them his various apartments, so that there was a clean sweep fore and aft and the impatient gun-crews could get at their charges, the pair of thirty-two-pounder carronades that Jack had installed in the coach.

They were too early, far too early: there were still miles of salt lake to pass. The harbour at the far end of the bay was still dim and misty in the shadow of the hills behind the town, and Jack had not the least notion of sailing into the enclosed water without surveying the whole of it: he ordered the courses to be hauled up in the brails, and now the *Worcester* and her consorts moved more slowly, under the usual fighting trim of topsails alone.

There were a fair number of country craft moving in and out in the morning light, tunny-boats and coral-fishers: and two corsair-xebecs with immense black lateen sails passed the *Worcester* on the opposite tack, low to the water, moving very fast. They were crammed with men and as they swept by scores of faces looked up, brown, shining black, sunburnt white, some bearded, some smooth, most turbanned or skull-capped, all keen and predatory. Jack glanced at them with strong dislike and looked away. 'Let us make a tour of the ship,' he said to Pullings.

As he had expected with such a first lieutenant, everything was in order – hatches laid, the decks so carefully dried not long ago now wetted and sanded, scuttle-butts

178

of fresh water amidships for the men to drink, shot-garlands full, arms-chests open: the guns were not run out yet, since the ship had not beat to quarters, but the slow-match for firing them was smouldering away in its little tubs, sending its fierce, well-remembered scent along the decks, and the boarders already had their cutlasses or those axes with a spike that some preferred in a hand-to-hand engagement. There were hands, both seamen and landsmen, who looked anxious, and some were over-excited, but most were gravely cheerful, quiet, and self-contained. It was a time of unusual freedom and those who had sailed into action with Jack before talked to him as he went round. 'Remember *Surprise*, your honour, and the dinner they give us in Calcutta?' 'The breeze lay just so when we took the big Spaniard.' And Joseph Plaice said something so witty about the *Sophie* that his own mirth made the end incomprehensible. Not that Jack had thoroughly understood even the beginning, since the cold had interfered with his hearing: it did not affect his sight, however, and when, having finished his tour, he climbed into the maintop with a telescope he saw Medina plain. The sun shone on the Golden Mosque, its dome and minaret, and on the inner harbour, too shallow for vessels of any draught, but the foretopsail cut off his view of the Goletta. 'Larboard a point,' he called, and as the ship turned so the long canal came into sight, with some merchantmen unloading at its wharfs and a good many smallcraft. At its seaward end two towers, one either side of the entrance, marking the end of the two long moles or breakwaters that closed the bottom of the bay, two curving lines of masonry on the colossal Phoenician and Roman scale that linked reefs and steep-to islands for a mile on either hand. And now as the *Worcester* steadied he saw the Frenchmen perfectly, a ship of the line and a frigate: they had moved since the *Dryad*'s visit and now they were moored a cable's length from the farther tower where the mole curved inward between two small islands, moored so close in that there was no passing between them

179

and the stonework. The French commander was obviously determined that there should be no repetition of the Nile: he had made sure that no enemy could double upon him, taking him between two fires, and he had also taken up such a position in his little bay that it would be impossible to lie athwart his hawse and rake him, since his bows were protected by the solid masonry. The frigate also lay snugly in this recess, and in her case the outward curve shielded her stern. Both ships were moored with their starboard broadsides to the sea, and between them there was a gap of some forty yards. The French boats were very busy in this gap, and for a while Jack could not make out what they were at. He leant on the barricade of tight-packed hammocks and focused more exactly: landing guns on the mole, that was what they were at, the dogs. Guns from their larboard broadsides to make a battery commanding the interval between the ships. Guns: and casks, spars and hammocks to protect them. Even if they shifted only the lighter, more get-at-able guns they would soon have the equivalent of the second frigate's broadside, judging by their present energy. And since their ships were moored, they would have all the hands they needed to fight them and as many again: an enormous increase in their fire-power.

'Let fall the fore-course,' he cried, and slinging his telescope he ran down on deck. 'Hoist out the launch and the cutters,' he said, and to the signal-midshipman, '*Dryad* and *Polyphemus*: captains repair aboard.'

The Worcesters were still making heavy weather of the ponderous launch when Babbington and Patterson came running up the side. 'You see the position, gentlemen,' said Jack. 'They are landing their guns as fast as they can: six are already in position. In an hour's time the place will be another God-damned Gibraltar, impossible to be attempted. I intend to engage the seventy-four yardarm to yardarm for five minutes and then to board her in the smoke. I desire you will cram your ships under my stern and second me at the given word, boarding her over the

bows or by way of our stern if you cannot get there. While
we are engaged, play upon her head and forecastle with
your small-arms – I doubt any of your great guns will
bear – but listen, gentlemen, listen: not a musket, not a
pistol, let alone a great gun, must be fired until they have
fired on us and I give the word loud and clear. Spread all
your officers and midshipmen among the hands with the
strictest possible orders to that effect. Tell them that any
man who fires before the word shall have five hundred
lashes and by God's name I mean five hundred lashes:
and the officer whose division he belongs to shall be broke.
That is clearly understood?'

'Yes, sir,' said Babbington.

Patterson smiled his rare smile and said he understood
perfectly; but they need not worry – he had never known
a Frenchman respect a port's neutrality in all his life, not
if the odds were on his side.

'I hope you are right, Mr Patterson,' said Jack. 'But
whether or no, those are my absolute orders. Now let us
go about our business, before the odds grow greater still.'
They shook hands and he saw them to the side; then,
turning to Pullings he said, 'Beat to quarters,' and loud
over the instant thunder of the drum, 'Pass the word for
Captain Harris.'

The Marine came running from his station on the
poop. 'Captain Harris,' said Jack, 'it is my intention to
board the seventy-four after a very short cannonade. In
the mean time you will take a party round the enemy's
stern in the boats, drive them from their battery on the
mole, and turn the guns against the frigate. Have you any
comments?'

'None, sir. Only that it would be an uncommon pretty
stroke.'

'Then take as many of your men from the guns as
you think fit – we can manage short-handed for a short
burst. Let them be in the boats and out of sight when
we are alongside the Frenchman, ready to pull round the
moment I give the signal.'

181

Word with the gunner: appropriate guns to be drawn and reloaded with chain-shot or bar for the first round, to destroy the enemy's boarding-netting. With the bosun: grapnels to make the Frenchman fast; prime hands in the tops to run out and lash his yardarms. With the master, on the course to steer, luffing up the second they were past the island that made the near corner of the bay. With Pullings, about leadsmen in the channels, so that they might keep as close inshore as possible, about the replacement of the Marines, a dozen other points. He was deeply pleased by the amount of intelligent anticipation he found: most of the things he called for were already on their way, most of the measures already in hand. He savoured this for a moment, watching the mole come nearer – its towers were a thousand yards away and the Frenchmen something farther – and waiting for the din of the top-chains being put to the yards to stop. There were many other things he would have liked to order, but with the Frenchmen landing their guns at this rate he must engage at once; and in any case the essential had been done. The yards were chained: the clashing stopped. 'Worcesters,' said Jack in as strong a croak as he could manage, 'I am going to lay the ship alongside that French seventy-four. We do not fire a shot until I give the word: she must fire first. That's the law. Then when I give the word we thump in four brisk broadsides and board her in the smoke. Those that have not boarded before will not go far wrong if they knock the nearest Frenchman on the head. But remember this: any man that fires before I give the word gets five hundred lashes.'

As an inspiriting harangue this did not perhaps rank very high, but Captain Aubrey was no orator and he had rarely done much better: in any case it seemed to satisfy the *Worcester*'s people and he left the deck to a murmured sound of approval: 'Four rounds brisk, then board.'

He stepped below to the half-deck, where Killick was waiting with his second-best uniform coat and his fighting sword, a heavy cavalry sabre. Many seamen clubbed their pigtails in time of action, but Killick rolled his up into a tight ball: this, combined with a pursed look of disapproval, gave him more the air of an ill-looking shrew than ever. He hated seeing good clothes put at risk and as he helped Jack on with the coat he muttered something about 'taking care of them epaulettes – cost the bleeding eyes out of your head.' For his own part he had changed the duck trousers and blue jacket that he wore as Captain's steward for a very squalid old shirt and petticoat breeches, which heightened the resemblance. Buckling on Jack's sword he said 'There is a fresh supply of wipes in both the pockets: which you could do with one now.'

'Thankee, Killick,' said Jack, blowing his nose. He had forgotten his cold until that moment, and he forgot it again when he returned to the quarterdeck. The enemy were now less than half a mile away, partly concealed by the island and the outward curve of the mole. The *Worcester*, under topsails, was making five knots; the launch and the cutters, full of Marines, were towing easily along on the larboard side, out of sight of the French; the *Dryad* and the *Polyphemus* lay exactly in their stations. No sound but the leadsman: 'By the deep eleven. By the deep eleven. By the mark ten.' In about three minutes they would pass the mouth of the Goletta, squaring main and mizen yards to reduce speed; and about two minutes after that the dust would begin to fly. It was a fairly hazardous stroke and much would depend on the Frenchmen's estimate of the *Polyphemus*. She was a large transport, capable of carrying the best part of a regiment, and if they thought she was full of soldiers they would be less likely to withstand the first decisive shock with full, aggressive confidence. But hazardous or not, it was the only attack he could launch at this short notice: in any event the die was cast and fate must look after the event. At present his chief anxiety was that no zealous excited hand should touch off the first shot and put the *Worcester* legally in the wrong. He knew the importance of the Barbary States' benevolent neutrality; he clearly remembered the words in his orders, *Scrupulous*

183

*respect will be paid to the laws of neutrality*; and he looked keenly along the deck. There was a midshipman to every two guns – he had stripped his quarterdeck – and an officer to every seven; and all the gun-captains were experienced man-of-war's men. Nothing could be safer.

He dismissed that anxiety: another instantly took its place. The ship was fast approaching the entrance to the Goletta; its two towers were fine on her starboard bow. And now, at this moment, from between them came a swarm of shrimp-boats, rushing out in some kind of a ceremony, to the sound of innumerable conchs. Presumably they expected the *Worcester* to turn right-handed into the channel, but whether or no they stood on, all sails set, right across her path, and Jack had only just time to back the foretopsail to avoid running down the nearest. His hoarse almost voiceless croak was not adequate to the occasion and he said to little Calamy, his only remaining aide-de-camp midshipman, 'Jump forward – tell Mr Hollar to hail 'em to bear up – we are standing on.'

From his station on the forecastle the bosun hailed them with enormous force, in what lingua franca he possessed, helped out by passionate gestures. They seemed to understand him, and turning to starboard they sailed along in a disorderly straggling heap, roughly in the same direction as the *Worcester* but slanting diagonally across her course, to gain the open sea while she proceeded along the mole.

The *Worcester* filled her foretopsail and surged on. Now the Goletta was astern with the Frenchmen's inlet sweeping close, and Jack's whole being was poised for the order that would carry the ship round the island and bring her grinding alongside the enemy – he and every seaman in the ship were so poised when part of the shrimping fleet suddenly steered inshore. For no conceivable reason they steered inshore and ran slowly past the island and along the mole. The island was at hand; the mainyard almost brushed it; the master said 'Port your helm' and here was the inlet with a score of brown lateen-sailed shrimpers and

184

beyond them the French ship of the line, colours flying, all gunports open wide.

There was not the least possibility of grappling her without crushing the shrimpers. 'Shall I squeeze 'em, sir?' asked the master from behind the wheel.

'No,' said Jack. 'Haul your wind.' In these few seconds an irretrievable space had passed by; the *Worcester* was already astern of the seventy-four and with this breeze no seamanship on earth could bring her back. 'Make sail,' said Jack, and followed by the *Dryad* and the *Polyphemus* the ship stood on, braced for the fire of the shore battery and the frigate, now abreast.

It did not come, and gathering speed they passed the second island, out of the French guns' reach. The extreme tension relaxed.

There had been no wild shot from the *Worcester* nor from her consorts. But none from the Frenchmen either: it was true that the country craft had partly masked the battery and the frigate as well as the ship of the line, but even so Jack had seen the small-arms men in their tops – he had seen their muskets trained on him, the gleam of the barrels as they followed his movements – yet not a shot had they fired.

Although there could no longer be any element of surprise, and although the *Polyphemus*'s inoffensive character was now evident, and although the landing-party of Marines had been clearly seen, the three ships tacked once they had made a decent offing. The breeze, which had been so kind, was growing fainter and veering south of east, so that a repetition of their course would be difficult indeed. Not that there could be any exact repetition, reflected Jack as he watched the Frenchmen through his telescope. He saw intense activity over there, in striking contrast to what he remembered as their total immobility during their few moments of near contact. His memory might be mistaken – it often was in moments of extremely vivid life – and there might had been some movement apart from that wicked creep of musket-barrels, the part of close action that he liked the least, when officers were picked off like sitting birds; but at all events they were very busy now, warping the seventy-four so close to the island that her bowsprit overhung the rock and it would no longer be possible for the *Dryad* and the *Polyphemus* to board her over the bows. They were also hurrying still more guns ashore.

Not that the *Worcester* was idle, with her Marines coming aboard again and her seamen getting a cable out of the aftermost larboard port, so that she could anchor bow and stern and perhaps come to grips again. There was also the straightforward manoeuvring to bring the ship back to somewhere near her point of departure.

'Sir,' said Harris, 'may I suggest landing my men on the landward side of the mole and approaching the battery from behind? It would be strange if the Frenchmen did not let fly, seeing us coming for them at the double with fixed bayonets.'

Jack did not answer for a moment. He stared at the crowds now hurrying along the mole to see the fun and in his mind's eye he saw the *Worcester*'s Marines among them, moving in neat platoons. Could such a spectacle conceivably be reconciled with neutrality? He did not know Harris and although the man certainly had courage he also had a deeply stupid face: could he be trusted not to fire first or indeed not to charge anything in sight? Including perhaps the Bey's troops, if they were to intervene. Then again any unforeseen delay on either side, anything but perfect synchronization, might expose the Marines to the fire of both ships' remaining larboard guns. It was a spirited suggestion, but without luck, intelligent dash, and exact timing it must lead to endless complications.

'A capital suggestion, Captain Harris,' he said, 'but this time I mean to shoot beyond her, dropping a stern-anchor to swing alongside with the breeze. There will be no room in the ship for the boarding.'

'Haul off all,' cried Pullings, and the mole with its Frenchmen vanished behind the foresail as the *Worcester* began her second run. More slowly now, as close-hauled as she could be, with the old quartermasters at the wheel staring up at the weather leeches of the sails, always on the edge of shivering. Jack blew his nose at some length and walked across to the starboard side. The Goletta mouth again, and as the ship passed the farther tower a man in a splendid turban made gestures towards him with a horse-tail banner. What the gestures meant he could not tell, nor could he put his mind to it, for here was the outward curve, the island, the corner they must turn to fall upon the enemy. And here was a party of Frenchmen dragging a heavy carronade to command the line of approach: a moment later and they could have raked him with a hail of grape.

'Steady, fore and aft,' he said. Then 'Stand by, the axes: stand by.'

'Hard over,' murmured the master in the silence.

'Hard over it is, sir,' said the helmsman and the *Worcester* came round into the Frenchmen's bay.

She hung there, her backed maintopsail exactly balancing the others' thrust, poised for the first gun and for the order that would carry her forward to cut away her anchors and so swing against the enemy's side there in his sheltered nook.

The first gun never came, nor yet the order. This same impression of stillness and silence: the French ship's side was higher than the *Worcester*'s and even by standing on a gun Jack could not see over the hammocks to her quarterdeck, which gave the strangest feeling of impersonality. All her ports were open, all her guns run out: her barricaded waist was lined with soldiers, their hats and muskets showing: thin wafts of smoke drifted from the lower ports, otherwise there was no movement at all, except in the tops, where the same musket-barrels pointed at him, gently varying their angle with the heave of the sea. After a few seconds it was clear to Jack that the French commander's orders about firing first were as rigid and as strictly obeyed as his own.

The minutes dropped by. With great skill the master kept the *Worcester* in equilibrium until an odd gust drove her a trifle out and she began forging very slowly ahead. The men stationed by the hanging anchors raised their axes, waiting for the word: but Jack shook his head. 'Fill the mainyard,' he said in his hoarse voice. The *Worcester* surged forward, moving across the face of the battery, now much stronger, but as quiet and unmoving as the seventy-four, and past the equally silent frigate. Here at least he could look down into her and on her quarterdeck he saw her captain, a short, capable, grave-looking man standing there with his hands behind his back, looking up. Their eyes met, and at the same moment each moved his hat to the other.

Jack was perfectly convinced that the Frenchman in command was determined not to fire the first shot, but since there might be some fool among the thousand men moored against the mole he led his ships up and down again. Fools there may well have been, but none in charge of a gun or even a musket, and the French were not to be provoked.

'May we not try just once more, sir, giving them a cheer as we go down?' asked Pullings in his ear.

'No, Tom: it will not do,' said he. 'If we stay here another half hour, with the breeze veering like this, we shall never get out of this God-damned bay – windbound for weeks, mewed up with these miserable brutes.' Turning from Pullings' bitter distress, he raised his voice, addressing the master: 'Mr Gill, pray lay her for Cape Mero, and then let us shape a course for Barka.'

He took a few turns up and down the quarterdeck in order not to evade the disappointed looks of the crews housing their guns, the sullen, disappointed atmosphere, the flat sense of anticlimax. The ship was profoundly dissatisfied with him: he was profoundly dissatisfied with himself.

# CHAPTER SEVEN

'And so, sir,' said Jack, 'I left them there and shaped a course for Barka, having first sent *Dryad* to inform you of their presence.'

'I see,' said Admiral Thornton, leaning back in his chair, putting on his spectacles, and inspecting him with a cold objectivity. 'Then before we return to the subject of Medina, give me a brief account of what happened at Barka,' he added after a disagreeable pause.

'Well sir, I am afraid that Barka was not altogether satisfactory either. When we arrived Esmin Pasha was being besieged by his son Muley and he asked us for guns as well as the presents. These I felt obliged to refuse until I could obtain your consent, but after consultation with Mr Consul Hamilton I sent my carpenter, gunner, and a dozen hands ashore to remount the cannon he possessed: most of their carriages were so decayed that they could not be attempted to be fired. But, however, his defences had hardly been put in a tolerable posture before a squadron came in from Constantinople bringing a new Pasha and an order for Esmin's recall. He did not see fit to obey it, and left by night with most of the presents and the guns to join his son, with the intention of besieging the new Pasha once the squadron had sailed. In the mean time the new man sent to say that it was customary to congratulate every newly-installed ruler of Barka with music, fireworks and gifts. The music and the fireworks I could manage,' said Jack with a nervous artificial smile. The nervous artificial smile met with no response whatsoever from the Admiral or his secretary, between whom it was divided: the expression of the first showed no change; the second looked down at his papers. Admiral Harte had no share in the smirk: nevertheless he saw fit to give a disapproving sniff.

It was a curious sight, the massive Jack Aubrey, a powerful fellow in the prime of life, long accustomed to authority, sitting there with an anxious, deferential expression, poised on the edge of his chair before a small, sick, bloated, old man he could have crushed with one hand. The service had enormous faults: its dockyards were corrupt and often incompetent, the recruitment of the lower deck was a national disgrace and that of the officers an utterly haphazard affair, while their promotion and employment often depended on influence and favouritism: yet still the Navy managed to throw up admirals who could make men like Jack Aubrey tremble. St Vincent, Keith, Duncan; and Admiral Thornton was one of their kind, or even more so. Now, after another pause, he said, 'You have seen Captain Babbington since your return to the fleet?'

'Yes, sir.' He had indeed – William Babbington pulling out in a double-banked cutter the moment the *Worcester* was in sight, pulling out over a sea so rough it was a wonder a boat could swim.

'Then you are no doubt aware that I have it in contemplation to call you both to a court-martial for disobedience of orders.'

'So Babbington gave me to understand, sir; and I told him at once that although I was extremely concerned at having displeased you, I flattered myself I could show that I had carried out my orders as I understood them to the best of my ability. And may I add, sir, that Captain Babbington acted under my direction at all times: if there was any fault in that direction, the responsibility is entirely mine.'

'Did you direct him to return from Medina without delivering the consul's dispatches?'

'In a manner of speaking, yes, I did. I particularly impressed upon him the necessity for respecting Medina's neutrality, and this he could not have done had he entered into conflict with the French. I wholly approved his return: had he entered the Goletta he must have been captured.'

'You wholly approved his defeating a carefully planned stratagem? Are you not aware, sir, that the *Dryad* or at least some similar vessel was intended to be captured? And that within five minutes of receiving news of her capture and of the Frenchmen's violation of neutrality I should have detached a squadron to depose the Bey and put in a friend of ours, at the same time clearing every French ship out of all the ports in his country? Had you no notion of this?'

'None whatsoever, sir, upon my honour.'

'Nonsense,' said Harte. 'I made it perfectly plain.'

'No, sir, you did not,' said Jack. 'You spoke in a general way about this being an important service requiring particular discretion, which puzzled me, since the carrying of presents and consular dispatches did not strike me as a task calling for exceptional abilities. You also dwelt upon the necessity of respecting the Barbary States' neutrality. When I referred to my written orders I found nothing whatsoever, not the slightest hint that they were to be understood in a special sense – that I was to send a ship under my command into a trap and oblige her to be captured, perhaps with heavy loss. And I do not wonder at it, sir,' said Jack, his choler rising at the idea of Babbington hauling down his colours at last under overwhelming fire, 'I do not wonder that you did not give me a plain direct order to send my friend in under such circumstances. On the other hand, my written orders did insist upon the respect due to neutrality, as did your verbal instructions; it was natural therefore to conclude that that was where the need for discretion lay. And I may say, sir,' he said looking Admiral Thornton in the eye, 'that I respected that neutrality to the very limit of human endurance.'

At some point in this statement, delivered with increasing force, the moral advantage changed sides; and now Jack Aubrey, sitting square in his chair, opened his orders at the relevant page and passed them to Admiral Thornton, saying, 'There. I appeal to your candour, sir: would not any man take that to be the heart of the matter?

*Scrupulous respect will be paid to the laws of neutrality.'*

While Sir John put on his spectacles again and ran through the orders Harte said that they were written in a great hurry, there not being a moment to lose; that he had not had time to read them over, and the clerk might have mistaken his drift; that a nod was as good as a wink to a blind horse; that he was nevertheless perfectly convinced that his verbal instructions had made his meaning clear – anyone could have told that something was afoot when a seventy-four was sent on such a mission and told to keep a full day's sail away – anyone could have told that the orders were to be obeyed to the letter. He had nothing to reproach himself with.

It was disconnected, angry, unskilful and somewhat embarrassing; Admiral Thornton made no reply, but said to Jack, 'International law must be obeyed, of course: yet even Roman virtue can be overdone, and there is such a thing as being too scrupulous by half, above all in a war of this kind, with an enemy that sticks at nothing. Letting fly first with a broadside in the presence of witnesses is one thing: a scuffle ashore, where the first blow might have come from anyone, is another. Did it never occur to you to land a party of Marines?'

'Yes, sir, it did. Indeed Captain Harris himself put the suggestion forward in the handsomest manner. I am not very much holier than thou, sir, I hope, in matters of this kind, and I should certainly have done so if my orders had not insisted so upon respect for neutrality.'

'They did nothing of the kind,' said Harte. 'Properly understood, they did nothing of the kind.'

Nobody saw fit to comment upon this and after a while Admiral Thornton said 'Very well, Captain Aubrey. Although the outcome of this affair is unfortunate in the extreme, I do not think we can usefully say any more. Good day to you.'

'Dear Lord above, sweetheart,' wrote Jack in his serial letter, 'I have never been so relieved in my life. All the way back in the boat I dared scarcely smile, or even

192

congratulate myself; and there was William Babbington waiting for me with such a look of mortal anxiety on his face, as well there might have been, he having beheld the Admiral in the first full flood of his wrath. I carried him into the stern-gallery, it being a sweet evening with a light breeze at SSW and the squadron standing due east under topgallantsails so that we had a capital sunset spread out before us, and gave him an exact account of what had passed. We were as gay as a pair of schoolboys that have escaped a most prodigious flogging and expulsion, and we called Pullings and Mowett in to sup with us. I could not in decency open my mind to them about the Rear-Admiral – I could not even say how painful it was to hear and see a man of his rank and age sounding and looking so very mean, so very like a scrub – but we understood one another pretty well and Mowett asked me whether I remembered a disrespectful song the hands had made up about him when I had the dear *Sophie*. It was not the sentiment that Mowett objected to, he said, but the metre, which, it appears, broke the laws of prosody.' Yet the sentiment was not wholly inoffensive either, since even the moderate chorus ran

> Bugger old Harte, bugger old Harte
> That red-faced son of a blue French fart

as Jack remembered very well.

'It was a charming supper-party, only wanting Stephen to make it complete; and even he will be with us, wind and weather permitting, in two days' time. For this morning the Admiral made my signal, received me kindly – no cold glare, no damned icy distance this time, no *Captain Aubrey* or *you, sir* – and gave me very welcome orders to proceed to Port Mahon to take certain stores on board and my surgeon, he having had leave of absence in those parts.' The orders had in fact continued, 'Now, Aubrey, I understand from Dr Maturin that you are acquainted with the nature of some of his more confidential expeditions: he also says that he places the utmost reliance on your

193

discretion, and had rather sail with you than any other captain on the list. At present his occasions take him to the French coast, something west of Villeneuve, I believe: you will therefore carry him to the most suitable point for landing and take him off again as and when you shall between you think best. And I do most sincerely hope that you will bring him back safe, with the least possible delay.' But obviously this could form no part of his letter. Nor could another subject that dwelt in his mind, rarely quitting his immediate consciousness. He could and did skirt round it, saying 'I do hope we have a brush with the enemy soon, if only to wipe out the fiasco at Medina. The officers and men who have sailed with me before know that upon the whole I am not wanting in conduct nor I believe I may say in ordinary courage; but most of the ship's company know little or nothing about me and I think some suppose I did not choose to fight. Now it is a very bad thing for men to sail under a commander they suspect of shyness. They cannot of course respect him, and without respect true discipline goes by the board . . .'

Discipline, as the essence of a fighting-ship, was certainly very dear to Jack Aubrey's heart; but there were some things dearer still and reputation was one of them. He had not had the least notion of how he valued it until both Harris and Patterson treated him not indeed with disrespect but with something considerably less than their former deference. This was not immediately after his most unpopular order to leave the Frenchmen lying there, when he knew very well that in the first flat anticlimax and disappointment, the letting-down of very high-wrought spirits, the ship would happily have seen him flogged, but some days after Medina. The incident, if anything so evanescent and impalpable could be called an incident, was followed by a series of unquestionable facts – the appearance of several names on the defaulters' list, charged with fighting, half of them former Skates, half of them men who had sailed with Jack before. Naval justice was crude and amateurish, with no rules

194

of evidence or procedure, but at this quarterdeck level, with the grating rigged for immediate execution, it was not calculated for delay, still less for concealing the real causes at issue, and quite often the truth came out at once, naked and sometimes inconvenient. In this case it appeared that the Skates, comparing Jack's conduct with that of Captain Allen, their last commander, maintained that Captain Aubrey was less enterprising by far. 'Captain Allen would have gone straight at 'em, says he, law or no law: Captain Allen was not near so careful of his health or his paintwork, he says. So I fetch him a little shove, or a nudge as you might call it, to remind him of his manners.'

This evidence explained the battered appearance of many hands who were not charged at all – Bonden, Davis, Martens and several more of Jack's lower-deck friends, even placid old Joe Plaice – the equally battered appearance of a number of Marines as well as former Skates, and the increased animosity between soldiers and seamen. It also led Jack to notice or to fancy he noticed changes in the attitude of some of his officers, a lack of the perhaps somewhat exaggerated awe and respect that they thought due to the genuine salamander's reputation that had surrounded him for so many years, that had made his work so very much easier, and that he accepted as a matter of course.

All this Jack could have put in his letter, and he might even have added his reflection about a man's losing his reputation and a woman's losing her beauty and each of them looking right and left for signs of the loss in much the same manner; but it would not have told Sophie much about her husband's real trouble, which was a dread that he might in fact have behaved cowardly.

He had a profound belief in the lower deck's corporate opinion. There might be a good many fools and landlubbers down there, but the seamen predominated not only in moral force but even in number; and in matters of this kind he had hardly ever known them to be wrong. He had

had no great heart for the fight in the first place, none of those tearing spirits and that joy and intense anticipation, like fox-hunting at its best, but fox-hunting raised to the hundredth power, which had preceded other actions. Yet that was neither here nor there: a man could be out of form without being chicken-hearted and he had certainly sought out the enemy with all possible zeal, directly offering a close engagement with the odds against him and even trying to provoke it. On the other hand he remembered his relief when he understood that the Frenchmen were not going to fight: an ignoble relief. Or was ignominious the word? Not at all: it was a perfectly reasonable relief at not having to throw an ill-prepared, unseasoned crew into a desperate fight, in which so many of them must certainly be killed, wounded, crippled, maimed. In actions of that kind there was always a most shocking butcher's bill, and with such a crew it would have been even worse, to say nothing of the strong possibility of defeat.

As for his refusing to land the Marines, on first recollection it had seemed to him perfectly innocent, decided in perfect good faith, his orders being what he had understood them to be. But the Admiral's words had shaken him horribly and by now he had argued the matter over with himself so often that what with accusation and indignant denial he could no longer tell just what the true nature of his intention had been: it was obscured by argument. Yet in this matter intention was everything and there was no point in putting the case to any other person on earth. Sophie for example would certainly tell him that he had behaved correctly, but that, though agreeable, would be no real comfort to him since even she could not get inside his head or heart or vitals to inspect his intentions – his intentions as they had been at that moment.

Nor could Stephen, for that matter: still, Jack looked forward extremely to their meeting, and in something less than two days' time, when the *Worcester* rounded to under Cape Mola, unable to enter Mahon harbour because of the north-wester, he took his barge, pulling through the narrow mouth and then beating right up the whole length, board upon board, although an exchange of signals with the officer in charge of Royal Naval stores had told him that nothing but a little Stockholm tar had yet arrived for the squadron. This was water that he and his coxswain and at least four of his bargemen knew as well as Spithead or Hamoaze and they sailed up with a kind of offhand cunning, shaving past the Lazaretto, catching the back-eddy by Cuckold's Reach (a spacious stretch in these warm latitudes), and slipping through the hospital channel, censuring all changes that had been made since their time. Not that there were many: the Spanish flag rather than the Union flew over various public buildings, and now the Spanish men-of-war in the harbour were not prizes to the Royal Navy but allies, yet upon the whole little had altered. The place still had much of the air of an English Georgian market-town and sea-port set down in an incongruous landscape of vines and olives, with the occasional palm, and a brilliant Mediterranean sky over all.

As they sailed along Jack pointed out the various places of interest to the youngster at his side, such as St Philip's, the powder mill, the ordnance-wharf and the mast-yard; but the gangling boy, a spotted first-voyager named Willet, was too much awed by his company, too eager to be ashore, and perhaps too stupid, to absorb much information and as they drew nearer to the town Jack fell silent. 'We will have a pint of sherry at Joselito's for old times' sake,' he said to himself, 'order a handsome dinner at the Crown – a beefsteak pudding, a solomon gundy, and those triangular almond cakes to finish with – and then walk about, looking at the places we used to know, until it is ready.' And then to Bonden, 'Captain of the port's office.'

The barge glided along under a high wall on the far side of the harbour, a wall with a discreet green door leading to the dove-house where he and Molly Harte had first made love. The wall was dotted with capers, growing wild in the interstices of the stones; they were now covered with their strange feathery flowers, as they had been on that occasion, and his mind was still ranging back with a mixture of lubricity and tenderness and indefinite regret when the barge sprang her luff and touched against the opposing wharf at the Capitania steps. 'Jump up to the captain of the port, Mr Willet,' said Jack. 'Give him my compliments and ask where the Doctor's victualler lays. Her name is *Els Set Dolors*.'

'Yes, sir,' said Willet, looking appalled. '*Els Set Dolors* it is, sir. What language shall I say it in, sir?'

'Spanish or French; and if that don't answer you may try Latin. Bonden will go with you.'

'The captain of the port's compliments, sir,' said the returning Willet, 'and the *Set Dolors* lays off la . . . la . . .'

'Dogana,' said Bonden.

'But Dr Maturin is gone to . . .'

'Ciudadela, on a mule.'

'And they do not look to see him back before Sunday evening.'

'Asking your pardon, sir,' said Bonden, 'Saturday, I believe.'

'He said Sabbath-oh,' cried Willet.

'So he did, sir: but the Sabbath is on Saturdays in these parts, we find. Sunday they call Dimanche-oh, or something very like.'

'Thank you, Mr Willet,' said Jack, deeply disappointed. 'However, I think we may as well have our dinner here, before returning to the ship.' He reflected for a moment, his eye on the unattached ladies gathering at the waterside: he had put half a guinea of the boy's allowance into his hand before leaving the *Worcester*, and although Willet was neither amiable nor intelligent Jack did not wish him to buy a pox with it. 'Eldon,' he said to the grizzled, hard-faced bow-oar, 'Mr Willet will have dinner at Bunce's, and then you will show him the sights of Mahon, the ordnance-store, the careenage, the proving-ground and the Protestant church, the slips if there is anything a-building, and the mad-house if there is time before six o'clock.' He arranged with Bonden for the bargemen's dinner, told them to draw straws for boat-keepers, and walked off unattended.

Sentimental pilgrimages had rarely succeeded with Jack Aubrey: in the few that he had ever deliberately under-taken something had nearly always happened to spoil not only the present but much of the past as well; yet it now seemed that perhaps this might be an exception. The day itself was brilliantly clear, as it had often been when he was in Minorca as a lieutenant and a commander, and it was warm, so that climbing the steps to the upper town he unbuttoned his coat, a far finer coat than that which he wore in those days but one that did not prevent him from being recognized and welcomed at Joselito's and the other places he called at on his way to the Crown.

Port Mahon still showed many signs of the long English connection: quite apart from the officers and men from the three Royal Navy vessels in the harbour – two sloops and a gun-brig on convoy-duty – pink faces and hair as bright yellow as Jack Aubrey's walked about the street. Tea and even buns were to be had, as well as English beer and tobacco, and at Joselito's there were copies of the London papers, not more than two or three months old. But the high days were gone, the days when the whole Mediterranean fleet lay in Port Mahon and power-ful garrisons filled St Philip's and the citadel: the Royal Navy now relied much more on Malta and Gibraltar; the Spanish navy kept only a couple of brigs in Mahon, while the troops amounted to no more than a few companies of local militia; so it was understandable that the town as a whole should seem rather sleepy, while the places that catered chiefly for sailors and soldiers should have a somewhat deserted air.

Jack walked into the Crown by the back way, through a courtyard full of orange-trees; and there he sat on the stone rim of the fountain in the middle to draw breath and cool himself after his walk. His cold was gone long since but he was out of form and in any case walking on the hard, unyielding land after weeks and months of having a live deck underfoot always made him gasp. From an upper window came the voice of a woman singing to herself, a long flamenco song with strange intervals and Moorish cadences, often interrupted by the beating of a pillow or the turning of a bed. The throaty contralto reminded Jack of Mercedes, a very, very pretty Minorcan girl he had known in this same inn before his promotion. What would have happened to her? Swept off by some soldier, no doubt; a mother many times over, and fat. But still jolly, he hoped.

The song ran on, a lovely dying fall, and Jack listened more and more attentively: there were few things that moved him as deeply as music. Yet he was not all ears, all spirit, either, and in a long pause while a bolster was thrust into a case too small his brute belly gave so eager a twinge that he got up and walked into the taproom, a broad, low, cool, shadowy place with vast barrels let into its walls and a sanded floor. 'You bloody old fool,' said a parrot quietly in the silence, but without real conviction.

Jack had known this place so thick with tobacco-smoke that you could hardly tell one uniform from another and so full of talk that orders had to be roared as though to the foretop. Now it was as though he were walking in a dream, a dream that respected the material surroundings to the last detail but emptied them of life, and to break the spell he called 'House. House, there. *La casa*, ho.'

No reply: but he was glad to see an enormous bull-mastiff come in from the hall, making the first marks in the newly-sprinkled sand. The Crown had always had fine English mastiffs, and this one, a young brindled bitch with a back broad enough to dine on, must be a granddaughter of those he had known very well. She had never seen him in her life, of course: she sniffed his hand with distant civility and then, obviously unimpressed, paced on to the patio. Jack stepped into the hall, a square hall with two staircases and two English longcase clocks in it, the whole full of brilliant sun: he called again and when the echo of his voice had died away he heard a distant screech of 'Coming' and the patter of feet on the corridor above.

He was contemplating one of the clocks, made by Wm Timmins of Gosport and ornamented with a creditable ship of the last age, a ship that still carried a lateen yard on the mizen, when the pattering feet reached the staircase on his right and looking up he saw Mercedes coming down – an unchanged Mercedes. Still pigeon-plump, but no vast spreading bulk, no moustache, no coarseness.

'Why, Mercy, my dear,' he cried. 'How happy I am to see you!' And stepping to the foot of the stairs he stood there with open arms.

Mercedes paused a moment in her course, and then, crying *'Capitan manyac!'* flung herself into them. It was as well that he was a powerful man and well braced, for Mercedes, though slim-waisted, was a solid girl and she had the advantage of the height: he stood the shock however, the padded, scented shock, and having squeezed the breath out of her body he lifted her up and gazed at her face with great complacency. Pleasure, freshness, gaiety and peach-like bloom he saw there, and he kissed her heartily, a delighted, frankly amorous kiss, heartily returned. Kisses were not unknown at the Crown; Jack and Mercedes had exchanged them before now without the roof falling in; but these set off a very shocking hullabaloo. Both clocks struck the hour, the front door and two windows slammed with a sudden gust of wind, four or five bull-mastiffs began to bay, and at the same moment the hall filled with people coming in from the street or the courtyard or down the other flight of stairs, all with messages or questions or orders that had to be shouted over the hollow roaring of the dogs. Mercedes banged and thumped the mastiffs, dealt with the questions in English, Spanish and Catalan, and between two of them she told a boy to lead the Captain to the Mermaid, a particularly comfortable little room up one pair of stairs.

And in this little room, the Crown grown calm again,

they sat very companionably together, eating their dinner at a small round table, the dishes coming up hot and hot from the kitchen by a plate-hoist let into the wall. Mercedes ate much less than Jack, but she talked much more, very much more: her English had never been accurate; it had slipped with the years, and now her rather wild remarks were interrupted by bubbling laughter and cries of 'Cat's English, *manyac*; kitchen-cat's English.' Nevertheless Jack perfectly understood the essence: Mercedes had married the Crown, a man much older than herself, a poor, thin, pitiful, weak-hammed cat as avaricious as a badger who had only made the offer to spite his family and save her wages. He had never made her a single present and even her ring was found to be brass and therefore neither valid nor binding: whereas the present Jack had given her long ago yet not so very long ago neither was close to her heart at this very moment: she had put on a new pinner for the occasion, and now undoing it she leant over the table, showing him the diamond pendant he had bought for her in the year two, one of the many charming fruits of a valuable prize, nestling low in her bosom. The Crown, that sordid creature, was away for some days, in Barcelona. Jack would have his old room, no doubt: it had been new-hung with crimson curtains!

'Oh damme, Mercy dear,' he cried, 'I am a captain now, you know, and must not sleep out of my ship.'

'Would you not even be allowed a little siesta after all that duck pie, and the day so hot?' asked Mercy, gazing at him with wide innocent eyes.

Jack's face, somewhat more florid than usual with fish soup, lobster, lamp chops, duck pie, Minorcan cheese and three bottles of wine, spread in a rosy smile so wide that his bright blue eyes vanished and Mercedes knew that he was about to say something droll. So he would have done too, as soon as he had hit just the right balance between 'not *sleeping*' and indelicacy, if Stephen had not made the most unwelcome entrance of his life. They had heard his harsh, disagreeable voice on the stairs and Mercedes had

had time to spring up and adopt the attitude of one waiting at table when he walked rapidly in, smelling of hot mule. 'Good day to you, young gentlewoman,' he said in Catalan and then without the slightest pause 'Come, brother, drink up your coffee. There is not a moment to lose. We must run to the boat.' He seized the water-jug, drained it, recognized Mercedes and said, 'Why, Mother of God, it is you, child, I am happy to see you. Pray run for the reckoning, my dear; the Captain must leave this minute. Is it a guest you have?' he asked Jack, observing the two places laid.

'No,' said Jack. 'That is to say, yes; most certainly – of course. Stephen, let us meet at the boat in a couple of hours' time – it is no good before then – I have given a youngster leave: he cannot be left behind.'

'Jack, I have run my poor mule nearly to death: you may certainly maroon a midshipman. Ten midshipmen.'

'Then again, I have some important communications to make to a friend here.'

'Are these communications of the very first importance to the service, tell?'

'They are more of a personal nature, but –'

'Then let us hear no more of them, I beg. Would I have rid the cruel long road from Ciudadela in the heat of the day – would I drag you from your coffee and your company and drink none myself, if there were no imperative haste? If it were not more important than amiable communications or even than spouse-breach for all love? Come, child, the Captain's hat and coat and sword, if you please: duty calls him away.'

Duty was obeyed, but with a sullen and a reluctant step; and it was clear to the coxswain and crew of the barge, hurriedly called from Florio's skittle-alley, that they had better watch out for squalls. A glance at their Captain's closed, forbidding face, a glance at one another, with an almost imperceptible jerk of the head or movement of an eyelid, and all was understood: the bargemen sat in their places, prim, mute, and correct as a Sunday-school while Bonden took the boat right down the harbour with a strong favourable breeze and the officers sat silent in the stern-sheets.

Jack's silence was that of extreme disappointment and frustration: Stephen's that of a mind busy far away, pre-occupied with motives and probabilities in the first place and then with questions of the distances to be covered by various men and the time required for their journeys. That morning he had received word of the meeting he and his colleagues had been working for, a meeting with men high in the service of the French and their allies that might lead to very great things: the meeting itself was confirmed, but to enable an important officer from Rochefort to attend it had been put forward three days. All the factors that Stephen could check agreed that the appointment could be kept by those on land, but there remained the *Worcester*'s ability to carry him to that obscure marshy rendezvous and as soon as they were in the fore-cabin he said to Jack, 'Pray, Jack, could you set me down at the mouth of the Aigouille by Tuesday evening?'

'Where is the Aigouille?' asked Jack coldly.

Stephen turned to the chart-table and ran his finger along the low flat coastline of Languedoc with its salt lagoons and brackish marshes, canals and small un-navigable rivers choked by sandbars, meandering through malarial fens, and said 'Here.'

Jack looked at the chart and whistled. 'As far as that?' cried he. 'I had supposed you meant something in these parts. How can I possibly answer for such a distance unless I can foretell the wind's direction and its force? Above all its direction. It is not quite foul at present, but it might haul forward until it is directly in our teeth any minute – dead on end, as they say. I wonder at your asking such a simple question: you must know by now that with the best will in the world a ship cannot lie closer than six points, and the *Worcester* will not come up so near. You must have heard of leeway – somebody must surely have told you of leeway and . . .'

'For God's love, Jack, just point the ship in as near the right direction as ever you can, and tell me about leeway afterwards. There is not a moment to be lost.' These words had so often been addressed to him during his years in the Navy that even in his present hurry of spirits he was pleased to be the one who uttered them, and he repeated, 'There is not a moment to be lost.'

'Do you wish me to slip?' asked Jack seriously; and to make his meaning even clearer, 'To slip the cable, leaving it and the anchor behind?'

'Would that save much time, so?'

'Not above a few minutes in this clean ground.'

'Then perhaps we should retain our anchor,' said Stephen. 'That invaluable implement – a precious standby.'

Jack made no reply to this but went on deck. 'I am afraid I have vexed him, the creature,' said Stephen to himself, and then sank back into his former train of thought. Half-consciously he heard the fiddle on the capstan-head, the stamp and go of the men at the bars, a strong cry of 'Heave and rally', the fiddle increase its tempo, and then the even stronger cry of 'Heave and aweigh.'

Two minutes later with the anchor catted the *Worcester* was making her ponderous way close-hauled for Cape Mola under topsails, driver and jib, swaying up her topgallantmasts as she went. As soon as she was well clear of the headland she took the true breeze, undeflected, a moderate tramontane, and Jack, standing by the helmsman with the master, said 'Luff and touch her.'

Up she came, spoke by spoke, until the weather-leech of the maintopsail began to shiver. 'Haul the bowlines,' called Jack.

'One, two, *three*. Belay oh!' The traditional howling chant came from the fore, main and mizen gangs in exact order and with immense spirit; and from the forecastle Mowett roared 'Bowlines hauled, sir,' with equal zeal, for Mowett, like all those who had sailed with Jack Aubrey in the *Sophie*, was used to these sudden departures from Mahon. In those days Jack had private sources of information about the sailing of enemy merchantmen and the *Sophie* would dart out to play havoc with French and Spanish commerce at a moment's notice, sending in prizes to such an extent that at one time Holborne's Quay had no room for any more and they were obliged to be moored in the fairway. It was then that the *Sophie*'s commander came by the nickname of Lucky Jack Aubrey, and his enterprise, good fortune and accurate intelligence had brought all the Sophies a great deal of money, which they liked. But even without the prize-money, or with much less of it, they would still have loved these cruises, the long-drawn-out chase with every possible turn of seamanship on either side, and then the capture – piracy with a clear conscience: and now, the word having spread from the former Sophies to all the present Worcesters with its usual electric speed, the hands hauled the bowlines and sharped the yards with far more than common energy. Jack noticed it, of course, just as he noticed Pullings' eager, questioning eye, and with a pang he realized that he was going to disappoint them all once more.

'Luff and touch her,' he said again, and the *Worcester*, braced so as to look as like a fore-and-aft vessel as her nature would allow or indeed rather more, came nearly half a point nearer the wind. He studied the angle of the dog-vane, called for an azimuth-compass to take the bearings of the wake and of Cape Mola, gazed long at the sky, the familiar clear tramontane sky with high white clouds moving in a steady procession toward Africa, and methodically began to pack on sail, causing the log to be heaved every five minutes.

Returning to the cabin at last he said to Stephen, 'If the breeze hold true, and there is a fair likelihood of its doing so, I may be able to carry you to the mouth of your river in time, by making three legs of it, the last profiting by the indraught close to the shore. But you are clearly to understand that at sea nothing whatsoever can be guaranteed.' He still spoke in a somewhat official tone, looking taller than usual, and stern; and even when Stephen had made all proper acknowledgements he went on in the same captain's voice, 'I am not sure what you meant by saying spouse-breach at the Crown just now, but if it means what I think it means, allow me to tell you that I resent the imputation extremely.'

Denial was on the tip of Stephen's tongue, denial or a rapid though necessarily fallacious explaining away: on the other hand it was exceedingly difficult to lie successfully to so intimate a friend. In the event he only had time to pass his tongue over his lips once or twice like an embarrassed guilty dog before Captain Aubrey stalked out of the cabin.

'Such asperity,' said Stephen to himself. 'Dear me, such asperity.' He stayed leaning over the chart for some time, studying the lines of approach to the hidden rendezvous: his colleagues and agents used it more often than most of their meeting-places in the southern parts, but he had not been there himself for many years. He remembered it well for all that: a lagoon at the river's mouth, then beyond it a great dyke dividing salt marsh from fresh; far along the dyke on the left hand a shepherd's hut by one of those vast buildings where wintering sheep were housed by night, and a rarely-inhabited shooting-box; away on the right hand the village of Mandiargues, almost depopulated by malaria, Malta fever and conscription but still served by an indifferent road; the whole, even beyond the distant village, deep in reed-beds, a paradise for duck, wading birds in great variety, mosquitoes, and the bearded titmouse. 'The bitterns may have arrived,' he said, partly to still an uneasiness that would keep rising in the depths of his mind, and he returned to his own part of the ship.

Here he found his assistants, and together they looked at the *Worcester*'s sparsely-inhabited sick-bay (a camel-bite, some broken bones), checked their accounts, and mustered their stores. Mr Lewis had dealt with the medical situation perfectly well in Stephen's absence, but there was a most unfortunate deficiency in the portable soup and port wine intended for invalids: they and two Winchester quarts of *Liquor Ammoniae Acetatis* had quite certainly been stolen by some criminal hand as yet unknown, misled by the *liquor* part of the label. 'Once he starts upon it we shall certainly know,' said Mr Lewis, 'and we shall no doubt recover what he and his messmates have not drunk; but the port and the soup are gone for ever. It was my own fault for not screwing them to the deck, and I shall have to make them good out of my own pocket. My one comfort is that there is said to be a monstrous fine prize in prospect that will enable me to do so without beggaring myself and Mrs Lewis – that will perhaps enable us to set up a carriage, ha, ha! What do you say to that, sir?'

'Nothing do I know of the future, Mr Lewis,' said Stephen. 'Still less of the immediate past. What is this Barka, where the camel bit young Williams?' Lewis told him about Barka in detail and about Medina, ending, '. . . and so all in all, sir, and by and large, and taking one thing with another, I believe I may say that I have rarely seen a ship's company so . . . so *deflated* is perhaps the proper word, seeing that the martial afflatus it was that was gone. Nor more discontented with their officers and the no doubt necessary state of affairs, nor more divided and apt to disagree – the two fractures and the tooth cases certainly arose from that, whatever the parties themselves may allege – nor more inclined to pick and steal. But I have no doubt that this prize will wipe out the sense of failure and set everything to rights. Our younger loblolly-boy is mess-mates with two old Sophies, and they tell him that Captain Aubrey never set out from Mahon in a hurry without bringing back a prize – never, they swear, not once. And if he did that with a fourteen-gun brig, what will he do with a ship of the line? A galleon is the least I reckon on: more probably two.'

'Mr Lewis,' said Stephen, holding up the lantern to see the pure gleam of cupidity more clearly, 'you forget we are no longer at war with the Spaniards.'

The gleam faded, then came obstinately back with the reflection that vast wealth was still carried by sea, even if galleons were gone. 'Remember the *Hermione*,' cried Lewis. 'The surgeon's share alone was above four thousand pound!'

Stephen went thoughtfully to bed. That is to say, his cast of mind was thoughtful and so was the expression on his face, but in fact he was so tired after his furious morning's ride on a more than ordinarily wicked mule that he could neither govern nor direct his thoughts. Notions, ideas, and statements presented themselves in no apparent order, with no apparent connection. This Medina business certainly explained some of Jack's asperity: what kind of rhinoceros was it, that Lewis described as having a *prehensile* upper lip?: how far was La Reynière (a sub-agent in Montpellier) to be trusted?: how had he, Stephen, come to say 'spouse-breach' at the Crown? The imputation was certainly true: it was also certainly impertinent, unwarranted, ill-bred, an unpardonable freedom. Was it impatience and fatigue on his own part, or a lurking jealousy at the sight of that fine, melting, amorous wench? In any event it was inaccurate, and since Mercedes was now married this would have been double: Spouse-breach . . . his eyes closed upon the word three times repeated, like a spell.

Long, long and late he slept, waking with a delicious sense of ease, his body moulded into the cot, almost immaterial. He lay for an indeterminate stretch, luxuriating, until an abrupt recollection of what the *Worcester* was carrying him to wiped the warm, benign, dozing pleasure from his face. At the same moment he saw his door open gently and Killick put his long red nose through the crack. How Stephen knew that Killick was doing so for the sixth or seventh time he could not tell, but he was as sure of it as he was sure of the words that Killick did then pronounce: if the Doctor happened to be awake, the Captain would be glad of his company at breakfast. Then the unexpected addition 'and any road there was something he did ought to see on deck.'

Jack had been on deck in the middle watch and again before dawn, when the breeze freshened. What little sleep he had had – and he was used to short snatches – had been deep and refreshing; the searching wind, right cold by night, and the driving spray had done away with much of his ill-humour; and although he had held back his real breakfast until Stephen should be awake, an early mug of coffee and a piece of bread and honey in his hand had restored much of the usual sweetness of his nature. 'Good morning to you, Doctor,' he said as Stephen came blinking into the brilliant light of the quarterdeck. 'Look at that. Ain't it prime? I do not believe that with all your experience of the sea you have beheld the like.'

The quarterdeck was crowded: all the officers and all the young gentlemen were there: there was a general atmosphere of excitement, and Stephen noticed that his particular friends were looking at him with a kindly triumph and expectancy, as though amazement might knock him flat at any moment now. He gazed at the pale blue morning sky, the darker white-laced sea, the quantities of sails. He was most unwilling to expose himself before so many comparative strangers, most unwilling to disappoint his friends, and with all the conviction and astonishment that could be summoned on an empty stomach he cried, 'I do not believe I ever have. A most remarkable sight, upon my word.'

'You can see 'em even better from the hances,' said Jack, leading him to the side, and carefully following the admiring gaze of all eyes on the quarterdeck Stephen perceived an array of overlapping triangular sails along the bowsprit and beyond it, well beyond it. 'There,' said Jack. 'There you have the whole shooting-match. Fore and foretopmast staysails, of course, inner jib, outer jib, flying jib, spindle jib, and jib of jibs!' He explained to Stephen at some length that after long experiment he had found this answer best with the *Worcester*'s present trim and with the present light breezes: he named a large number of other staysails, the spanker and driver, pointed out the total absence of square sails on the main and their rarity elsewhere, and assured Stephen earnestly that by so shifting the centre of rotation he was able to make good a course as close as six true points, so that now, with really able seamen at the helm and a prime quartermaster at the con, she could eat the wind out of any seventy-four of her class. 'When you have gazed your fill, come and eat breakfast with me. I have some prodigious fine Minorca bacon, and will set things in train.' He hurried away, and Pullings came up to wish the Doctor a good morning and congratulate him on having seen such a spectacle.

'Now you will really have something to tell your grandchildren,' observed Mowett; and pointing upwards he added, 'And you must not forget the mizen topgallant-staysail, whatever you do.'

'I served eight years with Sir Alan Howarth, and I do suppose he was the greatest flying-kite man in the service,' said Collins, 'but in all that time I never saw the whole shooting-match, not all at once.'

Stephen wondered how long he must in decency go on staring at the whole shooting-match: he smelt bacon, he smelt coffee: he slavered. 'Mr Pullings, my dear,' he began, but at that point the jib of jibs saw fit to part company with its sheet, and in the turmoil Stephen slipped away.

They were still breakfasting in the lavish naval fashion when the mate of the watch came bounding in, rather ahead of Jack's permission so to do. 'Mr Mowett's duty, sir,' he cried, 'and there are four sail of merchantmen fine on the larboard bow.'

'No men-of-war, Mr Honey?'

'Oh no, sir. Great fat greasy merchantmen all hud-dled together, ha, ha, ha!' In the gaiety of his heart Mr Honey laughed aloud, turning it into a cough when he met his Captain's cold eye. Jack dismissed him, and said to Stephen, 'I am afraid I am going to disappoint them cruelly again. But if we are to be off the mouth

211

of the Aiguouille by tomorrow evening there is no time for whoring after prizes.'

'I beg pardon, sir,' said Mowett in the doorway, 'but I am afraid Honey did not report quite right. There are four sail of merchantmen fine on the larboard bow, one of them very large; and if we do not alter course they will be windward of us in half a glass. May I put the ship about?'

'Are you quite certain they are merchantmen?'

'Dead certain, sir,' said Mowett, grinning wide, an amiable wolf.

'Then our course must still be east-north-east a half east.'

'Aye aye, sir,' said Mowett with creditable fortitude, 'east-north-east a half east it is.' The light left his face, and he left the cabin.

'There,' said Jack, 'I was afraid of it. A fine twelve-hour chase, with all hands on deck and every stitch of canvas set and drawing and the bow-guns playing long bowls would have pulled the people together wonderfully after the let-down at Medina. You have heard of it, Stephen?'

'I have too: at intolerable length.'

'I was obliged to disappoint them there . . . or so I thought. They have never been the same since. And for my part I have been most hellish ill-tempered – wake up angry in the morning – vex all too easy throughout the day. Tell me, Stephen, are there pills or draughts against the blue devils and ill-temper? I am most damnably hipped these days, as I am afraid you have noticed.' For a moment he thought of telling Stephen about the suspicion that dwelt in his mind, but recollecting what kind of rendezvous his friend was to keep he only said 'If you have finished, Stephen, pray smoke away. I am sure you bought some of your best mundungus in Mahon.'

'If you are sure you really do not find it disagreeable,' said Stephen, instantly feeling in his pockets, 'I believe I may. For me tobacco is the crown of the meal, the best opening to a day, a great enhancer of the quality of life.

The crackle and yield of this little paper cylinder,' he said, holding it up, 'gives me a sensual pleasure whose deeper origins I blush to contemplate, while the slow combustion of the whole yields a gratification that I should not readily abandon even if it did me harm, which it does not. Far from it. On the contrary, tobacco purges the mind of its gross humours, sharpens the wits, renders the judicious smoker sprightly and vivacious. And soon I shall need all my sprightliness and vivacity.'

'I wish to God you were not going,' said Jack in a low voice.

'There is no option,' said Stephen.

Jack nodded: to be sure, Stephen's landing in some remote creek had as little free choice about it as Jack's carrying his ship into action; yet there was something so horribly cold-blooded about the creek – cold-blooded, dark and solitary. He hated the idea: yet he drove the *Worcester* towards the place where the idea should become reality with all the skill he had acquired in a lifetime at sea. He drove her and her people hard, with jibs and staysails perpetually flashing in and out and with the utmost nicety of weather-helm, himself standing at the con watch after watch. The Worcesters were mystified: but those who understood seamanship were deeply impressed and those who did not were still so much affected by the sense of grave urgency that they too jumped to carry out all orders. He drove her so hard that in the event he made his landfall with hours to spare, intolerably dragging hours in which the *Worcester* stood on and off and the sun crept down the bright western sky. It set at last in a long golden blaze and the ship ran in on a kind but untrustworthy breeze, bringing the darkness with her: yet still another hour had to pass before she was close enough to send a boat off to that flat, desolate shore, and that hour was as burdensome as ten. All the preparations had been made, the letters written, the recommendations repeated several times: Jack fussed with the dark lantern, the blue signalling flare, the pistols, and the patent device

213

for striking a light that Stephen was to take with him. Jack also added a clasp-knife and a few fathoms of stout line. 'I have renewed your pistol flints,' he said again.

Again Stephen thanked him, and looked at his watch: only seven minutes had passed. 'Come,' he said, walked over to his 'cello case and said, 'Let us improvise.'

They growled and squeaked for a few minutes and passed the rosin to and fro; then Stephen struck out a phrase from a Haydn symphony they had heard together, a strange haunting inconclusive phrase, a faintly questioning voice from another world. Jack repeated it: they played it in unison once or twice and then handed it back and forth with an infinity of variations, sometimes by common accord playing together, sometimes separately. Neither was an excellent player but each was competent enough to express much of what he wished to express, and they so conversed without a pause until Pullings came in to say that the ship was in ten-fathom water and that the cutter had been veered astern.

After the lit cabin the deck seemed impenetrably dark, apart from the glow of the binnacles, and unseen hands guided Stephen to the ladder. The *Worcester* carried no top-lights, her great stern-lanterns were cold and unlit, the scuttles and stern-windows of cabin and wardroom had been carefully screened, and she was whispering gently towards the even darker shore through an unseen sea, her sails ghostly overhead: people spoke in undertones.

Stephen heaved himself up on to the rail: someone farther down the ladder set his searching feet on the first rung. He felt Jack's hand reaching for his, shook it, and made his way down into the boat.

A moment later Mowett said 'Shove off.' The *Worcester*'s tall stern moved smoothly on, even darker than the general night, shutting out a great stretch of star-filled sky. 'Give way,' said Mowett, and in a moment the boat was quite alone.

The breeze was coming off the shore, loaded with the scents of land: marsh reek, the smell of dew on reeds, the general smell of green. It was a long pull in but they took it easy: the moon would not rise for above an hour. Nobody spoke and Stephen found that sitting there in the darkness, with the rhythmic plash, the heave, and the sense of motion but of motion quite unseen, had the quality of a dream or more exactly that of another state of consciousness; yet presently his eyes grew used to the night and he could make out the land quite clearly. The starlight seemed to grow stronger, although clouds were drifting across the Milky Way, and he recognized several of the boat's crew – recognized them more from their general shapes then their faces however, or in the case of Fintrum Speldin by the depraved old wool hat from which he was never parted. All sober, discreet, solid men. Bonden, of course, he had known from the first.

'You have your cloak, Doctor?' said Mowett suddenly.

'I have not,' said Stephen. 'Nor do I feel the need of it. Sure it is a warm, even a balmy night.'

'So it is, sir. But I have a feeling the wind may back into the south – look how those clouds turn and tear – and if it does, we shall have rain.'

'The Doctor is sitting on his cloak,' said Bonden. 'I stowed it there myself.'

'Now you can see the tower pretty clear,' observed Mowett after a while. Stephen followed his pointing hand and there indeed the dark tower stood out against the sky, a square Roman tower built when the sea stretched five and even ten miles inland.

They said no more until they heard the small waves breaking and saw the faint line of white stretching out on either hand. 'We are just about a quarter of a mile south of the bar, sir,' said Mowett in a low voice, standing in the boat while the men rested on their oars. 'Would that answer?'

'Perfectly, I thank you,' said Stephen.

Mowett said 'Give way. Stretch out now.' The boat sprang into motion, moving faster and faster until it ran tilting up into the sand, checking with a hissing kiss. The bowman leapt out with a gangboard. Bonden led Stephen over the thwarts, said 'Mind your step, sir,' and he was ashore in France.

Five minutes, while Bonden struck a shaded light, lit Stephen's dark lantern and closed it, hung his other equipment round his neck in a little cloth bag, and made him put on his boat-cloak: then Mowett said very quietly, 'At half after four tomorrow morning in the same place, sir: or failing tomorrow the blue light at midnight and the next day at dawn.'

'Just so,' said Stephen absently. 'Good night to you, now.' He walked up the slope in the yielding sand and as he went he heard the rattle of the gangboard, the boat's kiss in reverse, and the stroke of oars. Where the dunes began he stopped and sat down facing the water. He could see the lapping wavelets as they ran up the shore, and the stars reflected for a great way out, and the horizon; but no ship anywhere at all, nor even the boat. The only sound was the wind over the dunes and the lapping water down there: it was in a way the world at the very beginning – the elements alone, and starlight.

He was extremely unwilling to move. The sense of personal invulnerability that helped at the beginning of the war had left him long ago: he had been a prisoner the last time he was in France and although he had come away unharmed at least two of the French intelligence services had identified him beyond any possibility of a doubt. If he were taken now he could expect no mercy at all: he could not hope to come away untortured or alive. In earlier days he had faced much the same kind of fate, but then there had always been a certain chance of deceiving the other side or of escape: and in those days he was not married – his aims were single-hearted and in any case he cared less about his life.

Directly before him a glow appeared at one point of the horizon: it grew brighter, still brighter, and then the rim of the moon heaved up, almost painfully brilliant to his night-accustomed eyes. When it was clear of the sea,

216

a gibbous, lumpish moon, he held his watch to his ear, pressed the repeater-stem, and counted the minute true chime. Both the watch and the moon told him that it was time to go, and standing up he paced deliberately down to the water's edge, where the wet sand not only made walking less laborious but also held no lasting trace.

Twice he stopped to argue with his unwillingness, and each time he looked out along the moon's path on the water: nothing whatsoever upon the sea, near or far. The bar at the mouth of the Aigouille lay before him at last, a broad strip of sand strewn with bleached tree-trunks: for except at times of flood most of the river stayed in its lagoons and marshes, the rest reaching the sea by a channel no wider than a man could leap. As he came to it he startled a night-heron fishing under the steep-to bank and for some reason the loud, harsh, familiar cry as it flew off, black and white in the moonlight, was a comfort to him. He made the leap successfully, whereas a few moments earlier he had been afraid that the bodily awkwardness that so often accompanies fear might make him blunder; and when he reached the far bank of the river he saw the two lights he was to look for, two lights one above the other far away in the direction of the shooting-box. His gentleman was there, and exact to the time; but to reach him Stephen must skirt the lagoon, following a fisherman's path to a wooded knoll, and then strike across through the reed-beds for the dyke, passing three small pools on his way.

At this end the path was clear enough and firm underfoot: it led him round a tongue of dry land to a shallow inlet full of wading birds that fled away with desolate fluting cries. And indeed, although the marsh gave an impression of silence – silent water gleaming under a silent moon – there was in fact a good deal of sound quite apart from the soughing of the wind in the reeds: over on his left he could hear the sleepy gabble of flamingoes, gooselike but deeper; duck flew overhead quite often, their wings creaking; and at the far edge of the reed-beds that he must traverse to reach the dyke, perhaps a mile away, a bittern began its foghorn song, boom, boom, boom, as regular as a minute-gun. He reached the knoll (an island once) with its tumbledown hut and the eel-traps hanging in a willow-tree: there were rabbits here, and while he was searching for his landmarks he heard one taken by a stoat.

On, and into the reed-beds: here it was night again, with very little moon coming down through the long leaves overhead. There was a path of sorts, and his lantern, unshaded now, showed him a cut reed here and there; but much of the way he had to push through, sometimes striding high over dead or fallen stems, often ankle-deep in ancient-smelling mud, always too hot in the cloak and sadly plagued by the mosquitoes he disturbed in his passage; and in any case there was little certainty about the path; others crossed it or merged with it or forked off, confusing the direction. These were certainly made by wild boars and at one point he heard a band of them moving about, snorting. But boars did not interest him very much: what almost frivolously occupied the top of his mind, riding above his eagerness for the meeting and its success, and above his deep and sometimes almost paralysing sense of fear, was the bittern. He was going directly towards it; the sound was astonishingly loud by now, and he thought the bird might be at the edge of the reeds fringing the next pool, whose far end was formed by the dyke itself. If only he could move quietly enough and if only luck were with him, he might see it standing in the moonlight. Though indeed the moon would not last much longer: every time he looked up out of his dense cover he saw more and more clouds in the sky, and although he could not be sure of the direction they now appeared to be coming from the south.

As far as luck was concerned, it seemed to be with him, decidedly with him so far, for although it was impossible to move without at least some rustling he was getting closer and closer, so close now that he could hear the bird's hoarse straining indraught and the small private

218

note that preceded the enormous boom. The bittern did not mind the noise he made; and perhaps mistaking him for a boar it did not even take fright when a false step sent him splashing knee-deep in the mud. But when a high, nervous voice called from the reeds ahead '*Halte là. Qui vive?*' it instantly fell silent, although it had taken a full breath.

'*Le docteur Ralphe,*' answered Stephen.

The voice made the agreed reply, claiming to be Voltaire, though from the sound it was clear to Stephen that he was an agent named Leclerc. 'I expected to find you on the dyke,' he said, examining Leclerc as the moon shone bright through parting clouds. Leclerc explained that he had heard movements on the farther marsh and that he had felt too visible, perched up there. Only cows, perhaps, but possibly poachers or smugglers – it was a great place for smugglers – and it was wiser not to call attention to himself. He had left the horses at the shooting-box, not liking to ride out, they being so nervous tonight. 'I do not wonder at it,' said Stephen to himself. 'If they have caught half your hurry of spirits they must be fit to take to the air.' Leclerc was a clever fellow, but Stephen would never have chosen him for this assignment; he was a townsman through and through, and townsmen were often ill at ease on a marsh or a mountainside by night. Besides, he had the wrong temperament entirely.

They were on the dyke, and from here the farther marsh could be seen, mostly rough pasture criss-crossed with shining ditches, but with clumps of tamarisks and taller trees here and there as well as great stretches of reed, and in places one could make out the windings of the road to Mandiargues and the canal of the same name. As they walked along Leclerc named the men who had arrived at the rendezvous by the time he left and he was speaking of those who were still expected when two large pure white shapes rose into the air from just under the dyke. 'Oh my God,' he cried, clutching Stephen's elbow. 'What was that?'

'Egrets,' said Stephen. 'And who else besides Pangloss?'

'Martineau and Egmont, as well as the Duroures. It is too many altogether. I was against it from the start. There is always the possibility of an indiscretion, an accident; and gathering so many people, some of whom we hardly know, in such a place as this . . . hush,' he whispered in an urgent voice, thrusting Stephen behind a clump of reeds, 'What is that?'

'Where?'

'On the corner, where the dyke turns to the left. It moves.'

In the shifting moonlight it was difficult to be sure of anything, but after a while Stephen said, 'I take it to be a gate-post with an owl upon it. There: the owl has flown. Pray put your pistol away.'

They walked on, Leclerc speaking of the organizers of this rendezvous with the waspish malignancy of a frightened man, and the gate-post proved to be in fact a lightning-blasted willow-tree. But they had scarcely passed it, they had scarcely turned the corner before there were shots in the marsh below them, a few hundred yards to the right. An exchange of shots from two separate places, orange stabs of flame in the darkness, crashing in a reed-bed over towards the road. A moment's stunned silence and Leclerc cried 'We are sold – betrayed,' and set off at a furious run towards the shooting-box.

Stephen slipped from the dyke and into the reeds, where he stood, listening intently. What he heard puzzled him: it was more the sound of a skirmish with both sides running off rather than that of a determined engagement or a pursuit. A good deal of sporadic shooting and then silence. An indistinct drumming sound, perhaps the galloping of horses a great way off, then nothing more. The clouds finally overcame the moon, and the night grew almost wholly dark.

The south wind, which had been blowing for some time in the higher regions of the air, now came in gusts across the marsh, making a noise like breakers in the tall reeds and bringing with it the first small sweeps of rain. The bittern began again, answered by another a great way off: Stephen pulled the hood of his boat-cloak over his head, against the drips.

When he had waited so long that it was certain that Leclerc was not coming back either on horse or foot Stephen climbed on to the dyke again. He now had to walk bowed against the strong south wind, but even so it was far below and he wanted to get away as soon as ever he could, back to the dunes before any organized search was possible.

Although he was worried by the thought that this wind might very soon work up such a surf that no boat could take him off, the deep and at times almost disabling dread that had been with him earlier had gone. It was less fear than anger, then, that he felt when he was walking along a stretch of dyke with water on either side of it and he saw a faint light ahead, a moving light but moving far too steadily for a will-o'-the-wisp and too clearly defined: almost certainly a lantern like his own, a dark-lantern slightly open.

He was unwilling to slip down into bare water of an uncertain depth, and there were no reed-beds for several hundred yards: indeed this was a singularly bare stretch, the only shelter being some stunted tamarisks. Rather than retreat, losing distance, he plunged into these, and with his hood drawn over his face to hide the whiteness, he crouched there waiting for the light to pass.

As it came nearer he became more and more convinced that it was carried by one man alone, not a party, and that this one man was not a soldier. His step was hesitant and slow, and sometimes he stopped altogether, though he did not appear to look round or search the marsh on either side.

Nearer, and Stephen lowered his eyes. A strong gust of wind, a squall of heavy rain, and clapping his hand to his hat the light-bearer stepped under the lee of the tamarisks and sat down. He was three yards from Stephen and a little beyond him; he sat there hunched with his back to the wind until the rain stopped as suddenly as it had begun. He stood up and they might well have passed if he had not suddenly sat down again, opening his lantern wide to inspect his naked foot. It was covered with mud, but as he wiped the dirt off with his handkerchief a red flow covered the white skin: he tried to staunch it with his neckcloth and in the reflected light Stephen saw Professor Graham's face, closed and hard with pain, but unmistakable.

# CHAPTER EIGHT

Once again the flagship made the approaching *Worcester*'s signal, requiring her captain to repair aboard; and once again Jack Aubrey sat primly on an upright chair in front of the Admiral's desk. But this time he did not sit so near the edge; his conscience was as clear as the pure Mediterranean sky; he had brought mail from Mahon as well as stores, and there was no hint of iciness in the great cabin.

'And so learning that the greater part of the spars had not arrived, sir,' he went on, 'I had the less scruple in complying with Dr Maturin's request that he should proceed to the French coast without delay. Fortunately the breeze served and I was able to set him ashore at the appointed place and time and to take him off the next morning, together with a wounded gentleman, the Mr Graham we carried out as far as Port Mahon.'

'Ah? Well, I am heartily glad you have brought Maturin back so soon: I was anxious for him. He is aboard? Very good, very good: I shall see him directly. But first tell me what they have sent us in the way of spars. I should give my eye-teeth for a comfortable supply of spars.'

Jack provided the Admiral with an exact, detailed account of the spars in question, and the Admiral gave Jack his views on the over-masting of ships, particularly of wall-sided ships, in the Mediterranean: or anywhere else, for that matter. While he was doing so, Dr Maturin and Mr Allen sat in the secretary's cabin, drinking marsala and eating Palermo biscuits. Stephen however was not reporting to Mr Allen – very far from it indeed – but rather offering remarks upon the unfortunate results of divided councils with his own recent expedition as an example. 'A better example you could not wish,' he said, 'for here you have a dark marsh with difficult, obscure paths – a pretty figure for this kind of warfare – and over these difficult obscure paths you have two bodies of men approaching one another in the black night, both moving to much the same rendezvous, both actuated by much the same motives, but neither knowing of the other's existence – they blunder into one another – mutual terror, foolish terror, flight – and the utter ruin of at least one carefully elaborated plan, to say nothing of the suspicions of indiscretion if not of downright treachery that make the renewing of contact almost impossible.'

'The man Graham must be a great fool,' observed Allen, 'A busy, pernicious fool.'

'I have expressed myself badly, I find,' said Stephen. 'I intended no reflection upon the individual, only upon a system that allows still another department of Government to set up an intelligence service of its own, working in isolation from the others and sometimes in its ignorance even directly against them. No, no: Professor Graham has shining parts. He was the gentleman responsible for the capitulation of Colombo, which made such a noise in its time.'

Allen was a newcomer to Intelligence in this restricted sense and he looked surprisingly blank for so clever a man; his lips silently formed the word Colombo twice; and Stephen said, 'Allow me to refresh your memory. When that Buonaparte seized Holland we seized, or attempted to seize, the Dutch possessions abroad, including of course those in Ceylon. The fortification of Colombo, the key to the whole position, threatened to present insuperable difficulties, particularly as the garrison was Swiss; for as the world in general knows the Swiss, if duly paid, are not easily dislodged nor yet bribed, persuaded, or overawed. Furthermore, the place was commanded by Hercule de Meuron, a Swiss officer of the most eminent military genius. But he was also an acquaintance of Mr Graham's, a close acquaintance as I understand it, even an intimate. Graham proceeds

224

to Colombo disguised as a Turk, enters into contact with Meuron by means of a message concealed – elegant stroke – in a Dutch cheese – reasons with him – convinces him – the Swiss march out, the English march in, and Buonaparte is denied the resources of Ceylon. What means Graham used I do not know, but I am morally certain that it was not money.'

'He must be an eloquent gentleman.'

'To be sure. But my immediate point is that he is also eloquent in Turkish: he is a Turkish scholar, and that is why I have brought him, so that he may be presented to the Admiral.'

'A trustworthy Turkish scholar would be unspeakably welcome – a Godsend. At present we have to make do with a most pitiful ancient one-eyed Greek eunuch and Dupin's chrestomathy. But would Mr Graham ever consent to serve?'

'Mr Graham has no choice. He quite understands that in natural justice he is now my property, my lawful prize; and when I desired him to remain aboard rather than leave the ship at Mahon he submitted without a murmur. After all, poaching on my preserve, the enemy coast, he undid all my careful legitimate web; and I took him off that coast, at very considerable inconvenience to myself since I had to prop him for miles through an evil bog, and at very great danger indeed to those devoted souls who came in through the surf – and such surf! – at the very minute of appointed time, while the horse-patrols were already searching the dunes, the country having been aroused by all that foolish running about and banging in the night. Nine several times they had to come in, now sideways, now backwards, at infinite peril, before they could fetch him away, and he lashed to a grating, three parts smothered in that universal roaring foam.'

Professor Graham still looked if not three parts smothered then at least very humble, very much reduced, when he was first brought limping aboard the flagship. His spirits revived a little when he was away from Stephen, whom he had so injured and to whom he owed such a burden of gratitude; but although he held a chair in no mean university it was long before he could recover his academic pride and sufficiency, since every time he put his stocking on or off he was reminded of his ignominious wound – for stumbling with a cocked pistol in his hand he had blasted off his little toe. Yet in the flagship he was once again the king of his company as far as moral philosophy was concerned, to say nothing of Turkish, Arabic, and modern Greek, and once more he was surrounded by the Navy's perhaps somewhat excessive respect for erudition, particularly classical erudition: and Stephen, coming across from a *Worcester* that had settled back into the monotonous routine of blockade, found a Professor Graham who had settled back into at least the appearance of his habitual self-esteem.

'I am come on behalf of the *Worcester*'s wardroom to invite you to dinner tomorrow,' he said.

'Honest fellows,' said Graham. 'I shall be happy to see them again so soon. I had not looked to visit the ship before the performance.'

'*Hamlet* is delayed once more, I am sorry to say; but the oratorio is in great forwardness – Mr Martin has come across several times to put a final polish to the shriller parts – and I believe we may hear it at last on Sunday. We expect a numerous audience, Mr Thornton having signified his approval.'

'Very good, very good: I shall be happy to be among them. And I shall be happy to dine with the *Worcester*'s wardroom again – a homelike gathering. It is still the same nest of genteel harmony, I make no doubt?'

'It is not, sir. As every schoolboy knows, the same grove cannot contain two nightingales: nor can the same wardroom contain two poets. It most unhappily appears that Mr Rowan, whom you will remember as the gentleman who attached you to the grating, sees fit to set up in rivalry with Mr Mowett; and what Mr Rowan may lack in talent he makes up in facility of composition and in fearless declamation. He has a considerable following, and the young gentlemen repeat his verses more readily than Mr Mowett's. Yet he is not satisfied with his performance and this morning he showed me these lines,' said Stephen, pulling a roll of paper from his pocket, 'desiring me to correct them: and if at the same time I could furnish him with some learned expressions he would be uncommonly obliged. For various reasons I declined the honour, but seeing his candid ingenuous disappointment I said that the squadron contained no more learned man than Professor Graham and that if he pleased I should carry the verses with me to the flagship. He was delighted. He submits himself entirely to your judgement, and begs you to strike out whatever does not please.'

Mr Graham pursed his lips, took the roll, and read

> But on arrival at the fleet's anchorage, there
> A very sad story we next did hear,
> That Buenos Ayres had been retaken
> And our little army very much shaken.
> But a small reinforcement from the Cape
> Induced the Commodore to try a feat
> To reduce Monte Video was his intent
> But which proved abortive in the event.

'You have begun at the end,' observed Stephen.

'Is the beginning of the same nature?' asked Graham.

'Rather more so, perhaps,' said Stephen.

'Clearly I am under great obligation to Mr Rowan,' said Graham, looking through the other pages with a melancholy air. 'But I am ashamed to say that as I was dragged through the surf I did not distinguish him as clearly as I should have done: is he indeed the very cheerful round-faced black-eyed gentleman, somewhat positive and absolute at table, who so often laughed and gambolled among the ropes with the midshipmen?'

'Himself.'

'Aye. Well, I shall do what I can for him, of course;

though the correction of verses is a thankless task.' Graham shook his head, whistling in an undertone and reflecting that perhaps being rescued was an expensive amusement; then he smiled and said, 'Speaking of midshipmen reminds me of young Milo of Crotona and his daily struggle with the bull-calf, and of his particular friend, the tow-haired boy Williamson. Pray, how do they come along, and how does the bull-calf do?'

'The bull-calf now luxuriates in whatever part of the vessel may be appropriate, eating the bread of idleness, since it has become so much a part of the ship's daily life that there can be no question of slaughtering it, nor even of castrating it, so that in time we shall no doubt have a very froward guest in the *Worcester*'s bowels. Yet it is Mr Williamson that gives me more immediate anxiety. As you may have heard, mumps is got into the ship, brought by a Maltese lad in a victualler; and Mr Williamson was the first and most thorough-going case.'

Mr Graham could never have been described as a merry companion: few things amused him at all and fewer still to the pitch of open mirth; but mumps was one of these rarities and he now uttered an explosive barking sound.

'It is no laughing matter,' said Stephen, privily wiping Graham's saliva from his neckcloth. 'Not only is our *Hamlet* brought to a halt for want of an Ophelia – for Mr Williamson was the only young gentleman with a tolerable voice – but the poor boy is in a fair way to becoming an alto, a counter-tenor for life.'

'Hoot,' said Graham, grinning still. 'Does the swelling affect the vocal cords?'

'The back of my hand to the vocal cords,' said Stephen. 'Have you not heard of orchitis? Of the swelling of the cods that may follow mumps?'

'Not I,' said Graham, his smile fading.

'Nor had my messmates,' said Stephen, 'though the Dear knows it is one of the not unusual sequelae of *cynanche parotidaea*, and one of real consequence to men. Yet to be sure there is something to be said in its

228

favour, as a more humane way of providing castrati for our choirs and operas.'

'Does it indeed emasculate?' cried Graham.

'Certainly. But be reassured: that is the utmost limit of its malignance. I do not believe that medical history records any fatal issue – a benign distemper, compared with many I could name. Yet Lord, how concerned my shipmates were, when I told them, for surprisingly few seem to have had the disease in youth –'

'I did not,' said Graham, unheard.

'Such anxiety!' said Stephen, smiling at the recollection. 'Such uneasiness of mind! One might have supposed it was a question of the bubonic plague. I urged them to consider how very little time was really spent in coition, but it had no effect. I spoke of the eunuch's tranquillity and peace of mind, his unimpaired intellectual powers – I cited Narses and Hermias. I urged them to reflect that a marriage of minds was far more significant than mere carnal copulation. I might have saved my breath: one could almost have supposed that seamen lived for the act of love.'

'The mumps is a contagious disease, I believe?' said Graham.

'Oh eminently so,' said Stephen absently, remembering Jack's grave, concerned expression, the grave concerned expressions in the wardroom, and upon the faces of a delegation from the gunroom that waited on him to learn what they could do to be saved; and smiling again he said, 'If eating were an act as secret as the deed of darkness, or *fugging*, as they say in their sea-jargon, would it be so obsessive, so omnipresent, the subject of almost all wit and mirth?'

Professor Graham, however, had moved almost to the very end of the *Ocean*'s empty wardroom, where he stood with his face by an open scuttle; and as Stephen approached he limped swiftly towards the door, pausing there to say, 'Upon recollection, I find I am compelled to decline the *Worcester*'s wardroom's most polite and obliging invitation, because of a previous engagement. You will present my best compliments and tell the gentlemen how much I regret not seeing them tomorrow.'

'They will be disappointed, I am sure,' said Stephen. 'But there is always the oratorio. You will see them all at the oratorio, on Sunday evening.'

'On *Sunday* evening?' cried Graham. 'Heuch: how unfortunate. I fear I cannot reconcile it with my conscience to be present at a public exhibition or display on the Sabbath, not even a performance that is far from profane; and must beg to be excused.'

Sunday evening came closer. Thursday, Friday, and on Saturday the mistral, which had been blowing for three days, setting the squadron far to the south of its usual station, suddenly shifted several points and turned dirty, bringing black cloud and rain-showers from the east-north-east. 'It will soon blow out,' said the harmonious Worcesters as they gathered, necessarily under hatches, for their grand dress-rehearsal. It had not been represented to them that neither costume nor action was usual in an oratorio, but as the sailmaker said, 'If we have no wimming to sing, we must have costumes: it stands to reason.' They certainly had no wimming, for the three or four warrant- and petty-officers' wives aboard were negligible quantities in the article of song (the oratorio was therefore strangely truncated) and the costumes were a matter of great concern to all the *Worcester*'s people. Although ship-visiting was discouraged in the squadron on blockade a good deal of intercourse in fact took place: it was perfectly well known, for example, that the *Orion*, having pressed the male part of a bankrupt travelling circus, had a fire-eater aboard and two jugglers, amazing in calm weather, while the *Canopus*'s weekly entertainments were always opened and closed by dancers that had appeared on the London stage. The *Worcester* passionately longed to wipe *Orion*'s eye, as well as *Canopus*'s; and since a large audience was expected, the Admiral having publicly, emphatically expressed his approval of the oratorio, it was absolutely essential that this audience should be struck all of a heap:

and elegant refined costumes were to do some of the striking.

Unhappily the victualler carrying the Aleppo muslin ordered from Malta was intercepted by a French privateer – it now adorned the whore-ladies of Marseilles – while Gibraltar sent nothing whatsoever; and the day came nearer with no elegant refined costumes within a thousand miles and all the purser's duck irrevocably turned into common slops long since. The sailmaker and his mates, indeed the whole ship's company, began to look wistfully at the rarely-used light and lofty sails, the kites, skyscrapers, royal and topgallant studdingsails: but the *Worcester* was a taut ship, a very taut ship; her Captain had already proved that he knew every last thing about capperbar, or the misappropriation of Government stores, and with the squadron so short of everything and so far from sources of supply it was impossible that he would tolerate even a modest degree of innocent theft. However, they sounded Mr Pullings, who was obviously concerned with the success of the performance and the honour of the ship, and at the same time they made devious approaches to the Captain by means of Bonden and Killick, to Dr Maturin through a small black boy who acted as his servant, and to Mr Mowett by 'ingenuous' requests for advice as to how to proceed. The whole matter had therefore been present in Jack's mind – present in the atmosphere and with a favourable bias – well before he was called upon to make a decision, and the decision came out with all the directness that the seamen looked for: any God-damned swab – any man that presumed to tamper with any sail, however thin, however worn in the bunt or chafed in the bands, should have his ears nailed to a four-inch plank and be set adrift with half a pound of cheese. On the other hand, there were seven untouched bolts of number eight canvas, and if Sails and his crew liked to shape the cloths for a fair-weather suit of upper sails, that might do the trick. Sails did not seem to comprehend: he looked stupid and despondent. 'Come, Sails,' said Jack, 'How

231

many two-foot cloths do you need for a main royal?'

'Seventeen at the head and twenty-two at the foot, your honour.'

'And how deep are they?'

'Seven and a quarter yards, not counting the tabling or the gores: which is all according.'

'Why then, there you are. You fold your cloth four times, tack a couple of grommets to each clew of the open ends, clap it over your shoulders fore and aft and there you are in an elegant refined costume in the classical taste very like a toga, and all without cutting canvas or wronging the ship.'

It was in these costumes then that they gathered for the dress rehearsal: but although the togas were not a week old they had already lost their classical simplicity. Many were embroidered, all had ribbons neatly sewn into the seams, and the general aim seemed to be to outdo *Orion*'s feathers and tinsel as quickly as possible – the cooper and his friends had come out in gilded keg-hoops by way of crowns. Yet although the choir looked a little strange, and would look stranger by far given time and leisure, they made a fine body of sound as they sang away, all crammed together below with the deck touching the cooper's crown, the taller men's heads, but so deep in the music that the discomfort counted for nothing.

In spite of the foul weather Captain Aubrey heard them on the wind-swept, rain-swept, spray-swept quarterdeck. He was not an extremely amorous man: hours or even days might pass without his thinking of women at all. But even so he had no notion of the eunuch's tranquillity and although he did his duty, visiting the sick-bay daily and standing doggedly by the cases of mumps for three full minutes he tended to avoid his friend Maturin, who wandered about in a most inconsiderate way, as though he did not mind spreading infection – as though it were all one to him if the entire ship's company piped like choir-boys rather than roaring away in this eminently manly fashion, so that the *Worcester*'s beams vibrated under foot. He stood by the weather-rail with his back to the rain, partly sheltered by the break of the poop, wearing a griego with the hood pulled up, and he stared forward in the dim late afternoon light at the *Orion*, his next ahead on the larboard tack, as the squadron stood westward under close-reefed topsails with the wind two points free: part of his mind was considering the effects of resonance and the harmonics of the hull, the singers being in rather than on the sound-box, while the rest concentrated upon the *Worcester*'s mainmast. This massive piece of timber, a hundred and twelve feet long and more than a yard across where it rose from the deck, complained every time the ship lifted to the short steep seas under her larboard bow. Fortunately there was no topgallantmast aloft to add its leverage on the roll, nor any great press of canvas, but even so the mast was suffering. He would give it another preventer travelling backstay, and if that did not answer he would turn to his old caper of getting light hawsers to the mastheads, however uncouth it might look. But the whole ship was suffering for that matter, not only the masts: the *Worcester* hated this particularly Mediterranean rhythm that caught her between two paces as it were, so she could neither trot easy nor canter, but had to force her way through the sea with one reef more out of her topsails than her better-built companions, many of them from French or Spanish yards.

Yet although hawsers might secure the masts, holding them even more strongly to the hull, if the *Worcester* did not mind looking lumpish and untidy, what measures could secure the hull itself? As Jack listened below the oratorio, below the complaining of the masts, below the innumerable voices of the sea and the wind right down to the deep confused groaning of the timbers themselves, out of tune and unhappy, he reflected that if she could not be provided with new knees in the course of a thorough refit he might eventually have to frap her whole carcass, winding cable round and round until it looked like an

233

enormous chrysalis. The idea made him smile, and smile all the wider since the choir forward had worked their way to their favourite chorus, and were now topping it the Covent Garden with all their might – with infinite relish, too. 'Halleluiah,' sang their Captain with them as a fresh sheet of rain struck the ship, drumming on the back of his hood, 'halleluiah,' until an unmistakable gunshot to leeward cut his note short and at the same moment the lookout hailed 'Sail ho! Sail on the larboard quarter.'

Jack plunged across the deck to the lee rail, helped on his way by the *Worcester*'s roll and lurch: hammocks had not been piped up that soaking day and there was no barrier between him and the sea to the southward. Yet nothing could he make out: he and Mowett, who had the watch, stood there searching the thick grey squall of rain.

'Just abaft the mizen backstay, sir,' called Pullings from the maintop, where he too had been sheltering from Dr Maturin: and the veil parting both Jack and Mowett cried out '*Surprise!*'

*Surprise* she was, far to leeward, so far and so directly to leeward that with all her fine sailing qualities she could never hope to join the squadron for a great while: but it was clear that she meant the squadron to join her, for as they watched she fired another gun and let fly her topsail sheets. At this distance and in this light and with this wind Jack could not make out the signal flying from her foremasthead, but he had no doubt whatsoever of its meaning. The French fleet was out: the frigate's entire appearance and all her behaviour said so in the loudest voice – her frightful press of sail (topgallants in this close-reef topsail breeze!), her wild conduct with her sheets and guns and now a blue light streaking away down the wind, could only mean one thing. The enemy was at sea, and the moment the signal reached the Admiral the line would wear round on to the starboard tack and bear up for the *Surprise*, to learn what more she might have to say.

'All hands to wear ship,' he cried: and the signal midshipman, who had had the wit not to take his eyes from the brig stationed outside the line to repeat signals from the almost invisible *Ocean*, bawled 'Flag to squadron, sir: *wear in succession: course south-east*' over the roaring of the bosun. Hollar and his senior mate, who both loathed Handel, happened to be on the poop ladder at the moment of Jack's order: they now raced forward towards the unconscious choir, towards the vigorous crescendo, the one shouting 'Rouse out, you nightingales' and the other piping 'All hands wear ship' with such force as almost to burst his silver call.

Seconds later, in a strange blank silence, the nightingales came flooding aft to their appointed stations. All the right sailors among them had discarded their togas, but a few of the landsmen had not, while the cooper still had his crown on his head. It so happened that his place was at the foresheet and that two of the togaed figures clapped on just behind him: they were all men of slow comprehension and they looked amazed, aggrieved, and so ludicrous that Jack laughed aloud, they being in his field of vision as he looked beyond them for the first movement of *Ocean*'s helm. His heart was bubbling high: that old splendid feeling of more, far more than common life.

The ships bore down on the distant frigate, packing on more sail as they went; and the moment the *Worcester* was settled on her new course Jack sent for the bosun, desired him to lay along the long-disused topgallantmasts – 'we shall need 'em soon, Mr Hollar, ha, ha, ha' – and explained his wishes about light hawsers to the mastheads. These wishes were not entirely new to the service: it was known that Lord Cochrane and Captain Aubrey and one or two other commanders had achieved surprising feats with these same hawsers: but the service as a whole was dead against them as innovations, ugly, untidy innovations, worthy of privateersmen or even, God forbid, of pirates. It needed very great authority or a peerage or preferably both to impose them on an old experienced

235

bosun, and the *Surprise* was quite near at hand before Hollar moved off, at least outwardly convinced that the *Worcester* must disgrace herself in appearance if, during the probable chase of the French fleet, she were not to disgrace herself in performance. The bosun done with, Jack looked across the water at the *Surprise*, and he observed with satisfaction that this was not a sea in which a boat could be launched, while the wind would make signalling slow and difficult: word of mouth it would surely be, and those without scruples might perhaps overhear the exchange between the frigate and the flagship.

The squadron heaved to: the *Surprise* worked as close alongside the *Ocean* as she dared and delivered her information in a roar that could be heard by the ships, the openly listening ships, well ahead and astern. Latham of the *Surprise* had a tremendous voice, and the Captain of the Fleet, speaking for the Admiral, an even louder one; but their brief conversation did not quite reach the *Worcester*. However, in this atmosphere of the utmost excitement, formality and even hard feeling went by the board, and as soon as the flag had signalled the new course together with the order *Make all sail with safety to the masts*, Wodehouse of the *Orion* appeared at the taffrail of his ship and hailed Jack, poised on the *Worcester*'s starboard cathead: the French were out with seventeen of the line, six of them three-deckers, and with five frigates. They had still been steering south when Admiral Mitchell sent the *Surprise* away in search of the squadron while he continued dogging them in the *San Josef*, detaching other messengers from time to time. From the greater zeal with which the French frigates had chased her to eastward, *Surprise* believed that the French fleet meant to go either to Sicily or right up the Mediterranean for Egypt or Turkey; but on being pressed admitted that this was little more than a guess.

'What is all this I hear about the French being out?' cried Stephen, suddenly appearing on the crowded quarterdeck in the midst of the swaying-up of the topgallantmasts and the sending of hawsers aloft, two delicate, complex, dangerous manoeuvres that called for all the skilled hands in the ship, an immense quantity of ropes, thick and thin, and, in this strong breeze and awkward sea, very exact timing and instant obedience to orders.

Stephen did not address himself directly to Captain Aubrey, who was standing by the windward hances, his eyes fixed on the maintopmast crosstrees, for that would have been improper; but Captain Aubrey had no such inhibitions and instantly roared out 'Go below, Doctor. Go below directly.'

Quite shocked by the vehemence of his cry Stephen turned: but even as he turned a party of seamen ran the stiff end of a cablet into his side, thrusting him under the fiferail and calling out 'By your leave, sir, by your leave,' as they did so. And as he was disentangling himself from the belaying-pins he happened to loop a fancy-line about his ankle and walk off with it until his old friend Tom Pullings bawled 'Stop playing with that fancy-line, and go below' with a ferocity that might have daunted Beelzebub.

It was the edge of darkness before he ventured up again, and then only because of a kindly message: 'The Captain's compliments and if the Doctor should wish to take the air, all was now cleared away and coiled down.'

There was air in plenty on deck: for the moment it was no longer mixed with rain, and it was coming in over the starboard rail even faster and in greater quantities than before. Jack shared the general belief that infection was far less to be dreaded in the open than between decks and he invited Stephen over to the windward side: in any event his mind was so eagerly aglow with life and the anticipation of battle – of a great decisive fleet action – that it had little time for disease. 'They are out with seventeen of the line,' he said. 'Give you joy of our prospects.'

'Is there a real likelihood of our finding them? We are sailing towards the east, I see,' said Stephen, nodding in the direction of the bloody remains of sunset on the *Worcester*'s starboard bow.

237

'Westwards, I believe, if you will forgive me,' said Jack. 'It appears that the sun is usually found to set westerly, in the Mediterranean.'

Stephen rarely suffered facetiousness patiently, but now he only said 'West, I mean. Are you persuaded they have gone to the westward?'

'I hope so, indeed. Had they meant to go up the Mediterranean I should have expected them to take some transports along; but according to *Surprise* there was nothing but men-of-war, and I am sure Latham took her in close enough to make certain. If we are wrong, and if they are destroying Sicily and our positions in the east while we are running west, there will be the Devil to pay and no pitch hot; but I trust the Admiral. He thinks they are making for the Atlantic, and he has shaped a course to intercept them somewhere north of Cape Cavaleria.'

'Do you think we shall do so? And if we do, can we attack seventeen with no more than twelve?'

'I believe we may see them in the morning. Any squadron bound for the Straits with this wind is very likely to pass within ten or fifteen leagues of Cavaleria. And as for the odds,' said Jack, laughing, 'I am sure the Admiral would not give a damn if they were twice as great. Besides, there will be Mitchell in *San Josef* together with what he has left of the inshore squadron, hanging on Emeriau's heels. No: if all goes as I hope it will go, we may bring them to action tomorrow.'

'God send we may,' said Stephen.

'A decisive action would clear the Mediterranean. We could go to America, and the Admiral could go home. Lord, how it would set him up. He would be a new man! So should I, for that matter. A decisive action, Stephen! It sets you up amazingly.'

'It might stop the war,' said Stephen. 'A decisive victory at this point might stop the war. Tell me, why do not you –'

'Turn the glass and strike the bell,' cried the quarter-master at the con.

238

'Turn the glass and strike the bell it is,' replied the Marine, stepping forward to the belfry.

At the second stroke a midshipman, wet from heaving the log, reported the ship's speed to the officer of the watch; he was followed by the carpenter, who reported the depth of water in the pump-well; and each time Mr Collins, the officer of the watch, paced across to Jack, took off his hat, and repeated the information: 'Eight knots and one fathom, sir, if you please.' 'Two foot eleven inches in the well, sir, if you please, and gaining fast.'

'Thank you, Mr Collins,' said Jack. 'Pray let the forward pumps be shipped as well.' Nearly three foot of water down there already: it was eighteen inches more than he had expected, although he knew that the ship had been working very heavily this last glass and more. They had already taken all the measures that could be taken at sea, and the only thing to do now was to pray that the chain pumps would not refuse their duty: though he might conceivably divert the stuffing-box pump . . . 'I beg your pardon?' he said.

'Why do we go no faster? Sure, this is a respectable pace for a common voyage, but with such an end in view should we not outstrip the wind – spread all sails we possess?'

'Well, the Admiral might take it amiss if we were to leave him behind: he lays down this rate of sailing so that even the slugs can just keep up. But what is much more to the point, what a set of clinchpoops we should look, was we to raise Cavaleria before the French. Always provided they come this way,' he added, bowing to Fate.

'But surely, surely,' cried Stephen, 'if you wish to stop an enemy, is it not best to throw yourself into his path – to be there first?'

'Oh dear me no,' said Jack. 'Not at sea. It would never answer at sea. Why, if the wind were to stay true, and if we were to reach Cape Cavaleria first, we should be throwing away all the advantage of the weather-gage. Mr Collins: we may come up the foresheet half a fathom, if you please.' He paced along the starboard gangway to the forecastle, gazing up at the sails, feeling the rigging – Hollar, though an excellent bosun in most respects, had a passion for smartness, for dead-straight shrouds and backstays, and whatever Jack might say he would set up the standing rigging so iron-taut that the masts were in danger of being wrung. All was well at present, however. Poor Hollar's pride had been brought so low by the hawsers to the mastheads that he had not taken his usual surreptitious heave at the lanyards and the shrouds were reasonably pliant. The hawsers and the hairy cablets did indeed look heavy, lumpish and untidy with these Irish pennants all along – not perhaps unseamanlike, but something that no crack spit-and-polish ship could bear for a moment. Yet on the other hand they did allow the *Worcester* to send up topgallantmasts without danger of rolling them by the board and above all to carry a fair press of sail. She had the wind on her starboard quarter, where she liked it best, and with her present trim she seemed to be running quite easy: but in fact she was still hauling under the chains – her seams opened on the upward roll and closed on the downward – and she was making much more water than she should. The main and forward pumps, turning steadily, were flinging two fine thick jets to leeward: the *Worcester* usually pumped ship for at least an hour a day even in calm weather and all hands were thoroughly used to the exercise. The larboard watch had the deck at present, and as Jack made his tour he saw that they had not forgiven him for Barka. It was not that there was any deliberate want of respect nor the least sign of discontent. Far from it: the men were in high spirits at the notion of meeting the French fleet, full of fun in spite of the disappointment over the oratorio. But as far as Jack was concerned there was a certain reserve. Intercourse between captain and lower deck was limited even in an unrated vessel with so small a crew that the commander knew each man intimately; there was no freedom of exchange, far less any flow of soul: in a ship of the line

240

with above six hundred hands the apparent interchange was even less. Yet for those attuned to it the language of eye, face and bodily attitude is tolerably expressive and Jack knew very well where he stood with those Worcesters who had not sailed with him before, the majority of the crew and particularly of the larboard watch. It was a pity, since the ship's efficiency as a fighting-machine was affected; but there was nothing he could do about it at this stage, and walking back to Stephen he said, 'Sometimes I wonder whether I express myself clearly; sometimes I wonder whether I make my meaning plain. I am not at all sure that you understand the weather-gage, even now.'

'You have often mentioned it,' said Stephen.

'Well now,' said Jack, 'consider one line of battle to windward and another to leeward. It is clear that the ships to windward, those that have the weather-gage, can force the action and decide when it shall take place. They can bear down when they choose; and then again their smoke, going to leeward before them, hides them, which is a great point when you come within musket-shot. You may say that with a heavy sea running and a close-reefed topsail breeze the windward ships cannot easily open their lower gun-ports as they come down, because they heel so; and that is profoundly true: but then on the other hand the squadron that has the weather-gage can break the enemy's line!'

'I am sure he can,' said Stephen.

'For example, the Admiral could order every other ship to pass through and so double up the Frenchman's van, two of ours engaging each one of his on either side, destroying or taking them before his rear division can come up, and then serving them the same way – not a single one to be left unsunk, unburnt, untaken! And you would fling all this away just for the satisfaction of being there first? It is rank treason.'

'I only threw out the remark,' said Stephen. 'I am no great naval strategist.'

'Sometimes I wonder whether you have really grasped

that it is the wind alone that moves us. You have often suggested that we should charge to the right or the left as the case might be, just as though we were flaming cavalry, and could go where we chose. I wonder you have not improved your time at sea better; you have, after all, seen a certain amount of action.'

'It may be that my genius, though liberal, is more of the land-borne kind. But you are also to consider, that whenever there is a battle, I am required to stay below stairs.'

'Yes,' said Jack, shaking his head, 'it is very unfortunate, very unfortunate indeed,' and in a gentler tone he asked whether Stephen would like to hear of a battle, ideal in all its stages – remote approach, inception, prosecution, and termination – the kind of battle the squadron might engage in tomorrow if the Admiral had guessed right about the Frenchmen's direction and if the wind remained true – 'for you must understand that everything, *everything* at sea depends on the wind.'

'I am fully persuaded of it, my dear; and should be happy to hear of our ideal encounter with Monsieur Emeriau.'

'Well then, let us suppose that the wind holds true and that we have calculated our course and our speed correctly – I may say that Mr Gill and I came to the same answer independently, give or take two miles – and that we have done the same for the French, which is probable, since they have two or three dull sailers with them, *Robuste*, *Borée* and maybe *Lion*, whose performance we know very well; and their squadron can sail no faster than the slowest. So we stand on all night in this loose formation, keeping our eyes fixed most religiously upon the Admiral's toplight when he hoists it; then at first light one of the frigates out ahead, and I do hope it will be dear *Surprise* – look, she is moving up to take her station now. She refitted at Cadiz, and they did wonders for her – brand-new knees, stringers, cant-pieces . . . how she flies.'

242

'She seems to be coming dangerously close to us,' observed Stephen, having stared for a while.

'I dare say Latham has thought of something witty to say about our hawsers and the Irish pennants. He has been peering at us through his glass this last hour and more, and cackling with his officers,' said Jack. 'Lord, how he does crack on! She must be making a clear thirteen knots off the reel – look at the feather she throws, Stephen.' He gazed fondly at his old command as she came racing through the gloom, all white sails, white bow-wave, white wake against the greyness; but the look of loving admiration vanished when she drew alongside, taking the wind out of the *Worcester*'s sails and checking her pace with a started sheet just long enough for Captain Latham to make an offer of his bosun's services, in case *Worcester* should wish to deal with all those Irish pennants.

'From the look of your rigging, I should never have thought you had a single seaman aboard, let along a bosun,' replied Jack with the full force of his lungs.

The Worcesters uttered a triumphant roar at this, and anonymous voices from open ports below begged to know whether they might favour *Surprise* with any ewes – an obvious and wounding reference to a recent court-martial in which the frigate's barber was sentenced to death for bestiality.

'That settled Latham's hash, I believe,' said Jack with quiet satisfaction as the *Surprise*, having run out of wit, filled and shot ahead.

'What did he mean with his Irish pennants?' asked Stephen.

'Those untidy flakes and wefts of hemp on the hawsers. They would be intolerably slipshod in regular rigging – there, do you see, and there. We call them Irish pennants.'

'Do you, indeed? Yet they are utterly unknown in Irish ships; and when they are perceived in others, they are universally termed Saxon standards.'

'Call 'em what you like, they are damned ill-looking uncouth objects and I knew very well the squadron would laugh and come it the satirical; but I will be b—d if I have a topmast carry away and so miss all the fun, and I will be damned if the Admiral throws out our signal to make more sail. And with a wall-sided, weak-kneed ship what can you . . . There goes his toplight, by the way.' Jack cocked his ear to the poop: he heard the utterly reliable Pullings' voice say 'Bear a hand now, and wipe *Orion*'s eye,' and the golden effulgence of the *Worcester*'s three stern lanterns lit the mizen topsail and the maincourse several seconds before those of any other ship in the squadron.

'You were telling me of your ideal battle, with a view to illustrating naval strategy,' said Stephen.

'Yes. The frigates tell us that the enemy is there under our lee – for the wind has stayed true, do you see – preferably straggling over a couple of miles of sea in two or three untidy heaps, as foreigners do, with the land no great way off to hamper their movements and to make it even easier for Admiral Thornton to decide the moment for the action. My bet is that he will instantly make a dash for it, before they can form their line – bear down immediately, forming our own as we go, double on his weakest part and so work up, taking, burning or sinking as we go. For it will take them a great while to make an orderly line, whereas we do so every day, and we practise the manoeuvre from the dispersed positions at least twice a week. Every man will slip into his place; and since the Admiral has explained his plans for half a dozen situations every man will know just what he is to do. There will be little signalling. The Admiral dislikes it except in the greatest emergency, and the last time he spoke to the captains he said that if any one of us was puzzled or could not make out the order of battle because of the smoke, he might take it upon himself to engage the nearest Frenchman yardarm to yardarm. But there are fewer of us, and since we must be able to compel a perhaps unwilling enemy to accept battle just when and where it suits us, all this, you understand, depends on our having the weather-gage: that is to say, that the wind shall blow from us to them. Lord, Stephen, I shall not be satisfied with anything under twenty prizes, and a dukedom for the Admiral.'

'Sure, I take your point about the wind,' said Stephen in a sombre voice. Although he longed for the final overthrow and destruction of Buonaparte and his whole system, the immediate prospect of huge slaughter depressed him extremely – apart from anything else his duties during battle and after it brought him to be intimately acquainted with war's most hideous side and with young men maimed; he did not mention this, however, but after a pause he asked 'Twenty? That is more than Monsieur Emeriau has with him.'

Jack had named the impossible number by way of conjuring fate: in fact he expected a very severe encounter indeed, for although from want of keeping the sea the French were often slow in manoeuvring, their gunnery was sometimes deadly accurate, and their ships were solid, well-found and new; but he was aware of what was in his friend's mind and he was about to pass his twenty off as a slip of the tongue when the *Renown*, quarter of a mile away on the *Worcester*'s starboard bow, hoisted a string of coloured lanterns to tell the Admiral that she was overpressed with sail.

'Overpressed with sail,' said Jack. 'And she will not be the only one. We shall see a good many topgallants gone in the morning, if the breeze keeps freshening like this, working up an ugly sea.'

'It is shockingly rough indeed. Even I have to cling on with both hands,' said Stephen, and as he spoke a packet of mixed water and froth struck the side of his face, running down inside his shirt. He considered for a while and added, 'Poor Graham will be in a sad way: *he* has not yet learnt the lithe gliding motion of the seaman. *He* has not learnt to anticipate the billow's force.'

'Perhaps you should turn in, Stephen. You may need all your strength tomorrow. I will have you called the moment the French fleet is seen, never fear – I promise you shall miss nothing.'

Yet the sun rose and no one woke Dr Maturin. A thin grey damp light straggled down to the cabin where he swung in his damp cot, dripped or even squirted upon each time the *Worcester* rolled, and still he lay, almost comatose after eight sleepless, tossing hours and then at last a small glass of laudanum. A more than usually violent lee-lurch sent a positive jet of water through the ship's side as her timbers opened and closed under the strain; and the jet, striking him in the face, plucked him from a dream of whales into the present world, and he woke with a confused sense of extreme urgency.

Sitting up and clinging to the lengths of baize-covered man-rope that had kindly been provided for his getting in and out he raised his voice in a grating howl, his nearest approach to the all-pervading sea-officer's call for his servant. Nothing happened. Perhaps his hail had been drowned by the omnipresent noise of grinding timber, pounding seas, and roaring wind. He said 'Damn the booby' and hurried into his damp breeches, tucking his wet nightshirt about him. He groped his way to the empty wardroom and there he hailed the wardroom steward ; but again he hailed in vain. Empty it was, the long table stretching away with fiddles upon it holding a few empty bowls while the bread-barge glided up and down as the *Worcester* pitched. The wardroom kept a barrel of small beer slung from the after beams for those who liked it and Stephen, dry within though damp without, was wondering whether the draught would be worth the journey when the *Worcester* plunged her stern deep into her own wake, so that he was obliged to crouch to keep his balance. There followed a quivering pause during which he considered small beer and then the forward part of her hull crashed down into a hollow of the sea with such extraordinary and quite unexpected violence that Stephen turned a double backward somersault, miraculously landing on his feet, quite unhurt.

'That was why I was dreaming of whales, no doubt – of the ship diving upon whales,' he reflected as he climbed the companion-ladder and put his head above the rim of the quarterdeck. A rough, blowing, overcast day he saw, with spray and packets of solid water flying through the air: a grim quarterdeck, with almost all the officers and young gentlemen upon it, looking grave, and a strong party at the pump by the mainmast, turning the winches fast, with reliefs standing by. Jack and Pullings over on the weather side, obviously discussing something high among the sails.

Even if Jack had not been so obviously engaged, Stephen would not have approached him: the Captain of the *Worcester* never allowed his young gentlemen to appear improperly dressed and he expected his officers to set a good example. He was himself rosy with new-shaving, although from his drawn face he had certainly not been to bed at all. Nor had a good many other people Stephen could see; and from their grey, jaded looks it appeared to him that both watches had been on deck all night. There was obviously some grave emergency, for one of the oldest, most strictly observed of all naval rules required that those who attended to the officers' comfort should never, never be called away unless instant dissolution threatened; yet here before him, at the cump-winches or waiting their turn, stood his own servant, the wardroom steward, Killick himself, and the Captain's cook.

Eager to know more, he crammed his nightcap into a pocket, passed his hand over his bristly skull by way of making himself more presentable, and climbed the remaining steps, with the intention of sidling along behind the midshipmen to the leeward beak of the poop, where the purser (a great tactician) was evidently explaining the situation to Stephen's two assistants and the Captain's clerk. But again he had reckoned without the *Worcester*'s strange surprising capers – he was on the rim itself, bending forward, when the ship dropped her bows sideways into the long vacancy, making that same

247

monstrous jerk and crash and bowling him diagonally across the deck to his Captain's feet.

'Bravo, Doctor,' cried Jack. 'You could set up for a tumbler, if all else fails. But you have no hat, I see – you have forgot your hat. Mr Seymour,' he called out to a midshipman, 'jump to my fore-cabin for the spare foul-weather hat by the barometer, and read the glass as you bring it away.'

'Twenty-eight inches and one sixteenth, sir, if you please,' said Mr Seymour, passing the hat. 'And sinking still.'

Jack clapped the hat on Stephen's head, Pullings fastened the tapes under his chin, and together they propelled him to the rail. 'But there they are,' he burst out, his voice cracking with emotion. 'There they are, for all love.'

And there they were indeed, the long line of French men-of-war covering a mile of torn, white-whipped sea, the rearmost division somewhat separated from the rest and not much above two miles from the English ships. 'Give you joy of your prophecy, Jack,' he cried but the words were hardly out before he wished them back. For the essence of the prophecy was not there: the strong, gusty wind was blowing from the enemy line and not towards it and that was the reason for the look of cruel, long-drawn-out disappointment on his friend's face. Emeriau it was who had the weather-gage, and he was making use of it to go home, declining battle.

The wind had veered steadily throughout the night, falling to a near calm in the middle watch and then suddenly springing up again and blowing harder from the north-west, so that although they found the French fleet off Cape Cavaleria as they had hoped, the whole situation was reversed. The enemy were now steering for home with the wind one point free, while the English line, close-hauled, crowded sail in the hope, the very faint hope, of cutting off the rear division.

'The trouble is, being new and clean they sail so much

better on a bowline than we do with our foul bottoms and old ships,' said Jack. 'But we still have a chance: the wind may back and favour us – it has often shifted these last hours – and they have the indraught and the Cavaleria current to contend with.'

'What is that frightful noise, that great resounding crash?'

'We call it slapping. Some of our northern ships do it when they stem these short hollow seas. It makes the Mediterranean builders laugh.'

'Perilous would it be, at all?'

Jack whistled. 'Why, as long as we do not spring a butt, we are not likely to founder,' he said. 'But it does make things a little damp between decks, and it does check our speed. Now you must forgive me. You would get a better general view from the poop: Mr Grimmond, Mr Savage, give the Doctor a hand to the poop. He would like to sit on the coaming where he can clap on to the fife-rail if it should get rough. Forecastle, there: is that spritsail-topsail laid along?'

He returned to the task of driving a heavy, partially-waterlogged and possibly disintegrating ship through a savage chaotic cross-sea, the Mediterranean at its sudden worst: and all the time he tried to persuade himself that the rearmost Frenchmen were not drawing away. The English line had changed a good deal since it was first formed at crack of dawn and the *Worcester* had moved up two places, the *Orion* dropping astern for want of foretopgallantmast and then the *Renown* with her bowsprit gone in the gammoning: the squadron was now sailing in a bow-and-quarter line, pelting along as hard as ever they could go, all their carefully-husbanded stores, cordage, sailcloth and spars now laid out with a reckless prodigality. Jack could see the Admiral, made fast to an elbow-chair clamped to the *Ocean*'s quarterdeck, his telescope often trained forward to fix Emeriau's flagship. Little time he had for watching the Admiral, however: this pace, close-hauled on a strong but capricious and veering wind that might lay the *Worcester* on her beam ends with a sudden furious gust or take her aback, called for the closest attention; and all this time the four experienced quartermasters at the wheel had to favour her to try to avoid the murderous slap, but without losing speed.

From his lonely, windswept, comfortless viewpoint abaft the mizenmast Stephen could make out little but a confused turmoil of water, high, sharp-pointed waves apparently running in every direction – a dirty sea with a great deal of yellowish foam blown violently over the surface, eddying here and there, and all this beneath a low yellow-grey sky with lightning under the western clouds. Far more impressive seas he had known: the enormous rollers of the high southern latitudes, for example, of the hurricane waters off Mauritius. But he had not seen a more wicked and as it were spiteful sea, with its steep, close-packed waves – a sea that threatened not the instant annihilation of the great antarctic monsters but a plucking apart, a worrying to death. Looking along the line he saw that several of the English ships had already been plucked to some degree – many a topgallantmast was gone, and even to his unprofessional eye there seemed to be some strange makeshift spars, sails and rigging, while far astern one unhappy ship could be seen sending up a jury mizen and at the same time trying everything humanly possible to keep pace. Yet there was not a ship but that was hurrying, racing along, with a prodigious expenditure of nautical skill and ingenuity and persistence, as though joining battle were the only felicity: a battle that seemed more and more improbable as time went by, measured for Stephen by the regular strokes on the *Worcester*'s bell and for the seamen by one emergency after another – the main pump choking, a gun breaking loose on the lower deck, the foretopsail blowing clean out of its boltrope.

At four bells Dr Maturin, changing into his old crusted black coat, crept down to make his rounds of the sick-bay: this was earlier than his usual time, but it was rare that a heavy, prolonged blow did not bring a fair number of casualties and in fact the sick-bay was busier than he had expected. His assistants had dealt with many of the sprains, contusions and broken bones, but some they had left for him, including a striking complex compound fracture, recently brought below.

'This will take us until after dinner, gentlemen,' he said, 'but it is much better to operate while he is unconscious: the muscles are relaxed, and we are not distracted by the poor fellow's screams.'

'In any case there will be nothing hot for dinner,' said Mr Lewis. 'The galley fires are out.'

'They say there are four feet of water in the hold,' said Mr Dunbar.

'They love to make our flesh creep,' said Stephen. 'Come, pledgets, ligatures, the leather-covered chain and my great double-handed retractor, if you please; and let us stand as steady as we can, bracing ourselves against these uprights.'

The compound fracture took even longer than they had expected, but eventually he was sewn up, splinted, bandaged, and lashed into a cot, there to swing until he was cured. Stephen hung his bloody coat to drip dry upon its nail and walked off. He looked into the wardroom, saw only the purser and two of the Marine officers wedged tight about their bottle, and returned to his place on the poop, carrying a tarpaulin jacket.

As far as he could make out little had changed. The *Worcester* and all the ships he could see ahead and astern were still tearing along at the same racing speed, carrying a great press of canvas and flinging the white broken water wide – a great impression of weight, power, and extreme urgency. On the decks below him there was still the same tension, with men jumping to make the innumerable slight changes that Jack called for from the place at the weather-rail that he had scarcely left for five minutes since the chase began, and where he was now eating a piece of cold meat. The pumps were still turning fast, and somewhere in the middle parts of the ship another had joined them, sending its jet in a fine curve far out to leeward. The French line still stretched half-way to the horizon, standing north-east for Toulon: they did not seem very much farther away if at all and it seemed to Stephen that this might continue indefinitely. To be sure, the *Worcester* was labouring cruelly, but she had been labouring cruelly for so long that there seemed no good reason why she should not go on. He watched attentively, therefore, and not without hope that some disaster among the French ships might allow the squadron to make up those few essential miles: he watched, fascinated by the spectacle of what he was tempted to call motionless – relatively motionless – hurry, with a sense of a perpetual, frozen present, unwilling to miss anything, until well on into the afternoon, when Mowett joined him.

'Well, Doctor,' said he, sitting wearily on the coaming, 'we did our best.'

'Is it over, so?' cried Stephen. 'I am amazed, amazed.'

'I am amazed it lasted so long. I never thought to see her take such a pounding, and still swim. Look at that,' he said, pointing to a length of caulking that had worked out of a seam in the deck. 'God love us, what a sight. She spewed the oakum from her sides long since, as you would have expected with such labouring; but to see it coming from a midships seam . . .'

'Is that why we must give up?'

'Oh no: it is the breeze that fails us.'

'Yet there seems to be a good deal still,' said Stephen, looking at the strip of mixed pitch and oakum as it lashed to and fro in the wind, the end shredding off in fragments that vanished over the side.

'But surely you must have seen how it has been hauling forward this last hour? We shall be dead to leeward presently. That is why the Admiral is taking his last chance. You did not notice the *Doris* repeating his signal, I suppose?'

'I did not. What did it signify?'

'He is sending our best sailers in to attack their rear.

252

If they can get there before the wind heads them, and if
Emeriau turns to support his ships, he hopes we shall be
able to come up in time to prevent ours being mauled.'

'A desperate stroke, Mr Mowett?'

'Well, sir, maybe, maybe. But maybe it will bring on a
most glorious action before the sun goes down. Look: here
they come. *San Josef, Berwick, Sultan, Leviathan*, and
just the two frigates to windward – no, sir, to *windward*
– *Pomone* and of course our dear old *Surprise*. All French
or Spanish ships, you see, and all with a fine tumblehome.
Some fellows have all the luck. I will fetch you a spyglass,
so that you miss nothing.

Now that they were no longer obliged to keep down
to the squadron's pace the four swift-sailing ships of the
line ran up in splendid style, steadily increasing sail as
they came. They passed up, forming as they went, and
each ship gave them a brief informal spontaneous cheer
as they went by: Stephen saw the cheerful Rear-Admiral
Mitchell in the *San Josef*, the surgeon of the *Leviathan*,
and perhaps a dozen other men he knew, all looking as
though they were going to a treat. And he waved to Mr
Martin on the *Berwick*'s quarterdeck; but Mr Martin, half
blinded by the spray sweeping aft from the *Berwick*'s eager
bow, did not see the signal.

Now they were well ahead, the *San Josef* leading, the
others in her wake, and all heading straight for the gap
between the French rear and centre divisions. Stephen
watched them closely with his glass: the finer points of
seamanship no doubt escaped him, yet he did see that
for the first hour they not only drew clear away from
their friends but they certainly gained on their enemies.

For the first hour: then between three bells and four
the situation hardly changed. All those heavily-armed,
densely-populated ships raced strenuously over the sea
in gratuitous motion, neither gaining nor losing. Or was
there indeed a loss, a slackening of the tension, the first
edge of sickening disappointment? Stephen peered over
the pooprail down at the quarterdeck, where Jack Aubrey

stood in his set place as though he were part of the ship; but little did he learn from that grave, closed, concentrated face.

At that point the *Worcester*'s captain was in fact even more part of his ship than usual: the master's, carpenter's, first lieutenant's reports had given him a fairly clear picture of what·was happening below and intuition provided the rest. He felt each of her monstrous plunges as though her bowels were his own; furthermore he knew that the immense purchases by which he had so far held the *Worcester*'s masts to her hull depended essentially upon the mechanical strength of her clamps and hanging-knees, that these must be near their limit, and that if they went he could not carry half his present sail – could not keep up with the squadron, but would have to fall to leeward with the other lame ducks. For a long while he had prayed that they might last long enough for the fighting to begin in the French rear and for the *Worcester* to come up; now, keener-sighted than his friend, he saw that there was to be no fighting. Long before Stephen saw the *San Josef* taken squarely aback, losing her maintopgallantmast with the shock, Jack realized that Mitchell's ships were being headed by the wind: he had seen the quivering weather-leeches, he had divined the furious bracing of the yards and the hauling of the bowlines, and he had measured the increasing gap between the English and the French, and it was clear to him that the advanced ships' slanting approach to the enemy could not succeed – that the long chase must end in slow disappointment and anticlimax.

But it was not over yet. 'Look at *Surprise* and *Pomone*, sir,' cried Pullings, and swinging his telescope from the *San Josef* Jack saw the two frigates draw ahead under a great press of sail and bear down under the rearmost Frenchman's lee, the *Robuste*, of eighty guns. They moved faster than any ship of the line and as soon as they were within range they opened with their bow-guns and then with their broadsides, firing high in the hope of knocking away some important spar.

'Luff up, luff up, for God's sake luff up,' said Jack aloud as he followed them in their perilous course along the *Robuste*'s side: very close range was everything in such a case. But neither *Surprise* nor *Pomone* luffed up. Both sides fired repeatedly at a distance; neither did any apparent damage, and after the frigate's first unsuccessful run Admiral Thornton threw out the signal of recall, emphasizing it with two guns: an engagement at that range, a distant peppering, would accomplish nothing, whereas the *Robuste*'s heavy metal might disable or even sink the smaller ships. And these two guns, together with those remote and ineffectual broadsides under the clouds to the north-east, were all the firing the squadron ever heard.

Almost immediately after the Admiral's second gun, and as though in answer to it, a particularly violent gust laid the *Worcester* over in a cloud of foam: she recovered heavily, all hands clinging to their holds; but as she came up and took the weather-strain so Jack heard the deep internal rending that he had dreaded. He and Pullings exchanged a glance: he stepped over to his larboard hawsers, felt their horrible slackness, and called to the signal-midshipman, 'Mr Savage, prepare the hoist; *I am overpressed with sail.*'

# CHAPTER NINE

When Jack Aubrey brought his ship into the fleet at the rendezvous south-east of Toulon she had three turns of twelve-inch cable frapped about her and a spare spritsail, thick with tarred oakum, drawn under her bottom. She had something of the chrysalis-look her captain had once imagined in the lightness of his heart, but at least she still possessed her masts and all her guns, though they had cost her people some cruel days of pumping, and at least she looked trim and clean as she glided cautiously in over a perfect sea, the deep, deep blue rippling under the caress of a languid southern breeze. The water still gushed in steady jets from her side, but she was no longer in danger of foundering.

The *Worcester* came in at such a gentle pace that Jack had plenty of time to survey the squadron. Some ships were missing, either because they had been sent to Malta to refit or because they had not yet rejoined; but on the other hand two seventy-fours and an eighty-gun ship had arrived from Cadiz, and at least some stores must have reached the fleet, since there were now only half a dozen jury-masts to be seen. The squadron, though battered and somewhat diminished, was still a powerful blockading force. He saw that clearly enough from a distance, and when his barge pulled along the line in answer to the flagship's signal he saw it more clearly still. On this calm, sunny day the ships all had their ports open to air the lower decks, and behind these ports he saw the guns, row after row of guns, with seamen titivating them. This sense of abiding strength and his exact falling-in with the squadron was a satisfaction to him, but the greater part of his mind was taken up with foreboding and concern. As the barge slipped along past the *Ocean*'s splendid gilded stern he heard the howling of the Admiral's little dog, and when Bonden hooked on at the entry-port, blundering for the first time in his life as captain's coxswain, Jack was obliged to compose himself for an instant before going aboard.

The ceremony of reception was muted; on all hands he saw faces as grave as his own; and the Admiral's secretary, leading him to the fore-cabin, said in a low voice, 'When I take you in, pray let the interview be as short and smooth as possible. He has had a long hard day of it: Dr Harrington is with him now.'

They stood there for a while, looking out through the half-port, beyond the dark rectangle to the brilliance and purity of the day, even purer and more brilliant for being framed: and still the dog howled. 'The doctor is with him,' reflected Jack. 'So they have put the pug into the coach: some dogs cannot bear seeing their masters touched.' The *Ocean* veered a quarter of a point, and now the frame contained a ship, a great way off and apparently floating above the nacreous surface of the farther sea. As seamen will, Jack tilted his head back and sideways to consider her: she was *Surprise*, of course, and she was presumably coming from the inshore squadron; yet her side was painted blue and what little he could make out of her pennant showed it as low as the crosstrees: the ship was in mourning. 'What happened to Captain Latham?' he asked.

'Can you indeed see as far as that?' said Allen, following his gaze. 'I am afraid he was killed. He and his first lieutenant were killed by the same ball as the *Surprise* was going down to attack the *Robuste*.'

Dr Harrington came out of the great cabin, bowed and sombre; he opened the coach door as he went by, and the little dog, scrambling fast across the deck, darted in before Jack and the secretary and flung itself down under the Admiral's desk.

Jack had expected to find the Admiral deeply saddened, even more infirm, possibly savage (he could be a Tartar on occasion), certainly very gravely affected indeed; but

257

he had not expected to find him removed from humanity, and it disconcerted him.

Admiral Thornton was perfectly civil and collected: he congratulated Aubrey on having brought the *Worcester* in, listened to a brief summary of the Statement of Condition that Jack laid on his desk and said the ship must clearly go to Malta for a complete refit – she would be of no use as a man-of-war for a great while, if at all; but her guns would be uncommonly useful at this juncture. His mind was alive – it dealt with the details of his command, rarely hesitating for a moment – but the man was not, or not wholly, and he looked at Jack from an immense distance: not coldly, still less severely, but from another plane; and Jack felt more and more embarrassed, ashamed of being alive while the other was already taking leave.

'But in the mean time, Aubrey,' said the Admiral, 'you will not be idle. As you may have heard, poor Latham was killed in his engagement with the *Robuste*, so you will proceed to the Seven Islands in *Surprise*. The death of one of the Turkish rulers on the Ionian coast has brought about a complex situation that may possibly allow us to expel the French from Marga, even from Paxo and Corfu, and we must have at least one frigate on the spot. I will not elaborate – I am leaving this station very shortly, you know – but Mr Allen will make the position clear and the Rear-Admiral will give you your orders. You will have the advice of Dr Maturin and Mr Graham. Does that suit you?'

'Yes, sir.'

'Then goodbye to you, Aubrey,' said the Admiral, holding out his hand. Yet it was not a human farewell: it was rather a gesture of civility to a being of another kind, very small and far away, at the wrong end of a telescope as it were, a being of no importance, in circumstances of no great importance, that nevertheless had to be dealt with correctly.

Only twice had Jack felt that the Admiral was still in contact with the ordinary world: once when he gently put his foot on the pug's back to stop it wheezing so loud, and once when he said 'leaving this station'. It was common knowledge that the *Ocean* was sailing for Mahon and Gibraltar in the morning, but the Admiral's meaning would have been clear to a man with even less religious sense than Jack Aubrey and the tone of unaffected humility and resignation moved him deeply.

Returning to the fore-cabin he found Stephen there with Mr Allen and Professor Graham. 'Captain Aubrey,' said Stephen, 'I have been telling Mr Allen that I must decline going with you to Admiral Harte's apartment. There are circumstances that make it improper for me to make any official appearance in this matter or in any other to do with Intelligence at present.'

'I quite agree,' said Graham.

'Besides,' added Stephen, 'I have to see Dr Harrington and our patient in fifteen minutes.'

'Very well,' said Allen. 'Then I shall send a messenger to tell Dr Harrington that you are here. Gentlemen, shall we wait on the Rear-Admiral?'

Rear-Admiral Harte had never held an independent command of any importance and the prospect of supporting the enormous responsibilities of Commander-in-Chief in the Mediterranean overwhelmed him. Although it was certain that the Admiralty would not leave him in a post so very far beyond his abilities but would send out a replacement as soon as the news of Admiral Thornton's incapacity reached London, Harte's manner and even his appearance were almost unrecognizable. His ill-looking, foxy, close-eyed face wore a look that Jack had never seen on it before, although they were old, old acquaintances – a look of earnest gravity. He was civil to Jack and almost deferential to Allen and Graham, who for their part treated him with no extraordinary respect. Harte had at no time been admitted to the Admiral's confidence in anything but purely naval matters: he knew almost nothing of the deeply involved political situation and nothing whatsoever about the Admiral's frail network of intelligence. Allen gave a short account of the position in the Seven Islands, and Harte could be seen straining his weak understanding to follow it: 'Now, sir,' said Allen, 'I advert not to the Seven Islands as such but to their former allies and dependencies on the mainland, particularly Kutali and Marga. As you know, the French are still in Marga, and they seem to be as firmly settled there as they are in Corfu: yet a little while ago it was represented to the Commander-in-Chief that the possessor of Kutali could cut Marga's aqueduct and take the town from behind; while a friendly base at Kutali would make it far easier for us to attack Paxo and Corfu, which even Buonaparte calls the keys of the Adriatic.'

'We are to take Kutali, then?' said Harte.

'Why, no, sir,' said Allen patiently. 'Kutali is Turkish, and we must not offend the Porte. Any evident, unprovoked aggression in this region would give our enemies in Constantinople a great advantage: it must never be forgotten that the French have some very intelligent men there, that the Sultan's mother is a Frenchwoman, and that Napoleon's recent successes have very much strengthened the French party. But it so happens that the town, which as you will recall was an independent Christian republic before the treaty of Pressburg, lies between three ill-defined beyliks, and its status has not yet been finally decided in Constantinople. The former governor, whose recent death brought this crisis about, was to hold office only while the town's position – its privileges and so on – were considered. It is a valuable place: the neighbouring rulers covet it exceedingly and two of them, Ismail and Mustapha, have already approached us for help, while the agent of the third is thought to be in Malta at present.'

'What kind of help do they want?' asked Harte.

'Guns, sir, and gunpowder.'

'Guns!' cried Harte, looking at the others: but he said no more, and when first Allen and then Graham explained that in the outlying provinces of the Turkish empire the valis, pashas, agas and beys, though in principle subject to the Sultan, often behaved like independent rulers, increasing their territories by usurpation or by making open war upon one another, he looked displeased.

'Ali Arslan of Iannina defeated and killed the Pasha of Scutari not long since,' said Graham. 'It is true that Scutari had rebelled: but the same cannot be said for the Derwend-Pasha of Rumelia, nor of Menoglu Bey.'

'The independence increases with the distance from Constantinople,' said Allen. 'In Algiers, for example, it is virtually complete, but here it is usually exercised with a certain discretion. They often go to war with one another, but they generally do so with cries of loyalty to the Sultan, for although the Porte will acquiesce in a *fait accompli* if it is accompanied by the proper offerings, a reasonably good case still has to be made out – the defeated man must be shown to have had treacherous intentions or to have been in correspondence with the enemy.'

'And except in cases where the pasha or vali throws off his allegiance and goes about to cut himself out a completely sovereign state, as Scutari and Pasanvoglu did not long ago and as Ali Pasha will almost certainly do as soon as he can be sure of the Morea – except in cases of total rebellion, I say, the Sultan's direct appointment is respected in these parts, when at last it is forthcoming in the form of an iradé or firman,' said Graham. 'The Sultan's iradé is sacred, except to rebels.'

'That is why all three beys also have their agents busy in Constantinople, jockeying for position,' said Allen. 'Though to be sure they expect to settle matters much more briskly by themselves, so that the fact of possession, and the increased wealth of possession, may plead in their favour. Unfortunately one of them has also seen fit to make interest with our embassy, which may complicate our task; for whereas the Commander-in-Chief inclines towards Mustapha as a seaman and a former acquaintance – they knew one another when Mustapha was in the Dardanelles – the embassy favours Ismail.'

'Who holds the place at present?' asked Jack.

'The third man, old Sciahan Bey. That is to say he is sitting quietly in the lower town and the suburbs. The Christians, the Kutaliotes, hold the citadel unmolested. For the moment there is an uneasy truce, no one of the three Turks daring to attack for fear of meeting a coalition of the other two, and the Christians biding their time; but the position will change the moment the cannon arrive.'

Harte stared for a while and then said, 'So they mean to fight one another, and we are to supply the guns. What do the various sides offer in exchange?'

'Their promises are the same: they will turn the guns against the French in Marga. Having settled us in Kutali they will join in our attack on Marga, the place being taken before there is time for the French party in Constantinople to interfere.'

'I see. Are the guns available?'

'Yes, sir. Two small transports have been prepared and are lying in Valetta. The trouble is we do not know which of the claimants to trust. Ismail openly states that General Donzelot, the commander of Corfu, has made him offers; but this may merely be intended to raise his price. Mustapha says nothing of the kind, but we have a certain amount of intelligence to show that he too may be in contact with the French. So bearing these things in mind, sir, and taking into account the necessity for rapid action, it was thought advisable to send Captain Aubrey, with a political adviser, to view the situation, to meet the beys, to make up his mind on the spot, and, if possible, to carry out the operation.'

'Just so,' said Harte.

'Perhaps it would be as well to couch the orders in the most general sense, leaving a great deal of room for discretion?'

'Certainly, certainly: just put "use his best endeavours" together with a general statement of the aim of the operation, and leave it at that. Do not tie his hands. Does that suit you, Aubrey? If it don't, just say the word and the orders shall be wrote to your dictation. I can't say fairer than that.'

Jack bowed, and there was a short silence.

'Then there is this point of the *Surprise*'s crew, sir,' said Allen. 'In view of the death of Captain Latham and his first lieutenant, the Commander-in-Chief thought you would agree that the best way of dealing with the situation would be to disperse the entire ship's company in small groups throughout the squadron and re-man the frigate from the ships that have to go in to refit.'

'God damn me,' said Harte, 'I should hang the mutinous buggers if I had my own way, every last one of them. But with both chief witnesses dead, I suppose it must be so.'

'Since *Worcester* must go in,' said Jack, 'I could pick an excellent frigate's crew from her people alone, men who are used to working together – several old Surprises among them.'

'Make it so, Aubrey, make it so,' said Harte: and in the same tone of awkward goodwill he continued, 'Of course you will have to have a sloop of some kind in company for this sort of expedition: if you like I will try to let you have Babbington in the *Dryad*.'

'Thank you very much, sir,' said Jack. 'I should like that of all things.'

' "I should like that of all things," said I, with a winning leer and a bob of my head,' wrote Jack Aubrey in his letter home, a letter dated from '*Surprise*, at sea'. 'But I hope, sweetheart, you will not think me ungenerous or mean-spirited when I say I do not trust him: that is to say, I do not trust the long continuance of his goodwill. If I choose the wrong man among these beys or if the operations do not go well, I think he will throw me to the dogs without the least hesitation; and William Babbington after me. Stephen don't trust him neither.' He paused; and reflecting that he could not very well describe his friend's vehement refusal to appear in the character of an intelligence-agent before 'a man so weak, so choleric, so little master of his passions, and so likely to be indiscreet' as Harte even though the Rear-Admiral might for the moment be acting Commander-in-Chief, he added 'which is very sad.' But the words were no sooner written than they struck him as ludicrous, and he was so very far from sad himself, that he laughed aloud.

'What now?' called Killick angrily from the sleeping-cabin: he was one of the very few who disliked the move into the *Surprise* and he had been in a most unpleasant temper ever since they left Malta. His immediate predecessor, Captain Latham's steward, a fornicating sodomite by the name of Hogg, had changed everything – nothing was the same. The night-locker where Killick had always kept needle and thread for small repairs had been moved from starboard to larboard: the midships scuttle under which he had always worked had been blocked up and painted over. He could no longer find anything, nor could he see to sew.

'I was only laughing,' said Jack.

'If I had that Hogg under my needle now,' said Killick, giving the hem of Captain Aubrey's best neckcloth a vicious stab, 'wouldn't I learn him to laugh? Oh no: not half I wouldn't . . .' His voice diminished in volume, but his nasal whine had a curiously penetrating quality and as Jack carried on with his letter he half-heard the stream of discontent flowing on: '. . . unhappy ship, and no wonder . . . everything changed . . . acres of fucking brass . . . closed up my scuttle . . . how can a poor unfortunate bugger see with no light, sewing black upon black?' This last was so shrill that it quite broke in upon Jack's line of thought. 'If you cannot see in there, carry it out into the stern-gallery,' he called, forgetting for a moment that they were no longer in the *Worcester*.

'Which there ain't no stern-gallery, sir, now we been degraded to a sixth-rate,' cried Killick with malignant triumph. 'Stern-galleries is for our betters, and I must toil and moil away in the dark.'

'Killick is in a horrid passion, I am sorry to say,' wrote

Jack, 'and will not be comforted until we are back in a ship of the line. For my part I do not care if I never see a ship of the line again: after these months of close blockade, a well-found frigate seems the ideal command to me, and I may say the same for all my officers. I am to dine with them today, and we are to have a grand poetic contest, a kind of sweepstake, to be judged by secret ballot. Killick,' he called, 'rouse out a glass of bitters, will you? And have one for yourself while you are about it.' The gunroom's dinner was earlier than Jack's usual hour, and he wanted to do honour to their feast.

'Which there ain't none left, sir,' replied Killick, pleased for the first time that day. 'Don't you remember the case dropped into the hold in consequence of the orlop-scuttle had been shifted, which they never told us, and was stove: so there ain't none left – all wasted, not even tasted, all gone into the bilge.'

'All wasted

Not even tasted

All gone into the bilge,' he repeated in a lugubrious chant.

'Oh well,' said Jack, 'I shall take a turn upon the quarterdeck: that will answer just as well.'

It answered even better. The hands had already eaten their dinner and drunk their grog but the midshipmen's berth was rounding out their pease-pudding and pig's trotters with toasted bloaters, laid in at Valetta, and the smell eddying aft from the galley brought water to his mouth. Yet the bloaters were not really necessary: happiness always gave Jack Aubrey an appetite and at present he was filled with irrational glee, a glee that redoubled as he stood on that familiar quarterdeck, so much nearer to the sea than the *Worcester*'s, and surveyed the noble spread of canvas that was urging the *Surprise* eastwards to her meeting with the *Dryad* at nearly three knots in a breeze so faint that many ships would not have had steerage-way, while at the same time he felt her supple lift and yield to the southern swell, a more living motion than that of any other ship he knew.

His was largely an irrational happiness and entirely on the surface: he had only to move down one layer in his mind to meet his very real distress for Admiral Thornton, one more for the shocking disappointment of the battle that had escaped them – a battle that might have ranked with St Vincent or the Nile and which would almost certainly have made Tom Pullings a commander (a move particularly near to Aubrey's heart) – another layer still for his own deeply worrying failure at Barka: and if he sank farther there were always his legal and financial worries at home and his anxiety about his father. The newspapers in Malta had spoken of General Aubrey's being returned for no less than two constituencies at once; and it appeared that the old gentleman was now twice as loquacious. He spoke against the ministry almost every day, and he was now doing so entirely in the more extreme Radical interest, alas, a real embarrassment to the ministry. And there was not much room for rational glee if Jack looked forward, either, but rather the prospect of an exceedingly difficult situation in which diplomacy rather than hard fighting would be called for, a situation in which he could rely on no support from his chief, a situation in which a mistaken choice might bring his naval career to an end.

Yet gleeful he was. The tedium of blockade on short commons in a heavy, ill-contrived ship that might publicly disgrace herself at any minute was behind him, at least for the immediate future; the wearisome and in some ways painful transfer, the paper-work and the wrangling with the authorities in Malta was over; the *Worcester*, that walking corpse, was the dockyard's corporate anxiety, not his; and although he had left the oratorio behind him he had also left the mumps, that fell disease. He had dispersed his more useless midshipmen and all his youngsters but for two, Calamy and Williamson, for whom he felt a particular responsibility. And he was aboard a thoroughbred frigate,

266

a ship he knew through and through and that he loved entirely, not only for her amiable qualities but because she was part of his youth – quite apart from the fact that he had commanded her in the Indian Ocean, where she had behaved quite beautifully, he had served in her long, long ago, and even the smell of her cramped and awkward midshipmen's berth made him feel young again. She was rather small (few smaller left in the service), she was rather old, and although she had been very much strengthened, almost rebuilt, in the Cadiz yard, it would never, never do to take her across to meet the heavy Americans; but he had found to his delight that her refitting had not altered her sailing qualities in the least – she was astonishingly fast for those who knew how to handle her, she could come about like a cutter, and she could eat the wind out of any ship on the station. For this kind of mission, and for the eastern Mediterranean in general, she was everything he could ask (except in broadside weight of metal), above all as he had had the most uncommon good fortune of being able to give her a crew of hand-picked seamen, in which even the afterguard could hand, reef and steer. There were still many who had not sailed with him before the *Worcester*, but a surprising proportion of the frigate's two hundred men had done so – all the first and second captains of the guns for example, and nearly all the petty officers – and wherever he looked he saw faces he knew. Even when they were not old shipmates he could put a name to them and a character, whereas in the *Worcester* far too many had been anonymous. And he observed that they looked remarkably cheerful, as though his own good humour had spread: certainly they had just had their grog, and the weather was fine, and this was a peaceful make-and-mend afternoon, but even so he had rarely seen a more cheerful crew, particularly the old Surprises. 'A *surprising* proportion of old Surprises,' he said to himself, and chuckled.

'The skipper's luck is in,' murmured Bonden, as he sat on the gangway, embroidering *Surprise* on the ribbon of his shore-going hat.

'Well, I hope so, I'm sure,' said his heavy cousin Joe. 'It's been out long enough. Get your great arse off of my new shirt, you whoreson lobster,' he said mildly to his other neighbour, a Marine.

'I only hope it's not come in too hearty, that's all,' said Bonden, reaching out for the solid wooden truck of number eight gun's carriage.

Joe nodded. Although he was a heavy man he perfectly grasped the meaning of Bonden's 'luck'. It was not chance, commonplace good fortune, far from it, but a different concept altogether, one of an almost religious nature, like the favour of some god or even in extreme cases like possession; and if it came in too hearty it might prove fatal – too fiery an embrace entirely. In any event it had to be treated with great respect, rarely named, referred to by allusion or alias, never explained. There was no clear necessary connection with moral worth nor with beauty but its possessors were generally well-liked men and tolerably good-looking: and it was often seen to go with a particular kind of happiness. It was this quality, much more than his prizes, the perceived cause rather than the effect, that had made the lower deck speak of Lucky Jack Aubrey early in his career; and it was a piety at the same old heathen level that now made Bonden deprecate any excess.

Captain Aubrey, staring out over the weather-rail, smiling as he recalled the simple fun he had had in this same ship as a boy, heard the crunch of the Marine drummers's boots coming aft. He cast a last automatic glance at the dog-vane, said 'Very well Dyce' to the helmsman, went below for his best neckcloth, and put it on while the drum beat Roast Beef of Old England; then bending low under the beams he walked into the gunroom just as Pullings took up his station at the door to welcome him.

'Come, this is altogether snugger and more homely,' said Jack, smiling at the friendly faces, eight of them tight-packed round the gunroom table; and homely it was for those brought up in sea-going slums, though perhaps a little snugger than could have been wished, since each had his servant behind his chair and since the day was uncommonly warm and still, with no air coming below. The fare was homely too, the main dish being the roast beef of Old Calabria, a great piece of one of those Italian buffaloes known as grey friars in the Navy and shipped to Malta when they were quite past work; and this was followed by figgy-dowdy.

'Now that is what I call a really good basis for literature,' said Jack, when the cloth had been drawn, the King's health drunk, and fresh decanters set upon the table. 'When is the sweepstake to begin?'

'Directly, sir,' said Pullings. 'Thompson, pass round the voting-papers, place the ballot-box, collect the stakes, and hand along the glass. We have agreed, sir, that each gentleman is to limit himself to a four-and-a-half-minute glass; but he may explain the rest of the poem in prose, speaking quick. And we have agreed, sir, that there is to be no applause, nor no cat-calls, for fear of influencing the vote. It is all to be as fair as Habeas Corpus.'

'Or *Nunc dimittis*,' said the purser. But although Mr Adams had been very active in framing the rules, he and others turned shy at the last moment, and the pearly nautilus passed round for the stakes held only a half-guinea, an assortment of English silver, and three pieces of eight, the contribution of the remaining competitors, Mowett, Rowan, and Driver, the new Marine officer shipped at Malta, a very ample, pink, amiable young man with weak eyes and a way of chuckling to himself. His powers were as yet unknown to the gunroom. They drew lots, and Rowan began. 'Now, gentlemen,' he said, speaking quick and in prose, 'this is part of a poem about the *Courageux*, Captain Wilkinson, running plumb on to the Anholt reef by night, wind at south-west, double-reefed topsails and forecourse, making eight knots. Turn the glass.' Pullings turned the sand-glass and without the slightest change of tone or pace or the least concession to the conventions of recital Rowan went straight on, his jolly round face beaming on the company,

'Dismal was this, many did despair
That her dissolution was very near;
She thumped heavy, and masts did play
That in their obedience to the prow, would jump
                                                away.

Awful the grinding noise of keel and heel
With an unusual motion made the crew to reel,
The rudder being most oppressed and bound
But soon it got released and went to the ground.

Sail first being set to press her over the reef,
But striking harder without relief
'Twas instantly chewed up and fasted again anew
With willingness and zeal by her gallant crew.

At last the deleterious order to prepare
To throw the cannon overboard. Oh what despair!
The officer of the third post ventured to state
Oh noble chieftan pray hesitate!

('I happened to have the watch, sir,' he said in an aside to Jack.)

Remember Sire, said this self same third,
With due submission, pray let me be heard,
Your own experiences of its baleful effects
As often tried and as often made wrecks.

Guns lying together on the sand equal to rocks
                                                annoy
The bottom of the bark, they may soon destroy;
And now it's blowing a gale of wind, what hopes
Impossible to save our lives could we get out
                                                the boats.

Stand fast, the bold commander said, 'Tis true
The wind has shifted for us. Set topsails anew
Square sails set and braced all aback. See hence

The wonderful care of Almighty's Providence.'

In spite of the rules there was a distinct murmur of approval at the ship's coming off, for it was clearly understood from Rowan's expression, and indeed from his presence among them, that the *Courageux* had come off; but there was an even more distinct expression of scepticism about the third lieutenant's words to his captain, Wilkinson being a testy gentleman: Rowan felt this, and observed, 'The piece about Noble Chieftan is poetic, you understand.'

'I never thought you would bring her off in time,' said Pullings. 'There were not above three grains of sand left. Next.'

Mowett took a draught of port, turned a little pale, and said, 'My piece is a fragment too, part of something in the epical line in three cantos about people sailing in these waters or to be more exact somewhat more easterly, off Cape Spado. They run into dirty weather, furl topsails, send down topgallant yards, and then reef courses; and this is a description of the manoeuvre. But it is preceded by a simile that I rather flatter myself – by a simile that would fall into place better if I went back to *Now to the north, from Afric's burning shore, A troop of porpoises their course explore* but I doubt I could get all that in and it may seem a little strange without but anyhow here goes.' He nodded to Pullings to turn the glass, and with his eyes fixed on the falling sand he began in a hollow moaning voice,

'Tossed on the tide she feels the tempest blow
And dreads the vengeance of so fell a foe
As the proud horse, with costly trappings gay,
Exulting, prances to the bloody fray,
Spurning the ground, he glories in his might,
But reels tumultuous in the shock of fight;
Even so, caparisoned in gaudy pride,
The bounding vessel dances on the tide.'

271

He looked quickly round for some reaction to his simile: he saw nothing but deep, universal stupidity, but this may only have been the reserve called for by the rules. In any case he hurried on to ground where everybody would be more at home:

> 'Fierce and more fierce the southern demon blew,
> And more incensed the roaring waters grew.
> The ship no longer can her topsails spread,
> And every hope of fairer skies is fled.
> Bowlines and halyards are relaxed again,
> Clewlines hauled down, and sheets let fly amain;
> Clewed up each topsail, and by braces squared,
> The seamen climb aloft on either yard.
> They furled the sails, and pointed to the wind
> The yard by rolling tackles then confined.
> While o'er the ship the gallant boatswain flies,
> Like a hoarse mastiff through the storm he cries:
> Prompt to direct th'unskilful still appears;
> Th'expert he praises, and the fearful cheers.
> Now some to strike topgallant yards attend:
> Some travellers up the weather-backstays send;
> At each masthead the top-ropes others bend.
> The youngest sailors from the yards above
> Their parrels, lifts, and braces soon remove:
> Then topped an-end, and to the travellers tied,
> Charged with their sails, they down the backstays
> slide.
> Their sails reduced, and all the rigging clear,
> Awhile the crew relax from toils severe.

But then it gets worse,' said Mowett, 'and the sun goes down – I skip the sunset, such a shame – I skip the moon and stars –

> The ship no longer can her courses bear;
> To reef the courses is the master's care:
> The sailors, summoned aft, a daring band!
> Attend th'enfolding brails at his command.

But he who strives the tempest to disarm
Will never first embrail the lee yardarm.
So to windward, and obedient to command,
To raise the tack, the ready sailors stand.
The sheet and weather-brace they then stand by,
The lee clew-garnet and the buntlines ply.
Thus all prepared – Let go the sheet! he cries.
Impetuous –'

'Time,' cried Pullings.

'Oh, Tom,' said Mowett, sinking in his chair, his afflatus gone.

'I am sorry, old fellow,' said Pullings, 'but fair's fair, you know, and the Royal Marines must have their whack.'

Mr Driver, always pink, was now the colour of his uniform coat; but whether this was port, or confusion, or the heat, could not yet be determined. He gave the gunroom to understand that his poem was not a fragment; oh no, not a piece of anything larger, if they understood him, but a whole, complete in itself, as he might say. By listening attentively they gathered that it was a cove thinking of getting married – advice to this cove from a knowing friend, a deep old file that had seen a thing or two in his time – but Mr Driver chuckled so extremely and spoke in so low and bumbling a voice, hanging his head, that they missed almost everything until

'Her person amiable, straight, and free
From natural or chance deformity.
Let not her years exceed, if equal thine;
For women past their vigour soon decline:
Her fortune competent; and, if thy sight
Can reach so far, take care 'tis gathered right.
If thine's enough, then hers may be the less:
Do not aspire to riches in excess.
For that which makes our lives delightful prove,
Is a genteel sufficiency and love.'

273

'Very good,' cried the purser as he wrote on his voting paper. 'Tell me, sir, what would you reckon a genteel sufficiency; supposing, I mean, a man only had his pay?'

Mr Driver laughed and wheezed and at last brought out 'Two hundred a year in the Funds, at her own disposal.'

'No remarks, gentlemen, if you please,' said Pullings, shaking his head at Professor Graham, who was obviously about to speak. 'No remarks before the voting.' He passed round the ballot-box, a sextant-case on this occasion, set it down filled in front of Jack, and said to Graham, 'I cut you short, sir: I beg your pardon.'

'I was only going to observe that Captain Driver's poem reminded me of Pomfret's *To his Friend Inclined to Marry*.'

'But it *is* Pomfret's *To his Friend*,' said Driver, surprised: and amidst the general outcry he could be heard to say, 'My guardian made me get it by rote.'

Battered on all sides, he appealed to Jack: 'How could a man have been expected to guess that it was to be original poetry? *Original* poetry, for God's sake! He had supposed it was to be a prize for elegant delivery.'

'Had it been a prize for elegant delivery,' said Jack, 'I dare say Mr Driver would have borne the bell away; but as things are, he must be scratched and given back his stake; and the ballots in his favour do not count. As for the remaining competitors,' he said, examining the votes, 'I find that Mr Rowan carries the day as far as poetry in the classical manner is concerned, whereas Mr Mowett wins for poetry in the modern style. The prize is therefore divided into two equal halves or moieties. And I think I do not misinterpret the company's sentiments when I urge both gentlemen to enter into contact with some respectable bookseller with a view to the publication of their works, both for the gratification of their friends and for the benefit of the service.'

'Hear him, hear him,' cried the rest of the gunroom, beating on the table.

'Murray is the man,' said Graham, with a significant look. 'John Murray of Albemarle Street. He has an excellent reputation; and I may observe for the credit of the booksellers that his father, who founded the shop, was the son, the legitimate son, of a lieutenant in the Marines.'

Mr Driver did not seem at all pleased. He said that if a cove had a son with no talent of any kind and no presence or personal beauty then the cove was quite justified in putting him to a shop: the family was not obliged to take notice of him after he grew up, unless he made himself an estate or at least a more than usually genteel competence. And anyhow a bookseller was not a common shopkeeper: many that Driver knew could read and write, and some spoke quite pretty.

'Just so,' said Graham, 'and this Mr Murray is a particularly well-conducted example; furthermore, he is comparatively free from the sordid parsimony that has brought the Trade, as it is emphatically called, so unenviable a reputation. I am told that he gave five hundred pounds, Five Hundred Pounds, gentlemen, for the first part of Lord Byron's *Childe Harold*.'

'Heavens,' said Stephen, 'What would the adult Harold have fetched entire?'

'Childe is an archaic term for a young man of good family,' said Graham.

'I should not expect so much,' said Rowan, 'not being a lord; but I should like to see my piece in print.'

In the evening, when the frigate was sailing very slowly into a mist that rose from the warm surface of the sea, a mist deeply tinged with rose from the setting sun, Jack said, 'I cannot tell you how happy I am to be in the dear *Surprise* again.'

'So I see,' said Stephen, 'and I give you joy of it.' He spoke a little shortly: the end of his 'cello bow had just come to pieces in his hand, and irritation was boiling up within. In Malta he had lain ashore, and Maltese bedbugs, fleas and mosquitoes had bitten him extremely, so that even now he itched from head to foot, and felt far hotter than he found agreeable. He was not positively malignant however, and he considered his friend attentively. Had Jack made some amorous conquest in Valetta, or rather (Jack being less enterprising than Babbington) had some odious wench led him by guile, by gentle force, to a pagan altar, persuading him that it was he the conquering hero? No, the look was not quite right for that: it had nothing of male self-complacency. Yet it was some heathen state of grace, he was sure; and when Jack, tucking his fiddle under his chin, struck out a strange leaping phrase and then began to improvise upon it he was surer still.

What with his self-taught technique and various wounds Jack could never be a very good player, but this evening he was making his fiddle sing so that it was a joy to hear. It was a wild, irregular song, expressing glee rather than any respect for rules, but a glee that was very, very far from being puerile; and contemplating Jack as he played away there by the stern-window Stephen wondered that a sixteen-stone post-captain, a scarred and battered gentleman with an incipient dewlap, could skip with such subtle grace, could possess such gaiety, could conceive such surprisingly witty and original concepts, and could express them so well. The dinner-table Jack Aubrey, delighted with a pun, was a different being: yet the two lived in the same skin together.

The 'cello bow was mended; the violin improvisation ended with an elfin shriek trilling up almost beyond the limit of human hearing; and they set to their old well-paced Scarlatti in C major, playing on into the middle watch.

'Will William Babbington have remembered my mastic, I ask myself?' said Stephen as they parted. 'He is a worthy young man, but the sight of a smock drives all other considerations from his mind; and Argostoli is renowned not only for mastic but also for handsome women.'

'I am sure he will have remembered it,' said Jack, 'but I doubt we meet him in the morning. Even we are making barely two knots, and that poor misbegotten rig, that Dutch tub of a *Dryad* is no use in light airs. Besides, if this mist don't clear tomorrow we may be becalmed altogether.'

Stephen had the utmost faith in Jack as a weatherprophet, a mariner and a sea-pope; but it so happened that his bites and the lack of air (the *Worcester*'s luxurious twenty square feet had made him forget the dank unventilated crib under the *Surprise*'s waterline) prevented him from sleeping – he was on deck at first dawn, when the pale mists were thinning and the handpumps wheezing up the water of the ritual scouring; and when the lookout called 'Sail ho! Sail on the larboard bow,' he looked in the right direction, saw the sail in question looming vaguely, but not so vaguely that he could not tell she was a brig, and said 'Fallible, fallible, Jack Aubrey. I shall have my mastic after all.' With this he walked forward, scratching himself; he picked his way among the sand and water sprinklers and passed the mate of the watch, who, perched on a carronade with his trousers rolled against the wet, was staring at the ghostly brig. Stephen said, 'There is Mr Babbington; perhaps he will come to breakfast,' but the youth, still staring, only answered with a vacant laugh. Stephen walked on as far as the starboard forechains, took off his nightcap and nightshirt, stuffed them under the dead-eyes, scratched himself industriously for a while, crept out on to the projecting shelf, and holding his nose with his left hand, crossing himself with his right, dropped with tightly-shut eyes into the sea, the infinitely refreshing sea.

He was not a powerful swimmer; indeed by ordinary standards he could hardly be called a swimmer at all, but with infinite pains Jack had taught him to keep afloat and beat his way through the water as far as fifty and even sixty yards at a time. His journey along the ship's side from the forechains to the boat towing astern was therefore well within his powers, particularly as the ship herself was in gentle forward motion, which made his relative progress towards the boat so much the faster.

It was without the slightest apprehension, then, that he plunged, although he had never done so alone before; and even as the bubbles rushed past his ears he thought 'I shall say to Jack "Ha, ha: I went a-swimming this morning," and watch his amazement.' But as he came to the surface, gasping and clearing the water from his eyes, he saw that the ship's side was strangely far from him. Almost at once he realized that she was turning to larboard and he struck out with all his might, uttering a howl each time a wave lifted his head well clear of the water. But all hands had been called and there was a great deal of piping and shouting and running about on board the *Surprise* as she continued her turn, packing on sail after sail as she did so; and since all those who had a moment to look away from the task in hand stared eagerly to larboard, it was only by a singular piece of good fortune that John Newby, turning to spit over the starboard rail, caught sight of his anguished face.

From about this point the exact sequence of events escaped him: he was conscious of swallowing a great deal of seawater, and then of sinking for a while, and then of finding that he had lost his direction as well as his strength and what little buoyancy he ever had, but soon he seemed to be in a perpetual agitated present in which things happened not in a given order but on different planes. The enormous voice that cried 'Back the foretopsail' high above his head, the renewed sinking into the depths, dark now from the shadow of the hull, the rough hands that grasped his ear, elbow and left heel, dragging him over the gunwale of a boat, and the midshipman's anxious 'Are you all right, sir?' might all have been contemporary. It was not until he had pondered for a while, gasping in the sternsheets, that occurrences took to following one another, so that 'Stretch out, stretch out, for God's sake' preceded the thump of the boat against the ship's side and the call for a line to be handed down; but he was quite himself by the time he heard, not without anxiety, bow-oar's confidential murmur to his neighbour of 'He won't half cop it, if the skipper misses of this prize, by reason of his topping it, the grampus.'

Bonden, almost speechless with indignation, bundled him up the side, and plucking at him like an angry nanny would have urged him below; but Stephen dodged under his arm and walked forward to where Captain Aubrey was standing by the larboard bow-chaser with Pullings and the gunner, while the gun's crew trained the beautiful long brass nine-pounder on the flying brig, now half a mile away and under a perfect cloud of canvas. All but Jack looked quickly away, adopting wooden, vacant expressions, as he came up and said, 'Good morning, sir. I beg your pardon for causing this disturbance. I was a-swimming.'

'Good morning, Doctor,' said Jack, with a cold glance. 'I was not aware that you were in the sea until the boat was beside you, thanks to Mr Calamy's presence of mind. But I must remind you that no one is allowed to leave the ship without permission: furthermore, this is not a proper dress in which to appear on deck. We will speak of this matter at a more suitable time: at present I desire you will go to your cabin. Master Gunner, lend the Doctor your apron, lay me the roundest shot in this garland, load with three and a quarter pound and two wads, and let us try the range.'

In his cabin Stephen heard the gun open a deliberate, careful fire. He felt cold and depressed: on his way below he had met nothing but disapproving looks, and when he called for his servant there was no reply. If it had not been for this vile prize – for the possibility of this vile prize – if it had not been for their greed, their grovelling cupidity – he would have been surrounded with loving care; he would have been caressed on all hands, and congratulated on his escape. Wrapping himself in a blanket he dropped into an improbable doze, then deeper, deeper, into a profound insensibility from which he was shaken, violently shaken, by Peter Calamy, who told him in a shrill bellow that 'old Borrell had cut her maintopsail halyards away at a thousand yards – all came down with a run – Lord, how they had roared! She was alongside now, and the Captain thought he might like to have a look at her.'

Ever since Dr Maturin had treated him for mumps, Calamy had grown very fond of him: this affection expressed itself by an odd confidential address – when, for example, Mr Calamy was to dine in the cabin he would take Stephen aside early in the day and say 'What's going to be for pudding, sir? Oh come on, sir, I'm sure you know what's for pudding,' – and by the assumption that in many respects he was the older of the two, an assumption much strengthened by this morning's events. He now compelled Stephen into quite formal clothes: 'No, sir; breeches it must be. The Captain may only be wearing trousers, but after this morning breeches and a frilled shirt is the least that can be expected.'

It was in something not very far from full dress, therefore, that Dr Maturin regained the deck, a deck now crowded with benevolent, smiling faces. 'There you are, Doctor,' said Jack, shaking his hand. 'I thought you might like to see our prize before I send her away.'

He led him to the side and they looked down on the captured brig, not indeed the *Dryad* nor anything resembling the *Dryad* except in the possession of two masts, but a genuine flyer, long and narrow, with a very fine entry, towering masts and a bowsprit of extraordinary length with a triple dolphin-striker, the *Bonhomme Richard*, that well-known blockade-runner. 'Whether we should have caught her by the end of the day, with the breeze freshening, I do not know,' said Jack, 'but Mr Borrell here made sure of it with a ball that cut away her topsail halyards at a thousand yards. Such a pretty shot!'

'It was mostly luck, sir,' said the gunner, laughing with delight.

'As you will recall,' said Jack, 'the halyards are the ropes

280

that haul the yards up, so when they are cut the yards fall
down. Unless they are well puddened, of course, which
was not the case,' he added.

'There is a great deal of blood on the deck,' said
Stephen. 'Did the falling yard crush many of her men?'

'Oh no. She had already been taken by Greek pirates,
their boats pulling aboard her in a dead calm. They killed
most of her people – that is where the blood comes from
– just keeping her master and a few others for ransom.'

'*Greek* pirates, alas?' said Stephen. He had an infinite
respect for ancient Greece; the cause of Greek independence was very near to his heart; and in spite of all the
evidence to the contrary he liked to think of modern
Greeks in an amiable light. 'I dare say they are very
rare.'

'Oh Lord, no: in these waters and eastward any
caique that sees a smaller one turns pirate directly,
unless the other is from the same village or the same
island, just as everything from the Barbary Coast turns
corsair whenever the chance offers. In spite of the Turks
they haunt this channel, since it has all the shipping from
the Levant to the Adriatic ports. These fellows came
up on the Frenchman in their felucca without a sign
of hostility – they hailed one another, and passed the
time of day, her master tells me – and then in the
night, when it fell dead calm, they carried him with
their boats, as I say. And when the yard came down
they took to these same boats again and pulled away
like fury, keeping the Frenchman between our guns and
them. Do you choose to step over? It is an interesting
sight.'

The bloody deck was neither new nor interesting,
nor were the pillaged cabins and quarters below, but
Jack led him down and down into the hold, dim in spite
of the open hatches, and extraordinarily aromatic, almost
unbreathably scented.

'They had begun breaking bulk, the goddamn fools,'
said Jack; and as his eyes grew used to the twilight

281

Stephen saw that they were walking on nutmegs, cinnamon, cloves and turmeric, spilt from torn bales. 'Is it all spice?' he asked, pausing by the extraordinary pungency of a cracked pot of musk.

'No,' said Jack. 'The master tells me that the spice was only his last lading, at Scanderoon: the chief of the cargo is indigo, with a few casks of cochineal. But what those vermin were after,' he said, referring to the Greeks and leading Stephen along the shadowy hold through slanting pillars of scented, dust-filled sunlight, 'and what I am delighted to say they did not have time to carry to their infernal boats, was this.' They turned the corner of a carefully-stowed wall of indigo bales, ducking under the shores, and there in a recess lay a heap of silver, a deep sloping heap of pieces of eight and Maria Theresa dollars that had spilled from an open tilting chest. By the light of lanterns two strong ship's boys, guarded by the sergeant of Marines and the master-at-arms, were shovelling it into canvas bags: the boys' faces gleamed with sweat and satisfied desire. They and their guardians beamed on the Captain.

'That will make a pleasant little distribution,' observed Jack; and as he led the way back to the *Surprise*, handing Stephen carefully along the cat-walk set up for the bags of dollars, he pointed out the flying Greeks. Their boats had reached the felucca, and it was sailing away eastwards under its two lateens, helped by its long, heavy sweeps.

'Shall you pursue them, so?' asked Stephen.

'No. If I caught them I should have to carry them back to Malta to be tried, and I cannot spare the time. If I could deal with them in the Turks' brisk fashion, it would be different; and in any case I shall give them a gun or two if ever we come within range, which is precious unlikely,' said Jack, and he called, 'Pass the word for Mr Rowan.' For much of the rest of the watch he was taken up with the prize and with giving Rowan, the prize-master, very serious advice about his course and conduct. Then, just after eight bells, 'Where away?' he called, in answer to the lookout's cry of a sail.

'Broad on the starboard beam, sir. A brig, ha, ha, ha.'

It was rare for merry laughter to accompany replies in a ship under Captain Aubrey's command, but this was an uncommon day, and in any event it was clear from the lookout's satirical tone and his mirth and from the brig's bearing that this must be the unfortunate *Dryad* – unfortunate in that a slightly earlier appearance would have earned her a share in this fine plump prize. If she had even been on the horizon during the chase she must have shared, and the Surprises, to a man, were heartily glad that she had been delayed. 'You will get your mastic at last,' said Jack, laughing too. 'But poor Babbington will be as blue as a Barbary ape. Still, he has only himself to blame: I always told him as a boy to waste not a minute, ha, ha, ha. Mr Pullings, when the clerk is ready, we will muster by the open list.'

This was not a regular day for mustering: the Surprises had neither clean shirts nor shaved faces, and although some made an effort to look trim, replaiting their pigtails and putting on their best blue jackets, most came straight from their work on the prize's damaged rigging. They all looked very cheerful however, and at the bosun's pipe they formed their usual irregular mass on the larboard side of the quarterdeck and along the gangway in a high state of expectant greed, for it was seen that Mr Ward, the Captain's clerk, had taken up his station by the capstan rather than just forward of the wheel and that there were several sailcloth bags at his feet, and all those who had sailed with Captain Aubrey before knew his habit of circumventing the Admiralty courts and their long, long delays.

'Silence fore and aft,' called Pullings: and turning to Jack he said 'All present, clean and sober, sir, if you please.'

'Thank you, Mr Pullings,' said Jack. 'Then we will muster by the open list.' He raised his voice: 'Listen, men: there was some silver in the Frenchman, so rather than wait six months for the prize-court, we will have a first distribution now. Carry on, Mr Ward.'

'Abraham Witsover,' called the clerk, and Abraham Witsover pushed his way out of the throng, crossed the deck, saluted his captain, had his name checked on the roll and received, paid down on the capstan-head, twenty-five dollars, the equivalent of three months' pay, which he put into his hat, moving over to the starboard gangway, chuckling to himself. It was necessarily a long muster, though a satisfying one, and before it was over the *Dryad* had drawn so close with the freshening breeze that even without his telescope Jack could see what looked very like a group of women right aft.

With his telescope he saw that it was quite certainly women, clustered about the *Dryad*'s captain. Another parcel, somewhat larger, stood near the mainmast, presumably surrounding the *Dryad*'s officers, while a female crowd lined the rail as far as the bows, among the hands. He had known women put off to a man-of-war coming into port in such numbers that the ship would settle a strake under their weight, but such proportions as this – more women than foremast jacks – he had never beheld, even in the most licentious ships and on the West Indies station: and this was at sea, on active service!

The last man crossed the deck: the clinking ship's company was dismissed, and Jack said to the signal-midshipman, 'To *Dryad*: *Captain repair aboard at once.*' He then turned to Rowan and said, 'You may part company as soon as I hear from Captain Babbington whether the transports are in Cephalonia or not; then you will not lose a moment of this beautiful leading breeze. Here he is. Captain Babbington, good day to you. Are the transports in Cephalonia? Is all well?'

'Yes, sir.'

'Mr Rowan, report to the Commander-in-Chief, with my duty, that the transports are in Cephalonia, and that all is well. You need not mention the fact that you saw one of the squadron crammed with women from head to stern; you need not report this open and I may say shameless violation of the Articles of War, for that disagreeable task falls to your superiors; nor need you make any observations about floating brothels or the relaxation of discipline in the warmer eastern waters, for these observations will naturally occur to the Commander-in-Chief without your help. Now pray go aboard our prize and proceed to Malta without the loss of a minute: not all of us can spare the time to dally with the sex.'

'Oh sir,' cried Babbington, as Rowan darted over the side, 'I really must be allowed to protest – to deny –'

'You will not deny that they are women, surely? I can tell the difference between Adam and Eve as quick as the next man, even if you cannot; just as I can tell the difference between an active zealous officer and a lubber that lies in port indulging his whims. It is of no use trying to impose upon me.'

'No, sir. But these are all respectable women.'

'Then why are they leering over the side like that, and making gestures?'

'It is only their way, sir. They are all Lesbians –'

'And no doubt they are all parsons' daughters, your cousins in the third degree, like that wench in Ceylon.'

'– and Lesbians always join their hands like that, to show respect.'

'You are becoming an authority on the motions of Greek women, it appears.'

'Oh sir,' cried Babbington, his voice growing shriller still. 'I know you do not like women aboard –'

'I believe I have had occasion to mention it to you some fifty or sixty times in the last ten years.'

'But if you will allow me to explain –'

'It would be interesting to hear how the presence of thirty-seven, no, thirty-eight young women in one of His Majesty's sloops can be explained; but since I like some decency to be preserved on my quarterdeck, perhaps the explanation had better take place in the cabin.' And in the cabin he said, 'Upon my word, William, this is coming it pretty high. Thirty-eight wenches at a time is coming it pretty high.'

'So it would be, sir, if there were any guilty or even shall I say cheerful intent; but upon my honour, I am blameless in thought, word, and deed. Well, in word and deed, anyhow.'

'Perhaps you had better begin the explanation.'

'Well, sir, as soon as I had seen the transports into Argostoli I shaped a course for the Strophades, and towards the end of the day we sighted a sail far to leeward, flying signals of distress. She proved to be a Tunis corsair that had been dismasted in a squall and had run clean out of water, having so many prisoners aboard. She had been raiding the islands for women, and she had done far better than she expected – chanced upon a kind of sewing-bee on the shore at Naxos and then all the young female part of a wedding in Lesbos, taken as they were crossing Peramo harbour in boats.'

'The dogs,' said Jack. 'So these are the women?'

'Not all of them, sir,' said Babbington. 'We told the Moors, of course, that the Christians must be given up, in the nature of things; and we told the women that they should be taken back to Greece. But then it appeared that those from Naxos, who had been aboard quite a long time, did not want to be parted from their corsairs, whereas those from Lesbos did – they were absolutely passionate about going home. We could not quite make it out at first, but presently the Naxiotes and the Lesbians started calling names and pulling one another's hair, and everything became quite clear. So we separated them as gently as we could – my bosun was bitten to the bone, and several hands cruelly scratched – helped the Moors set up a jury-mast, gave them biscuit and water enough to carry them home, and made all possible sail to join you at the rendezvous. And here I am, sir, quite happy to be publicly reproached, abused, and amazingly vilified, so long as I am conscious of having done my duty.'

'Well, damme, William, I am sorry: I am very sorry, indeed I am. But injustice is a rule of the service, as you know very well; and since you have to have a good deal of undeserved abuse, you might just as well have it from your friends.'

'Certainly, sir. And now, sir, what must I do?'

'You must drink a few glasses of madeira, and then you must turn about while the wind serves, and take all your pretty creatures, your *virgoes intactoes* I am sure, to Cephalonia and entrust them to Major de Bosset, the governor. He is an uncommon energetic, reliable officer and understands the Greek; he will look after them, victualling them on the shore establishment, until he finds a good stolid trader going to Lesbos. Killick,' he called, raising his voice from habit, although his steward could be heard breathing heavily on the other side of the bulkhead, eavesdropping as usual, 'Killick, light along some madeira, and ask the Doctor and Mr Pullings if they would like to step below.'

'I must tell the Doctor of a prodigious kind of pelican that flew over us off Zante,' said Babbington. 'And I must not forget the Turkish frigate we saw not long before I met you. She gave us a civil gun when we showed our colours, and I returned it; but we did not speak, because she was chasing a felucca to leeward, cracking on most surprising for a Turk, studdingsails aloft and alow on either side.'

The Turkish frigate, said Professor Graham, who had a recent list of the Sultan's men-of-war, was the *Torgud* of thirty guns. She and the *Kitabi* of twenty guns, together with a few smaller things, constituted the command of Mustapha, the ruler of Karia and the Capitan-Bey or senior naval officer in these waters: indeed, they might be said to belong to Mustapha himself, since he used them just as he saw fit, without any reference to Constantinople. And this was fair enough, since Constantinople never produced the men's wages, and Mustapha was obliged to feed and pay them himself. He was said, however, to be an active, zealous officer, and after they had been sailing an hour or two, with the mainland of Epirus looming high and jagged ahead and the *Bonhomme Richard* and the *Dryad* lost to view long since, they came across signs of his activity and zeal – the charred remains of a felucca, shattered by gunfire but still just awash and still just recognizable. Then, perfectly recognizable, twenty or thirty corpses drifting in a line along the current: all Greek, all stripped, some headless, some with their throats cut, some impaled, and three roughly crucified, Saint Andrew fashion, on the felucca's broken sweeps.

# CHAPTER TEN

The *Surprise* lay off Mesenteron, moored in fifteen fathom water, pitching gently as she gazed at the harbour, a harbour silted up long since and now full of tree-trunks from the last flood of the river that meandered through the low-lying unhealthy town. Two castles guarded the tree-trunks and the score of smallcraft inside the harbour: the castles had once belonged to Venice and the winged lion of St Mark still stood in bold relief upon their outward walls, but now they flew the Turkish crescent. The frigate had saluted them on dropping anchor and they had replied, the roar of cannon sending up clouds of pelicans from an unseen lagoon.

But since then nothing had happened: nothing to the purpose, that is to say. The pelicans had recovered their wits, flying back in long straight lines to their brackish mud, and the fishing-boats continued to mill about in the harbour, spearing squids as they rose to the surface in the ecstasies of ten-armed copulation; yet no canopied official boat shoved off from the castle jetty, no pasha showed his horse-tail banner, and aboard the frigate there was a distinct sense of anticlimax.

A sailor's eye would have seen that she was even trimmer than usual, with her furled sails skinned up in the bunt and her head-braces lying in perfect Flemish fakes, while even a landsman would have noticed that the officers had abandoned their usual working clothes of easy nankeen pantaloons and light jackets for undress uniform and Hessian boots, while the bargemen were already in their snowy trousers, bright blue jackets and best straw hats, ready to row their Captain ashore as soon as he was invited. Yet the invitation did not come. The castle showed no sign of life and Captain Aubrey was certainly not going to make the first move: he sat in his great cabin, elegantly and even splendidly dressed but for the fact that his gold-laced coat lay on a chair with his Patriotic Fund hundred-guinea sword beside it, while his neckcloth was as yet untied and his breeches unbuckled at the knee. He was drinking a supplementary pot of coffee and eating biscuits with a fine equanimity, fully prepared either to see Ismail Bey, if that gentleman appeared or sent a proper message, or to sail northward for an interview with Mustapha. Or failing Mustapha, then with Sciahan Bey in Kutali itself. He had wished to see his three Turks in regular succession, travelling up the coast from Ismail's Mesenteron to Mustapha's Karia and so past Marga and its Frenchmen to Kutali, thus spending the least possible time in preliminaries. But with such a delicate mission as this he was certainly not going to allow himself to fret over details, and if his Turks did not chance to be at home as he passed by, then he would take them in another order: in any event he intended to be at sea, well out at sea, before the evening. At quarters yesterday the ship's gunnery had disappointed him, and although the hands' tearing high spirits over the prize had something to do with their criminal levity and indifferent shooting it was also true that they were not yet quite at home with the frigate's guns. A couple of hours' steady practice, live practice, would do wonders, even though it meant burning much of the powder he had taken out of the prize.

Ismail's absence did not vex him unduly, therefore, but it did puzzle him: in these circumstances, where the cannon he could provide would probably mean victory to any one of the three sides, he had expected an eager welcome – janissaries playing a Turkish march, fireworks, perhaps an oriental carpet laid out. Was this apparent indifference Turkish policy, a common manoeuvre in the East? He would have liked to ask Professor Graham: but early in the day, as soon as the mountains of Epirus grew clear on the eastern sky, the Professor and Dr Maturin had made their way into the maintop, helped and guarded

290

by Honey and Maitland, both master's mates and both powerful young men, there to survey the classic ground. It was not Attica, it was not even Boeotia, but it was still just Greece, and the poor young gentlemen were bored to a galloping pallor, intolerably bored with accounts of Theopompus and the Molossians, of Agathocles and the Molossians, of Themistocles and the Molossians with his speech at full length, of the Actian games, and even of the battle of Actium itself, though neither Graham nor Maturin could remember which side had the weather-gage. Their only relief from boredom came when Graham, in the heat of declamation (Plutarch on Pyrrhus), stepped backwards into the lubber's hole, and when they were sent down for maps and an azimuth compass so that it might be determined which mountain on the skyline concealed Dodona and its speaking oak – 'Dodona, young gentlemen, which Homer describes as the hole of the Selli, who sleep upon the ground and do not wash their feet.'

'Perhaps that is Graham,' thought Jack, hearing someone speaking to the sentry at the cabin door. But no, it was Stephen, attracted by the smell of coffee wafting up and perhaps a little overcome by Graham's elephantine memory (he was now treating the master's mates to Polybius, Dionysius of Halicarnassus, and Pausanias, all of them on the subject of Pyrrhus, born and nurtured in those blue-grey mountains ahead.)

'I was thinking of Graham,' said Jack.

'So was I,' Stephen instantly replied. 'The other day he explained to me that the Navy was a school for cowardice, and I meant to ask you for some heads of argument on the other side. I was reminded of his contention as I came down just now, because I heard a midshipman reproving a foremast hand.'

'How did Graham make this out?' asked Jack. 'Killick, light along another cup.'

'He began by saying that he had seen an admiral throw an inkwell at a post-captain, and that the post-captain, a

291

choleric and masterful man, overcame his desire to retaliate by a very great exertion of self-discipline, explaining afterwards that if he had raised his hand to his superior officer it would have been the end of his career – even in theory of his life. Graham observed that the admiral could blackguard and even assault the captain with impunity, just as the captain could blackguard and even assault his lieutenants and they their inferiors and so on to the penultimate member of the ship's company. He said that the admiral, from his earliest days in the Navy, had seen the cowardly practice of abusing and beating men who could not reply, their hands being tied; and that, his mind having been long schooled in cowardice and he wearing the impregnable armour of the King's commission, it now appeared quite natural to him to do so. I did not answer directly, meaning to ask your views first: I was reminded of it by hearing this boy revile a seaman and threaten him with a rope's end, when in a state of nature the man would have put him to silence. Even in the present unnatural conditions the sailor was sufficiently human and incautious to reply.'

'Who was the midshipman?' asked Jack with strong displeasure.

'My dear, I am sorry that my face should look at all like an informer's,' said Stephen. 'But tell me now, how can I best confound Professor Graham?'

'Why, as to that,' said Jack, blowing on his coffee-cup and staring out of the stern-window at the harbour, 'as to that . . . if you do not choose to call him a pragmatical clinchpoop and kick his breech, which you might think ungenteel, perhaps you could tell him to judge the pudding by its fruit.'

'You mean, prove the tree by its eating.'

'No, no, Stephen, you are quite out: eating a tree would prove nothing. And then you might ask him, had he ever seen many poltroons in the Navy?'

'I am not quite sure what you mean by poltroons.'

'You might describe them as something that cannot be

attempted to be tolerated in the Navy – like wombats,' he added, with a sudden recollection of the creatures Stephen had brought aboard an earlier command. 'Mean-spirited worthless wretches: cowards, to put it in a word.'

'You are unjust to wombats, Jack; and you were unjust to my three-toed sloth – such illiberal reflections. But leaving wombats to one side, and confining ourselves to your poltroons, Graham might reply that he had seen a good many bullies in the Navy; and for him, perhaps, the two are much the same.'

'But they ain't, you know. They ain't the same thing at all. I thought they were once, when I was a youngster in the *Queen*, and I stood up to a tyrannical brute, quite sure he would prove a barnyard cock and turn shy. Lord, how he did bang me up and down,' – laughing heartily at the recollection – 'and when I could no longer hear or see or keep my feet he stood over me with a cobbing-board . . .' For some minutes he had been watching a remote whirl of activity at the foot of the nearer castle, between the gate-house and the shore, and now he broke off to say, 'They are launching a boat at last, a caique with an awning.' He reached for his telescope. 'Yes. It is something official: I see an old gentleman with a beard being lifted in by two blackamoors. Killick, pass the word for Professor Graham. Tell Mr Gill with my compliments that he is to be brought down by both master's mates together. Lord, what a set of lubbers' – nodding towards the distant boat – 'They have fouled a tree-trunk. Now they have jibed, God help them. There will be plenty of time before we have to put on our coats.'

This was the opinion of the quarterdeck as well. All those officers who were not on duty went back to their game of shove-groat in the gunroom: a great competition had been going on since Malta, and although the prize of twelve and sixpence seemed trifling since the capture of the *Bonhomme Richard*, they still played with the greatest eagerness, as careless of the glorious sky, the perfect sea, the spectacular Ionian shore, and even of Pyrrhus and the Dalmatian pelicans as they had been in some sunless convoy, far out in the drizzling German Ocean. Pullings glanced at his perfect decks, the white-gloved sideboys and the new-covered manropes ready to bring the visitor aboard, the powdered and pipe-clayed Marines prepared to stamp and clash by way of martial compliment, the bosun and his mates waiting with their shining silver calls, and then hurried below himself, to shove a groat, emerging only when the caique was within hailing distance. On deck Gill, the officer of the watch, had everything well in hand: in the cabin below Killick had arranged cushions in the Oriental manner under Professor Graham's direction, and had lit the hubblebubble laid in for the purpose at Valetta – tobacco-smoke rose from the cabin-skylight, and the afterguard breathed it in greedily.

The caique upset all natural calculations by suddenly darting round to the larboard mainchains at the last moment; but the Navy, accustomed to the wild vagaries of foreigners, dealt with the situation directly, facing about and providing a mirror-image of the proper ceremonies, bringing the old gentleman aboard without a feather of the splendid aigrette in his turban being ruffled.

He was led to the cabin, where Jack welcomed him, Graham acting as the interpreter: his only function was to invite Captain Aubrey to dine with the Bey, and to apologize for the lateness of the invitation – the Bey had been hunting in the marshes and the news of the frigate's arrival had not reached him for a great while: he was desolated; he lay in ashes.

'What was the Bey hunting?' asked Jack, who was interested in these things and who in any case felt that some polite conversation might compensate for Killick's lukewarm version of sherbet and the plain Navy twist in the hubblebubble, neither of which seemed quite to the company's taste.

'Jews,' said Graham, relaying the question and the answer.

'Pray ask the Effendi whether the pelicans nest here,'

294

said Stephen, after the slightest pause. 'I am aware that the Turks have a great kindness for the stork, and never molest her; perhaps their humanity may extend to the pelican, there being a superficial resemblance.'

'I beg your pardon, sir,' said Pullings, coming in, 'but the caique has sunk alongside. We have made it fast to the tyes, head and stern, and the crew are aboard us.'

'Very good, Mr Pullings: I dare say they would like something to eat – anything but swinesflesh, you know. Tell them No porco, pas porco. And let the barge be lowered down: I am going ashore. Mr Graham, please convey the sad news to the Effendi, and tell him our carpenters will probably be able to repair the damage.'

The old gentleman did not seem much moved. He said that it was clearly God's will, and that he for his part had never put to sea without a disaster of some kind. Indeed, the contrary would surprise him.

'Then let us hope that the Effendi will be surprised on his return voyage,' said Jack, 'for it is clear he must make it in my barge.'

Thursday, at sea

'. . . so I took the old gentleman ashore, telling my bargemen to row dry, and as luck would have it we shipped not a drop all the way,' wrote Jack in his letter home, 'though navigation in that choked-up harbour, with whole trees aground or floating, was neither beer nor yet skittles. But, however, Bonden knew that our honour depended on it, and he brought us alongside the jetty in great style: there I was pleased to see that they had spread out a perfectly beautiful blue carpet with a close pattern of rosy flowers, just the size to fit the breakfast parlour at home. Standing in the middle of it was Ismail Bey, the ruler of these parts, who welcomed me very civilly and led me to an uncommon fine horse, a bright bay stallion of rather better than sixteen hands, to carry me the three hundred yards into the castle. We passed through several courts, and in the last, which was full of orange-trees trimmed neat, they had spread an awning and laid the table – a precious short-legged table I may say, but since there were no chairs, only cushions raised on a low bench, it was just as well – and a pleasant thing was that through an empty gun-embrasure opposite my place I could see the dear *Surprise*, exactly framed.

'We sat down six: the Bey and I, his vizier and Professor Graham, and his astrologer with Stephen. The Bulbuljibashi, the keeper of the nightingales, and the Tournajibashi, the keeper of the cranes, had been brought to tell Stephen about pelicans, but they were not admitted to the table. We had no plates or knives or forks (though we each had a tortoiseshell spoon) and dinner was not served quite in our way either, there being no removes, but dishes following one another separately, to the number of thirty-six, not counting the sweetmeats. Each came in to the sound of kettledrums, brought by black men who put them down on a monstrous fine gold salver nestling in an embroidered cushion in the middle of the table: then we all reached out and took lumps with our fingers, unless it was very soft, when we used our spoons. One of the dishes was a roasted lamb with a pudding of bright yellow rice in its belly, and the Bey seized it by the legs, tearing it very neatly to pieces for us. Graham was a great help, keeping up a fine flow of talk in Turkish and telling us how to behave: you would have laughed to hear him say, every so often and without looking at Stephen, 'Feed the keeper of the nightingales – feed the keeper of the cranes', and Stephen would gravely put a piece into the waiting mouth behind. And sometimes he would say, in Killick's very words, 'Captain A, your sleeve is in your dinner,' which I am afraid it often was, a uniform coat not being designed for plunging wrist-deep into a common dish. But apart from that it was a forbiddingly grave and solemn meal, with scarcely a smile from start to finish. We drank only water until the end, when we reached coffee, which was poured into odd little china cups without handles that stood in gold stands all set with diamonds and rubies and emeralds. Mine was all emeralds, and I was incautious enough to admire it: Ismail at once ordered it to be put up in a box and carried to the barge, and it was only Graham's firmly and repeatedly stating that for people of our nation this was a most inauspicious day for giving or receiving presents that saved the situation. For indeed it would never have done to lay myself under an obligation to the Bey: although he is in so much favour with our embassy in Constantinople and although he certainly has smooth, obliging, caressing manners, I found him a disagreeably oily gentleman – not my idea of a Turk at all and indeed Graham tells me that he is the grandson of a Greek apostate, while his mother was Egyptian – and it would not have answered at the end of the feast, when most of the company was dismissed and we came to talk about the real point of our meeting. I will not trouble you with the details of our negotiations, but will only observe, that although my profession requires me to suffer for my King and country, the agony of sitting cross-legged with one's breeches buckles grinding into one's very bone, is, after the first three hours, far, far beyond the call of duty. In any case, I must resume our conversation for the Commander-in-Chief, and to write it out twice would be tedious indeed, particularly as it was so unsatisfactory.'

This was only the second instalment of a new letter, since he had posted the last in Malta, and he ran over it from the beginning – the extraordinary luck of having *Surprise*, with a hand-picked crew, if only for this single cruise – the delightful little prize – not a floating Golconda, not a *Santa Brigida*, not a capture that would do away with all the difficulties at home, but at least one that would give him room to turn around: and Sophie was to buy herself a new pelisse, a fine new tippet – Babbington and the Grecian women – the noble coast-line of Epirus. And he felt a certain twinge as he reread the lines in which he desired his daughters to find out Epirus on the map, and his son to read about Pyrrhus in Gregory's *Polite Education*, 'for it would be a great shame, was George

297

to be found ignorant of Pyrrhus when he grew up': Jack had never been a hypocrite until he became a father, and even now it did not come easy.

Then he considered the paper he was to write, the memorandum of his conversation with Ismail Bey. The conclusion was plain enough: if the British guns were to be paid for by effective action against the French in Marga, Jack thought he could take them to a better market. Ismail seemed to him, and to his advisers, much more a politician than a warrior: he had no coherent military plan for taking Kutali, still less Marga, but seemed to think that the town must necessarily fall into his hands as soon as he had the cannon. Nor could he be brought to state the exact number of troops he would bring to the two operations: 'there would be a great many, far more than would be needed; he would have been delighted to show them, parading in the square, but two regiments and most of his best officers were away, putting down rebels in the north, while thousands of men were dispersed along the frontiers. But if Captain Aubrey would give him a little notice before he next came to Mesenteron, there would be a magnificent review: Captain Aubrey would see a splendid body of men, devoted to the British cause, burning to see the downfall of the French, and perfectly equipped, except in the article of guns.' Much of this sounded false, and all the falser for coming over in translation, separated from the significant looks and gestures that accompanied the original words: one of Jack's few certainties was that the Bey's notion of urgency and even of time itself was quite unlike his own.

But by far the greater part of Ismail's discourse was concerned with his excellent relations with the British embassy and with the characters of Mustapha and Sciahan, his rivals for the possession of Kutali. They were a sad pair, it seemed, in whom wickedness and greed struggled with ineptitude and cowardice for the mastery: they would of course endeavour to deceive Captain Aubrey, but Captain Aubrey would instantly perceive that the first was nothing but an illiterate corsair, scarcely better than a pirate, a person whose word no man relied on, while the second was a man of doubtful loyalty to the Sultan, completely under the influence of the notorious Ali Pasha of Iannina, and as impotent in the field of battle as he was in the harem: and both were devoted to Napoleon.

Graham had warned him of the slowness of Oriental negotiation, and of the different standards of acceptable duplicity; he had also said that Ismail's vizier, coming to ask what present Captain Aubrey would expect for his good offices in this affair, had offered the professor a personal commission of eight hundred and forty piastres for each gun delivered. It was not an encouraging beginning, and perhaps the other Beys would be much the same: it was not impossible that the embassy was right, and that Ismail was the depressing best of the bunch. 'Come in,' he said in a low, dispirited voice, and Elphinstone, a midshipman, walked in, trim and shining. 'Good morning, sir,' he said. 'You wished to see me?'

'Oh, Mr Elphinstone: yes. You have three men down in the defaulters' list. Two are trifling cases and five-water grog for a couple of days will deal with them, but you bring Davis up on a serious charge, a flogging charge. If nobody speaks up for him and if he cannot convincingly deny it, I must give him at least a dozen, though I very much dislike seeing men beaten. Do you like seeing men beaten?'

'Oh no, sir; but is it not necessary for discipline?'

'Some people think so, and with some men perhaps it is; but I have known commanders go a year and more without any flogging, taut commanders of crack ships.'

'Davis answered, sir: he answered very rudely when I told him to strop the block again – said something about me "still shitting yellow" which made the others laugh.'

'Davis is a special case. He is a little odd and he has always been allowed rather more leeway than the others. He was at sea long before you were born, and although he is still not very good at stropping a block nor serving a cable he has other seamanlike qualities that will no doubt occur to your mind. He is enormously strong, for one thing; he is always the first to board and he is a most terrifying sight on the enemy's deck: mad bulls ain't in it. But I was forgetting, you have yet to see that kind of service. That is all I have to say for the moment, Mr Elphinstone: good day to you. Pray give my steward a hail as you go by.'

'It ain't no bleeding good, sir,' said Killick in an angry whine, coming in with Jack's best coat over his arm. 'This nasty foreign mess will not come out, not if it's ever so, and now I've tried to cover it with saffron over the gold lace it looks even worse. Time and time again I've said "Your sleeve's in your dinner, sir" when it was only beef and pudding or drowned baby or the like, and that's been bad enough; but this here foreign mess — why . . .'

'Come, Killick, pipe down and give me my coat,' said Jack. 'There is not a moment to be lost.'

'On your own head be it,' said Killick, helping him into the heavy full-dress coat; and he added something mutinous about 'laughing-stock' under his breath.

Yet no very great degree of mirth greeted Captain Aubrey when he stepped on to his quarterdeck: this was a Wednesday, and at six bells in the forenoon watch on Wednesdays it was customary for all hands to be piped aft to witness punishment, a solemn occasion. Six bells struck: all the officers and young gentlemen were present, all in uniform: the grating was rigged and the bosun's mates stood by it, prepared to seize up any guilty man at the Captain's word and flog him with the cat-o'-nine-tails that Mr Hollar had ready in its baize bag.

The cat was not needed for the earlier defaulters. They were all mild cases of profane oaths, cursings, execrations, reproachful and provoking speeches or gestures, of uncleanliness or of drunkenness, and they were dealt with by suspension or dilution of grog or by extra duties; but when Davis' name was called and his offence made known and admitted or at least not denied, the bosun began untying the baize bag's strings. 'This is a damned bad state of affairs, Davis,' said Jack. 'There you are, a man rated able these twenty years and more, answering an officer. You must have heard the Articles read out some hundreds of times, and yet there you are, answering an officer! Mr Ward, let us hear number twenty-two, the second part.'

'The twenty-second Article of War, sir: the second part,' said the clerk, and he continued in a hieratic boom, 'If any mariner, or other person in the fleet, shall presume to quarrel with any of his superior officers, being in the execution of his office, or shall disobey any lawful command of any of his superior officers; every such person being convicted of any such offence by the sentence of a court-martial, shall suffer death.' Here he paused and repeated '*shall suffer death*' before going on in a perfunctory manner 'or such other punishment as shall, according to the nature and degree of his offence, be inflicted on him by the sentence of a court-martial.'

'There you are,' said Jack, looking at Davis, who looked steadily at the deck. 'How can you hope to escape flogging? Have you anything to say for yourself?' Davis made no reply, but began to take off his shirt. 'Has anyone else anything to say for him, then?'

'If you please, sir,' said Elphinstone, taking off the cocked hat he had put on for the occasion, 'he is in my division and has always been diligent and attentive hitherto, obedient to command and respectful.' At this one of Davis' messmates, out of sight in the throng, burst out in a coarse hoot of laughter, but Elphinstone, blushing painfully, went on, 'I believe it was only a temporary lapse, sir; and should like to beg him off his punishment.'

'Come, that is handsomely put,' said Jack. 'Do you hear, Davis? Mr Elphinstone begs you off your flogging.' He then delivered a particularly dreary homily on right and wrong, whose only merit was that it was fairly short and that it made him smile within.

He was smiling openly when Stephen walked in, looking shrewish. Like many large, florid, good-natured men, Jack Aubrey was afflicted with an undue proportion of small pale, meagre friends of a shrewish turn. One of his earliest shipmates and closest acquaintances, Heneage Dundas, had already earned himself the name of Vinegar Joe throughout the service; Jack's steward was a confirmed nagger; and at times even Sophie . . . He was therefore peculiarly sensitive to the quality of shrewishness and even before Stephen opened his mouth Jack knew that he was about to say something disagreeable.

'I ask only for information,' he said, 'and without the least personal bearing: but tell me, when captains set themselves up as judges and lay down the moral as well as the military law, extolling virtues that they rarely if ever practise, do they often feel the spiritual squalor of their conduct?'

'I dare say they do,' said Jack, smiling still. 'I know I have often wondered that I was not struck down by a levinflash. But there you are – no ship carries a man rated spotless Christian hero, so the captain has to do what he can, for the sake of discipline.'

'I see,' said Stephen. 'So it is not for the sake of exalting him in his own opinion, it is not for the sake of airing his own views before an audience that dare not stir or disagree, it is not for the deeply discreditable, nay, wicked pleasure of exercising his almost unlimited power: nor is it that our gentleman is unaware of the true nature of his act. No, no: it is all for discipline, for the country's good. Very well: I am content.' He sniffed, and went on, 'Pray, what is this I hear about passing for a gentleman?'

With a flash of insight Jack perceived that Stephen had been talking to Driver, the new Marine officer they had shipped at Malta, a great admirer of kings, titles of honour, ancient families, coats of arms, hereditary office and privilege in general. 'Well,' he said, 'you know what we mean by passing for lieutenant? When a mid has served his six years he attends the Board with his certificates and

302

his logs, the captains present examine him, and if they find he understands his profession he passes for lieutenant.'

'Sure, I have heard of it many, many times; and I remember poor Babbington's trembling anxiety. But I calmed his spirits with three drops of the essence of hellebore on a piece of sugar, and he passed with sailing colours.'

'Flying colours.'

'Let us not be pedantical, for all love.'

'But,' said Jack, 'so many have passed since the beginning of the war, and so many have been made lieutenants, that now there are more on the list than there can be employment for, let alone promotion; so some years ago men of no particular family found they were being left on shore. They had not passed for gentlemen, and they did not possess the friends or connections that could make interest for them, though sometimes they were capital seamen. Tom Pullings could not find a ship for a great while: and of course no ship, no promotion. I did my best, naturally, but I was away much of the time, and anyhow one scheme after another came to nothing: just before they gave me the *Worcester* I took him to dine at Slaughter's with Rowlands of the *Hebe*, who had lost a lieutenant overboard. They got along well enough, but afterwards Rowlands told me he did not choose to have anyone on his quarterdeck who did not say balcóny, and unfortunately poor Tom had said bálcony. It is the old story of the gentleman captains and the tarpaulins all over again.'

'What is your view of the matter?'

'I have no very clear view. There are so many factors; and so much depends on what you mean by gentleman. But suppose it is no more than the usual notion of someone whose family has had a certain amount of money for two or three generations, someone with reasonably good manners and at least a scrape of education – why then, seamanship being equal, I should rather have the gentleman than not, partly because it is easier for the officers to live together if they have roughly the same ideas of behaviour, but even more because the foremost hands value birth so highly, perhaps much more highly than they should.'

'Your ideal is a gentleman who is also a seaman?'

'I suppose so. But that would exclude Cook and many other men of the very first rate. As a rough rule it might answer for the common run, but it seems to me that your really good sea-officer is always an exceptional being, and one that ordinary rules scarcely apply to. Tom Pullings, for example: he may not be another Howe or Nelson, but I am quite certain he would make a far better captain than most – we do not often have occasion to talk of balconies at sea. I have tried to get him made again and again, as you know very well; but pushing don't always answer, and too much may do harm. Look at this,' he said, passing a letter from among the papers on his open desk.

'Sir,' read Stephen, 'The Board not having considered the service (alluded to in your letter of the 14th) performed under the direction of Lieutenant Pullings of the description that entitles him to promotion, I must confess my surprise at the manner in which you have thought fit to address me on the subject of it. Very sincerely, your humble servant, Melville.'

'That was years ago,' said Jack. 'The cutting-out of the *Rosa*. But things are no better now – rather worse indeed, with my old father cutting his capers in the Commons and shedding such a blight on any recommendation of mine – and Tom's only hope is a successful action. That is why we were so very disappointed when Emeriau slipped away, and why I do so very much hope that this next Turk, this Mustapha, may show more promise than the last. Turning the French out of Marga would almost certainly count as a frigate-action, with a step for the first lieutenant. With this breeze we should reach Karia tomorrow, and form some notion of the Capitan-Bey.'

In the event they formed their notion of him a good deal earlier. The *Surprise* was standing northward, surrounded by a cloud of her own making, when the lookout gave news of two ships on the starboard quarter, two ships under the land. He would have given the news sooner if he had not been watching the competition between the watches with such passionate interest, and now his hail had an anxious quality, for the ships were already hull-up, and this was one of the offences that Captain Aubrey rarely overlooked. By way of covering up he added details – 'Turkish frigate, coming up hand over hand – stuns'ls aloft and alow – t'other maybe a twenty-gun ship, Turk likewise – all plain sail – holds her course under the land – very hard to see.'

The starboard watch had just shattered a floating cask at four hundred yards, at the end of an exercise in which they had attained a thoroughly satisfactory rate of accurate fire: Jack said, 'House your guns. Starbowlines win by two points. A creditable exercise, Mr Pullings.' Then walking to the taffrail he directed his telescope at the newcomer and her distant consort. Graham and Stephen were standing by the stern-lantern, and to them he said with a smile, 'We are in luck. Here we have the whole Turkish navy this side of the Archipelago: that is the *Torgud* coming up and the *Kitabi* over there under the land, and I make no doubt the Capitan-Bey is aboard the frigate.' Raising his voice he gave the order that brought the *Surprise* close to the wind on the starboard tack, steering a course that would cross the *Torgud*'s bows.

Jack moved up to the forecastle as the ship turned and studied the Turk intently. She was built in the European manner, probably in a French or Venetian yard, and although the people on her deck wore turbans or scarlet skullcaps she was sailed in the European manner too. Pretty well handled: far better than her lumpish consort over the way, who was most shamefully brought by the lee, rounding a headland, just as he turned his glass on her.

The *Torgud* threw a fine bow-wave under her press of sail – she was obviously quite fast when going large – and as the *Surprise* was always happy on a bowline the

305

two frigates came together at a spanking pace. For a while they were almost head-on, but then the angle opened as the *Torgud* altered course to swing wide and cross the *Surprise*'s wake; she turned with a fine gleam of brass cannon all along her side and now for the first time Jack could really see what she was like: she was rather heavier than the *Surprise* and she mounted another pair of guns – damned odd gunports amidships, too – but he had the impression that they overpressed her, that she would not handle easy and that she might be slack in stays: from the churning of her wake she must carry an uncommon strong weather-helm. But there was little time for staring. 'Sir,' said Pullings, 'I believe they mean to come under our stern.'

'Come, that is civil,' said Jack. 'Professor Graham, do you understand the Turkish naval etiquette?'

'No, sir, I do not,' said Graham. 'But in general they follow the French.'

'Silly dogs,' said Jack. 'However, he means to be polite. Mr Borrell, stand by to give him thirteen guns the moment his jib comes in.'

The Turkish frigate ran down, put her helm hard over and rounded to, lying there under the *Surprise*'s lee. It was pretty well done: scarcely Navy-fashion – the taking in of the studdingsails was far too ragged for that and there was a sad want of coordination in the rising of the tacks, a general raggedness – but few merchantmen or privateers could have beat the *Torgud*'s performance.

And none could have outdone her in briskness of lowering a boat. It splashed down with an almighty thump from her quarter-davits and its crew tumbled over the rail in a most surprising fashion, followed almost as rapidly by men in robes, presumably officers. Jack had expected a long shouted exchange of civilities from ship to ship, but he had hardly had time to return to the quarterdeck before the Turkish boat was half-way across. Its bargemen were not elegantly dressed (one had nothing more than a torn pair of calico drawers), nor did they row pretty, but from their urgency and concentrated effort they might have been pulling for a prize; and facing the rowers, acting as his own coxswain, sat a man in a purple turban, a red beard down to his swelling belly, and purple baggy trousers, so big a man it was a wonder the boat was not grossly by the stern.

Jack clapped on the cocked hat that Killick silently passed him, glanced fore and aft and saw that Pullings, quicker-witted than his commander, had already turned out the Marines and laid on a proper reception. Then he heard the boat hook on, and looking over the rail he saw the big man reach for the manropes – the *Surprise* gave a distinct heel as he grasped them – and come running up the side as nimbly as a boy. Reaching the quarterdeck he put his hand to his forehead, then to his heart, bowing with a magnificence that might have seemed excessive in a smaller man: but Mustapha was huge in person and in presence. Though not quite as tall as Jack he was broader by far, and his vast purple Turkish trousers made his bulk seem even greater: 'Mustapha, Capitan-Bey,' he said in a resounding boom, and the wispy officer who had followed him said the same, adding in Greek and something like English, 'Commander of the Grand Turk's ships in these waters, and lord of Karia.'

'Welcome aboard, sir,' said Jack, stepping forward with his hand held out. 'Professor Graham, pray tell the gentlemen they are welcome aboard, and suggest that we should take coffee in the cabin.'

'So you speak Turkish,' said Mustapha, gently patting Graham's cheek. 'Very good, very good. Then Ulusan can go back to the boat.'

'Would he not like to take some refreshment in the gunroom?' asked Jack, seeing Ulusan bow and turn away.

'The Capitan-Bey says he might be tempted to drink wine and even spirits, forbidden to Mussulmans,' said Graham. 'He is better in the boat.'

In the cabin Jack was pleased to find that the Capitan-Bey could smile and even laugh. The extreme gravity of his

307

hosts at Mesenteron had weighed upon his spirits, making an already serious matter positively funereal: furthermore Ismail and his advisers had always looked at the table when addressing him – a part of Turkish manners, perhaps, but disconcerting; and now, with Mustapha's shrewd, knowing, often amused eye fixed steadily on his he felt much more at home. They were curious orange-yellow eyes, and they looked small in that huge face: smaller still when Mustapha smiled. The red-dyed beard would part, showing a broad gleam of teeth, and the eyes would almost vanish in the luxuriant bristling hair. This happened more and more often as the afternoon wore on and it was found that Mustapha could quite easily be tempted to drink wine and even spirits.

They had been for a tour of the frigate, during which it had become evident that Mustapha, though a judge of a ship, was even more devoted to a gun. He was fascinated by the improvements that Jack had borrowed from Philip Broke of the *Shannon*, at least for his chasers, and he fairly gloated over the heavy carronades, the genuine smashers, that lined the *Surprise*'s quarterdeck; for his ideal engagement was a furious battery at ever-diminishing range, followed by boarding.

'I love guns,' he said when they were back in the cabin, smoking the hubblebubble and drinking punch. 'They are not to be had, now that Venice is gone, and I need all I can get to take Kutali. I am delighted you have brought me so many.'

'And I should be delighted to give them to a fellow-seaman,' said Jack, smiling. 'But they are my master's guns and I must deliver them to the ally best suited for helping us to turn the French out of Marga. As I believe you know, two other gentlemen have proposed their services, and in justice I must hear what all those concerned may have to say.'

'I can tell you what Ismail has said,' cried Mustapha. 'He has said that I am an illiterate corsair, hand in glove with the French, not to be trusted for a moment. And

308

Sciahan will tell you I am in league with Ali Pasha, plotting to rebel against the Sultan – not to be trusted for a moment, ha, ha, ha! But neither can say I did not conquer Djerba and pacify the Morea in a two years' campaign – a hundred towns and villages in flames! And neither can be of the least use in helping you to turn the French out of Marga: Ismail is a mere Egyptian eunuch, terrified by the sound and sight of battle, and Sciahan is too old for anything like war – negotiation is his line, and that will never answer with the French. Whereas once I hold Kutali, the thing is done! We attack from land and sea, while at the same moment all the Mussulmans in the town rise up. Nothing can withstand the shock – believe me, Captain, nothing can withstand the shock. Come and look at my ship: you will see what she is capable of: you will see what kind of men I have aboard.'

'Hairy buggers,' muttered Bonden, gazing up the side as his Captain went aboard the *Torgud*, welcomed by the clash of cymbals; and by this he meant not only bearded but savage, fierce, dark, passionate, rough, fiery, vicious and tigerish. Jack had much the same impression, and he had more of a right to it since he saw the whole crew, the surprisingly numerous crew: they all had a certain family look although they were of many different races and colours, from shining black to the sour-cheese grey of Bessarabians; they were presumably united by religion, certainly by their awe of the Capitan-Bey – defaulters in the *Torgud* were cut up for bait – and they visibly trembled before him. The officers all appeared to be Turks, and judging from the knowledgeable zeal with which they showed their great guns and small arms they understood the fighting part of their profession, while the way the ship had rounded served to prove that at least some of them were competent seamen; yet none seemed to have the slightest notion of order, discipline, or cleanliness, except as far as the guns were concerned. These were all brass, and they all gleamed nobly in the declining sun; apart from that the *Torgud* appeared to possess no first lieutenant, no bosun, no captain of the sweepers. The rigging was knotted rather than spliced when repair was needed, the planking of the deck could not be seen at all for dirt, and between the guns lay little heaps of human excrement. Yet in spite of this the *Torgud* was evidently a formidable vessel, not unlike a larger, much more dangerous version of the pirate ships Jack had seen in the West Indies: he had little time for reflection however, because as Mustapha showed his ship he also expounded his plan of attack on Kutali, explained it with an exuberant vitality that called for the closest attention, particularly as Graham was sometimes at a loss for a sea-term. In essence the attack was to be a bombardment by shallow-draught gunboats armed with the cannon Jack would supply, and this would be followed by a general assault. Mustapha had nearly forty suitable caiques up and down the coast; they would open half a dozen breeches in the wall, and his men would carry the place by storm. He looked attentively at Jack, but Jack, having nothing to say about an attack on a town whose shore he did not know and whose defenders and fortifications he had never seen, merely bent his head politely. In any case, much of his mind was taken up by the extraordinary half-seen spectacle of the midships cannon. The middle gun in the long row of brass eighteen-pounders seemed to tower over its fellows in the strangest way; but its uncommonly large portlid was shut at the moment and the sailmaker had spread his work over much of its bulk.

'This is my heart's delight,' said Mustapha, waving the canvas away; and to his astonishment Jack beheld a thirty-six-pounder, an unheard-of, preposterous weapon for a frigate – even a first-rate line-of-battle ship carried no more than thirty-two pounders and those only on the lowest tier – and so massive that it dwarfed its neighbours. And over against it, on the larboard side, there was its fellow, its necessary counterpoise.

'I have never seen such a beautiful gun,' cried Jack, examining the dolphins that twined round the King of

Portugal's arms and the well-worn touch-hole. 'But do you indeed find they answer the weight and the confusion?' he asked, looking keenly at the reinforced deck and side and the triple ringbolts; and until they reached the cabin they discussed the advantages and disadvantages of the arrangement – the inconvenience of different calibres on the same deck, the extra weight so high in the ship and its effect on her roll in heavy weather, as opposed to the crippling effect of thirty-six pound shot hitting the enemy at a distance.

In the cabin itself, a singularly gorgeous room hung with crimson damask, the appearance of coffee broke the thread, and in any case it was evident that Jack was about to leave: he could not be persuaded to stay any longer, nor to visit the nearby port of Karia, because he had a rendezvous with his consort the *Dryad*. This being established Mustapha went over his plan of attack again, with a reasonably convincing account of the forces at his disposal, and once again he stated his opinion of Sciahan Bey and Ismail.

Sciahan's chief crime, apart from greed and avarice, was age, cold-blooded, incompetent age, and Jack had the impression that although Mustapha would certainly expel Sciahan from Kutali if he could, perhaps killing him in the process, he did not really dislike him. With Ismail it was quite a different matter: here there were detailed, persuasive charges of faithlessness, hypocrisy and disloyalty – Mustapha's voice grew even stronger, his eye more terrible: he called upon God to curse his children's children if ever he allowed that vile unmanly traitor to get the better of him.

Jack had seen some passionate men, but none who seemed to swell so much, nor whose great clenched fist trembled so with rage, none whose eyes became more suffused with red. Clearly there was something very much more than competition for the disputed town between Mustapha and Ismail: though on the other hand there was no doubt that Mustapha was also extremely eager to possess Kutali.

311

The Capitan-Bey boomed organ-toned, and in the barge alongside Bonden said, 'How their skipper does carry on, to be sure: like a bull in a barn.'

At this the portlid of the starboard thirty-six-pounder opened and a hairy, turbanned face peered out. 'Well, you'll know me again, mate,' observed Bonden, having been stared at for a full unwinking minute.

'Barret Bonden,' said the hairy face, 'you don't remember me.'

'I can't say as how I do, mate, behind all them whiskers.'

'Ezekiel Edwards, quarter-gunner in *Isis* when you was captain of the foretop. Zeke Edwards: ran when we was off of Tiberoon.'

'Zeke Edwards,' said Bonden, nodding his head. 'Yes.' Then, 'What are you doing in this barky? Was you took? Are you a prisoner?'

'No. Which I belong to her. Gunner's mate.'

Bonden considered him for a moment, and said, 'So you turned Turk, and grew a full set, and clapped a pudding-cloth round your head.'

'That's right, mate. Being I never was brought up religious; and being I was circumcised already, any gate.'

The other bargemen had been gazing steadily at Edwards with their mouths open; they now closed them and stared with wooden disapproval out to sea: but he had spoken with such an awkward, urgent, pleading tone, as though longing beyond expression to hear and utter Christian sounds, that Bonden replied. Rather severely he asked what Edwards was doing with that thirty-six-pounder – what a thirty-six-pounder was doing in a frigate, for Christ's sake, a long thirty-six-pounder?

This released a flood of words, a stumbling confidential rush with scraps of Greek and Turkish and lingua franca mixed with the burring West Country English, all delivered into Bonden's disapproving, half-averted ear. The guns were from Corfu, from the French general in Corfu; and he had let the skipper have them because why? Because they was Portuguese and did not take the

312

French thirty-six-pound ball, nor any other bloody ball now made, that was why. But the Capitan-Bey did not care for that: he had marble round-shot made by the Greeks in the island of Paros, smooth as glass. The trouble was, they often cracked if not stowed very careful; and then they cost a mint of money. You could not blaze away with half a dozen rounds just to keep your hand in – you could not fling marble balls about, not marble balls at nineteen piastres a piece.

'Marble balls,' said Bonden, obscurely feeling some reflection upon the *Surprise* and her plain iron round-shot. 'Marble balls my arse.'

'I never seen such a filthy mud-scow as this here in all my life,' remarked bow-oar, spitting to leeward. 'Don't they never wash down the heads?'

Edwards instantly grasped the implication and he cried out very humbly that he had not meant to top it the nob nor to come it the heavy; he did not go for to make them believe the shot-locker was crammed with marble balls – no, no, there was not but five for the starboard gun and four for t'other, one of them chipped. More he could not say, for now cymbals clashed, shrill drums beat and conchs brayed loud as Captain Aubrey made his farewells and stepped down into the barge with Professor Graham, sitting thoughtful and silent as they were rowed back in the twilight.

Thoughtful and silent again on this quarterdeck at dawn, with Marga almost vanishing on the starboard quarter: he levelled his telescope, took a last look at the rock-built citadel, the great Venetian mole, and resumed his pacing. Silent: partly because it had long been his habit to go up and down the windward side of whatever vessel he commanded as long as he could without disturbing the ship's routine, and partly because neither of his advisers was awake, they having discussed Mustapha and Ismail well into the middle watch. Thoughtful, because although Mustapha was a fine fellow in some ways, he was not likely to show much zeal in turning the French out of Marga if he was on such friendly terms with General Donzelot in Corfu: Bonden's report had reached him through Killick with his first cup of coffee, and then Bonden had confirmed it himself.

As he turned his eye caught the flash of a sail in the offing, far beyond the *Dryad*: she had joined at nightfall and she was now keeping her station abreast of the *Surprise*, they being spread out in the faint hope of snapping up some vessel bound for the French in Corfu, or better still one from the French in Corfu to their friends in Marga. Automatically he pointed his telescope, but realizing that he could not possibly spare the time to chase anything at such a distance – it was only a little trabaccolo in any case – he shifted his gaze to the *Dryad* and found himself looking straight at Babbington, who was leaning on the quarter-rail with a very pretty young woman in a sort of pink, lacy garment. He was showing her something over the side, and they were both laughing very cheerfully.

Jack clapped his glass to. He remembered that Babbington, coming aboard to report, had muttered something about giving a lift to a respectable Italian matron, an officer's widow, from Cephalonia to Santa Maura – being compelled to keep her aboard, the wind not serving for Santa Maura and he being so unwilling to delay Captain Aubrey at the rendezvous. A matron could of course be no more than twenty and a widow could perfectly well be cheerful: but it would not do – it really would not do.

The next turn brought him face to face with something else that would not do. Young Williamson, the midshipman of the watch, was looking wretchedly peaked and ill again: the boy was not strong enough for a life at sea and Jack would never have taken him if he had not been Dick Williamson's son. He had wanted no first voyagers, no children who should not relieve the deck at four in the morning on an empty belly, and here he was, still answerable to their mothers for two of them at a time when he needed all his powers for infinitely more important problems than the moral and physical welfare of a pair of squeakers. He would invite the boy to breakfast and at the same time beg Stephen to look at him. In any case Stephen ought to be up by now: Cape Stavro was already looming on the starboard bow, and he must not miss the opening of Kutali Bay.

'Mr Williamson,' he called, and the boy gave a guilty start, 'pray go down to Dr Maturin's cabin, and if he is awake tell him with my compliments that we are about to open Kutali Bay, which is reckoned a prodigious fine spectacle. And perhaps you would give us the pleasure of your company at breakfast.'

While he waited for Stephen, and a long wait it was, Dr Maturin having ensured sleep at last by four successive doses, Jack watched the shore go by, a prodigious fine spectacle in itself, now that they were drawing in with the land – a steep-to shore of towering light-grey cliffs rising straight from deep water and backed by mountains, precipitous, jagged mountains reaching high up the sky with the early light cutting across them from a little south of east so that they stood out clear, range after range of them, seven deep, the vast forests green on the sunward side, the bald crags shining grey. Ordinarily Jack disliked being near any coast at all; he was a blue-water sailor, one who liked plenty of sea-room under his lee, fifty leagues or so; but here he had a hundred fathoms beneath his keel within gunshot of the land and in any case the weather had been unusually kind. It was now treating them to a topgallant zephyr a point or so before the beam that might have been specially ordained to carry them round the cape and into the bay: but whether it would waft them eastwards again to Kutali was doubtful; it had a somewhat languishing, dying air and perhaps they should be obliged to wait for the sea-breeze to set in to complete their voyage round the great peninsula.

In fact the zephyr dropped entirely while they were still at breakfast. But this was an unusually prolonged meal and there had been time not only for the *Surprise* to round the cape and reach the middle of the bay but for Dr Maturin to recover his humanity. He had begun the day in a very sullen, dogged, and unappreciative mood indeed, opposed to natural beauties of any kind; but now, led out, well-fed, well-coffee'd, to smoke his morning cigar and admire the view he was perfectly ready to admit that he had seen few more glorious sights than Kutali and its setting. The water of the bay was gently rippled in some few places but glass-smooth in others, and in the purest of these natural mirrors they could see the astonishing peaks that rose from the sea with the whole town at their feet – all this reversed, and superimposed upon the image stood ships and boats, most as it were suspended, hanging motionless, a few creeping across the surface with sweeps or sculls. The dead calm, the cloudless sky, the stillness of the ship and perhaps this sense of being on or even in a looking-glass gave an extraordinary impression of silence and people spoke unnaturally low.

The close-packed town itself had the appearance of a double cone – grey battlements, red roofs, white walls repeated in the mirror-image – until a chance air destroyed the reflection. This did not affect the walls of the upper town or the citadel, but with its double vanishing the lower town's ramparts suddenly shrank to half its height. It no longer looked very formidable, and Jack saw that Mustapha's plan of battering it with gunboats was perfectly feasible.

Although at first sight Kutali looked compact, rising in one triangular mass from the sea up the mountainside, it was in fact built in three parts: the lowest straggled out on either side of the fortified harbour and here the wall had been spread too far, too thin. It was vulnerable, and as far as Jack could see, looking steadily through his telescope, the defences of the middle town would not stand any very determined assault either. But, he reflected, looking up at the heavily fortified upper town, the Christian town with its church towers showing above the battlements, even a small battery of cannon up there, even three or four twelve-pounders, well plied, would make the attack impossible, by sinking the gunboats as they came within range. There was no need for massive fortifications below, so long as the sea and the lower ground was commanded by artillery.

Mustapha swore that the Christians had only two guns, old and honeycombed, and some mangonels, but that even if they had a dozen he should still carry out his attack on Sciahan, because the Christians would not interfere in a quarrel between Mussulmans: and that might very well be so, thought Jack, now surveying the harbour as a naval base – a fine roomy naval base, with fresh water just at hand, deep-water repairing docks, and any amount of timber, capital Valona oak.

'That is the Christian town up there,' said Graham at his side. 'You will perceive that no mosque has been built within the walls. A mixed mercantile community occupies the middle town, and mariners, ship-builders and so on the sea-shore. The Turks live mostly in the suburb to the right, on the far side of the stream, and you can make out the governor's kiosk beyond what I take to be the ruined temple of the Pelasgian Zeus. Yes: I see Sciahan's banner. He is an alai-bey, the equivalent of a brigadier; he therefore displays a single horse-tail.'

Stephen was about to say 'A galley is putting off from the strand,' but as he, Jack, Graham and Pullings were all standing on the forecastle, gazing steadily in that direction, he saved his breath.

'Thirteen guns for a brigadier, sir?' asked Pullings.

Jack paused, focused his telescope with the utmost care. 'That is no brigadier,' he said at last. 'No brigadier I have ever seen, one-tailed or two. I believe it is a Greek parson, the kind they call a pope in these parts.'

The Surprises' reception of a pope, a square-topped, black-hooded Orthodox pope, was less certain than their reception of brigadiers, but they carried it off well enough, and in the cabin those chiefly concerned with

317

his entertainment very soon lost their Sunday expressions when it appeared that Father Andros was not only the representative of the Christians of Kutali but also one of the Bey's political advisers and his emissary on this occasion. The Bey was unwell, and although he would be overjoyed to see Captain Aubrey as soon as he was recovered the need for dispatch was so great that he had asked Father Andros to wait upon the Captain with his best compliments and to lay the position before him, at the same time conveying the Bey's specific requests and his corresponding propositions. By way of credentials Father Andros passed Jack a beautifully written document with a seal to it, saying in an aside to Graham, 'I bring you the greetings of Osman the Smyrniot.'

'Is he in Kutali?'

'No. He was called to Iannina, to Ali Pasha, the day you saw Ismail.'

'This is a most elegant letter,' said Jack, passing the document on to Graham. 'But pray tell the gentleman that he could bring no better credentials than his cloth and his countenance.'

It was clear that Killick shared his Captain's favourable impression of Father Andros (who was indeed a fine manly-looking priest) because at this point he brought in a decanter of Jack's very best madeira, the kind with the yellow seal. Father Andros too could be tempted to drink wine, but even if it had been much later in the day it would obviously have been no use offering him spirits; nor was he much given to smiles or laughter. His business was too serious for either, and he laid it out in a direct, methodical, and, Jack would have sworn, reasonably candid way.

Sciahan's claim to Kutali was perfectly justified by Turkish law and custom and it would no doubt be vindicated by the Sultan's iradé in the course of time, but Father Andros would not go into that: he would confine himself to the immediate practical issues. It was understood that the British Admiral wished to use Kutali

318

as a base for his attack upon the French in Marga, and as a place of refuge and supply for his ships in the Ionian Sea; and that in exchange for the base he offered a certain number of cannon, providing these cannon were also used against the French.

Marga could be attacked only from the heights behind the town, and to reach these heights one necessarily had to pass by Kutali: and at Kutali alone could Marga's aqueduct be cut. Both Ismail Bey and Mustapha would have to fight exceedingly hard for Kutali, because apart from his own troops Sciahan would have the backing of the Christians, who were extremely unwilling to be ruled by either Mustapha or Ismail, both being not only notoriously rapacious but also bigoted Mussulmans, while Mustapha, who was in practice very little removed from a common pirate, was odious to the whole mercantile class, the shipowners and the mariners, Mussulmans and Christians alike; so that in the unlikely event of a victory the winner's few surviving men would be of very little use against the French, even if Ismail or Mustapha ever kept his word and joined in the attack, which Father Andros begged leave to doubt extremely. It also followed that neither Ismail nor Mustapha could count on any support whatsoever from the Christians of Marga, an essential point if the attack were to succeed at once, rather than drag out in a long siege that would give the French party in Constantinople time to intervene. Most of the Margiotes were Christian. Sciahan Bey, on the other hand, was already in possession of Kutali. He had continued the mild, almost imperceptible rule of the former vali, leaving the Christians their own courts and the possession of the citadel: he was on such good terms with the various communities, the Albanians, Vlachs and Greeks, that they had guaranteed him six hundred and eighty fighting men, many of them Mirdite Ghegs. Indeed he was the ideal ally for the English Admiral: his military reputation reposed on twenty-three distinct campaigns, two of them in Syria and Egypt in conjunction with the British, whom he esteemed, against the French, whom he loathed. He was a true Turk, a man of his word; he was not a descendant of Egyptian slaves or Algerian renegades, nor a man who would receive the cannon and then discover fresh needs or reasons for declining to attack the French. He invited Captain Aubrey to come ashore, to view his troops and to tour the city with Father Andros, seeing its strengths and its admitted weaknesses for himself.

'Come, he cannot say fairer than that,' said Jack. 'Killick, my barge.'

'This coast is familiar to you, I believe,' said Stephen to Graham as they walked up through the busy town behind Captain Aubrey and Father Andros.

'I have not been just here before,' said Graham, 'but I have visited Ragusa and Cattaro, which are not unlike, and some of the inland parts.'

'Then no doubt you can tell me what these cheerful souls in short white gathered petticoats and red caps and such a quantity of weapons may be.'

'They are Tosks, southern Albanians. My good friend Ali Pasha is a Tosk. He is a Mussulman of course; but many Tosks, perhaps most in these parts, are Orthodox Christians. Observe the deference with which they treat this worthy priest.'

It was quite true: as the worthy priest led the way with an elastic, bounding step up the steep, crowded, central street or rather flight of stairs the people fell away on either hand, bowing, smiling, pushing mules, asses and children against the wall.

'Yet not all are quite so respectful,' remarked Stephen a little later. 'The person in the doorway there, with the moustachioes of the world and a pair of pistols and a curious sword and two daggers in his belt – the person in crimson pantaloons and a short gold-laced jacket, is secretly biting his thumb, in a gesture of contempt or defiance.'

'He is a Gheg, from the north,' said Graham. 'Sad

fellows, much given to murder and rapine. I dare say he is a Romanist or a Mussulman: the curious sword is a yataghan. Now there is a Gheg who is certainly a Romanist – the fellow in the long white tunic with a red sash and white trousers. Do not look too pointedly: they are very apt to take offence, and as you see he carries a perfect arsenal. He is a Mirdite, an entirely Catholic tribe of Ghegs: there is a large colony of them in the neighbourhood, though their home is in the northern highlands.'

'They must feel at home here, then,' said Stephen. 'This town is built for the chamois and her kind, or the true mountain capricorn.'

The street, growing somewhat steeper, turned abruptly to the left, so that now as they climbed the strong sun beat upon their backs; and still Father Andros strode on, his black robe billowing out behind as he pointed out the various quarters, Venetian, Greek, Jewish, Armenian and Vlach, all separately fortified in the days of the republic.

Apart from a few hours in Malta and at Mesenteron Jack had not set foot on land for months, and his boots were killing him. So was his uniform coat, put on to review the troops in the Maidan far below, and so were his breeches, his sword-belt and his neckcloth. The younger Jack would have climbed on, blind and gasping, till he burst: now, after a decent interval of suffering, the present Captain Aubrey cried 'Hold hard. Hold hard for a moment – you will kill your allies.'

Andros led them to a square with a fountain under an immense nettle-tree with a smooth grey trunk, and as he sat recovering in the green shade, drinking ice-cold retsina brought from a nearby house, Jack mused upon his use of that word 'allies'.

It was a busy square, with a market at its far end by the church, and people of half a dozen races walked to and fro across it, most of the men armed, many of the women veiled. They were all intensely curious but all, even the children, remarkably discreet: yet at one point Stephen noticed a tall, martial man leave a group of Catholic Ghegs and come deliberately towards them, twirling his moustache with a hand adorned with a magnificent amethyst: he had two silver-mounted pistols in the belt of what looked very like a cassock and a musket or perhaps a fowling-piece – no, a musket – over his shoulder, a pectoral cross showing beneath its butt. Stephen was aware of a tension, and he noticed that Andros and the stranger timed their salutes with the utmost exactness, so that neither was half a second before the other.

'This is the Catholic Bishop of Prizren, who accompanies part of his Mirdite flock,' said Father Andros.

Jack and Graham rose and bowed: Stephen kissed the Bishop's ring and they conversed in Latin for a while, the Bishop being very urgent to know whether it was true that the King of England was about to be converted and whether the British Admiral might be induced to guarantee the independence of the republic of Kutali. Stephen could satisfy them on neither point but they parted on the kindest terms, and it was observable that the morose Ghegs looked more favourably upon the party now that it was known that at least one member was of the right way of thinking.

This was particularly evident when they reached the citadel, which at this time of day was guarded by the Ghegs alone, a proud, haughty, dark and sullen band that blossomed into smiling humanity when one of the many accompanying children told them the news. But neither children nor other followers were admitted beyond the gate, and beyond the gate Father Andros' lively flow of talk ceased entirely. His face was graver than ever as he led them up the winding path to the ultimate platform, a half-moon battery that took its rise in the living rock on either hand, curving out to dominate the sea, the lower town and its approaches. As the path mounted, crossing and recrossing the precipitous rock-face, Jack counted the embrasures up there: twenty-one of them, all filled; more than enough guns to deal with a powerful squadron, if reasonably well handled. Yet at the last turning, at the last iron wicket, Father Andros hesitated. 'We are perfectly candid, as you see,' he said, unlocking the gate at last. 'Sciahan Bey has repeatedly said that he relies entirely upon the honour of an English naval officer.'

The remark was not well received. 'If he is so sure he need scarcely say it once, let alone keep up a perpetual harping on the subject,' reflected Jack, and Stephen said 'This is a clumsy form of blackmail' to himself, while the whole tone of Graham's translation conveyed disapproval. Andros however was far too agitated to notice: he took them into the battery, and once the small group of gunners who manned it had stood clear Jack saw the cause of his emotion: all the guns but three were made of painted wood and of the others two had had their trunnions beaten off, so that they could not be pointed with any sort of accuracy, while the third, an archaic brass piece, had once been spiked, and the person who bored out its touch-hole had made a sad botch of it. Mustapha could bring in his gunboats at high noon if he chose and batter away at the lower walls to his heart's content: there was nothing in Kutali to stop him.

'These two we use for firing salutes,' said Andros, 'to deceive the world in general. The third we dare not touch.'

'Has the Bey no field-pieces?' asked Jack.

'Only one, and it throws no more than a three-pound ball. He keeps it in his camp. If it were brought up here people might suspect the real state of affairs.'

Jack nodded, and leaning out over the parapet he considered the possibility of splicing four cables an-end and winching up cannon made fast to well-greased travellers, directly from the shore. After all, an eighteen-pounder weighed no more than his bower anchors, and half a dozen would make this place perfectly impregnable: but getting even one or two up those impossible, narrow, twisting, ladder-like streets would be a labour of weeks.

The hold-fast this end and of course the prodigious tension would be the main difficulties . . . but they would deal with that problem when they came to it: Tom Pullings could always be relied upon to do wonders in the line of seamanship.

'A romantic prospect, is it not?' said Father Andros. His anxiety seemed to have diminished, as though he had read Jack's mind, and he spoke quite easily, smiling for perhaps the first time since they came ashore.

'Eh?' said Jack. 'Why, I suppose it is.' He straightened and took his bearings: Cape Stavro ran out to the south-west, the long promontory with Marga at its southern base and Kutali at its northern, the two separated by thirty miles of sea but only three of land. Yet those three were so mountainous that it was not easy to see how the journey could be made. 'Where is the aqueduct that goes to Marga?' he asked.

'You cannot see it from here,' said Andros. 'But I can easily show it to you. It is no distance at all, and there is a wild romantic view from the crag above it. I am aware that English travellers are partial to wild romantic views.'

'Pray ask him what he means by no distance at all,' said Jack.

'Not an hour by the goats' path,' said Graham after the translation. 'But he says that we could take horse and go by the smooth way, if you do not mind missing the wild romantic view.'

'I am afraid that we are not here to indulge ourselves in wild romantic views,' said Jack. 'Duty requires that we should take horse.'

The smooth way led them between the mountains over a firm springy sward, up and down and down again to a grassy saddle, where the priest dismounted and said 'Here.'

'Where?' cried Jack, gazing about for a noble series of arches marching across the landscape.

'Here,' said the priest again, thumping a limestone slab half-buried in the turf. 'Listen.' And bending their heads in the silence they could hear water running underground. The spring was on Mount Shkrel and a gently-sloping covered channel carried it all the way to the heights behind Marga: 'You can see it, like a green road following the curves of the hillside, where it plunges straight down, and I will show you many places where it can easily be cut.'

Looking down on Marga Jack felt inclined to say that he would not be in that commanding officer's shoes with his water cut off and a battery opening upon him from such a height: for he had no doubt that although guns and even carronades were notoriously awkward things to carry across country, above all mountainous country, he could move a competent number over this firm dry turf, keeping to the channel as it followed, or very nearly followed, the contour-line, if once he could get them up to the citadel. But he never liked to tempt fate either by land or sea, and he only observed 'that perhaps they should be getting back now; he for one was so hellish peckish that he could eat an ox and then call for more.'

They rode back therefore, and at a fine pace, the horses eager for their stables, the men for their mangers; and on the way they met a Turkish officer. He and Father Andros exchanged a few private words – the language incomprehensible but not the tone of satisfaction – and the priest announced with what little spontaneity he could summon that the Bey, having recovered from his indisposition, would be happy to invite Captain Aubrey to a . . . 'It is an unusual term, Albanian in origin, I believe,' said Graham. 'Perhaps it should be translated as a snap, a slight or hasty meal.'

A more accurate version would have been fat-tailed sheep stewed with saffron, preceded by three made dishes and followed by three more. During part of the feast, so that Graham should have leisure to eat, Sciahan spoke through a Moldavian dragoman, telling Jack about the Syrian campaign in 1799, when he and Sir Sidney Smith repelled Buonaparte from Acre, and then about his manoeuvres with the Naval Brigade in the days that led up to the battle of Aboukir. Sir Sidney was somewhat too showy to qualify as Jack's favourite public character, but sincere and reasoned praise of the Navy, above all from a fighting man as scarred and battered as the Bey, was quite another matter, and Jack looked upon him with great complacency. Though indeed he would have liked his host in any case, a small, compact, grey-bearded man with great natural dignity, direct, and apart from his diplomatic illness and his sending of Father Andros so that the position should be put to Aubrey by a fellow-Christian, devoid of artifice. He was much more what Jack had expected of a Turk: a plain man, and one that he could trust. Towards the end of the meal Sciahan said, 'I am happy to learn from Father Andros that you have seen the state of Kutali. I understand that your Admiral wishes to be able to use the port for his ships and that he wishes us to help him expel the French from Marga. If he will give me the cannon I and the Kutaliotes will do our part.'

'Very well,' said Jack. 'I shall send my consort to Cephalonia for the guns as soon as the wind turns into the north.'

# CHAPTER ELEVEN

Matins and lauds, prime, terce, sext, nones, vespers
and compline: at each of the canonical hours and often
between them, prayers for a north wind rose from the
churches of Kutali, prayers far more fervent than Jack
or his advisers had imagined at first. The Kutaliotes
loathed and dreaded Ismail Bey, but they loathed and
dreaded Mustapha even more; they knew him directly or
by reputation as an exceedingly violent cruel man, subject
to huge, ungovernable rages; and few of the Greeks had
not lost relatives in the burning villages or devastated
countryside of the Morea. And it was Mustapha whom
they all looked upon as the most likely attacker, he being
sea-borne and immensely active. One measure of their
dread was their kindness to the sailors ashore and their
eager cooperation when it was understood that the officers
wished to settle the true line for an enormous rope running
from the mole to the citadel, a rope that must necessarily
sag but that must nevertheless have a clear path between
its supports. The officer chiefly concerned, Mr Pullings,
or the Maiden as the Kutaliotes called him because of his
mild face and gentle manners, had but to hint that a wall,
outhouse, chimney, dovecote might be in the way for it
to vanish, plucked down if not by its owners then by his
neighbours and the rest of the community.

The prayers for a north wind were not answered at
once, which was just as well, since it gave Captain Aubrey
time to write his dispatch for the *Dryad* to carry to the
Commander-in-Chief, a long and detailed account of his
proceedings, together with a request for more Marines for
the final assault, at least two sloops for diversionary actions
and to prevent reinforcements and supplies being thrown
into Marga from Corfu, and for money to enroll three

327

troops of Mirdites and one of Moslem Ghegs for three weeks at nine Argyrokastro piastres a calendar month, they to find themselves in arms and victuals: Jack had little hope of the sloops, but it was thought that he could rely on the money, just as he could be sure that the *Dryad* would bring back the officers and men of the prize-crew, perhaps with news of the *Bonhomme Richard*'s condemnation and sale, and with any letters from home that might have arrived in their absence. It also allowed time for his furious quarrel with Professor Graham not indeed to die away nor yet to be composed, since each maintained his original position, but at least to reach a stage where they could disagree with the outward appearance of civility.

The quarrel had begun at Sciahan's table, when Graham choked over his stuffed vine-leaves on hearing Jack say 'Very well. I shall send for the guns.'

'But for that vile pragmatical Moldavian dragoman those words would never have been conveyed,' he cried as soon as they were alone. 'I should have refused to interpret such an extreme indiscretion.' An angry, loud-breathing pause, and he burst out 'You had all the advantages a negotiator could desire: and without consultation, nay, apparently without the least reflection you took it upon yourself to throw them away. Throw them away.'

He developed his theme at considerable length: even if Captain Aubrey had not seen fit to consult with his advisers on the attitude to be adopted to Sciahan Bey he must surely have seen that he was in a position to insist upon the most favourable terms. Before committing himself in any way he could have required a detailed agreement, a properly established treaty, with security for the observation of its terms. The Bey would certainly have given one of his nephews as a hostage and the various Kutaliote communities would have done the same. In all negotiation, and *a fortiori* all Oriental negotiation, each side was expected to extract all possible profit from the balance of forces: if either did not do so it was because there was some hidden weakness – a plain unconditional acquiescence in a demand must necessarily be taken as the greatest proof of weakness. And quite apart from the hostages and the guarantees for the free use of the port there were innumerable other aspects that should have been gone into before any agreement was reached: for example, Sciahan and his advisers, who were intelligent men, accustomed to business, would undoubtedly have examined the possibility of disarming Mustapha by offering him compensation for the loss of Kutali in the form of a share of the territory of Marga, to be acquired by both Sciahan and Mustapha according to the terms of an offensive and defensive alliance that would also strengthen both against Ismail. Fortunately it was not too late; Captain Aubrey's ill-judged remark was in no way binding; it could be explained as a mere feast-time formula of politeness and the real negotiations could begin between the advisers on both sides.

Jack replied coldly that he regarded his words as wholly binding, that he was convinced that he and Sciahan understood one another, and that in any event the responsibility lay with the Captain of the *Surprise*. That was the last cool remark in the discussion, which presently grew not only warm but even personal. Graham wished to hear no more of this parrot-cry of responsibility: if an invaluable opportunity was lost the country through frowardness and ignorance it was of little or no comfort to an injured public to fasten the responsibility upon some particular one of its servants. It was the duty of those engaged in warfare, and above all in the political side of warfare, to consider the situation with the impartiality of a natural philosopher watching the action of spirits of salt upon hartshorn, of the electric fluid on a dead frog's thigh; all sentiment and personal preference must be laid aside; and other purely objective and informed opinion must be sought. Throughout this inauspicious day however Captain Aubrey had been clearly guided by his personal likes and dislikes and by the fact that these people called themselves Christians; he had made up his mind on sentimental grounds. This had been evident from the moment

329

they set foot on shore until the moment they left and it was of no use for Captain Aubrey to prate about respect and discipline. Professor Graham was not one of Captain Aubrey's subordinates – the cruel and bloody lash which he had seen, with bitter regret, so disgracefully used upon this very ship, was not for him – and even if he were a subordinate, that would not prevent him from doing his duty or protesting, officially and with the utmost vehemence, against this ill-considered course of action. Nor was it of any use for Captain Aubrey to look big and talk loud; Professor Graham was not a man to be bullied. If, like some other military forms of life, Captain Aubrey was a being that confused superior force with superior reason, that was Captain Aubrey's affair: nothing would prevent Professor Graham from telling the truth, calmly and without raising his voice. Volume of sound was in no way related to volume of veracity. Captain Aubrey might speak violently, if he chose; it made no difference to the truth. If Captain Aubrey were to turn his cannon – the *ultima ratio regum*, and of other bullies – on Professor Graham, the truth would remain unaltered. No, said Professor Graham, now quite hoarse from bellowing, he did not suppose that he possessed a monopoly of wisdom – the remark he might observe in passing was wholly irrelevant and as illiberal as if Professor Graham had referred to Captain Aubrey's remarkable bulk or to his lack of education – but in this particular case an impartial observer comparing Professor Graham's not inconsiderable knowledge of Turkish history, language, literature, policy, and customs with the encyclopedic ignorance and presumption of those who contradicted him, might be tempted to think so. Furthermore . . . At this juncture Stephen broke in and maintained a rapid, vapid flow of talk, refusing to be interrupted until the blessed beating of the drum enabled him to lead Graham away undefeated to the gunroom, where amidst a silent consternation (for both gentlemen had been tolerably audible, the cabin bulkheads being not much above ordinary match-boarding in thickness, whereas even nine-inch plank would scarcely have sufficed to keep so passionate a disagreement in) he savagely dismembered a pair of Kutaliote fowls.

In the course of this disagreement Jack had suffered from his usual want of eloquence (well-chosen words came fairly pouring out of Graham) and from the fact that he had not had the support he expected from Stephen. 'I really think you might have stood up for me a little more,' he said. 'I should have taken it friendly, was you to have flashed out a piece of Latin or Greek, when he checked me with my bulk.'

'Well, brother, you had already let fall some remarks about meagre wizened bookworms: by that time you were both calling names, which is the end of all discourse. Earlier, when you were conversing like Christians rather than roaring like Turks, I did not intervene because I thought there was substance in Graham's contention.'

'Do you think I did wrong? In negotiations of this kind, and with men like Sciahan, the natural spontaneous word may do better than any amount of tortuous haggling and formal treaties.'

'I think you should have consulted Graham beforehand – he is after all an eminent authority on Turkish affairs and you have wounded him extremely by not doing so – and I think he may have been right about Mustapha. The more I hear of the Capitan-Bey and the more I reflect upon the situation, the more I am persuaded that he is less concerned with the possession of Kutali than with keeping Ismail out of it, and more generally with doing Ismail in the eye, as the seamen say. I hear accounts of his obsessive hatred for the man on all hands; and I think that if you had not committed yourself so thoroughly to Sciahan you might have been wise to take this into account. After all, it may be held that in war there is neither Turk nor Christian nor moral consideration.'

'A war like that would not be worth fighting,' said Jack.

'And yet the Dear knows war is not a game,' said Stephen.

331

'No,' said Jack. 'Perhaps I should have said not worth winning.'

The breeze came northerly; the *Dryad* sailed for Cephalonia and Malta; the Bey clapped an embargo on all shipping so that the news should not reach Marga before the first cannon-ball and the first summons to surrender; and the Surprises set about rigging their ropeway.

At one point they had hopes of completing it by the time the transports could be expected from Cephalonia – four or five days, with the usual variable breezes at this season of the year – but it was soon found that their first plan had been too sanguine and that at least a week would be necessary, since the Kutaliotes' goodwill did not extend to the destruction of three particularly valued church towers and a raised cemetery in which the dead lay as though in pigeon-holes and the only way of avoiding them was to start right over at the far corner of the mole, a much more considerable undertaking. However, they made a vigorous beginning, the merchants and shipowners of Kutali coming forward with massive windlasses and great quantities of cordage (though nothing that the Navy could possibly look upon in the light of a cable), and presently the system took on its general form, with light hawsers running by stages from bottom to top. This was only a beginning, of course: true cables, seventeen-inch cables a hundred and twenty fathoms long apiece, spliced end to end and heaved as near twanging-tight as human ingenuity could heave them, were to take the hawsers' place.

But just as the prayers of the Catholic Albanians, Orthodox Greeks and the various minorities such as Melchites, Copts, Jews and Nestorians for a north wind had been immoderate, so was the response: the north wind came, but although it carried the *Dryad* racing down to Cephalonia it also kept the transports pinned there, and quite soon it worked up such a heavy sea that it was impossible to stay on that exposed corner of the mole. Pullings, the bosun and their men were obliged to confine themselves to finework at the top or on the intermediate stages, walking up and down the sunny town day after day, growing thoroughly familiar with its geography and its people, talking to them in fearless naval Albanian or Greek or even both.

At the beginning Jack divided his time between the ropeway and the road the chosen guns would have to take to batter Marga: he also took his gunner and the Marine officer to consider sites for the batteries; but it was thought unwise to spend much time up there, for fear of arousing suspicion, and he was happy to accept Sciahan Bey's invitation to hunt the wolf. He took his sickly midshipman Williamson with him, feeling that the boy could do with an airing, and he adjured him to keep close to the Bey's nephews, who would show him what to do, and perhaps keep him from being eaten by the quarry. They had a pleasant day of it, but for the fact that Jack's horse, though of the famous Epirotic breed, was not up to its rider's weight. Towards the evening the wolf retired to a dank forest, the haunt of many of its kind, and here in a clearing the horse refused to go any farther. They were alone, the Bey, his nephews, Mr Williamson and the mixed bag of dogs having vanished among the trees some time ago; and as Jack sat there on his trembling, sweating mount in the twilight he realized that persuasion would be useless: the horse could do no more. He dismounted and heard it gasp with relief: he looped the reins over his arm and they walked quietly back, meaning to leave the forest where they had first entered it, at a grassy place by a brook. From time to time the horse looked into his face with its lustrous and (for a horse) intelligent eyes, as though to express something – possibly doubt, for the darkness gathered under the trees, and the grassy place did not appear. Then, while Jack was considering what little sky he could see through the leaves to get his bearings, they heard a wolf's voice away on the right, and another beyond it. The horse at once began to dance, thoroughly revived by now; and although Jack had it firmly by the head he could not mount. They spun round one another faster and faster until he managed to thrust its rump against a tree, which gave him just enough time to make a froglike spring, swarm into the saddle and away. When he had recovered both stirrups – a long process – and something like control they were out of the trees, labouring up a ferny slope, the horse's ears brought to bear on a dimly-seen dell right ahead. Again the cry of wolves to the left and the right, and now from the very dell itself, followed almost immediately afterwards by the hail 'Captain Aubrey, ahoy.' He distinguished Williamson and one of the Bey's younger nephews against the skyline as they emerged from the dell; they howled again, coming down to meet him, and he said, 'Why are you making that goddam row, youngster?'

'We are imitating the wolves, sir. Suleiman here can do it so well, they answer almost every time. Ain't it fun! How the other chaps will envy us.'

Stephen also had some modest fun while the north wind kept the guns in Cephalonia. In his life he had never seen a spotted eagle: he longed to see a spotted eagle, and since this was a country in which spotted eagles might reasonably be expected to be seen he made his wishes known. Father Andros knew nothing about eagles, spotted or plain, but there was a family of shepherds behind Vostitsa who were said to know everything about birds, how to call and how to speak to them by name: they collected nestling falcons and trained them up for hawking. The mother of these young men, on being called, asserted that she knew the spotted eagle well, intimately well, that her husband had frequently pointed it out when they were in the mountains together, and that her boys would certainly find the gentleman a very spotted one. Stephen believed in her goodwill but little else; she had agreed with every description he proposed and in her desire to please the priest she would in all likelihood have promised him a cassowary. It was with no great expectations therefore that he set out on his seventeen-mile ride into the mountains: but it was in a state of singular happiness and contained satisfaction that he came staggering, stiff and bandy-legged, into the cabin and said, 'Jack, give me joy: I have seen five spotted eagles, two old and three young.'

Professor Graham, on the other hand, spent his days in conference with the Mirdite bishop, Father Andros and other Christian leaders, with the Bey's Turkish counsellors and with certain travelling government officials, old acquaintances from his days in Constantinople. When he was speaking Turkish or Greek his schoolmasterly arrogance tended to drop away: he was a more amiable man and a more efficient intelligence agent, and during this period he gathered a surprising amount of information about Ismail's relations with the French, the various complex treacheries of the inland pashas, the Egyptian viceroy's appeal to the English to support him in a revolt against the Sultan, and the history of the friendship, the quarrel, and the reconciliation between Mustapha and Ali Pasha of Iannina. All this he summarized for Stephen's benefit; for although, as he said, his advice might be neither required nor regarded, he still had a conscience; and it was possible that Dr M's voice might be heard when his was not. Graham was able to devote a long time to this task, far longer than he had expected, for although the heavy sea died down, allowing the work on the mole to continue, the wind remained obstinately in the north. And in fact the ropeway was complete before they had even so much as a smell of the transports: the entire midshipmen's berth and all the ship's boys had, on one pretext or another, walked, crawled, and finally climbed the whole majestic catenary curve from bottom to top and one thirty-two-pounder carronade and one long twelve-pounder had already made the trial voyage successfully, there and back. In a word, everything was ready, except for the essential cannon; and spies sent into Marga by the mountain paths reported that no one there had the least notion of an attack.

335

But still the north wind blew: day after day the north wind blew. And it was now, when the waiting time was growing not only tedious but barely tolerable, when the time was full-ripe and perhaps on the turn to rotten-ripe, and when Jack was haunted by the feeling that the excellent beginning was in extreme danger, if for no other reason than that the news must leak out and the effect of surprise be lost, for with Sciahan's embargo the busy port was becoming more and more crowded with shipping, and the cause must soon be evident – it was now, when he and Stephen were sitting in the cabin, silent between two pieces of music as the frigate lay rocking gently alongside Kutali mole, that Graham came aboard, unusually late at night. They heard the sentry's challenge; they heard Graham's habitually harsh and ungracious reply; and some moments later Killick came in to say that the Professor would like to see the Captain.

'I have this to report, sir,' said he in a cold, formal tone. 'There is a rumour in the Turkish camp that Ismail has been appointed governor of Kutali, and that the Sultan has signed the iradé, and that the document has already reached Nicopolis.'

The thought, 'Oh my God I have backed the wrong man' flashed through Jack's mind together with a whole train of other bitter reflections as he laid his fiddle on the locker. 'How much truth is there in it, do you think?' he asked.

'I do not know,' said Graham. 'It would be unusual for the Porte to come to a decision so soon in a matter of this kind, but on the other hand our embassy has been very busy, I am afraid: perhaps fatally busy.'

'Why do you say fatally busy?'

'Because if Ismail is installed that is the end of our attack on Marga. As Dr Maturin may have told you, I have undeniable evidence of his relations with the French: they are a source of very great profit to him.'

'Do you know the origin of the rumour?'

'The most probable origin is a courier who passed through on his way to Ali Pasha: the account may be exaggerated, but it is likely to have some foundation. A man would have little temptation to invent such unwelcome news.'

'If it is true, what do you think we should do?'

'Are you asking my advice, sir?'

'Yes, sir, I am.'

'I cannot give you a considered reply. I have only caught a fag-end of the tale at third-hand, no doubt distorted. I must see the Bey in the morning: fortunately he is an early riser.'

The old Turk walked out of his kiosk to mount his horse before dawn, but he did not outrise Captain Aubrey, for Jack had not gone to bed at all. Much of the night he spent on deck, watching the clouds scud from the north as he paced up and down, irritating the harbour-watch and absolutely terrifying Mowett as he crept back from a venereal assignation; and as he paced so some critic in his mind kept up a very unprofitable nagging about what he ought to have done, outlining various courses that would infallibly have led to success. He ought for example to have closed with Mustapha right away and to have sent for the transports by that same tide: the wind would then have served admirably, Mustapha would have taken Kutali out of hand, and by now they would be battering Marga together; for the Capitan-Bey, though something of an explosive and unpredictable ruffian, was at least a man of action. Nonsense, he replied: Kutali would have had to be conquered street by street, if it had been conquered at all, even with the guns destroying its walls and houses. And Mustapha was quite untrustworthy, as far as Marga was concerned. When he had had enough, and more than enough, of this nagging, Jack went below, and having stared for some time at charts of the passage north from Cephalonia – charts he knew by heart – he turned to his unfinished letter home. '. . . so much, my dear,

337

for the public side, the service side, for the lost time and opportunity and treasure if all this turns out to be true,' he wrote. 'Now, since we are the same person, I can speak of the personal side: if the expedition returns to Malta with its cargo of guns, having accomplished nothing, Harte's expressions of goodwill and support will not amount to much. They will certainly not prevent him from tossing me over the side. He can say that I backed the wrong man, and I cannot deny it. The responsibility and the blame will rest on me and no amount of justification on my part (though I could produce a great deal) will make a scrap of difference to the outcome. With ill-will it could be made to look very bad indeed, and even with a friendly report (which I cannot expect) it must be a very black mark against my name; and that, coming after the fiasco at Medina, will do me no good at all in Whitehall. What particularly grieves me is that it will put it even farther out of my power to do anything for Tom Pullings. If he is ever to be promoted commander *and employed in that rank*, it must be tolerably soon; for no one wants a greybeard in a sloop of war, nor even a man of thirty-five. Yet on the other hand I now know that the people of Kutali would have resisted Mustapha, however much he had battered their walls; and when I think what his men would have done in the town I am glad I had no hand in it.' His thoughts moved on to Andrew Wray, to the unholy alliance between Harte and Wray; to the large number of influential men he had contrived to disoblige in one way or another; to his father . . .

Eight bells, and piercing through his reflections came the shrill piping of *All hands* at the main hatchway and the muffled bellowing of bosun's mates 'Starbowlines hoy, starbowlines hey. Rise and shine, there, rise and shine. Here I come with a sharp knife and a clear conscience. Oh rise and shine. Out or down. Tumble up, you idle hounds,' and a remote howl of laughter as Sleeper Parslow's hammock was in fact cut down.

Eight bells, and Killick removed the deadlights from

the stern window, admitting a grey morning and peering in himself with an inquisitive expression on his ratlike face. Inquisitive and ratlike, certainly, but also shining with cleanliness: how he did it Jack could not tell, remembering his own days on the lower deck and the total absence of anything to wash in before the forenoon watch and precious little then. Clean, and benevolent today, since it was evident that Jack was low in his spirits: for Killick was not unlike a partner on a seesaw, often being at his most shrewish when Jack's cheerfulness was at its height, and the other way about. He reported the wind, still north-north-east, and the weather, medium fair, and then went to fetch the coffee. 'Professor's gone ashore, sir,' he said in a conversational tone, bringing it in. 'Most uncommon early.'

'Is he?' said Jack. 'I shall look forward to seeing him, when he returns. Let me know the moment he comes aboard.'

After a long blank interval in which the decks were cleaned with the usual din of holystones and swabs and sluicing water, and hammocks were piped up to the sound of a furious rush of more than two hundred men, many of them shouting, a stampede repeated almost immediately afterwards as the same horde was piped to breakfast, Stephen came in, and they waited for Graham together, eating buttered toast without the slightest appetite. 'At least,' said Jack, 'the glass is beginning to fall.'

'What does that signify?'

'A change of weather, with the wind almost certainly coming easterly or even south of east. Lord, how I hope so. Even a few points east would bring the transports up: I know Venable and Allen are both keen, enterprising men, and I am sure they would sail the moment they possibly could. It is not much above two days' sailing, with a brisk full-topsail breeze even one point free. Good morning, Tom,' he said, looking up in surprise. 'Sit down and take a bite.'

'I beg pardon for bursting in like this, sir,' said

Pullings, 'but I am just come from the mole and the works, and the town is all of a screech. As far as I can make out, that Ismail is to be governor and they want us to land guns to protect them from him. There is a party coming to see you, sir. They are in such a pitiful taking I said I was sure you would receive 'em.'

'Oh Christ, Pullings,' began Jack, but it was too late: the party was aboard and nothing would keep them out. They were mostly priests of the different denominations – though Father Andros was not there – but some were laymen, middle-aged or elderly merchants, senators in the time of the republic, and they put it to Captain Aubrey that it was his duty to protect his fellow-Christians: to guarantee if not the independence then at least the privileged status of Kutali. The city was Turkish, nominally Turkish, rather than part of the Republic of the Seven Islands only by an error that the Powers would soon put right. Jack said that he was no more than an officer acting under orders; he could not commit his Admiral, far less his King's government. They explained Kutali's special position, a position that had been guaranteed in the first place by their possession of the citadel and that had been respected by Sciahan Bey; Ismail would not respect it, and the citadel was now known to be naked – an empty threat. Twenty guns, no more, would enable them to impose terms on Ismail. They were very urgent with Captain Aubrey to send at least his upper-deck cannon to the citadel and repay himself from the transports, which must arrive very soon now: one of the former senators, a ship-owner and a man of great experience, said that down off Cephalonia the wind would already be in the east; with this cloud-formation he had known it again and again.

Jack said that what they asked him was impossible: this ship and everything in her belonged to his master. They then described to him the taking of a Christian city by Turkish troops, particularly by the irregulars, the utterly undisciplined bashi-bazouks employed by Ismail: murder of course, with women raped and men and children

340

sodomized, but also monstrous desecration of churches, graves and everything holy. It was extremely painful: it was as painful as anything Jack had even known, to have elderly dignified men kneeling to him there in the great cabin.

'Gentlemen, gentlemen,' cried Stephen, 'We are running too far ahead entirely. All this is no more than a rumour, mere words blowing in the wind. Let me implore you, before you take any desperate measures, even any measures at all that might give the Turks just cause for resentment, to wait on Sciahan Bey to learn where the truth lies and what steps he intends to take.'

'Have you ever known an evil rumour that was not true?' asked a tall white-bearded man.

'God help them, poor people, poor people,' muttered Jack, watching them cross the gangway. And aloud he said, 'Mr Gill, let the ship be warped out a cable's length into the fairway,' for women, veiled or shawled, were gathering fast on the mole, and he could not bear their coming aboard to plead with him. The hands who carried out the kedge and who cast off the moorings knew very well what they were about, and they and their officers and their Captain looked mean, hang-dog, and ashamed as the frigate, that powerful battery of guns, edged away from the silent crowded wharf.

It was noon before Graham came back. He was wearing Turkish clothes, looking so natural in them that after a moment neither Jack nor Stephen noticed the odds, and he said, 'I have got to the bottom of it, I believe: I have reached the underlying truth. The position seems to be this: the tsarfetim, a kind of preliminary appointment, has been made out in Ismail's favour, but the Sultan has not signed the iradé, and no iradé has reached Nicopolis or anywhere else. The tsarfetim may have done so, since it is not unusual to send these – these announcements to the regions concerned to see how they are received. There is some slight analogy with the banns of marriage. I propose riding post to Constantinople to put the case before

341

the embassy. When I confront them with the proof of Ismail's intimate connection with the French I have no doubt that they will not only withdraw their support but press for the revocation of the tsarfetim. Furthermore both Sciahan and the Kutaliotes have given me drafts for a sum of money that should certainly ensure this revocation and almost certainly the eventual appointment of Sciahan. They have also supplied me with a guard of Albanian horses.'

'You relieve my mind extremely, Professor,' said Jack. 'We may carry out our attack on Marga yet.'

'I hope so, I am sure,' said Graham. 'But Sciahan has some lingering superstitious doubts about the iradé and in any case, without risking the bowstring he cannot move until the tsarfetim is withdrawn. Once that is settled however he says he will certainly carry out his part of the agreement: and by then the guns are more likely to be here.'

'With the wind as it lies, I believe we may look for them the day after tomorrow,' said Jack. 'But tell me, Professor, is not this a most prodigious wearisome ride you are undertaking? Should you not prefer one of these fine taut caiques? They can sail wonderfully close to the wind, and I have known them log two hundred miles from one noon observation to the next. And this breeze serves for up or down.'

'No doubt,' said Graham, 'but the sea is an uncertain chancy whimsical female lunar element: you advance one mile upon its surface and at the same time the whole body of water has retired a league. I prefer the honest earth, where my advance is absolute, however arduous; and I am no more a seaman than is a Turk or a tib-cat. Now, gentlemen, have you any commands for Constantinople? If not, I must beg to take my leave.'

Stephen accompanied him to the shore, and as they walked to the Maidan, where the horses were waiting, Graham said, 'I shall go by Iannina, where Ali Pasha will tell me how things stand at the Palace, and where I shall have a conference with his Christian Greek advisers and with Osman the Smyrniote, who knows a great deal about the workings of the Porte – he was the author of the Pera reports that you admired so much.'

'You are well with Ali Pasha?'

'I was able to do him a kindness once, and though he is a man of blood he is not ungrateful. He will offer me a larger guard, but I shall not take it.'

'Why is this, colleague?'

'Because Ali is strongly suspected of disloyalty, of wishing to set up as an independent ruler, as so many pashas have done or tried to do; and if only he could be rid of Mustapha, who is in a position to hinder him by sea, I am convinced he would do that very thing. So the less I am seen with him or his men the better. Here are my Ghegs. Good day to you, Maturin.'

It was Captain Aubrey's intention to put to sea until the probable time of Graham's return, to gather his transports on their way north and with them to look into Paxo and Corfu and other places held by the French, partly to harass the enemy if the opportunity offered and partly because so long a stay in such a welcoming port was bad for the ship's health and discipline, but far, far more because an even longer stay must make the French commander in Marga uneasy. For embargo or no embargo, news spread in this country as it were by the wind alone, and Father Andros, putting off with the present of a buck from Sciahan, told him that various versions of the rumour about Ismail were already to be heard in the remotest mountain villages. Yet Captain Aubrey, his first lieutenant, and above all his bosun, were extremely unwilling to put to sea with so many of their cables, and those her best, stretched between the mole and the citadel: a ship often needed to veer out a great scope of cable if it came on to blow, two and even three on end; and proper simpletons they would look, dragging their anchors on a lee shore, having left half a mile of prime seventeen-inch stuff behind them, dangling on a mountain-side. On the other hand, although the people of Kutali were a little less agitated than they had been at first, there were still continual processions to the churches, and Jack hesitated to give the word to unrig the ropeway.

It was not usual for him to discuss his orders with anyone, since in his opinion a ship, and above all a man-of-war, was not 'a God-damned debating society' nor yet 'an infernal House of Commons', but on this occasion he said privately to Pullings, 'What do you think about it, Tom?'

'I think there would be a riot, sir,' said Pullings. 'They would be sure we were deserting them. I know if I touched so much as a limmer-line, Annie would have a fit of the mother.'

'Who is Annie?' asked Jack.

'Oh, sir,' cried Pullings, blushing crimson, 'she is only a young person where I go to have a cup of coffee sometimes – a very small cup of coffee – and to learn a little of the language – the customs of the country.'

Stephen asked Father Andros his opinion, and Father Andros, having pulled his beard and looked anxious for a while, admitted that it might be better to wait for a day or two, while the people grew accustomed to the notion that their fears had been exaggerated, that matters were likely to be arranged satisfactorily, and that the ship's going was not definitive. 'One can do a great deal with rumour – with word of mouth properly employed,' he said with a look that surprised Stephen. 'If you had asked me, I should have put it in hand earlier.'

Very late on Friday night, therefore, the *Surprise* was lying at single anchor, riding easy with her head to the moderate south-east wind and hoping to get her cables in next morning, and her Captain and surgeon were sawing away fortissimo, building up to the climax of their Corelli in C major, when the door burst open and Graham appeared in the opening. His appearance was so extraordinary that neither said a word, but merely stared: the sound fled out of the room and he cried 'Mustapha is

344

at sea. He has taken the transports. You may catch him
if you are quick.'

'Where away?' asked Jack.

'He is taking them into Antipaxo, and from there he
goes straight on to meet Ali Pasha at Makeni, sailing at
dawn.'

Jack strode across the great cabin, through the fore-
cabin, and whipped up the quarterdeck ladder in the
darkness: he was strongly tempted to slip the cable, but the
notion of putting to sea with almost nothing to hold him
to the sea-bed was so abhorrent, so against all his feelings
of what was right, so nearly impious, that he changed his
order to 'All hands to weigh', and by the time he left the
deck the capstan-bars were already being swifted and the
barrel had already made a preliminary turn or so, with
the musical click of the pawls. Three top-lanterns and a
few battle-lanterns on deck and between-decks were all
they had to see by, but it was wonderful how a really
seasoned crew of man-of-war's men worked together,
rapidly, accurately, with little noise and no fuss, although
half of them had been asleep in their hammocks not five
minutes before.

When he returned to the cabin Stephen was easing
Graham's boots off and mopping the places where they
had chafed him raw. 'You have had a hard ride of it,
Professor,' he said. 'Where have you come from?'

'Only Iannina.'

'That is far enough, in all conscience. Should you
not take a glass of brandy, perhaps, and then something
to eat? Killick! Killick, there.'

'You are very good. If I might be indulged in a little
cocoa, with milk, and a lightly boiled egg: but they are
already preparing.'

'When you have recovered a little, you must tell
us how Mustapha came to do this extraordinary thing.'

The cocoa came in, but Graham's hands were trembling
so that he could scarcely drink from the mug: however, the
ship was on an even keel, so he put it down on Diana's

music-stand and drank by suction. 'That's a braw whet,' he said, holding out his mug for more. 'I will tell you now. Mustapha is in open rebellion. He has thrown off his allegiance to the Sultan and has raised his own standard. He needed the guns, and so he has taken them.'

'Was there an action? Has he hurt many of our people?'

'No. He decoyed them in. He is treating them well, in hopes of an arrangement.'

'And his course is from Antipaxo to Makeni, sailing at dawn? You are sure of that?'

'As sure as I can be of anything in this world of false-seeming,' said Graham. 'He has a rendezvous with Ali Pasha at Makeni tomorrow evening, and he goes there in his ship the *Torgud*.'

'Forgive me a moment,' said Jack. On deck the capstan was turning steadily, the ship gliding across the quiet black water, and as Jack turned into the master's day-cabin, calling for a light, he heard the bosun on the forecastle cry 'Right up and down, sir,' and Pullings' reply, 'Thick and dry for weighing.'

He studied the charts by the flaring lamp. Antipaxo to Makeni, the wind steady at south-east, a topgallant breeze: he laid off Mustapha's course and another to intercept it in the approaches to the Corfu channel, where the narrowing of the shores must correct even the wildest Turkish navigation. He worked it out twice, with the known performance of both ships, and it appeared to him that they could scarcely fail to meet. Mr Gill, yawning and unshaved but quick, keen and accurate with figures nevertheless, came to the same conclusion independently. Turning the course over in his mind Jack walked forward to see the anchor catted; and as he stood there he caught the ship's mood – eager excitement at the prospect of a dust-up, intense curiosity about their opponent, and a lively anticipation of orders for a middle-watcher, that uncovenanted refreshment that some of the humaner captains, Aubrey among them, sometimes called for when all hands had been turned up, particularly from harbour-watch, at a more ungodly hour than usual. He walked back along the starboard gangway, watching the few remaining lights of Kutali glide slowly astern, and reaching the quarterdeck he said to the officer of the watch, 'Due north to clear the headland – give it a wide berth, Mr Mowett, I beg – and when we are clear west by south a half west: topsails and jib.'

'Due north and a wide berth it is, sir; then west by south and a half west. Topsails and jib.'

Professor Graham was sitting in front of his uneaten eggs, an unbitten piece of bread and butter in his hand: he looked old, surprisingly frail, unwell.

'Now sir,' said Jack to him, 'we are heading out to sea. If your information about Mustapha is correct, and if the breeze holds steady, we may hope to meet him some time in the afternoon tomorrow.'

'I believe it is correct,' said Graham. 'Let me tell you the circumstances.' An expectant silence, with only the sound of the ship gathering way, the gentle creaking of innumerable ropes, blocks and spars, and the run of water along her side, the more and more urgent heel as her sails were braced to take the wind: then he said, 'I am too worn and stupid to give you anything but the baldest account, and I may leave out some important points. Well, now: the whole tale of Ismail was a flam, a piece of deception invented and engineered by Ali Pasha. It deceived the whole countryside – it deceived me, I am ashamed to say – and it deceived Mustapha, which was the whole object.'

'Why Mustapha?'

'To push him over the edge into rebellion: he was very near it in any case. The news of Ismail's success was perfectly intolerable, and it threw Mustapha into a frenzy of rage and jealousy; and Ali had a confidential friend there to spur him on – he and Ali would join forces and divide the western provinces – and to urge him to make the first bold stroke immediately, seizing the transports while they were within his reach and then

347

coming on to confer with Ali for their campaign against Ismail.'

'What were Ali's motives?'

'He means to rebel himself: a loyal Mustapha was one of the few men who could stand in his way. If Ali sends Mustapha's head to Constantinople, that not only does away with the suspicions about his fidelity to the Sultan but also leaves the field quite clear. Besides, there was an old enmity between them, more or less patched up but never forgotten by Ali Pasha.'

'So Ali means to take his head off at their conference?'

'Yes, if Mustapha ever reaches it. But I think Ali really expects you to deal with the situation first, while he contents himself with confiscating Mustapha's treasure, harem, and beylik in the Sultan's name. That is why his counsellors gave me such very precise information about Mustapha's movements.'

'It is hardly believable.'

Graham said 'No . . . no,' in a vague, unmeaning voice and then begged to be excused – he could say no more.

For the ten thousandth time Jack woke to the sound of holystones on deck: the *Surprise* might be going into action later in the day, but she was certainly going into it titivated to the nines, and the first lieutenant could be heard calling with unusual insistence for the removal of three spots of tar. Jack's whole massive form was utterly relaxed, yielding to the slow easy lift and roll: he had been on deck twice during the graveyard watch, but since then he had had some hours of deep, deep velvet sleep, and he felt perfectly rested, actively and positively well. The tension of that interminable waiting for the transports was gone, and with it his uncertainty and his immediate distress about Kutali and all the falsity and double-dealing on shore: his present course of action was clear-cut and perfectly direct at last, an operation that he was fully qualified to undertake by training, inclination, and the splendid instrument at his disposal, and one in which he needed no man's advice.

Yet although he had been a great way down, the thought of their probable encounter with the *Torgud* had never left him: he had fallen asleep working out the weight of her broadside and now that he was awake his mind carried on the sum. But could the shocking great thirty-six-pounders be counted? Was the renegado to be believed when he said there were only nine rounds for them altogether? And then what was the Turks' gunnery like? A great deal would depend on that. If it was no better than their seamanship it would not be very formidable; but the two did not necessarily go together. As for numbers, the *Torgud* probably had about a hundred and fifty more men than *Surprise* when he saw her, but she would have lost a good many in her prize-crews, more than enough to compensate for the Surprises now in Malta or on their way back in the *Dryad*. He was on the point of exclaiming 'Thank God *Dryad* ain't here,' – for even an unhandy butter-box of her size would upset the fairly even match and take all the glory away – when he realized that nothing could be more presumptuous or unlucky, and choking back even the enunciation of the thought he sprang out of his cot, singing 'The lily, the lily, a rose I lay, The bailey beareth the bell away,' in his powerful melodious bass.

Like a horizontal jack-in-a-box Killick shot in, carrying shaving-water; and lathering away Jack said to him, 'Breeches today, Killick. There are chances we may see action.'

With Killick's goodwill Jack would never have worn anything but scrubbed old nankeen pantaloons and a threadbare coat with the lace taken off, while his good uniforms all lay in tissue-paper where no damp or sun could get at them. He now objected to any change on the grounds that a Turk and above all a rebellious Turk did not rate breeches. 'Lay out the breeches and top your boom,' said Jack firmly, when the nagging had been going on for some time. But when he pulled off his nightshirt and turned, he found that although the letter of the order had been obeyed the spirit, as usual, had not – before him lay a barely reputable pair of darned breeches, thread stockings, yesterday's shirt, and the coat whose sleeve he had ruined in Ismail's dinner. Of his own authority he opened a locker and took out the splendid affair he wore to visit admirals, pashas and governors; in this he walked on to the already crowded quarterdeck, and after a general 'Good morning' he surveyed the scene. A brilliant day with a high dappled sky and the sun a handsbreadth up astern; the breeze steady; the sea flecked with white where the wind caught the remains of the dying northern swell. From the traverse-board and the log-board it was clear that the *Surprise* was almost exactly where he had meant her to be: Cape Doro would lie a little abaft the beam over the starboard horizon, and right ahead Phanari should loom up within an hour or two. He took a couple of turns the whole length of the ship, breathing the sea-smell deep in after the closeness of his sleeping-cabin, and with it the damp fresh scent of newly-scrubbed planks: most of the ship's company were on deck, and he moved among faces he knew perfectly well. The men had had their breakfast, and they looked at him cheerfully, knowingly, expectantly, with a certain connivance or complicity; some were engaged in beautifying the long seams of the larboard gangway with a shining black preparation invented by Mr Pullings, but most were busy with such things as the breechings of the great guns or the chipping of round-shot to make it more perfectly spherical, truer in its flight, more deadly. The armourer was at his grindstone under the forecastle with a group of seamen round him relaying one another at the crank and giving advice; he had rows of shining cutlasses and boarding axes and officers' swords at his feet, and his mates were checking pistols by the score, while in a separate body a little farther aft the Marines, looking quite human in their shirt-sleeves, polished their already spotless muskets and bayonets.

350

A couple of turns, and then saying to the officer of the watch, 'Mr Gill, pray lend me your glass,' he swung up over the hammocks, tightly packed in their netting, and so up and up for the pleasure of climbing, the strong easy motion of going aloft. The lookout, warned by the creaking of the shrouds, moved out apelike on the topgallant yard to make room and Jack installed himself at the crosstrees, gazing all round the vast blue disc spread taut below him and reaching to the sky on every hand: there to starboard lay Cape Doro, where it ought to be within half a point; and he believed he could just make out Phanari ahead. 'Simms,' he called to the man on the yard, 'keep a good lookout, d'ye hear me there? Our gentleman is likely to come up from the south, but since he is a Turk, he might come from anywhere.'

With this he returned to the deck, where he found Stephen and Graham. He invited them to breakfast, together with Pullings and two youngsters, Calamy and Williamson; and while it was preparing he talked to the gunner about the amount of cartridge filled and to the carpenter about the provision of plugs to deal with forty-pound-ball shot-holes. 'For,' he said, 'our possible adversary – and I say only *possible*, Mr Watson . . .'

'Or hypothetical, as you might put it, sir.'

'Exactly so – is the *Torgud*, and she carries two Portuguese thirty-sixes, which is our forty-pounder, give or take a trifle.'

'Hypothetical,' muttered Killick with great contempt, and then very loud, drowning the carpenter's reply, 'Wittles is up, sir, if you please.'

It was a cheerful meal. Jack was a good host, and when he had time to concern himself with them he was fond of the little brutes from the midshipmen's berth; furthermore he was in remarkably high spirits and he amused himself and the young gentlemen extremely by dwelling at length on the fact that the country they had just quitted was practically the same as Dalmatia - a mere continuation of Dalmatia – so famous for its spotted dogs. He himself had

351

seen quantities of spotted dogs – had even hunted behind a couple of braces – spotted dogs in a pack of hounds, oh Lord! – while the town of Kutali was positively infested with spotted youths and maidens, and now the Doctor swore he had seen spotted eagles . . . Jack laughed until the tears came into his eyes. In a Dalmatian inn, he said, by way of pudding you could call for spotted dick, give pieces of it to a spotted dog, and throw the remains to the spotted eagles.

While the others were enlarging upon the possibilities, Graham said to Stephen in a low voice, 'what is this spotted eagle? Is it a joke?'

'The *aquila maculosa* or *discolor* of some authors, Linnaeus' *aquila clanga*. The captain is pleased to be arch. He is frequently arch of a morning.'

'I beg your pardon, sir,' cried the midshipman of the watch, fairly racing in. 'Mr Mowett's duty and two sail on the larboard beam, topsails up from the masthead.'

'Two?' said Jack. 'Are they ships?'

'He cannot make out yet, sir.'

'May I go, sir?' asked Pullings, half out of his chair, his face alive with eagerness.

'Aye, do,' said Jack. 'We will eat up your bacon for you.'

Ships they were. Turkish ships they were, although it was so early, and men-of-war: the *Torgud* and the *Kitabi*. Mustapha had sailed far sooner than had been expected; and being now perhaps less confident of Ali's good faith he had brought his consort with him.

'Oh what a damnable thing,' cried Graham, when this was established beyond the tremor of a doubt. 'Oh what a bitter, bitter disappointment. Yet I am sure Osman gave me the best intelligence he had.' He fairly wrung his hands, and Jack said, 'Never be so concerned, sir: it will be somewhat harder, to be sure, but we must not despair of the republic.'

'You cannot possibly attack both of them,' said Graham angrily. 'The *Torgud* carries thirty-two guns in all and nearly four hundred men, and the *Kitabi* twenty guns and a hundred and eighty. You are outnumbered by more than a hundred and eighty. There is no shame in retiring before such odds.'

As he said this some of the people on the quarterdeck nodded; others adopted reserved, remote expressions; only Pullings and Mowett frowned with evident disapproval. Stephen thought he detected a predominant sense of agreement with Graham's remark: for his own part he did not feel qualified to form a naval opinion, but he did know how passionately Jack wished to wipe out the wretched affair at Medina and he suspected that desire might warp his judgement.

'Why, Professor,' said Jack pleasantly, 'I believe you are almost in danger of poaching upon my province,' and Graham, recollecting himself, begged pardon and withdrew.

Leaning over the hammocks in the starboard netting Jack watched them over the sparkling sea: the frigate and the twenty-gun ship were now not much above two miles away, keeping steadily to their original course under all plain sail while the *Surprise* stood towards them on the larboard tack, the south-east wind one point free.

'Lord, how glad I am we weighed directly,' he said to himself. He smiled at the thought of his mad frustration had they arrived too late, all for the sake of the cables and hawsers ashore: he smiled and even chuckled aloud.

By now the quarterdeck had all its officers and young gentlemen, all its proper foremast hands, signalmen, messengers and timoneers, together with everyone else in the ship who had a right to walk upon it, and Stephen and Professor Graham were wedged against the hances, behind the Captain's clerk and the purser.

'It seems an uncouth long wait before anything happens,' said Graham in a low voice. 'I dare say you have seen many actions at sea?'

'I have seen the beginnings of several,' said Stephen, 'but as soon as it grows dangerous I retire to a place of safety below.'

'You are all very arch and jocose this morning,' said Graham discontentedly. Then, nodding towards the other side, where Jack and Pullings were discussing some point of their approach and laughing heartily as they did so, he said, 'Do you know the word *fey*, that we use in the north?'

'I do not,' said Stephen. He was perfectly well acquainted with the word, but he did not wish to discuss his friend's dangerous high spirits with Graham.

'I am not a superstitious man; but if those gentlemen are married and if their wives . . .'

'All hands aft,' said Jack, and the howling of the calls and the sound of hundreds of feet drowned Graham's words.

'I am not going to make a speech,' said Captain Aubrey to his men. 'We know one another too well to go on about duty. Very well. Now when we were in Medina I had to tell you not to fire into the enemy first, and since he would not begin we were obliged to come away without doing anything. Some of you were not quite pleased. This time it will be different. Those two Turkish men-of-war over there have rebelled against their Sultan.' The wrongs of the Sultan of Turkey left the Surprises quite unmoved: their expressions did not change in the slightest degree: they looked attentively at their Captain, who continued, 'And what is more they have taken our transports. So it stands to reason we must knock some sense into their heads, and get our prisoners and ships and cannon back. As I dare say you know, they have a good many men in them, so we are not likely to board very soon, but rather hammer them from a distance. You must fire into their hulls, right into their hulls, mind: fire low and true, deliberate fire with post paid on every ball. Mr Pullings, we may clear for action, and beat to quarters.'

Very little required doing. All the warrant and petty officers had had plenty of warning and they had taken their measures: Mr Hollar, for example, had had his puddings and dolphins in the tops these hours past. Killick had already taken Jack's better clothes and possessions below, and Diana's dressing-case, horribly ringed and stained by Graham's cocoa, lay in its elaborate double case in the bread-room. All that remained was for the galley fires to be put out, for the carpenters to knock down the bulkheads of Jack's and the master's cabins, and for the gun-crews to take possession of the massive brutes that had been Jack's stable-companions, and it was done.

The various officers reported to Pullings, and Pullings stepped up to Jack, saluted and said, 'A clean sweep fore and aft, sir, if you please.'

'Thank you, Mr Pullings,' said Jack, and they stood there side by side, smiling and looking forward, over the starboard bow, at the immediate future coming towards them.

The *Surprise* was silent, most of her men grave, as they usually were before action: grave, but not very much concerned, since there were few who had not run down on the enemy like this many times over. On the other hand, not many had run down to quite such odds, and some thought the skipper had bitten off more than he could chew. Most hands knew very well that Medina rankled at his heart, and the few stupid fellows were soon told. 'That is all wery fine and large,' said William Pole, on hearing the news. 'All wery fine and large, so long as I don't have to pay for it with my skin.'

'For shame, Bill Pole,' said the rest of the gun-team.

The *Surprise* bore down, therefore, under her fighting-sails, with her master at the con, her guns run out, powder-boys sitting well behind them on their leather cartridge-cases, shot-garlands full, splinter-netting rigged, scuttle-butts all along, decks damped and sanded, and wet fearnought screens over the hatches leading to the magazine far below, where the gunner sat among his little deadly kegs. Mowett had the forward division of guns on the maindeck, Honey, the senior master's mate, the after division, with midshipmen attending three aside each – the oldsters, that is to say, for Jack kept the boys who had

breakfasted with him on the quarterdeck as aides-de-camp.
Those Marines who were not quartered at the guns lined
the gangway, looking particularly trim, their red coats
strikingly brilliant against the white hammock-cloths and
the now intense blue of the sea, in this powerful sunlight.
Their lieutenant now stood amidships, with the purser and
the captain's clerk, none of them speaking but all looking
steadily forward at the Turks.

In this silence Graham turned to Stephen, who had
not yet gone below to his battle-station, and close to his
ear said, 'What did Mr Aubrey mean by desiring the men
to put *post paid* on every ball?'

'In English law it is a capital offence to stop His
Majesty's mails: by extension the stopping of any object
marked post paid is also mortal. And indeed the man who
stops a cannon-ball is unlikely to survive.'

'So it was a joke?'

'Just so.'

'A joke at a time like this, good God forgive us?
Such a man would be facetious at his father's burial.'

In the last few minutes the ships had approached to
within random shot, the Turks on *Surprise*'s starboard
bow holding their course without the slightest deviation,
with the *Kitabi* abreast of the *Torgud*, a quarter of a
mile to leeward. Bonden, the captain of the gun, kept
the starboard chaser steadily trained on the *Torgud*'s
bows, perpetually shifting it with his handspike. They
were drawing together at a combined speed of ten miles
an hour, and just before they came to point-blank range
the silence was ripped apart by a great screaming blast of
Turkish trumpets, harsh and shrill.

'God, how it lifts your heart,' said Jack, and he
gave the orders 'Colours at the fore and main.' With
his glass he watched the crowded Turkish deck: saw the
man at the halyards, followed the flags as they ran up in
reply, and on seeing the regular Turkish ensign break out
he reflected, 'He thinks we do not know yet: perhaps he
hopes to slip by. But his guns are manned,' and aloud he

356

called 'Professor Graham, pray come and stand by me. Mr Gill, wear round to the starboard tack and lay me within pistol-shot of his starboard side.'

Now high seamanship showed its splendid powers: the sail-trimmer sprang from their guns; forecourse, staysails and jibs flashed out; the frigate leapt forward like a spurred horse and made her quick tight turn, as Jack knew she would do, bringing her larboard guns to bear when the Turks were still expecting her on the other side.

'Shiver the foretopsail,' called Jack, with his eye on the *Torgud*'s quarterdeck and her burly captain right under his lee. 'Mr Graham, call out to him that he must surrender directly. Larboard guns stand by.'

Graham shouted loud and clear. Jack saw Mustapha's red beard part in a white gleam as he roared back his answer, a long answer.

'In effect he refuses,' said Graham.

'Fire.'

The *Surprise*'s entire broadside went off in a single explosion that shook both ships from truck to keelson and for a moment deadened the air; and now in the thick smoke rolling to leeward over the *Torgud* began the great hammering, red flashes in the gloom, iron crashing into the hulls on either side or howling overhead, an enormous all-pervading din, with ropes parting, blocks falling, jagged pieces of wood struck from the rails, the bulwark, the decks, and whistling across. After their hesitant start, they being caught on the wrong foot, the Turks fired hard and fast, though with no attempt at regularity, and the first shot of their starboard thirty-six-pounder tore a great gap in the hammocks, scored an eighteen-inch groove in the mainmast yet extraordinarily killed no men. But if the *Torgud* was firing pretty well or at least pretty fast, the *Surprise* was excelling herself: now that the broadsides were no longer simultaneous, the guns being out of step after the third or fourth discharge, it was hard to be sure, but judging by number seven, just under him, they were achieving something like a round in seventy seconds, while the quarterdeck carronades were doing even better; and Jack was very sure that their aim was a great deal truer than the Turks'. Glancing to windward he saw a wide area of sea torn up by Turkish grape and round-shot that must have missed by as much as twenty or thirty yards, and then as he paced up and down he stared to leeward, trying to pierce the smoke: 'I wonder the Turk bears it so long,' he said, and as he spoke he saw the *Torgud*'s topsails bracing round as she edged away to join the *Kitabi* to leeward. He caught the master's eye: Gill nodded – he was already following the movement.

After a few minutes of this gradual turn the smoke would blow away ahead and the sharpshooters would have a chance. He bent to his youngsters, and shouting loud through the uproar and the general deafness that affected all hands he said, 'Mr Calamy, jump up to the tops and tell them to annoy the Turk's thirty-six-pounder. Mr Williamson, tell Mr Mowett and Mr Honey we are reducing the charges up here by a third. Mr Pullings, make it so.'

At this furious rate of fire the guns heated excessively and they kicked with even greater force when they went off: indeed, as he moved towards the taffrail, trying to see through the smoke, one of the quarterdeck carronades did in fact break its breeching and overset.

As he bent to snub a trailing side-tackle the waft of the thirty-six-pound ball sweeping over the deck a foot from his head made him stagger; and now, as the iron hail beat furiously on and about the *Surprise*, ball, grape and bar flying through the continuous thunder, with the crackle of musketry above it, there was a new note. The *Torgud*, with the *Surprise* following her, had edged down much closer to the *Kitabi*, and now the *Kitabi* opened with her shrill twelve-pounders. Up until this point the *Surprise* had not suffered badly, except perhaps in her hull; but this present hail knocked one of the forward guns half across the deck, striking it on its own recoil and maiming three of its crew, and again the thirty-six-pounder roared out:

its great crash was followed by a screaming below that for two minutes pierced even the united gunfire. And now a bloody trail on the deck showed where the wounded were carried down to the orlop.

Yet the frigate's fire scarcely slackened from its first tremendous pace: powder and shot ran smoothly up from the magazines, the gun-teams rattled their massive pieces in and out with a magnificent zeal, sponging, loading, ramming, heaving up and firing with a racing coordination that it was a pleasure to watch. Although it was still impossible to see at all clearly Jack was sure that they must already have mauled the *Torgud* very severely; she was certainly not firing so fast nor from so many guns, and he was expecting her to wear in the smoke, either to run or to present her undamaged larboard broadside, when he heard the fierce harsh trumpets bray out again. The *Torgud* was going to board.

'Grape,' he said to Pullings and his messengers, and very loud, 'Sail-trimmers stand by.' The *Torgud*'s fire died away except for her bow guns; the smoke cleared, and there she was, turning into the wind, steering straight for the *Surprise*, her bowsprit and even her jibboom crowded with people, willing to take the risk of a raking fire for the sake of boarding. 'Wait for it,' cried Jack. To tack his ship before the Turk could run her aboard, to tack her in so short a space of time and sea as though she were a cutter, was appallingly dangerous; but he knew her through and through, and as he calculated the wind's strength, the ship's impetus, and the living force of the water he called again, 'Wait for it. Wait. Fire.' And then the second his voice could be heard, 'Hands about ship.'

The *Surprise* came about, but only just: the *Torgud* did not. She lay there, taken aback; and as they passed, the Surprises cheering like maniacs, Jack saw that the storm of grape had cleared her head of men, a most shocking butchery.

'Warm work, Professor,' he said to Graham in the momentary pause.

'Is it, indeed? This is my first naval battle of any consequence.'

'Quite warm, I assure you: but the Turks cannot keep it up. That is the disadvantage of your brass guns. If you keep on firing at this rate, they melt. They are pretty, to be sure; but they cannot keep it up. Mr Gill, we will lie on her larboard quarter, if you please, and rake her from there.'

The *Torgud*, falling off, had put before the wind, and now the *Surprise* bore up and made sail in pursuit; no guns but the bow-chaser could be trained round far enough to bear, and all up and down the ship men straightened and stood easy. Some went to the scuttle-butts to drink or dash the water in their faces; most were stripped to the waist, shining with sweat; all were in tearing spirits. At one of the quarterdeck carronades a young fellow was showing his mates a lost finger. 'I never noticed it,' he kept saying. 'Never noticed it go at all.'

But now here, against all expectation, was the *Kitabi*, coming up fast with the obvious intention of passing between the *Surprise* and the *Torgud* and then presumably of hauling her wind to take the *Surprise* between two fires.

'That will not do, my friend,' said Jack, watching her approach. 'It is very gallant, but it really will not do. Round-shot,' he called, 'and fire steady from forward aft: fire at the word.' Some minutes later, when the relative positions of the three ships were such that the *Torgud* was directly to leeward of her consort and unable to give her any support, Jack shivered the main and mizen topsails, slanting down towards the *Kitabi*, making no reply to her high, rapid, nervous, largely ineffectual fire until they were a cable's length apart, no more.

They gave her six deliberate rolling broadsides, beating five of her midships gun-ports into one and silencing her entirely. At the sixth there was a violent explosion aboard her, and the beginning of a fire: the *Surprise* passed on, leaving her drifting before the wind, her people running with buckets and hose.

The breeze had faded, perhaps stunned by the cannon-ade, and the *Surprise* set her topgallantsails to pursue the *Torgud*: not that the Turk was evidently flying – he had no great speed of canvas – but he was steering steadily on his original course, perhaps in the hope of reaching Ali Pasha; and right ahead the mainland could now be seen, mountain-peaks nicking the horizon, while the low Morali islands must be nearer still. In this wonderfully silent pause, while the bosun and his mates sprang about the rigging, knotting and splicing, Jack stared at the *Torgud* for a moment, watching them throw their dead over the side – a trail of dead in her wake – and then made a quick tour of the ship. He found less damage than he had feared: one gun dismounted, the side pierced by three thirty-six-pounder balls and some others, but none of the holes dangerously low, while in Stephen's hands there were no more than six badly wounded men and three sewn into their hammocks, remarkably few for such a furious bout.

On deck again he saw that the breeze had recovered, and that the *Surprise* was overhauling the *Torgud* fast. They were already within gunshot, but with land in sight it seemed to Jack that so long as he could avoid being boarded close action was called for, and it was not until they were drawing abreast, close enough to see men's faces clearly, that he reduced sail and the hammering began again. This was the *Torgud*'s larboard broadside, hitherto unengaged and undamaged, and the Turks blazed away with as much spirit as before: again a thirty-six-pound ball passed so close to Jack's head that it made him stagger – he actually saw the dark blur of its passing – and he said to Driver of the Marines, 'Let your men amidships concentrate on the loader of that damned heavy gun.' Graham, who was just at hand, said 'May I take a musket, sir? I might do some good, and I feel uneasy, useless and exposed standing here.'

He was indeed exposed. Now that both ships had the wind aft the smoke blew clear away forward; the *Torgud* was shooting more accurately than before and as her shot hit the *Surprise*'s bulwark or upper hull so showers of splinters flew across her deck, some trifling, some deadly. Graham had already been knocked over twice, and most of those on deck had been more or less banged about.

The *Torgud* was still full of fight, and she still had a surprising number of men. After a particularly violent salvo she clapped her helm hard over, meaning to board again, and again her people crowded thick into her bows and along her bowsprit. This time the *Surprise* had no room to tack, but she had her forecourse in the brails for just such an emergency, and dropping it now she shot ahead: though none too fast, since the *Torgud*'s jibboom caught in her mizen topgallant backstays. She shot ahead nevertheless, her stern-chasers blasting grape into the close-packed Turks, a red slaughter that checked even the gun-crew's cheers; and the moment she had way enough she crossed the *Torgud*'s stern, raking her as she did so. The *Surprise* let fly her sheets, and the *Torgud*, ranging up, engaged again with her starboard broadside, shockingly ravaged from that first bout, with at least seven guns dismounted, ports blackened and battered in, the scuppers and even the bare sides thick with blood.

Ravaged, but still dangerous: now, when some opponents might have struck, she let fly with a dozen or thirteen guns and two of these did more damage than all she had fired hitherto. One struck the uppermost pintle and wedged the rudder, and another, the last of her huge round-shot, caught the *Surprise* just as she was on the lift, showing her copper, and made a shocking great hole under her waterline. And a third, fired as Jack was giving Williamson orders to carry forward, took the boy's arm off at the elbow. Jack saw his amazed face go paper-white – not pain but amazement and concern and disbelief – whipped a handkerchief round the stump, twisted it tight, staunched the jetting blood and passed him to a quartermaster to carry below.

By the time the *Surprise* had dealt with the steering

and the leak the *Torgud* was much nearer the land. Apart from a few shots from her stern-chasers as she drew ahead she had not tried to profit by her advantage, still less to board. It was possible that she was unaware of the damage she had inflicted: it was certain that the last encounter, the last raking, had killed a great number of her men. She sailed away, therefore, and in her wake there now sailed the *Kitabi*, she having pursued a course with no turnings since the *Surprise* left her; and both Turks were clearly steering for the same port.

'All sail she will bear, Mr Pullings,' said Jack, going forward to study the *Torgud* through a borrowed telescope – a musket-shot had broken his own as he held it: the tube shattered, his hand untouched. The *Torgud* had suffered terribly, there was no doubt of that; she was sailing low and heavy and although the *Surprise* was now gathering way fast as Pullings spread topgallantsails and even weather studdingsails in his passionate eagerness, the *Torgud* seemed unwilling and unable to make any increase. And even now the bodies were still splashing over the side.

'No,' said Jack to Bonden at the starboard bow-chaser as they came within easy range of the Turk's stern, moving faster every moment. 'Do not fire. We must not check her way. Boarding is the only thing for it, and the sooner the better.'

'Anyhow, sir,' said Bonden, 'that damned fool is in the way.' This was the *Kitabi*. Convinced that the *Surprise* was in pursuit of her, she had cracked on the most extraordinary amount of canvas to rejoin the *Torgud* and now she lay directly between the two.

Jack walked aft, and as he passed the boarders in each gun-crew smiled at him, or nodded, or said 'Coming up now, sir,' or cheerful words of that kind; and again he felt the rising of that enormous excitement of immediate battle, greater than any other he had ever known in the world.

He spoke to the Marines, who were now to come

into their own, and after a few more turns he ran down the ladders to the lantern-lit orlop. 'Stephen,' he said privately, 'How is the boy?'

'He will do, I believe.'

'I hope so, indeed. As soon as we come up, we mean to board.'

They shook hands and he ran on deck again. Pullings was already taking in the studdingsails, not to overrun the *Torgud*: and there, still absurdly ahead, fled the *Kitabi*, between the two frigates. She fired not a gun: she seemed to have lost her head entirely. 'Forward, there,' called Jack to the bow-chaser guns, 'Send a ball over her deck.'

'By God,' cried the master, as the *Kitabi* jigged at the shot, 'She'll run the *Torgud* aboard if she don't take care – by God, she can't avoid her – by God, she's doing it.'

With a rending, crashing sound that came clear to their ears at four hundred yards the *Kitabi* ground slanting into the *Torgud*'s starboard side, her foremast falling over the frigate's waist.

'Lay me athwart her stern,' cried Jack, and then very loud, 'One broadside at the word, and board her in the smoke.'

As the *Surprise* began her turn he stepped forward to the great gap in the starboard hammock-netting torn by the Turks, loosening his sword, easing his pistols. Pullings was at his right hand, his eyes sparkling, and from nowhere had appeared the grim man Davis, jostling against Bonden on the left, looking perfectly mad with a line of white spittle between his lips and a butcher's cleaver in his hand.

The last sweeping movement, the easy, yielding crunch of the ship's sides, and the roar of the great guns as Jack gave the word. Then calling 'Boarders away' he leapt through the smoke down to the *Kitabi*'s deck. Perhaps forty Turks stood against them, an irresolute line almost instantly overwhelmed and beaten back, and there in the clearing eddies was an officer holding out his sword, hilt first, and crying, 'Rendre, rendre.'

'Mr Gill, take charge,' said Jack, and as the *Torgud*

364

fired her remaining after-guns straight into the *Kitabi* he raced through the billowing smoke into the bows, roaring 'Come on, come on, come on with me.'

It was no great leap across, for the *Torgud* was low, low in the water, the sea washing into her shattered midship ports and flowing out red, and one flying stride took him on to her quarterdeck rail.

Here it was different. Here though her decks were bloody and ploughed with shot they were still full of men: most were facing aft into the smoke, but one whipped round and cut at him directly. Jack caught the blade on his sword and from his height on the rail gave the Turk a great thrust with his foot that sent him flying into the waist of the ship – into the water that swilled over the waist of the settling, almost sinking ship.

He leapt down on to the deck: he had never felt stronger or more lithe or more wholly in form and when a pike came piercing through the confusion, thrusting straight at his belly, he slashed it with such force and precision that he struck the point clean from its shaft. Almost at once the fight took on a pattern. Jack, Pullings and most of the boarders were crowding into the forward starboard corner of the *Torgud*'s quarterdeck, trying to force their way aft from there and the gangway. Some others and all the Marines were doing their best to storm the stern-windows and the taffrail.

It was the usual furious melée, with a huge amount of shouting and striving, very little room to move because of both friends and enemies, little in the way of skill in swordsmanship – an enormous pushing, thrusting, lashing out at a venture, quick stabs in the tumult, short-armed blows, kicking: the physical weight of both sides and the moral weight of both sides.

The mass heaved to and fro: turbans, skull-caps, yellow bloodshot eyes, swarthy bearded faces on the one hand, pale on the other, but both with the same extremity of naked murderous violence; a prodigiously strenuous, vehement mass, sometimes clearing between the two fronts for a short burst of individual, direct and often deadly fighting: then it closed again, the men face to face, even chest to chest, immediately touching. And hitherto neither had a clear advantage: Jack's hundred or so had won a few yards to fight in, but there they were blocked; and the people astern seemed to have lost their foothold. Jack had felt two or three wounds – the searing lash of a pistol-ball across his ribs, a sword-thrust, half-parried, on the other side, while once Davis had very nearly brought him down with the back-stroke of his cleaver that opened a blunt gash on his forehead – and he knew that he had given some very shrewd blows. And all the time he looked for Mustapha: never a glimpse of him, though his enormous voice could be heard.

Abruptly there was room in front of him, breathing-space as some of the Turks eased back, still fighting. On Jack's right Pullings lunged into this space, thrusting at his opponent, caught his foot on a ring-bolt and fell. For a fragment of time his ingenuous face was turned to Jack, then the Turk's sword flashed down and the fight closed in again. 'No, no, no,' roared Jack, driving forward with enormous strength. He had his heavy sabre in both hands and taking no guard he hacked and slashed, standing astride over Pullings' body. Now men scattered before his extreme fury; they fell back; the moral advantage was established. Shouting to Davis to stand by, to stand guard, to carry the body under the ladder, he charged aft, followed by all the rest. At the same time the Marines, repulsed from the stern and reformed farther forward, came thundering down both gangways with bayonets fixed.

The crowd of Turks thinned, some running, most retreating steadily towards the taffrail, and there abaft the tottering mizzen sat Mustapha at a table covered with pistols, most of them discharged. His leg had been broken early in the day and it rested on a blood-stained drum. Two of his officers were holding his hands down and a third called to Jack 'We surrender.' This was Ulusan, who had come aboard the *Surprise* with Mustapha: he stepped forward, hauled down the colours and slipped the ensign free. The others at last made Mustapha give up his sword: Ulusan, wrapping the flag about it, offered both to Jack in the unearthly silence. Mustapha rose up, grasping the table, and flung himself on the deck in a paroxysm of rage or grief, his head striking against the wood like a mallet. Jack glanced at him with frigid indifference. 'Give you joy, sir,' said Mowett at his side. 'You have come it the Nelson's bridge at last.'

Jack turned a pale, hard face on him. 'Have you seen Pullings?' he asked.

'Why, yes, sir,' said Mowett, looking surprised. 'They have fairly ruined his waistcoat and knocked his wits astray; but that don't depress his spirits, I find.'

'You had better get back to the barky, sir,' said Bonden in a low voice, tucking the ensign and the other officers' swords under his arm. 'This here is going to Kingdom Come.'

# In Which We Serve

## JOHN BAYLEY

IN ALDOUS HUXLEY'S first novel, *Crome Yellow*, a man of
action recounts an escapade of his youth, and comments that
such things are only really agreeable to look back on after
the event. Nothing is exciting as it happens. Warriors in
heroic times only knew what they had been through when
they heard about it from the bard in the mead-hall. Armchair
warriors who have never performed such feats can nonetheless become connoisseurs of them at second-hand. In the
same way, it is possible to become an expert on the apparatus
of the old-time naval world – backstays and top-gallants,
twenty-four pounders and hardtack – without having the
faintest idea how to fire a gun, reef a sail, or fother a ship's
bottom. Naval novels today are unique among the genre in
this engaging respect: author and reader are alike innocent
of the experience graphically conveyed by the one and eagerly
appreciated by the other.

This may seem a good reason for not taking such books
very seriously. The Marryat who wrote *Mr. Midshipman
Easy* and the Melville who wrote *Moby-Dick* had themselves
been to sea, as frigate officer and as a whaling hand: they
knew what they were talking about. So too with Joseph
Conrad. But that is scarcely relevant to the genre of nautical
fiction today, which can seem more like the genre of science
fiction or fantasy, even of 'magic realism'. The fashionable
thing in the theory of the novel at the present time is to do
it, so to speak, without hands; to recognise the totality of
fiction, its arbitrariness, its success not in relation to 'life'
but in purely literary terms. On the other side the new his-
toricism has created a genuinely authoritative style of fiction
– Gore Vidal and Simon Schama are formidable expo-
nents of it – which researches the legend of the past while

demonstrating the seductive unknowability of the real thing. Gore Vidal's *Lincoln* is a special and incontrovertible masterpiece of such a kind.

Like his compatriots, J. G. Farrell and John Banville, Patrick O'Brian does not really fit into any of these more up-to-date categories. In their own different ways they are at once too traditional and too idiosyncratic. Loosely linked by the theme of an empire in its decline, the novels of Farrell's trilogy – *Troubles, The Siege of Krishnapur,* and *The Singapore Grip* – were a great success from the fashion in which they combined fantasy and erudition with an original imagination of how a particular culture saw itself, spoke, and showed off to itself. They made something new, fresh and hilarious, out of being bookish. In his own subtle and leisurely style Patrick O'Brian does something of the same sort, making extensive use of the pleasure that fiction addicts find in feeling at home, recognising old faces, old jokes, the same social occasions and regimes, the same sort of exciting situation. His most time-honoured ploy is the two-man partnership, the accidental coming together of a dissimilar pair – Don Quixote and Sancho Panza, Holmes and Watson, Hergé's Tintin and Captain Haddock – who from then on are indissolubly wedded in terms of the reader's expectations and the novels' success.

O'Brian's couples are Jack Aubrey and Stephen Maturin, who meet at Port Mahon in Minorca in the year 1802, when Jack is a lieutenant in the British Navy hoping for promotion to commander, and Stephen is a bit of a mystery man, a half-Irish half-Catalan scholar in medicine and botany, down on his luck. After a mild quarrel at a concert – passionate music lovers both, Jack will play the violin and Stephen his cello throughout many a subsequent saga – they take to each other, and Jack offers Stephen a berth as surgeon in his first command, the fourteen-gun sloop *Sophie. Master and Commander*, the first in a series now approaching its fifteenth volume, inaugurates a relationship which will continue through the vicissitudes of the service in every ocean and latitude, through marriages and bankruptcies, promotions, dismissals, windfalls, and losses of prize money, until with *The Nutmeg of Consolation* (the name is that of a jewel of a little corvette built in Borneo to replace the shipwrecked HMS Surprise) we end up on the shores of Botany Bay, among the convicts of the new colony of Australia.

In strict terms of time and sequence the war against Napoleon should by now be over, and the Treaty of Ghent signed that ended the war of 1812 between England and the USA. But O'Brian has cunningly allowed history to expand, as it were, so that his own episodes can continue while the larger process marks time. In a recent introduction he confesses to this method, for he is too sound a chronicler to play fast and loose with what actually occurred. In the middling novels of the series there are memorable accounts of historic actions, like those of the French and English frigates and East Indiamen at Mauritius, and the unequal but epic fight in the Indian Ocean between HMS *Java* and the USS *Constitution*. *The Fortune of War* actually ended with the battle outside Boston harbour of the *Shannon* and *Chesopeake*, while *The Surgeon's Mate* opens with the burial at Halifax of Captain Lawrence, the *Chesapeake*'s gallant commander.

But by the time we reach *The Nutmeg of Consolation* such main events have tractfully withdrawn into the background and the chief action – a very thrilling one to be sure – is an attack by Dyaks and their pirate queen on the shipwrecked crew of the *Surprise*. (This frigate was Jack's favourite command and gave her name to the third novel in the series.) The flora and fauna of the far Orient, and of Australia itself, are of the deepest interest to Stephen and his chaplain assistant, and *The Nutmeg* ends with a marvellous account of the duckbill platypus and the hazardous consequences of being bitten by one.

The above may give the idea that adventure is paramount in the series, and that the novels are further examples of the naval-romantic genre inaugurated by C. S. Forester with the exploits of Captain Hornblower, and copied since by several inferior cutlass-and-carronade performers. Nothing could be further from the truth. Many of the Hornblower books were superb examples of their craft, and Forester remains unequalled for dynamism of narrative and precision of encounter; his single ship actions are surely the best ever described. O'Brian's technique and achievement are of quite a different kind. For a start, although he is dutiful about giving us marine warfare, meticulously reconstructed and fleshed out from the dry pages of naval historians like Brenton and James, his real interest is in the ships and the crews, in naval custom, habit, and routine, the daily ritual of shipboard life and the interplay of personality in the confinement of a wooden world. His ships are as intimate to us as are Sterne's Shandy Hall or Jane Austen's village of Highbury in *Emma*. Like Jane Austen, O'Brian is really happiest working on two or three inches of ivory and turning to art the daily lives of three or four families in a locality – except that his village happens to be a wooden ship of war at the apogee of a great Navy's world sea-power in the days of sail, and famous for the skill and discipline of its officers and men. Jane Austen, two of whose brothers ended up as admirals, would have understood all this very well, and would no doubt warmly have approved O'Brian's spacious but modest undertaking.

Stephen is being shown over the *Sophie* by young Mowett, a midshipman with a taste for writing verse, by no means a rare accomplishment at a time when learning to play the German flute was a popular relaxation in the gunroom, and captains might stitch *petit point* in the lofty seclusion of the great cabin.

'You are studying trigonometry, sir?' said Stephen, whose eyes, accustomed to the darkness, could now distinguish an inky triangle.

'Yes, sir, if you please,' said Babbington. 'And I believe I have nearly found out the answer.' (And should have, if that great ox had not come barging in, he added, privately.)

'In canvassed berth, profoundly deep in thought,
His busy mind with sines and tangents fraught,
  A Mid reclines! In calculation lost.
  His efforts still by some intruder crost,'

said Mowett. 'Upon my word and honour, sir, I am rather proud of that.'

'And well you may be,' said Stephen, his eyes dwelling on the little ships drawn all round the triangle. 'And pray, what in sea-language is meant by a ship?'

'She must have three square-rigged masts, sir,' they told him kindly, 'and a bowsprit; and the masts must be in three – lower, top and topgallant – for we never call a polacre a ship.'

'Don't you, though?' said Stephen.[1]

In one sense the technique – clueless landsman much respected nonetheless as a doctor – is as time-honoured as it is in Smollett, but O'Brian contrives to give it back a sort of innocence, which goes with his extraordinarily adroit individualisation of minor figures. Two novels later in the series Jack is giving a dinner party on board his new command (he has just become a post captain) and is as relieved as a suburban hostess would be that the burgundy and the plum duff ('Figgy-dowdy' to the service) are doing their job in loosening tongues and promoting social ease. Stephen is in conversation with the marine lieutenant, a Highlander called Macdonald, and they are growing a little warm over the Ossian question, Stephen pointing out the absence of manuscript sources:

'Do you expect a Highland gentleman to produce his manuscripts upon compulsion?' said Macdonald to Stephen, and to Jack, 'Dr Johnson, sir, was capable of very inaccurate statements. He affected to see no trees

1. Patrick O'Brian, *Master and Commander* (London: Collins, 1970), pp. 88–89.

in his tour of the kingdom: now I have travelled the very same road many times, and I know several trees within a hundred yards of it – ten, or even more. I do not regard him as any authority upon any subject. I appeal to your candour, sir – what do you say to a man who defines the mainsheet as the largest sail in a ship, or to belay as to splice, or a bight as the circumference of a rope? And that in a buke that professes to be a dictionary of the English language? Hoot, toot.'

'Did he indeed say that?' cried Jack. 'I shall never think the same of him again. I have no doubt your Ossian was a very honest fellow.'

'He did, sir, upon my honour,' cried Macdonald, laying his right hand flat upon the table. 'And falsum in uno, falsum in omnibus, I say.'

'Why, yes,' said Jack, who was well acquainted with old omnibus as any man there present.[2]

Not only do the natural passions – indeed obsessions – present in any small community receive at the author's hands the most skilful and sympathetic testimony, but he makes graphic if unobtrusive display of the diversity of types, interests, and nationalities always present in a naval context. The hazards too. A day or two later Stephen has to amputate Macdonald's arm after a cutting-out expedition, and they take up their conversation again in the hospital.

O'Brian is equally and fascinatingly meticulous on questions of geography and natural history. *The Nutmeg of Consolation* is embroidered with the flora and fauna of the East Indies; and an extraordinarily gripping sequence in the previous novel, *The Thirteen-Gun Salute*, recounts the danger to a sailing vessel of approaching too near in a calm to the nine-hundred-foot cliffs of Inaccessible Island, which rise sheer out of the depths of the South Atlantic not far from Tristan da Cunha. Whalers had been drawn by the mountainous swell into the giant kelp at the cliffs' foot and perished with all hands. The crew of the *Surprise* are

2. Patrick O'Brian, *Post Captain* (London: Collins, 1972), p. 224.

enjoying a routine Sunday morning when this danger threatens, and are plucked from divine service by the urgent need to get out the boats and row the becalmed frigate clear into safety. It is then revealed by a white-faced carpenter that the long boat had a couple of rotten strakes which he has cut out, and not yet had time to replace. Like the young captain in Conrad's *The Shadow Line*, who fails to check that what is inside the bottle in the ship's medicine store is indeed quinine, Jack Aubrey is faced – and not for the first time – with the implacable crises of life at sea, to survive which every last detail must be kept in mind and under eye. There is nothing in the least approximate or merely picturesque about O'Brian's handling of any marine situation, or even the most conventionally spectacular kind of naval action. In *Master and Commander* he took us, together with the unskilled Sophies, through every detail of the drill required to fire a single gun of the broadside.

Of course he has his failures – what novelist embarked on so amply comprehensive an undertaking could not have them? The women are a problem; although it seems unfair they should turn out to be, for Jack's amiable fiancée and then wife, his far from amiable mother-in-law, and Stephen's own heartbreaker, Diana Villiers, with whom he is on and off through several books, are as vigorously and subtly portrayed as the men, and come alive as much as thy do. No more than Conrad is O'Brian what used to be called a man's man, and he has as many women as men among his fans. Nonetheless it is with a feeling of relief that we leave Jacks' Sophia in the little house near Portsmouth, or Diana in Mayfair, and embark upon our next commission. The reason is plain. It is not that O'Brian's women are less interesting than his men, but that a single domestic background is essential to the richness and vivacity of the work. Not being a bird, as the Irishman said, O'Brian cannot be in two places at once; and he cannot successfully locate the women in one background and his seagoing population in another. Were he able to take his ladies to sea (he does have some memorable gunners' wives and East India misses) it would be another matter, but there history is against him – naval wives often took passage but could not be closely involved in the life of the ship – and O'Brian has total respect for the niceties of contemporary usage and custom.

Another important narrative theme is more suitably ambiguous. Almost unknown to Jack, at least in the earlier books of the sequence, Stephen is an undercover agent of naval intelligence. Nothing improbable in that, and it does lead to some interesting situations, although the reader may feel that such goings-on are there more for the benefit of plot and adventure than real assets to the felt life of the fiction. The two traitors inside the Admiralty who are a feature of the later novels bear a not altogether comfortable resemblance to more recent traitors like Burgess and Maclean. There are moments, too, when Stephen's erudition and expertise in all matters except love become a little oppressive, as does Jack's superb seamanship and childlike lack of business sense. But these are the kinds of irritation we feel at times with those who have become old friends. Stephen and Jack have their occasional quarrels too, and their moments of mutual dissatisfaction.

For indeed the most striking thing about the series is the high degree of fictional reality, of Henry James's 'felt life', that it has managed to generate. This may be partly because we grow accustomed and familiar, as in the homelier case of the comic strip; and yet the more surprising and impressive virtue in the novels is their wide range of feeling and of literary sensibility. At least two tragic characters – Lieutenant James Dillon in the opening novel, and the erratic Lord Clonfert who makes a mess of things in *The Mauritius Command* – have their psychology subtly and sympathetically explored; and there are some scenes too in the series of almost supernatural fear and strangeness: two pathetic lovers seeking sanctuary on a Pacific island, or the weird and grisly chapter, like something out of *Moby-Dick*, when a Dutch seventy-four pursues Jack's smaller vessel implacably through the icebergs and mountainous waves of the great southern ocean. And no other writer, not even Melville, has described the whale or the wandering albatross with O'Brian's studious and yet lyrical accuracy.

The vicissitudes in Jack's naval career – the many fiascos and disasters as well as the occasional triumphs – come from naval careers of the period, like that of Lord Cochrane and his brother, who was dismissed from the service for alleged financial irregularities. Such resourceful heroes often made a second career for themselves – Cochrane became a Chilean admiral in the South American war of liberation – and there seems every hope that Jack and Stephen may turn up in those parts when their author can no longer put off the conclusion of hostilities in Europe. Most historical novels suffer from the fatal twin defects of emphasising the pastness of the past too much while at the same time seeking to be over-familiar with it ('Have some more of this Chian,' drawled Alcibiades). O'Brian does neither. Indeed 'history' as such does not seem greatly to interest him: his originality consists in the unpretentious use he makes of it to invent a new style of fiction.

That unpretentiousness has become a rare asset among novelists. The reader today has become conditioned, partly by academic critics, to look in Melville and Conrad for the larger issues and deeper significances, rather than enjoying the play of life, the humour and detail of the performance. Yet surface is what matters in good fiction, and Melville on the whale, and on the *Pequod*'s crew, is more absorbing to his readers in the long run that is the parabolic significance of Captain Ahab. Patrick O'Brian has contrived to invent a new world that is almost entirely, in this sense, a world of enchanting fictional surfaces, and all the better for it. As narrator he never obtrudes his own personality, is himself never present in the role of author at all; but we know well what most pleases, intrigues, and fascinates him; and there is a kind of sweetness in his books, an enthusiasm and love for the setting of the fiction, which will remind older readers of Sir Walter Scott. It is worth remembering that Melville too worshipped Scott, and that the young Conrad pored over the Waverley novels in Poland long before he went to sea.

This retrospective review first appeared in November 1991 in *The New York Review of Books*. It is reproduced here with the kind permission of Professor Bayley.

378

# The Works of Patrick O'Brian

*Aubrey-Maturin Novels*

MASTER AND COMMANDER
POST CAPTAIN
HMS SURPRISE
THE MAURITIUS COMMAND
DESOLATION ISLAND
THE FORTUNE OF WAR
THE SURGEON'S MATE
THE IONIAN MISSION
TREASON'S HARBOUR
THE FAR SIDE OF THE WORLD
THE REVERSE OF THE MEDAL
THE LETTER OF MARQUE
THE THIRTEEN-GUN SALUTE
THE NUTMEG OF CONSOLATION
CLARISSA OAKES
THE WINE-DARK SEA
THE COMMODORE
THE YELLOW ADMIRAL

*Novels*

TESTIMONIES
THE CATALANS
THE GOLDEN OCEAN
THE UNKNOWN SHORE
RICHARD TEMPLE

*Tales*

THE LAST POOL
THE WALKER
LYING IN THE SUN
THE CHIAN WINE
COLLECTED SHORT STORIES

*Biography*

PICASSO
JOSEPH BANKS

*Anthology*

A BOOK OF VOYAGES

# Master and Commander

*Master and Commander* is the first of Patrick O'Brian's now famous Aubrey/Maturin novels, regarded by many as the greatest series of historical novels ever written. It establishes the friendship between Captain Jack Aubrey R. N. and Stephen Maturin, who becomes his secretive ship's surgeon and an intelligence agent. It contains all the action and excitement which could possibly be hoped for in a historical novel, but it also displays the qualities which have put O'Brian far ahead of any of his competitors: his depiction of the detail of life aboard a Nelsonic man-of-war, of weapons, food, conversation and ambience, of the landscape and of the sea. O'Brian's portrayal of each of these is faultless and the sense of period throughout is acute. His power of characterisation is above all masterly. This brilliant historical novel marked the début of a writer who has grown into one of the most remarkable literary novelists now writing, the author of what Alan Judd, writing in the *Sunday Times*, has described as 'the most significant extended story since Anthony Powell's *A Dance to the Music of Time*'.

'It is as though, under Mr O'Brian's touch, those great sea-paintings at Greenwich had stirred and come alive.'

TOM POCOCK, *Evening Standard*

'*Master and Commander* recreates with delightful subtlety the flavour of life aboard a midget British man-of-war, plying the western Mediterranean in the year 1800, a year of indecisive naval skirmishes with France and Spain. Even for a reader not especially interested in matters nautical, the author's easy command of the philosophical, political, sensual and social temper of the times flavours a rich entertainment.'

MARTIN LEVIN, *New York Times Book Review*

ISBN: 0 00 649915 5

# Post Captain

*Post Captain* is the second novel in Patrick O'Brian's remarkable Aubrey/Maturin series and led Mary Renault to write: '*Master and Commander* raised dangerously high expectations; *Post Captain* triumphantly surpasses them.'

The tale begins with Jack Aubrey arriving home from his exploits in the Mediterranean to find England at peace following the Treaty of Amiens. He and his friend Stephen Maturin, surgeon and secret agent, begin to live the lives of country gentlemen, hunting, entertaining and enjoying more amorous adventures. Their comfortable existence, however, is cut short when Jack is overnight reduced to a pauper with enough debts to keep him in prison for life. He flees to the continent to seek refuge: instead he finds himself a hunted fugitive as Napoleon has ordered the internment of all Englishmen in France. Aubrey's adventures in escaping from France and the debtors' prison will grip the reader as fast as his unequalled actions at sea.

'Mr O'Brian is a master of his period, in which his characters are firmly placed, while remaining three-dimensional, intensely human beings. This book sets him at the very top of his genre . . . It is brilliant.'

MARY RENAULT

ISBN: 0 00 649916 3

# H. M. S. Surprise

*H.M.S. Surprise* follows the variable fortunes of Captain Jack Aubrey's career in Nelson's navy as he attempts to hold his ground against admirals, colleagues and the enemy, accepting a commission to convey a British ambassador to the East Indies. The voyage takes him and his friend Stephen Maturin to the strange sights and smells of the Indian sub-continent, and through the archipelago of spice islands where the French have a near-overwhelming local superiority.

Rarely has a novel managed to convey more vividly the fragility of a sailing ship in a wild sea. Rarely has a historical novelist combined action and lyricism of style in the way that O'Brian does. His superb sense of place, brilliant characterisation and a vigour and joy of writing lifts O'Brian above any but the most exalted of comparisons.

'He is perhaps unique . . . in that his books can absorb and enthral landlubbers who do not even know the difference between a jib-boom and a taffrail.'

VALERIE WEBSTER, *Scotsman*

'*H.M.S. Surprise* is the third in the series, and one can hardly give it higher praise than to say that it maintains the level of the other two. The language is just right, with a full late eighteenth-century weightiness that is still free from any trace of strain or affectation.'        JULIAN SYMONS, *Sunday Times*

ISBN: 0 00 649917 1

# The Mauritius Command

Captain Jack Aubrey is ashore, married with twin daughters, living in a damp cottage in Hampshire on half-pay and without a command – until Stephen Maturin arrives with secret orders for Aubrey to take the frigate, *Boadicea* to the Cape of Good Hope, under a Commodore's pennant. But the difficulties of carrying out his orders are compounded by two of his own captains – Lord Clonfert, a pleasure seeking dilettante, and Captain Corbett, whose severity can push his crews to the verge of mutiny.

'Patrick O'Brian has written splendid novels – of which *The Mauritius Command* is the latest – recounting episodes in the lives of the naval officer Jack Aubrey and his friend the saturnine Irish physician, Stephen Maturin... Taken together, the novels are a brilliant achievement. They display staggering erudition on almost all aspects of early nineteenth-century life, with impeccable period detail.'

T.J. BINYON, *Times Literary Supplement*

'During the Napoleonic Wars, Captain Jack Aubrey reaches middle age and is beached with domesticity: wife, daughters, mother-in-law, several servants, all packed into a little cottage like the Black Hole . . . He jumps at the chance to escape. What's more, he'll be with some great old friends, including ship's surgeon Stephen Maturin – with whom he loves to fiddle two-part Mozart inventions over port in the ship's cabin.'

*Kirkus*

ISBN: 0 00 649918 X

# Desolation Island

In *Desolation Island*, Jack Aubrey exchanges the Indian Ocean of *The Mauritius Command* for colder and lonelier seas. Commissioned to rescue Governor Bligh of Bounty fame, Jack Aubrey and Stephen Maturin sail the *Leopard* to Australia with a hold full of convicts. Among them is a beautiful and dangerous spy - and a treacherous disease which decimates the crew. The ingredients of a powerful and dramatic novel are heightened by descriptive writing of rare quality. Nowhere in contemporary prose has the majesty and terror of the sea been more effectively rendered than in the thrilling chase through an Antarctic storm in which Jack's ship, outmanned and outgunned, is the quarry not the hunter.

'Without intending sacrilege to C.S. Forester, for me Mr O'Brian's timbers are as sound, his historical soundings as deep, his power to impress and excite with the mystique of a ship under sail as great, and he packs more humour and writing into his books.'  STEPHEN VAUGHAN, *Observer*

'Patrick O'Brian is a literary conjuror who can cure boredom with the flick of a pen. There is enough here to cure anything. When you start reading Jack Aubrey's adventures you will soon get to know that you are in for many a thrill and the occasional narrow squeak.'  *Nautical Magazine*

'Seldom has it been my pleasure and thrill to have the terror and majesty of the sea more graphically depicted.'

*Irish Independant*

ISBN: 0 00 649924 4

# The Fortune of War

As *The Fortune of War* opens Captain Jack Aubrey, R.N., sails the storm-beaten H.M.S. *Leopard* into harbour in the Dutch East Indies to find himself appointed to the command of the fastest and best-armed frigate in the Navy. He and Stephen Maturin take passage for England in a despatch vessel. But the War of 1812 against the United States breaks out while they are en route. Bloody actions precipitate them both into new and unexpected scenes where Stephen's past activities as a secret agent return on him with a vengeance.

'Captain Aubrey and his surgeon, Stephen Maturin, compose one of those complex and fascinating pairs of characters which have inspired thrilling stories of all kinds since the Iliad.'

JOHN BAYLEY, IRIS MURDOCH

ISBN: 0 00 649919 8

# The Surgeon's Mate

Jack Aubrey and Stephen Maturin are ordered home by despatch vessel to bring the news of their latest victory to the government. But Maturin is a marked man for the havoc he has wrought in the French intelligence network in the New World and the attentions of two privateers soon become menacing. The chase that follows through the fogs and shallows of the Grand Banks is as thrilling, as tense and as unexpected in its culmination as anything Patrick O'Brian has written. Then, among other things, follows a shipwreck and a particularly sinister internment in the notorious Temple Prison in Paris. Once again the tigerish and fascinating Diana Villiers redresses the balance in this man's world of seamanship and war.

'Captain Jack Aubrey and Stephen Maturin . . . undertake a secret mission in the Baltic; are later wrecked on the coast of Brittany; are imprisoned in Paris, but are surreptitiously aided to escape . . . One must admire once again Patrick O'Brian's subtle and persuasive re-creation of the past. Here there is nothing of your ordinary historical novel . . . instead each incident or description is saturated by a mass of complex and convincing detail. Such details might be overwhelming . . . were they not reduced to their proper status as background by the superabundant liveliness and lifelikeness of the characters; and by the pace and excitement of the narrative. So eventful, indeed, are the novels, it is easy to ignore the fact that . . . they are, on one level, addressing themselves to questions of human actions and behaviour far beyond the compass of the normal adventure story.'     T.J. BINYON, *Times Literary Supplement*

ISBN: 0 00 649921 X

# Treason's Harbour

Uniquely among authors of naval fiction, Patrick O'Brian allows his characters to develop with experience. The Jack Aubrey of *Treason's Harbour* has a record of successes equal to that of the most brilliant of Nelson's band of brothers, and he is no less formidable or decisive in action or strategy. But he is wiser, kinder, gentler too.

Much of the plot of *Treason's Harbour* depends on intelligence and counter-intelligence, a field in which Aubrey's friend Stephen Maturin excels. Through him we get a clearer insight into the life and habits of the sea officers of Nelson's time than we would ever obtain seeing things through their own eyes. There is plenty of action and excitement in this novel but it is the atmosphere of a Malta crowded with senior officers, waiting for news of what the French are up to and wondering whether the war will end before their turn comes for prize money and for fame, that is here so freshly and vividly conveyed.

'Patrick O'Brian's engaging Captain Jack Aubrey is the best thing afloat since Horatio Hornblower and notably less austere ashore.'
STEPHEN VAUGHAN, *Observer*

ISBN: 0 00 649923 6

# The Far Side of the World

It is still the War of 1812. Patrick O'Brian takes his hero Jack Aubrey and his tetchy, sardonic friend Stephen Maturin on a voyage as fascinating as anything he has ever written. They set course across the South Atlantic to intercept a powerful American frigate outward bound to play havoc with the British whaling trade. If they do not come up with her before she rounds the Horn they must follow her into the Great South Sea and as far across the Pacific as she may lead them. It is a commission after Jack's own heart. Maturin has fish of his own to fry in the world of secret intelligence.

Aubrey has to cope with a succession of disasters – men overboard, castaways, encounters with savages, storms, typhoons, groundings, shipwrecks, to say nothing of murder and criminal insanity. That the enemy is in fact faithfully dealt with no-one who has the honour of Captain Aubrey's acquaintance can take leave to doubt.

'All true lovers of the sea will find this a most enjoyable book.'
*Nautical Magazine*

'Aubrey has rarely undertaken a more hazardous mission or one more packed with exciting incident.' *Gloucester Citizen*

ISBN: 0 00 649925 2

# The Reverse of the Medal

*The Reverse of the Medal* is in all respects an unconventional naval tale. Jack Aubrey returns from his duties protecting whalers off South America and is persuaded by a casual acquaintance to make investments in the City on the strength of supposedly certain information. From there he is led into the half-worlds of the London criminal underground and of government espionage – the province of his friend, Stephen Maturin, on whom alone he can rely.

Those who are already devoted readers of Patrick O'Brian will find here all the brilliance of characterisation and sparkle of dialogue which they have come to expect. For those who will read him for the first time there will be the pleasure of discovering, quite unexpectedly, a novelist of unique character.

'Taken together the novels are a brilliant achievement. They display staggering erudition on almost all aspects of eighteenth-century life, with impeccable period detail.'

*Times Literary Supplement*

'These books are works of scholarship, classics of contemporary literature, joys to read. Savour *The Reverse of the Medal* – and seek out its predecessors. You rob yourself by neglecting them.'

*Western Morning News*

ISBN: 0 00 649926 0

# The Letter of Marque

Jack Aubrey is a naval officer, a post-captain of experience and capacity. When *The Letter of Marque* opens he has been struck off the Navy List for a crime he has not committed, and, because he is the man he is, there is no position that could cause him greater unhappiness. With Aubrey is his friend and ship's surgeon Stephen Maturin, who is also an unofficial British intelligence agent. Maturin has bought for Aubrey his old ship the *Surprise* so that the misery of ejection from the service can be palliated by the command of what Aubrey calls 'a private man-of-war' – a letter of marque, a privateer. Together they sail on a voyage which, if successful might restore Aubrey to the rank, and the raison d'etre whose loss he so much regrets.

Around these simple, ostensibly familiar elements Patrick O'Brian has written a novel of great narrative power, exploring his extraordinary world once more, in a tale full of human feeling and rarely matched in its drama.

'Delicacy and generosity of feeling are constant themes in O'Brian's novels. *The Letter of Marque* is both serious and light-hearted, true and sentimental, as comic opera can be.'
*London Review of Books*

'He does not just have the chief qualifications of a first-class historical novelist, he has them all.' MARY RENAULT

ISBN: 0 00 649927 9

# The Thirteen-Gun Salute

As *The Thirteen-Gun Salute* opens Jack Aubrey has been re-instated to his command, and he and his old friend Dr Maturin are sailing on a secret mission with a hand-picked crew, most of them ship-mates from the adventures and lucrative voyages of earlier years. But Patrick O'Brian's resourcefulness is a sure warrant that things will not turn out as his readers or his characters expect. Twists and turns, sub-plots, echoes from the past, these are the only certainties in this astonishing *roman fleuve*. Distant waters, exotic scenes, flora and fauna to satisfy Maturin's innocent curiosity as well as scope for his cloak and dagger work enrich its flow. The ending of the book leaves the reader more than usually impatient for its successor.

'In *The Thirteen-Gun Salute* we sail on a secret mission to the East with those two devoted and disparate shipmates Aubrey and Maturin, characters not tacked on to their period but inhabiting it as completely as though the author were their contemporary. For those unlucky enough not to have crossed their bows, Captain Aubrey is a lion afloat and a bit of a lost sheep ashore, Stephen Maturin, surgeon, naturalist, secret agent . . . is an innocent of a different stamp; their friendship, developed with subtlety and feeling, is an endearing and enduring achievement. Here Aubrey is restored to the Navy List, French intrigues in Malaysia are attacked, and Maturin has a wonderful time, conveyed with a real sense of wonder, among the strange flora and fauna.'

CHRISTOPHER WORDSWORTH, *Guardian*

ISBN: 0 00 649928 7

# The Nutmeg of Consolation

Patrick O'Brian is regarded by many as the greatest living historical novelist writing in English. In *The Nutmeg of Consolation,* Jack Aubrey and Stephen Maturin begin stranded on an uninhabited island in the Dutch East Indies, attacked by ferocious Malay pirates. They contrive their escape, but after a stay in Batavia and a change of ship they are caught up in a night chase in fiercely tidal waters and then embroiled in the much more insidious conflicts of the terrifying penal settlements of New South Wales. It is one of O'Brian's most accomplished and gripping books.

'*The Nutmeg of Consolation* brings his achievement to a new height. Any contemporary novelist should recognize in Patrick O'Brian a Master of the Art.'       ALAN JUDD, *Sunday Telegraph*

'In length the series is unique; as far as quality is concerned, it cannot but be ranked with the best of twentieth-century historical novels.'       T.J. BINYON, *Independant*

ISBN: 0 00 649929 5

# Clarissa Oakes

As *Clarissa Oakes* opens, Captain Jack Aubrey, a lion in action but somewhat at sea on land, sails away from the hated Australian prison colonies in his favourite vessel the *Surprise*, pondering as he does so on middle age and sexual frustration. He soon becomes aware that he is out of touch with the mood of his ship: to his astonishment he finds that in spite of a lifetime's experience he does not know what the foremost hands or even his own officers are thinking. They know, as he does not, that the *Surprise* has a stranger aboard: and what they, for their part, do not know is that the stranger is potentially as dangerous as a light in the powder magazine itself.

The author is a master of tension. A chase by an ostensibly friendly but strangely persistent cutter, the swell of disorder in the ship's company and the unpredictability of her captain's reactions carry the reader forward to a fierce battle on a Pacific island full of the drama and colour which his admirers have come to expect.

'Few books so entertaintaining and readable are based on such strong research and grasp of human nature. One moment you laugh aloud at comedy rooted in character, and the next, storm-ing adventure or danger grips you by the throat . . . good writing allied to must-read-on storytelling.'

SHAUN USHER, *Daily Mail*

'What is so gripping about O'Brian's novels is the completeness with which he invents a world which is our own and not our own . . . O'Brian is a brilliant observer.'

A. S. BYATT, *Evening Standard*

ISBN: 0 00 649930 9

# The Wine-Dark Sea

At the opening of a voyage filled with disaster and delight, Jack Aubrey and Stephen Maturin are in pursuit of a privateer sailing under American colours through the Great South Sea. Stephen's objective is to set the revolutionary tinder of South America ablaze to relieve the pressure on the British government which, already engaged in a death-struggle with a Europe dominated by Napoleon, has blundered into war with the young and uncomfortably vigorous United States.

The shock and barbarity of hand-to-hand fighting are sharpened by O'Brian's exact sense of period, his eye for landscape and his feel for a ship under sail. His thrilling descriptions of hair-raising and bloody actions make the reader grateful that he is watching from a distance.

'To read Patrick O'Brian is to turn the pages of literary history. His series of novels comprises the most significant extended story since Anthony Powell's *A Dance to the Music of Time*.'

ALAN JUDD, *Sunday Times*

'O'Brian has shown us that in our literary silver age, authentic gold can still be mined . . . He is a man whose books you would dare to give Sterne; whose conversation would have delighted Coleridge. It is his misfortune, but our great good luck, that he is our contemporary, and not theirs.'

WILLIAM WALDEGRAVE, *The Times*

ISBN: 0 00 649931 7

# The Commodore

Jack Aubrey's long service is at last rewarded: he is promoted to the rank of Commodore, and given a squadron of ships to command. His mission is twofold – to make a large dent in the slave trade off the coast of Africa and, on his return, to intercept a French fleet set for Bantry Bay with a cargo of weapons for the disaffected among the Irish.

But might the nature of the secret mission on which the squadron is sent present a conflict of loyalties for the complicated and inscrutable figure of Stephen Maturin, Jack's indispensable ship's surgeon and close friend? Invention and surprise follow at every turn in this tale of nineteenth-century seamanship, as rich, as compelling, as masterly as any of its predecessors.

'While his stories tell of men at war, he is a novelist of great gentleness of spirit. A pervasive serenity, a generosity towards human frailty, are among the qualities which have made his books irresistible . . . All the familiar virtues of O'Brian are here: effortless command of period dialogue, seamanship, culture and manners: intimate understanding of a small floating world dominated by the vagaries of the wind; droll observation of human idiosyncrasy . . .'  MAX HASTINGS, *Daily Telegraph*

'In English fiction my chief pleasures this year came from reading four books in the series about Captain Jack Aubrey, RN by Patrick O'Brian, a writer whose work I have discovered late in the day, and who writes the sort of elegant, civilized and humorous prose that ought, in my opinion, just now and then to win the Booker Prize.'

JAN MORRIS, *Independent Books of the Year*

ISBN: 0 00 649932 5

# The Yellow Admiral

Life ashore may once again be the undoing of Jack Aubrey in Patrick O'Brian's long-awaited sequel to *The Commodore*. Aubrey, now a considerable though impoverished landowner, has dimmed his prospects at the Admiralty by his erratic voting as a Member of Parliament; he is feuding with his neighbour, a man with strong Navy connections who wants to enclose the common land between their estates; he is on even worse terms with his wife, Sophie, whose mother has ferreted out a most damaging trove of old personal letters. Even Jack's exploits at sea turn sour: in the storm waters off Brest he captures a French privateer laden with gold and ivory, but this at the expense of missing a signal and deserting his post. Worst of all, in the spring of 1814, peace breaks out.

Fortunately, Jack is not left to his own devices. Stephen Maturin returns from a mission in France with news that the Chileans, to secure their independence, require a navy, and the service of English officers. Jack is savouring this apparent reprieve for his career, as well as Sophie's forgiveness, when he receives an urgent despatch ordering him to Gibraltar: Napoleon has escaped from Elba.

'. . . Patrick O'Brian is unquestionably the Homer of the Napoleonic wars.'              JAMES HAMILTON-PATERSON

ISBN: 0 00 225561 8

# The Golden Ocean

In the year 1740, Commodore Anson embarked on a voyage that would become one of the most famous exploits in British naval history. Sailing through poorly charted waters, Anson and his men circumnavigated the globe, encountering disease, disaster and astonishing success, and seizing a nearly incalculable sum of Spanish gold and silver. But only one of the five ships survived the voyage.

This is the background to *The Golden Ocean*, the first novel Patrick O'Brian ever wrote about the sea, a precursor to the critically acclaimed Aubrey/Maturin series. This novel shares the same sense of excitement, and the rich humour of those books, invoking the eloquent style and attention to historical detail that O'Brian readers admire so much. The protagonist of this story is Peter Palafox, son of a poor Irish parson, who signs on as a midshipman, never before having seen a ship. He is a fellow who would have delighted the young Stephen Maturin or Jack Aubrey . . . and quarrelled with them as well. Together with his life-long friend Sean, Peter sets out to seek his fortune, embarking on a journey of danger, disappointment, foreign lands and excitement. Written in 1956, this is a tale certain to please not only the many admirers of O'Brian, but any reader with an adventurous soul.

'As always, the author's erudition and humor are on display . . . the attention to period speech and detail is uncompromising and while the cascades of natural lore can be dizzying, both aficionados and newcomers will be swept up by the richness of Mr O'Brian's prodigious imagination.'

SCOTT VEALE, *New York Times*

ISBN: 0 00 225408 5